Nae Mammie's KISSES

Nae Mammie's KISSES

MHAIRI PYOTT

authorHOUSE®

AuthorHouse™ UK Ltd.
1663 Liberty Drive
Bloomington, IN 47403 USA
www.authorhouse.co.uk
Phone: 0800.197.4150

Published by AuthorHouse 08/19/2013

ISBN: 978-1-4918-7577-3 (sc)
ISBN: 978-1-4918-7576-6 (hc)
ISBN: 978-1-4918-7578-0 (e)

Dedicated to my children who will always
have a mother's love and kisses.

CHAPTER ONE

THE HORSE PULLED the cart along the canal side at a good pace. David Chalmers walked beside the horse deep in thought. Things at home had not been going well for him these last few months. Mary and the children would still be asleep. He would try to get home for breakfast about nine o'clock. Half past five now, he would have time to unload at the yard for eight. Mary did not cope so well since the youngest was born. She never really settled into life at Port Dundas.

Her heart was at home in Islay, where everyone was "family." People to help, to speak with, even have some understanding.

The horse knew the job so well, it plodded on as if the cartload of wood weighed nothing at all. David hung on the reins like an ornamental harness attachment.

Maybe if they moved to Islay things would be better. He could try for a distillery job again. Certainly he had the experience—foreman for fifteen years. Anyone could be unlucky. He had been stupid.

He should never have got involved with the men, emptying the washings from the maturing sherry barrels. That had been the whole problem, drinking, losing his job because of it and Mary having found comfort from hiding in the hazy corners of life slowed down by gin.

The house was never tidy. Even the children looked uncared for and dirty. Mary never bothered to prepare meals for them.

The horse was gathering speed as if it knew David's plight and anxiety to get home.

"Good lad Blue," said David and hopped up on the front of the cart. "Soon be time for food"

The woodyard was in sight

"Breakfast time for us, boy."

When David got upstairs to the door of his home he could hear no sounds from inside. The children would miss school again if they were not out of bed. Sure enough, the only movement was from the cat, jumping from the table, still not cleared from the previous day's use. Dirty dishes and papers, no sign of food except a small piece of bread.

"Mary lass, you've slept in," David shouted. "The bairns are late for school again."

Mary sat up quickly in the bed recessed in the kitchen.

"Oh David, I'd no idea it was so late. Get Davy and Maggie up, they'll make it to the school before nine. Charlie can stay at home and play with Alex."

Davy, Maggie and Charlie slept 'through the room'. "Come on bairns, hurry up for the school."

David went back to the kitchen, to put the kettle on the fire. Damn it was out—have to kindle it again.

"Come on Mary, get up. The bairns will need breakfast. Put on some porridge.

I'll see if I can get some milk from the milkman's cart in the street."

"Oh David, my head is pounding so much. I just cannot lift it off the pillow."

"Mary, there's little time to speak of it now but you'll have to pull yourself together lass. Get up. The bairns can stay off school again today. Maybe they'll get this place sorted out. God knows, it could do with a clean up."

"Don't nag David, I just never feel fit enough these days. I've no energy. Everything is a bother, the life's just gone out of me."

"Maybe if you cut out some of the gin you'd feel better. Now get up. I'll see what I can get for the bairns to eat."

David banged the door as he left.

Maggie ran into the kitchen.

"Mammie, where's the key for the place? I'm bursting."

Mary was out of the bed, standing holding her head in her hands.

"Oh lassie, I've no idea, I'm bursting too, through the back of my head. Fetch me a wee drop of water."

Maggie ran to the corner where there was a table with a bucket.

"Mammie there's no water. You forgot to bring it in last night."

"Take the big jug lass and run down to the well and fill it before Dada gets back, there's a good lass. Davy can get Alex dressed. Come on Davy, Charlie, your Dada will be back in a minute."

Maggie lifted the jug from the shelf and the key for the "place" was beside it. She ran her fingers through her tousled hair, before leaving the house. Half way down the four flights of stairs she met her father coming up.

"Where are you going, Maggie?" he asked.

"I'm going for a pee and to fetch a drink for Mammie. She's a sore head again today."

"Hurry then, I've got milk for your porridge, bring enough water for it with you. There's a good lass. I'll need to go away back to work. Look after Mammie and Alex, get the boys to help you tidy the house. See if Mammie can make some supper for us tonight."

David carried on upstairs, while Maggie rushed away to attend to nature's call.

The two toilets that served the tenement building were in the back yard next to the wash-house. Beside the toilet door was a water tap. The residents of the tenement thought themselves lucky to have their own 'well' and 'privvies.'

Maggie tried the door of the privy allocated to their side of the building.

"Occupied," was gasped out from behind the door. It's that wife McNair from the first landing she decided.

"Hurry up please. I'm bursting," pleaded Maggie.

Maggie jumped from one foot to the other. Mammie would be waiting for water for the porridge and for a drink.

"Hurry up in there."

I could do it in the bucket upstairs I suppose. No never make it back up she decided.

"Look missus, squeeze and fart a bit quicker, let other people get a chance."

"You cheeky wee bitch, I'll be out in a minute to skelp your ear for you."

Good, thought Maggie, then I'll get a pee.

Mrs McNair unbolted the door and stepped out. It was amazing that so much bosom and backside could have been folded into such a small confined space. Maggie ducked down below her ample breasts, slipped in behind her and bolted the door.

"Just you wait until I see your father madam, take the wind out of your sails."

"Be lucky if I'm still breathing after this stink," Maggie shouted.

When the coast was clear she came out, filled the jug at the well, then hurried as best she could up the four flights of stairs.

Maggie was nine and a half years old but life had made her capable of looking after herself. Davy, her older brother, was eleven. He was a quiet gentle boy. Maggie could "sort out" the ones she thought were taking "the loan of him." Charlie her younger brother was eight. He was the type of boy who could make everybody laugh. At times he would be so annoying and have his parents so angry, then he would make a comment and everyone would laugh. When she back chatted Mrs McNair, Maggie was sure that was what Charlie would have shouted. Alex was the baby, he was only a year old, starting to walk around things. Maggie looked after him a lot because of Mary's "sore head attacks." Lately Mary had to lie down in bed quite a lot.

"Come on lassie with the water, your father is away without anything but a bit of bread."

"Sorry Mammie, that wifie McNair was in and I had to wait."

Mary put the porridge pot on the fire, bending over to stir the contents. Half stooping at the fire she found it difficult to keep her balance. It felt as though her head was too heavy for her neck and shoulders.

"Maggie, stir this for me lass, I feel dizzy. That woman McNair will be reporting us for not sending you to the school."

Maggie took over the cooking. Davy appeared from the room, with Charlie and baby Alex.

"Go lie down a wee while Mammie, until you feel better. Maggie and I will manage."

When Mary got out of bed at midday the house was tidied up, and she could hear the bairns in the room laughing. Charlie was singing something about "Mrs McNair had a hat, she blew it off with a great big fart."

Mary laughed to herself. What a long time since she found something to amuse her. The children were a blessing. Poor David, he was so good to her, so patient. He was right, she must get herself pulled together. What would her family think if they knew how she had let things slide. It was different here in Glasgow. Despite all those thousands of people she still felt lonely. At times she felt as though she was a bird in a cage. At home her mother's hens had more freedom. Oh, to walk along the shore with the sound of the waves on the shingle and feel the wind on her face. On a day like this her mother and father would be out on the moss cutting the peats for drying. Free in the open air.

Here she was shut up in this sectioned off building, like a hen and chicks in a nesting box. Even a hen looks after its chicks.

David, he was a good husband and father.

"Come on through bairns, I'm feeling better now."

The children ran into the kitchen.

"Are you sure that you feel fine?" Davy asked.

"Aye laddie, my head is much better. Maggie you've been a good girl, the house is looking fine. Charlie, did I hear you making fun of Mrs McNair? You know not to ridicule your elders."

Mary turned and picked Alex up from the floor to keep the children from seeing the smile on her face.

"Davy, we will need some wood for the fire. Maybe you could find Dada at the woodyard and get some? Take Charlie with you. Maggie will run to the Society for bread. We will get some tripe from the cooked food shop for the tea."

"You are feeling better Mam," said Maggie. "I'm so pleased to see you like yourself."

"Good job you're not like Mrs McNair, Mam," said Charlie.

"What's wrong with Mrs McNair then?" said Mary.

"Well we'd never get past her chest to kiss her. Bend down, it's easy to kiss you, Mam."

Mary bent down, Charlie kissed her cheek, Davy squeezed her hand.

"Getting quite the young man now, Davy lad. On you go boys for the wood. If you see Dada tell him I'm much better, I'll have his supper ready."

After the boys left Mary sat Alex on the bed. She filled the black iron kettle on the hearth then hung it on the sweigh over the low burning fire.

"We'll have a strupach Maggie, before you go to the society. Bring the cups, lass."

Maggie and Mary sat at the table drinking their tea.

"Will you need to go to the shop for your medicine, Mam?" asked Maggie.

"No lass, I'm not for out. I'm going to wash my hair and get the tea ready for Dada coming home."

"He will be so happy you're better Mam. I'm pleased too."

Maggie got up from her side of the table, walked around and sat down on her mother's knee. She put her arms around her mother's neck. "I love you so much Mam. Sing to me like you used to do, please."

Mary held her daughter's frail body close to her and in a pure clear voice sang in her native Gaelic tongue Ho ro my nut brown maiden . . .

At the end Maggie kissed her mother.

"Oh I'm so happy you are well again Mam."

David was tired. Slowly he climbed the stairs wondering what was in store for him behind the closed door. Davy had said Mary was better but he'd heard that story before. At the last turn of the stair he could hear singing. It was Mary, singing the mouth music. There was laughing too. David hurried the last few steps and opened the door. The smell of onions cooking filled his nostrils. A cheery fire burned in the grate. The bairns were dancing and enjoying themselves.

Mary was bouncing Alex on her knee to the rhythm of the song.

"You're home Dada," shouted Maggie. "Mam is better again."

"Yes, it certainly looks like she is," said David, lifting Alex from Mary's knee, at the same time bending and kissing the top of Mary's head.

"Let's sit down at the table then," said David, still with Alex on his knee. "Davy I think on a happy occasion such as this you should say grace and give thanks to God for all his mercies and goodness we enjoy."

Mary hung the socks and stockings along the brass rail below the mantelpiece.

"That will be fine for the school tomorrow. Are they asleep yet David?"

"Aye I think so. They were quiet when I came back in with the water. Would you fancy a wee cup of tea lass?"

"That would be good."

David filled the kettle. As he passed to hang it over the fire he put his arm around Mary's waist.

"Tonight has been like old times again, Mary."

He looked at her, the firelight showing her high cheekbones and fine facial structure. Mary was a handsome looking woman for her thirty-eight years despite the self-abuse and personal neglect over the past two.

"You are as bonnie as ever, darling," he said as he took her in his arms.

"Oh David, I feel so ashamed sometimes."

She started to cry.

"Wheesht wumman, Davy will think we are fighting again."

"That's it, poor wee souls, what have I done to them? I love them so much yet when I feel alone and so unhappy they have to pay the price. Poor Maggie tidied the house, they looked after Alex, got the shopping. Davy and Charlie seen to the fire, emptied the buckets, swept the stairs. They are just bits o' bairns yet do nothing but work."

Tears ran down her cheeks.

"Well lass, if you are feeling a wee bit better now you could do these things yourself again. I've been thinking myself how they have suffered because of me losing my job at the distillery. How can we make it up to them?"

Mary poured the tea into the two china cups, taken down from the mantelpiece. They were all that remained of their wedding china her sister Janet gave them as a wedding present when they were married fourteen years before . . . if Janet had known how, in a drunken temper, Mary had thrown the china at David she would have been mortified.

The sisters, though very close to each other, were so different in looks and temperaments. Janet was broader built, plain looking, but with a very pleasant calm disposition. Mary, fortunate with good looks, had a fiery temper, which exploded regularly depending on her mood swing, from deliriously happy to depressed and despondent.

They had both started off working in domestic service together. Mary fourteen and Janet had been sixteen. They left home at the farm on Islay to take up work in the "big house" on the neighbouring island of Gigha, Mary as laundry maid, Janet as scullery maid.

She had done well, had Janet. She was the housekeeper to the laird and had married the island blacksmith.

Although she had done well in some ways, Janet's marriage had never been blessed with children.

They both sat quietly sipping their tea and staring into the fire. David broke the silence.

"Would your family know if there were any houses we could rent back home?"

Mary sat bolt upright.

"What do you mean David?"

She had never dreamed that he would even think of such a thing. David had always lived in Glasgow, although his father was reputed to be a wealthy farmer; his mother Jean was unmarried. Like so many other young girls in service she had found herself "in trouble" and cleared off to the big city to find work and get lost.

Jean still kept house for an elderly gentleman but years of scrubbing and hard work had taken its toll. Her poor hands were very crippled with arthritis. Her employer, an unmarried solicitor, knew her worth and left her in charge of his household. If ever her job came to an end she would have to live with David and Mary, as she was so handicapped no-one would employ her again. She was used to the extra comforts her employer provided. Good food, her own room and she reigned supreme over the servants' hall. Jean had one day off each week. Since they moved into the tenement two years ago she had never managed to visit. The stairs kept Jean from viewing the poor living conditions since Mary had lost interest in home and family. David had taken the children to visit their grandmother on an occasional Sunday afternoon, but only on two occasions in the past eighteen months. Mary was unable to visit because of her "headaches".

"All day I have been thinking of the life Maggie and the boys have here. It's no life for them Mary. Surely it would be better for them in the fresh air. I could get some kind of work if we had a place to live. A new start for us all."

"You said so many times that you would not leave your mother here on her own in Glasgow. What will she do?"

David picked up the poker and stirred the few blackened sticks in the grate before answering.

"Well I think I owe my mother a lot but my children have to come first. This is no life for them Mary. It's not the life we planned together. We have to do something. Start over. What do you think?"

Mary jumped up from her chair and kissed David.

"Oh darling, we will get some place to live. Maybe your mother could come with us. I know it will work out."

David sat Mary down on his knee.

"Now lass, this is a new start and means no more drinking, you'll be among your own folks so things will have to be alright. My mother will manage away fine as she is in the meantime. Once things are settled we can see if there is room for her."

"Oh David, you are such a good man. I have been such a rotten wife to you lately. Those horrible things I've said and done. I don't really deserve someone like you. I do love you."

"I know that lass, come on now, let's get to bed or you will be sleeping in again. The bairns cannot be late for school. It's a new start for them tomorrow as well."

Mary was so excited that she could not sleep. David was snoring regularly. He could relax in deep sleep. No need to listen for the children. Mary was sober and would be able to cope. Mary's mind moved on at such a pace, thinking of houses, the children playing on the shore. Maybe go to the school at Kilchoman where she had been. Maggie could visit her grandmother who she had been named after. They could get a few of her mother's hens, maybe a cow and a few sheep. David would get work. He was a big able man. Physically fit and at the prime of life at forty. She would tell the children in the morning they would be moving soon.

David eased his arm from below Mary's head. She was still asleep. He tiptoed about the room cleaning the fireplace and lighting the fire. He made some tea.

"Mary," he shook her by the shoulder. "Here's a cup of tea lass. It's five o'clock and I'm away to work."

Mary pulled herself up the bed, leaning on one arm while she took the cup.

"Don't worry David. I'll get the bairns off to school all right. I promise there will be no drink. Things are going to be all right again.

I'll write a letter to my mother about a house. Maybe I'll go and see if anyone going on the steamer to Islay will take it to my mother."

David put on his jacket and bonnet then kissed Mary on the cheek.

"I'll see you when I get finished for dinner then. I won't come home for breakfast when you are feeling good. Take care and look after the bairns."

Mary lay back on the pillows.

There might even be work for David on Gigha where they would be beside Janet and her husband Alex. Maybe once the baby was older she would get work in the "big house". There might even be a horseman's job for David. Mary got up, washed and dressed. The baby was still asleep at the back of the bed. Mary swept and washed the floor, dusted the mantelpiece, then polished the brass rail and fender. The words on the fender gleamed "Home Sweet Home".

It will be, Mary promised herself.

After their breakfast the children were ready for school with time to spare. Maggie played with Alex in front of the fire, clapping his hands.

"You will be all right Mam?"

"Fine, Maggie; you just get away to school and pay attention to the teacher. You're going to a new school soon and I don't want folk to think that you are stupid."

"What new school?" asked Davy.

Mary sat down by the fire beckoning them all to come close to her.

"Well, Dada and I have been speaking and we think it would be fine if we all moved to the country to live. What do you think?"

"What country are we going to Mam? Italy, where Hokey Pokey Joe's from?" said Charlie excitedly.

"No not there," said Mary. "To where your grandmother or Aunt Janet stays."

"Would I get to feed the cows and sheep and work on the land like grandfather?" quizzed Davy.

"Probably; everybody will have to work hard to make our new life succeed. No more time to talk about it now though. Away to school and do your lessons well. I'll make rice pudding for your dinner."

"We should go to Italy Mam and you could make ice cream like Joe," said Charlie.

Mary pulled down the sleeve of his jumper. It was far too short.

"Get away now or you will be late."

After playing with Alex, Mary found a piece of paper that had not been scribbled on, a pen with a nib that looked as if it would write. There was still a drop or two in the bottom of the ink bottle. Mary added a few drops of water then wrote her letters.

She wrapped Alex inside her shawl and left the house hoping that the letters would be despatched before David came home at dinnertime.

Blue pulled the cart along automatically by the side of the canal. David sat on the shafts whistling happily. He thought of working extra hours. It would help to pay for all the expenses of moving. He was glad that he and Mary had the talk. She would have to try to improve, with her mother seeing what was going on and keeping a check on the children. The future really looked promising.

A huge rat ran from the side of the path followed by a cat. They ran right between Blue's front legs. The startled horse reared up. The wood on the cart shifted to the side, then the whole cart toppled over into the canal, the hoses legs flailing the air. Less than ten seconds after the splash only a few bubbles breaking the water surface was evidence that the horse cart and driver ever existed.

Two men ran from the woodyard gate. Where the cart had gone over was soup thick with mud. Pieces of wood were floating up.

"Poor devil must be trapped down there with the horse, Jock."

Both men were pulling off their boots and jackets. They dived into the debris. Three times they surfaced for air. The fourth time they came up with David between them. They pulled him to the side. More workmen were now there, on the bank and pulled the three out to dry land. The two rescuers coughed and spluttered, covered in the muddy water.

David lay still. One man took off his scarf and wiped the mud off David's face.

"Too bad lads, poor soul is dead."

Mary's morning had been busy. The letters were already on the way to Islay and Gigha. She had got a bone and vegetables and made soup to go with the rice pudding. The bairns had snapped up their meal and were away back to school. Mary wondered why David had not been in for his dinner. Maybe the horse had needed to be seen by the farrier or something. She busied herself tidying about the house, then put the girdle on the fire to make some bannocks and scones. Half past three. David would not be in now until suppertime.

There was a knock at the door. Mrs McNair stood on the landing with a policeman. Mary was quickly on the defensive.

"What's she saying the bairns have been up to this time? The greetin' faced auld scunner!"

The policeman stepped inside the door.

"Can we come in and sit down Mrs Chalmers? It's not about the children."

"Well, what is she wanting?" shouted Mary

"I've brought her with me," said the officer, gently pushing Mary into the room. "Make some tea please, Mrs McNair."

He sat Mary down on the bed.

"Mrs Chalmers, I've got bad news for you. David has been in an accident. I'm afraid he's dead."

"Don't speak rubbish," said Mary. "How can he be, we've just sent letters to say we are moving away from Glasgow, and her kind," pointing at Mrs McNair.

"David was drowned this morning when his horse bolted with the load and fell into the canal."

Mary started to laugh hysterically then scream.

Mrs McNair took her in her arms and held her close to her ample bosoms.

"Now dear, I'll no leave you, come on, try a wee drop of tea."

The voices came to Mary from a far distance. She found it difficult to reason with what was said. How could David be dead? They were leaving Glasgow to give the bairns a better chance.

"Drink up your tea Mrs Chalmers, that's the thing. Come on with me Alex and I'll give you something to eat."

Mrs McNair sat down at the table with Alex on her knee.

The policeman fetched a chair and sat beside Mary.

"Now, Mrs Chalmers, have you any friends or relations here to help you with all the formalities?"

"Nobody at all," said Mary, "My family are all in Kilchoman; we're going back there to stay."

The officer turned to Mrs McNair.

"Is there anyone you could get to help with the children or come to be with Mrs Chalmers?"

Mrs McNair kept on feeding the scone to Alex.

"They don't seem to have anyone who comes to the house. At least not that I have seen. I'll be able to manage the bairns. They'll be home from school shortly. They seem to be well able to cope themselves already."

Mary sat gazing into the fire oblivious to her surroundings.

"Come on lass, put your coat on and come with me to the station. There's one or two things you'll have to see too. Is there no man that can help?"

Mary stood up; her legs felt like jelly.

"No, there's not. David never knew his father and it would take days to get in touch with mine, to bring him here."

Suddenly she wondered who would tell Jean what had happened.

Probably best to send Maggie round.

Mary felt her knees buckle.

"What will I tell the bairns? Oh David, what am I to do?"

Mrs McNair got up from the table, handed Alex to the policeman.

"I have some brandy in the house. I'll go and fetch it."

Mary was on her knees at the hearth, wailing and rocking to and fro.

Mrs McNair came back with the bottle and a glass. She poured some into the glass then handed it to Mary.

"It's just like medicine, drink it all over in one swallow. It will make you feel better."

No more persuasion was needed. Mary swallowed the brandy in a gulp.

"There now, sit up on the chair again lass," said the policeman, helping Mary up from the floor. "A wee drink is not a bad thing at times like these, helps to ease the pain."

"Could I have a wee drop more please?" said Mary, holding out the empty glass.

Mrs McNair looked at the officer.

"There's plenty in the bottle if you think it will be alright."

"Yes, give her another," he said "Then we might be able to get through this identification business."

The three children skipped along the street in the bright September sunshine.

"If you step on the lines you'll have bad luck," said Charlie, jumping from one paving stone to the next.

"What rubbish you speak sometimes," said Davy, "How could walking on the pavement bring bad luck?"

"Come on, let's look at the fire station, see if the doors are open," suggested Maggie.

They had to pass nearby to get to Maitland Street.

"We'd best get home, see how Mam is," David told her. "She'll be wondering where we are if she needs messages."

"Will we be near shops when we move beside Grandma?" asked Charlie.

Davy took his hand and pulled him along.

"I don't know what it's like at all. Mam tells us about what it's like but I don't think she's been there at home since she got married to Dada. Maybe even longer."

Maggie was now walking with one foot on the pavement one in the gutter while singing "up today and down the morn".

They turned the corner of Maitland Street.

"Race you, Maggie, first to the close doesn't fetch the water."

Charlie tore off. His fat little legs pounding on. Maggie knew fine it would not matter if he lost anyhow because Charlie was lucky—he never fetched the water. Mam said he was too little. It would either be Davy or herself. What a surprise when they opened the door. There was Mrs McNair sitting in their house with their baby Alex on her knee.

"Where's our Mam?" said Maggie, "That's our baby."

Davy lifted Alex into his arms.

"Come on wee fella, I'll give you a piggy-back."

Charlie ran back through from the room.

"Mam's no lying down through there. Where is she?"

Mrs McNair looked flustered, pulled down her blouse, dragged her hand over her forehead.

"Look bairns, sit down at the table. Your Mam is all right, she's had to go out on some business."

"Where's she gone, Mrs McNair, and left Alex?" quizzed Davy.

"Oh laddie, this is not easy to explain. Your Mam has had to go to the police station."

Maggie looked at Mrs McNair's worried expression.

"That's all right though, wifie, never worry, she'll be away to see about us moving to the country, everything will be great, she'll tell you when she gets back."

Mrs McNair put her arms around Maggie.

"No my wee lamb, that's not what she's doing. A terrible thing has happened. An accident. Your father's had an accident."

Davy jumped round from the bed where he had been bouncing Alex up and down.

"What's happened to our Dada?" he shouted.

"He was drowned in the canal this morning laddie. Nobody could save him. Oh, bairns I'm so sorry to have to tell you."

Charlie turned and punched Maggie in the back.

"I told you not to walk on the lines—it would bring bad luck."

"It's not my fault. I never did anything, I just want my Dada." She started to scream. "You're just saying this because you don't like us. Get out; our Mam will fix you when she gets back. Go on out."

Mrs McNair was in tears herself, but still very much in command.

"That's enough now, stop your screaming. You bairns will have to stick together and help your Mam. No carrying on. It's not easy but things cannot be changed."

Davy disappeared through the room with Alex.

Mrs McNair pointed in the direction of the door.

"Charlie, go and bring your brothers back here. You'll need to pull together and be here when your Mam comes back with the policeman."

"Mrs McNair, what's the policeman got our Mam for? She'll have such a sore head." said Maggie.

"Aye lassie, and a sore broken heart to go with it for a long time. You'll need to be a big girl now and do as much as you can about the house."

"What's she with the police for? Is our Dada in a coffin? Where is he?"

"Oh bairns," said Mrs McNair, "I don't know what's going on. I'm just to be with you until your mother gets back, whenever that may be. Have you got any aunties or uncles you could go to?"

Davy came back into the kitchen, squeezing Alex close to him.

"Yes, we have our Grandma and Grandpa McKinnon in Islay. Our Granny Fraser lives in Glasgow, auntie Janet and uncle Alex live at the smithy on Gigha. We've got two uncles, Donald and John who live far away in New Zealand."

"Well now, Davy, where does your granny Fraser stay? Do you know how to get there?"

"Yes, I'm sure I could find the house; it's in Kelvinside," said Davy.

"Your granny must be well off to live their bairns."

"Oh she is, it's a huge house," said Maggie, "There's a cook and maids and granny Fraser bosses them all around."

"Right then," said Mrs McNair, a bit puzzled as to why, if this was correct, the family lived in such poor circumstances.

"Davy, you will have to go and tell your granny Fraser that your mother is badly in need of help. Get her around here to be with you all."

Maggie seemed to have already forgotten what was the cause of all the upheaval and did not wish to miss out on a visit to the big house.

"I'll come with you Davy, show you the way. Charlie can play with Alex until we get back."

"That would be fine," said Mrs McNair, relieved that the children were no longer upset and screaming, and also that help was on the way.

"Charlie and Alex you can come to my house and have your tea."

It was after seven when the pair stood on the front steps to the stately house. Davy rang the doorbell while Maggie tried to peer through the small leaded panes of glass on the inside door.

"You can't see a thing Davy, but I can smell polish. Maybe it's elbow grease, that's what Mam says puts a shine on things."

A young girl in a black dress with a white frilly cap and apron opened the door.

"What do you want here? No begging." She looked at the sorry state of the children. "Go round to the back door and cook will give you a piece."

Davy stepped up into the vestibule beside Maggie.

"Can we speak to our granny Fraser please.?" He asked.

The maid looked puzzled.

Davy tried to explain.

"It's our Dada's mother—Jean Fraser."

At the mention of her father Maggie started to wail.

"Our Dada's been drowned, he's in a coffin, Mam's away with a policeman. Mrs McNair's taken our Charlie and Alex. I want my Mam."

She was now screaming hysterically and pulling at the young maid's apron.

"Stop all the noise," she said, "You'll have the master disturbed at his dinner."

Davy took hold of Maggie around the shoulders.

"She can't help it," he sobbed, "We want to speak to our Granny."

"Come on in and keep quiet. I'll take you into the servants' hall. Mrs Fraser is at dinner with the master. I'll fetch her later. Now no noise."

As was the usual custom the master and the housekeeper had their evening meal together. This gave Jean time to discuss the various details associated with the management of the house. It also saved the master from a solitary mealtime. In the servants" hall a cheery fire burned in the grate. A brass companion set gleamed beside a filled brass coalscuttle.

"No sticks for them," said Davy.

"Mam would love some of that coal."

Maggie picked up two fist sized lumps and shoved them up the leg of her knickers.

The maid came back into the room, followed by Jean Fraser.

"Mercy bairns, what brings you here and in such a state?"

Davy and Maggie's clothes were dirty and shabby. She had wiped the tears from her face with the coal-blackened hands. Davy with a visibly trembling lip started to tell the woman they called Granny, twice a year on hourly visits, why they were there.

He sobbed, "Mrs McNair sent us to fetch you; she's got our Alex and Charlie. Mam is away with the policeman."

Jean took a clean handkerchief from her pocket and blew Maggie's nose.

"Now, now it will be all right; is your father working?"

Davy wiped his nose on his sleeve, then managed to squeeze those awful words from his throat.

"Dada is dead, he was drowned in the canal."

Jean looked at the boy, her flesh and blood. The words rang through her head like vibrations of a gong. She felt a tightening in her chest like a steel band crushing the breath from her. David, her son, dead. Pain shot up the side of her jaw, her arms felt heavy and numb. Jean felt herself slide through a curtain of blackness into oblivion.

The hansom cab took them back to Maitland Street. No one to come with them to help. The master of the big house told them Granny would be all right and well looked after.

Everything seemed chaotic at first. The maid screaming for help. The cook shouting for the master and the master shouting for a doctor.

All the time Granny lay on the floor not moving. Maggie volunteered information. "She'll be fine, just taken too much of the headache medicine. Mam's often like that. Put her to bed and she'll be fine in the morning."

The master asked who the children were, yet without waiting for the details ordered "Get them in a cab and home safely away from here."

As they got down from the cab Maggie dropped one of her pieces of coal she had retrieved from her undergarments.

"Mam will get a fine heat off this."

The gas light was on. Mrs McNair was sitting by the bed.

Mary was lying flat, her head rolling from side to side on the pillow. She was talking to herself.

"What will I do now you've left me, David? How will I feed your bairns?"

"Wheesht now and try to sleep, Mrs Chalmers. Here's the bairns back. Could your Granny not come with you?" questioned Mrs McNair.

"No, she's had to lie down with a sore head like Mam's," said Maggie.

"Mam we were for a hurl in a hansom cab."

Davy knelt on the bed and leaned over his mother.

"Where's Alex, Mam, do you know?"

Mrs McNair pulled him back.

"Alex is asleep; a neighbour's looking after him. Your mam had a bit too much brandy to get her over the shock. She'll be fine in the morning. You bairns get away to your beds as well."

Maggie went to the fireplace and threw the coal onto the dying cinders of the fire.

"I want my Dada," she cried.

CHAPTER TWO

T HE DAY OF the funeral was wet and windy. The water fell from the sky like transparent sheets blowing before the wind. Large blobs bounced off the ground like clear rubber balls. Mary, the Church Minister and four men from the wood yard stood beside the open ground.

"Ashes to ashes, dust to dust, life everlasting."

What life, thought Mary. She had five shillings to provide lasting life for the four bairns and herself. Things were going from bad to worse. Granny Fraser was still hanging between life and death, too ill to be moved to the Infirmary. The doctor said her heart was in a bad way. This very morning Mary had a letter from the Minister at Kilchoman telling her that her message home had been passed on to him. The letter said her father had died years ago. The farm had been given up. Mary's mother had moved away to live on another part of the island. He would try to get the letter to her mother. In the meantime he "hoped that all was well and God was good to them."

What God? Surely it's an evil power that has brought me to this.

The minister had stopped praying. He stepped forward taking Mary's hand in his.

"David is at the right hand of God now, he's in the place that's been prepared for him."

Mary pulled her hand away, stood straight, with head held high.

"Tell me then, Minister, who prepared this bloody hellish place for me and my fatherless bairns? Was it God or was it the Devil? Who will prepare a place for them to sleep or eat?"

The Minister was taken aback and as he bowed his head, the water poured like a waterfall from the brim of his hat.

"You poor, distraught woman. I'll pray for you that the Lord will bless you and provide for you."

"He had best make it bloody quick then," said Mary, "For five shillings'll not last hellish long to provide for them."

Mrs McNair tried to calm Mary down.

"Come on now Mary, the bairns will be needing you. They'll be waiting for their tea."

This set Mary going again.

"They'll wait a bloody long time for tea if they wait for the good Lord making it. The Lord should have left me with my man and the bairns their father."

The minister was like a clockwork toy shaking hands with the four men in turn, side stepping as fast as he could to move away from the graveside and Mary.

October and November were bleak months with high winds and rain. Mary tried hard to find a way to earn a little money. She had sent Maggie and Davy to some of the big houses in the "better off" parts of town, offering her services as a washerwoman. At first this worked rather well. Mary tackled the laundry in the communal wash-house.

Mrs McNair, true to her word, had been a good friend. She looked after Alex and always made sure that the older ones had something to eat, a bowl of soup or bread and jam.

All day in the steaming wash-house and standing by the hot fire ironing, tired Mary out. She told herself that a wee drink would perk her up and help her to see the job finished. The wee drinks got bigger and the work got less.

Things were at a desperate stage. It was the twenty-sixth of November. In two days" time the rent was due. Mary lay on the bed in a drunken stupor. There was not a penny in the house. Mrs McNair entered the room. She looked at the prone figure on the bed. The fireplace was running over with ashes, odds and ends of clothes lay scattered around. Beside the bed stood a chipped enamel bucket full of urine. The stench was awful.

This is no use, thought Mrs McNair; those poor bairns are living like animals. She could hear them in the room.

"Davy are you there?" she shouted.

"Aye, we're fine, Mrs McNair," he answered.

"Come on ben, I want to speak to you."

The bairns were a sorry sight. They were so thin. Charlie's face was like a frame around gigantic eyes. His curly golden hair hung in ringlets down about his shoulders. Maggie's face was dirty, her nose bright red with green trails hanging down on to he upper lip. She was holding Alex by the hand. He was wearing no clothes on his lower half. Every few minutes he gave a whimper.

Maggie told him "You be quiet, Mam will be better in a minute and give us something to eat."

Davy just stood, head bowed, looking at the floor.

"What have you had to eat today?" asked Mrs McNair.

"We aren't hungry, Mrs McNair, we'll get tea when Mam's head is better," said Maggie.

Mrs McNair took Alex in her arms.

"You're needing something anyhow, you are frozen. Why is his bum bare?"

"He keeps peeing his clothes; there's nothing dry to put on him," Davy explained.

Mrs McNair took a piece of rag from the pocket of her overall and wiped Maggie's nose.

"Blow hard; see if you can keep the snotters from running into your mouth. Davy get a blanket, coat or something, and wrap it around Alex before he gets pneumonia. You'll all better come downstairs with me."

"Will Mam be all right though? She's sick sometimes when she is in bed," said a worried Maggie.

"You'll all be sick if this goes on. She'll be fine for a wee while. Come on, hurry up."

Mrs McNair sat them around the table; they each had a large bowl of soup in front of them.

"Take a bit of loaf now and dip it in your soup. I'll see to you, wee man."

She picked up a piece of torn sheet, deftly folded it into a square, and then pinned it around Alex's blue posterior.

"This is a lovely house," said Maggie. "You've so many treasures and pictures on your mantelpiece."

"Aye," said Mrs McNair, "That was my man, he was an engine driver."

"That's what I want to be," said Davy. "I'd like to work with engines. I'm not going to be a carter like my Dada. Sometimes I think I'd like to work on a farm. My Granddad had a farm, but he's dead now."

"We were going to stay beside them in Italy." said Charlie.

"Mam would learn to make ice-cream same as Hokey Pokey Joe."

Mrs McNair listened to the chatter. They were good bairns. What could she do for them? It was a disaster. She could not afford to keep them herself. Really she did not feel able. Next year she would be sixty-eight years old. Mary was never to be any better. She had given her as much help as she could. Mary could have taken the place of the daughter she never had. Being sorry for Mary did no good. She just could not face up to looking after her family. There was nothing else for it, she would have to go to the police, see if they might know what to do. Mary was in need of help; the bairns were needing to be cared for. She would have to do something.

"Now listen bairns, I'll have to go a message for a minute. You'll be fine supping your broth until I get back."

"I'll go for you Mrs McNair," offered Maggie, jumping down from her chair.

"No, no my bairns, you finish your soup."

"Aye, it's really good," said Charlie his face glowing from eating the hot food.

"Davy, you make sure that Alex gets enough, keep him warm. I'll be back soon. Everything is going to be all right."

"We will manage by ourselves, thank you," said Davy. "You are very good to us, Mrs McNair. You know we didn't like you very much at first but now that we know you better you really are our friend."

The old woman felt a lump in her throat. Was she doing the right thing?

Maggie started to cough. The bairns were not well; they deserved to be cared for properly.

"Now, behave until I get back," she said as she pulled her shawl round her shoulders. "Don't touch the fire."

The desk sergeant at the Northern Police Station was a busy man.

What did this woman want him to do next—look after neglected bairns?

"Look missus, if you've got the bairns they'll be fine with you," he said.

"Aye, but that's just in the meantime," said a frustrated Mrs McNair. Now that she had plucked up the courage to do the right thing by the bairns, she was not to be put off by an overfed, well cared for male, with no understanding of what these bairns had suffered.

"Look, I'm not to tell you again. These poor wee souls have gone through hell since their father died in September. Their mother is seldom sober. They haven't had a decent meal for months. Never been at the school. Their home worse than a pig-sty. The rags they wear for clothes are filthy. Not a bite to eat in the house and as usual their mother is lying absolutely pissed out of her mind with gin. Mind you there are times that I canna blame the lassie. She canna support four weans on nothing."

"Enough missus, I'm busy at the moment myself but I'll send a constable round to see what is going on. Where do you live?"

Mrs McNair was glad it was over. The responsibility was hers no longer.

"Seventy-three Maitland Street, the top landing. I stay down stairs. The bairns are in my house just now, poor wee lambs."

"Stay here a minute and I'll get an officer to go back with you."

The sergeant left the counter and returned minutes later with the same officer who had gone for Mrs McNair on that dreadful day David Chalmers drowned.

"I know this woman and the family you are talking about. Remember the poor chap was drowned at the canal when his horse was spooked by a rat? It's his family."

"Right I mind o' that now," replied the sergeant, "The wife had to identify the body and attend the Fiscal's enquiry by herself, poor woman."

"Poor bairns more like," interrupted Mrs McNair, "She's never been sober since."

The constable escorted Mrs McNair past her own door to the flat upstairs. Mary still lay flat on the bed. She had been sick. The vomit was on her neck, hair and the already filthy pillow.

"She's going to choke herself yet," said Mrs McNair.

"If she doesn't stop breathing first from the stink in here," blurted out the constable, "This is awful. In two months what a change. I can see why you're concerned, missus."

"Well, what are you going to do about it? The weans canna live here any more."

"Have they got any relatives to take them?"

Mrs McNair thought for a minute.

"Well Maggie did tell me once that her Granny lived in Kelvinside, but I think it was in her imagination for when Davy went to look for her, some posh man sent them back in a hansom cab. Their other grandparents are from Italy."

"Are they Roman Catholics then? Maybe the priest could help?"

"No I don't think they belong to any church. The parish minister buried the husband, but Mary left him without a name."

"Well missus, there's nothing for it but for me to have her charged with being drunk and in charge of the children, then take them all back to the police station."

What a sensation it caused in the street. The horse-drawn Black Maria standing at the close mouth. A crowd gathered to watch the entertainment. The bairns were led out by a sergeant. Mary, being supported by two burly law officers, was not at all pleased at being disturbed and wakened to face reality.

She was shouting "You fat buggers, dragging a poor widow woman from her sick-bed. Leave me alone, you cowards."

She was a sorry sight, dangling between them, her feet dragging behind. Her hair was matted to her forehead with dried vomit.

"You're just trying to make a fool of me in front of my bairns and neighbours."

They pushed her up the two steps into the van and shut the door.

The children sat on a bench facing the sergeant, who was writing into a big book on the counter. Alex was on Maggie's knee. Charlie stood huddled into Day's side.

"What's going on, Davy?" whispered Maggie. "Where have they taken our Mam?"

"I don't know," he answered. "I'm just glad not to hear her shouting and swearing."

Maggie started to cry. "I wish my Dada was here. I'm so frightened they lock us up."

"We haven't done anything wrong, Maggie," he assured her.

"No, but Mam has. She bit that bobby's hand and kicked the other one between the legs. Do you think that Mrs McNair will come for us?"

"I don't know, Maggie. She got the police."

A stern looking woman in a tight fitting black coat with a high collar and black hat collected them from the police station.

"I don't want any nonsense from you," she said. "Be glad you paupers are to have a roof over your head at the poor house. Follow me and no dawdling." Maggie tried to hurry but Alex was clinging to her neck. Davy carried Charlie who was crying.

"What's a pauper Davy?" gasped Maggie trying to keep up.

"I don't know Maggie, but by the way she said it I don't think it's nice."

It was a sombre looking building from the outside. Inside was all scrubbed wooden floors with the walls painted dark brown and dark green.

Alex was taken away from Maggie.

Two girls, about fifteen, were told to take her to the wash-house.

"Give her a good scrub with carbolic soap and no doubt she's got head lice, so cut her hair short then put on the oil."

Maggie felt sick with fear. The girls pulled her clothes off, threw them on the floor, then they set about her emaciated body with scrubbing brushes and soap.

"Stop that you bitches," she screamed.

The bigger girl pushed the bar of soap into Maggie's mouth.

"That'll learn you to keep quiet!"

Maggie retched and spat.

"I'm going to die. Stop it or my brother Davy will get you."

Little did Maggie know that she was never to see her brother Davy again.

Mary's head pounded. Her tongue was stuck to the roof of her mouth. She forced her eyes open to see four bare walls. One with a barred aperture high up near the ceiling. She lay on the floor. Her soiled clothing stank.

"Oh please, God help me," she cried." Where are my bairns?"

She tried to stand up. A wave of sickness made her drop on to all fours. Green bile poured from her mouth and nose. "God please don't let me die. I love my bairns, what have I done?"

The heavy door opened slowly, a uniformed officer stood well back from the entry. "No feeling so frisky and fighting fit now then?"

Mary tried to get up and face him. With one hand against the wall she was able to stand. "What's happened to my bairns, you dirty bastard?" she screamed.

"Ho ho, smell yourself if you can't see who is dirty. Shit yourself as well and I'm dirty! Here's a bucket of water; clean yourself up for the court at ten o'clock."

Mary drank some of the water from the bucket, then started to wash. Surely this was a nightmare and she would wake up in bed beside David.

The cold water and washing helped her to accept this disaster was reality. Mrs McNair would have the bairns. The shame of being lifted by the police and going to court hit her with full force of the seriousness and probable consequences. Mary felt her body shake until her teeth chattered. "God help me, I'll never drink again. Let me home to my bairns."

Mary sat in court, head lowered until her chin touched her chest. The constable read his story from a notebook. The bailie, a staunch rechabite, listened intently. Mary could feel shame and embarrassment for her behaviour. Her very toes curled until the nails scraped the floor.

"Where are the children now, constable?" queried the bailie.

"Being destitute sir, we had no alternative but have them admitted to the poor house."

Mary wailed "Oh, my poor bairns!"

"Before passing sentence, has the accused anything to say?"

No words would come. She shook her head.

"Having considered all the relevant details, I have decided that five days in prison will give the offender time to contemplate her children's future in a sober state. Take her away."

Maggie lay quiet on the straw mattress covered with a coarse grey blanket. Her hair cropped short and liberally soaked in strong smelling oil, was covered with a cotton cap. The two girls who had assisted Maggie to wash, were among the eight sleeping figures in the room. Wishing no further lessons from them Maggie lay still trying to stifle her sobs, with her hands over her mouth. Where were Mam and the boys? Why was she separated from them? She hoped that Davy was looking after Alex and Charlie.

Charlie and Alex were seated at the table with the old men at breakfast. Maggie sat with the two girls and five old women. Breakfast was a bowl of porridge, skimmed milk and a piece of bread.

Maggie rose from her place at the table and ran towards her brothers.

"Where's Davy gone, Charlie?" she shouted before her two minders pulled her back to the table.

"Eat your food and be grateful to your provider, for caring," said one.

"Shut your face you plooky bitch. My brother Davy is away for my Mam, she could fight the police so she'll bash you." boasted Maggie.

Maggie was rewarded for her outburst with a sharp kick in the backside.

"Eat up and shut up or I'll put my fist in your mouth"

Maggie gingerly sat down on her painful buttocks and supped the lumpy porridge.

The bailie was a wise man. The withdrawal of drink and shame of Mary's actions was a tremendous punishment. She was glad to be free and to make amends for her madness. She hurried along the street; the neighbours would all be watching from behind the twitching curtains.

Glad for the refuge of the close, Mary ran up the stairs longing for the shelter of her own home. The door was locked. Mary rattled it in desperation.

Mrs McNair came up the stairs to investigate the noise.

"It's yourself, Mary lass. How are you?

"I'm all right but I can't get this door open"

"Oh Mary, I'm sorry. The factor was round. You never paid the rent, so he's let it to someone else."

"This is grand start anyhow. Talk about kicking a dog when it's down. What has happened to my belongings?"

"They were all dumped out the backies. I've tried to save as much as I could. You know what happens with the neighbours. Nobody has very much, so they helped themselves to what was there. Come on down, I'll show you what I've got and we can have a cup of tea."

Mary was crying.

"How can I get my bairns back? I've no place to take them. Nothing at all to call my own."

"You're a strong young woman Mary. Put all this behind you and do the best you can for Davy, Maggie, Charlie and Alex. Surely you have some family that can help you?"

"I'll write to my mother and sister and see what they can do. Of course they might not want to know me after the mess I've made of things."

"The important thing is, Mary, that you realise where you were wrong; you want to change and do the best you can by your family. Write to them and for now you can stay with me lass."

While Mary was writing to her mother and Janet, she thought of David's mother Jean. Was she still alive? Could she help?

She would go this afternoon and find out, before she collected the bairns.

Jean Fraser ushered Mary into her own sitting room. The master had been good to her. The housemaid was now her assistant and a young girl had been brought in to help. Jean still controlled the running of the house but was required to rest several times each day.

"It's been a long time since I've seen you Mary. How's the family?"

Mary could not look at the older woman in the face. She looked down at her hands folded on her lap.

"That's why I've come to see you, for the sake of the bairns."

Mary started to sob. "I'm so ashamed, what a mess I've made of things."

An hour later Jean was aware of the problems that had faced her daughter in law since her son David's untimely death. Jean was well aware of the difficulties of providing for a child with no man behind you. Mary's problem was four times worse. Mary's weakness and refuge in drink did not help matters.

"Look lassie, I've no home of my own to take you and my grandchildren.

We've got to get them out of the poor house. Poor wee things."

Jean went across the room to the top drawer of a chest and brought out a small leather purse. Into Mary's hand she put five gold sovereigns.

"Take this, lassie, and get somewhere to stay with the bairns. It's what I had put aside for my burial. By the time it's needed I'll be past bothering. The worry of you and my David's children are more important."

Mary kissed Jean on the cheek. She had always been afraid of this staid old woman who always spoke with authority. The eyes were the same as her David's.

"Thank you for the chance. I'll be forever grateful to you. I'll get them round to see you."

"Just spend the money wisely and take heed of the hard lesson you've had. Keep away from the drink or don't ever come back to me."

Mrs McNair and Mary sat at the other side of the desk facing the poorhouse superintendent.

"Yes Mrs Chalmers, the board decided that young David should be given a chance in life, so he has been sent to Mossbank Industrial School to learn a trade."

"The board decided! What right did they have to say what should happen to my son?" screamed Mary who was almost hysterical.

"Every right; the children were destitute and paupers. You were in jail unfit to make any choice as to the children's future. It's in the lad's best interest to be taught how to be self sufficient and support himself."

"You sneaking, ferret-faced bastard. How do you know what's best for the boy? Probably never been able to father a son of your own, so you interfere in the lives of other people."

"That's just about enough from you. Any more and I'll call the police."

"Call the bloody Queen if you want. She's a mother. She'd understand. I want my bairns."

Mrs McNair pulled Mary around to face her and in a quiet voice told her to calm down or she might not get Maggie, Charlie and Alex released into her care.

Maggie's heart was thumping so hard she could feel it in her ears. Her Mam was there to waiting to collect her. She rushed from the room filled with old women.

Her Mam was standing in the hall beside a table with a big potted aspidistra. Mrs McNair sat beside the door on a high-backed chair. She showed no sign of recognition as Maggie came through the door.

"Oh Mam, take me home," cried Maggie.

Her mother turned at the sound of the familiar voice.

"In the name of God, what have they done to you, my wee lamb?" exclaimed Mary, looking with sober eyes, for the first time in months, at her only daughter. Maggie's cropped, greasy hair, cold sores on her lips and nose did nothing to enhance her thin skinny body.

"I'm fine Mam. Is your sore head better? Are we all going home? The boys as well?"

Mary could not answer at first. She was filled with shame and remorse. This was the daughter that she and David had wanted so much. The plans they had made together for this bairn. How she would be brought up well-mannered, well educated. Maybe a governess or a teacher, then marry into money. Life is a fickle bitch decided Mary, but I'll beat it yet.

"Aye my wee darling, the boys are just coming and we are off to Mrs McNair's for the night."

The excitement of the next day kept Maggie and Charlie from nagging too much as to the whereabouts of Davy. First thing in the morning they went round to Water Street where a Mrs Davidson at number seventy-four had a furnished attic for let. It was small but neat and tidy. There were two double beds fitted into the "fall ins" of the roof slopes. That would be adequate for them. Maggie would sleep with Mary and Alex when Davy came home. The rent had to be paid a quarter in advance but it still left enough to buy some clothes for them to wear. Mary carried the few belongings saved by Mrs McNair up to their attic haven. Mrs Davidson had set the fire ready to light. They settled in quickly; it was a cosy wee home.

Mary managed to find work scrubbing. Things were working out not too bad.

If only Davy was home. Mary had not even seen him since that dreadful day she was arrested.

"This is Hogmanay Mam. What does that mean?" asked Charlie.

"It's the last day of the old year. Tomorrow is the start of a New Year," she explained.

"What happens then Mam," chimed in Maggie. "Will things be different?"

Maggie took her mother's hand in hers.

"Things are better now, Mam. You've no more sore heads, Alex has stopped peeing himself and Charlie doesn't wet the bed anymore."

"You're right lassie, we should be thankful for small mercies."

The children were fast asleep. Mary sat by the fire as the last hours of the old year ticked away. Her mind was full of questions and thoughts of her family. What did the future hold for her and her bairns? Was her mother coping on her own in Tormisdale?

Margaret McKinnon was nearly seventy. She had never left her native Islay in all those years. Mary thought her mother must feel as alone as she did at that moment in time. Charles, her father was dead, her brothers in New Zealand and Janet away in Gigha. Aye, her mother must be thinking of her bairns as well. Mother was typical of the Islay stock, programmed to work at anything from weaving, fishing crofting, even making whisky; father had been a farmer. Mary remembered those warm sunny days helping to cole the hay, lifting the potatoes, baiting the lobster creels. It was a good life. The long summer evenings, walking up the hill to see the sun sink like a scarlet ball beyond the rim of the Earth. The ceilidhs and story telling. Mary loved to hear some of her mother's tales of her cousin Colin McLiver, who joined the army and put down the Indian mutiny. He was a Lord now and a friend of Queen Victoria. Strange, when here she was in a furnished room, miles from kith and kin. Her mother was in much the same position.

Mary decided she would write to her sister Janet. It would be good if she would visit and bring her up to date with island news. It would be such a treat to have a conversation in her own native tongue. Things could be better, yet on the other hand they could revert to being much worse.

Mary had resisted the temptation of drink. Mrs McNair had primarily been the strength behind her abstinence, never allowing her to forget that dreadful week in jail. The shock of seeing what she had done to her children would live with her forever.

Mary's thoughts then turned to Davy. Yes, he would do better with a trade, but the emotional cost was high.

When she slipped into bed, Maggie stirred "Oh it's you Mam. Love you" she then folded her arms around Mary's neck.

Maggie and Charlie were excited—they were getting a visitor.

Auntie Janet was coming from Gigha. She was to land at the Broomielaw on the steamer from Campbeltown.

"What does she look like, Mam?" asked Maggie.

"Gosh lassie, I wonder myself. It will be twenty years since I've seen her."

"Is she as old as Granny McNair?" questioned Charlie.

"No. She's my sister. Not my mother. She's two years older than me."

Alex was toddling around the baggage stacked on the quay.

"Maggie fetch him back until I watch for Janet, she might walk past us."

Janet McMillan could see her younger sister standing with three of her four children.

"Mary, I'm over here."

It was an emotional reunion for the sisters. They had both thought of each other as they had parted twenty years before. Now they were two matronly women embracing and crying.

"I thought you wanted to see each other, not hide in each other's collar'" said Charlie.

They both laughed at his remark.

Janet smiling looked at her nephew, "You must be Charlie."

"Yes. I'm named after your father, Charles."

"That's right; and this is Maggie named after my mother. Who are you named after Alex?"

"The doctor who delivered him," replied Mary.

"Where's your oldest boy David? Is he at home?"

Poor Mary did not know what to say. A lump came up in her throat fit to choke her.

"He's at school just now. Hurry along bairns, Auntie Janet will be ready for her tea."

Mary was afraid that Maggie, who had a knack of blurting out the truth, might expand on the explanation.

Janet had never lived in a town. She was amazed at the cramped living conditions that housed her sister and family. She was surprised at Mary allowing her oldest boy to go to a trades school. Admittedly there was not much room for him here. Not much of a life for any of them in this small room with two double beds, a table and chairs. Janet considered the house she kept for the Scarletts with its massive reception rooms. The housemaids cupboard was about the same square footage as his sister's home.

The women sat well into the night reminiscing. There was laughter, tears, anger, even thought and hopes for the future.

Janet chose her moment carefully before suggesting to Mary, "Charlie would have a good life with us on Gigha. With no children of our own Alex, could apprentice him as a blacksmith then he could take over the business. Think about it Mary; we could give him a life in the open air, just as David and you planned."

All night long she considered Janet's offer. There was no future here in Glasgow for Charlie. If she felt trapped in a cage, then it would be best to release her son from that captivity. At least she would be comforted by knowing Janet would treat him as her son. It would not be the great unknown that her beloved Davy was facing.

Two days later Mary, Maggie and Alex stood on the quay, waving goodbye to Janet and Charlie.

Mary wiped her eyes then blew her nose.

"I'll never leave you and Alex, Mam, we'll always be together."

"Always is a long time Maggie."

"Well nearly always then. Come on Alex, we're going to Granny McNair's for tea."

Mrs McNair was in bed. She had a bad cold, which had settled in her chest. She sat propped up against the pillows.

"Och, I'll manage Mary. Never died of winter yet." She tried to joke. Mary could hear her wheezing.

"Have you had the doctor?"

"Lord no, lassie how could I afford the doctor? I've been having a wee drop of toddy and a bit of butter rolled in sugar that stops the cough."

Mary made certain that everything she could do to help was done. This was as near a mother as she would get. Deep down Mary had grown to love this woman, who was there for her in her hour of need. This woman who was unstinting in the love she gave the bairns.

"Stay in bed, I'll be back first thing in the morning. If you are no better then to hell with the cost, it's the doctor for you."

Mary was up and about early; she got Maggie ready for school. Momentarily she thought about Charlie.

"Come on Alex, we'd better check on how Granny McNair is today."

The door was unlocked.

"Cooee, it's just me," shouted Mary.

Mrs McNair was still sitting up in bed; her face was dark blue, with her tongue protruding from her mouth.

"In the name of Jesus, she's dead," she announced to the empty room. "In God's name what am I to do?"

She picked up Alex and ran to the Northern Police Station.

"I've just found my friend Mrs McNair dead," she told the duty constable at the counter.

"And where would that be that you found her?" he asked.

"In her bed of course, at seventy-three Maitland Street. What the hell am I going to do?"

"Calm down for a start, before you have a heart attack yourself," was the suggestion. Only then did Mary appreciate that her dear friend was no longer alive.

"I'm a jinx; anything I care for is taken from me. I'm not allowed to love or care."

The sergeant appeared from the door behind the counter.

"Oh it's you Mrs Chalmers. Not to give us any bother are you?"

"No. I've just found my best friend Mrs McNair dead in her bed. I'm not sure what to do."

"I'll come with you myself lassie," said the sergeant, putting on his helmet.

Turning towards the counter he ordered "Get the doctor to attend at seventy three Maitland Street as soon as possible. Come on Mary let's see what has happened."

Mary sat staring into the embers of the fire. Maggie and Alex were asleep. The funeral had gone without a fuss. Mrs McNair's family had paid their last respects, locked up the house and promptly left for

Edinburgh. They had packed a basket with what food there was in the house and given it to Mary.

"No need to waste it, after all it's still good," they had said.

Mary lifted it from behind the door, where she has laid it down. It was heavy. There was jam, sugar, eggs, tea and an almost full bottle of Brandy.

Mary looked at the bottle, her tongue rolled around inside her mouth. She set the bottle on the table. No she would not touch it. She returned to her seat beside the fire. How she missed her boys. How many more nights would she sit here alone with just her memories and no hope or plans for the future?

Mrs McNair herself and the constable had told her—a wee drink did no harm at a time like this to ease the pain.

She would just take one wee drink.

The empty bottle stood on the table. Mary had never been to bed. As daylight broke she left the house to walk in the fresh air. She wandered down the street as if drawn like metal to a magnet, to the canal side. Oh David, what is it about me that courts disaster? She'd loved David from the first time they met at the Highlandman's Umbrella. He was gentle, kind, protective. Mary leaned over to look into the black flowing water. What was that she could see down there beneath the surface? She knelt over the edge to get a better look. It was David, beckoning her to come join him. Mary longed so to be in the warm safety of his arms. "Darling, I'm coming to be with you," she said.

There was no splash as her body slid into the water and disappeared below the surface; Mary had joined her beloved David and had found peace in his arms.

CHAPTER THREE

ALEX' CRYING WAKENED Maggie. "Mam, what time is it?" When she got no answer Maggie rose from her bed. Alex was there alone. "Shut up and stop your greetin." Mam must be away to the lav." Despite scolding, she got in beside him and cuddled her close in her arms. "Mam will be back in a minute." When Mary never appeared Maggie got up and looked at the food on the table.

"Here's an eggie for your breakfast. You'd enjoy that eh,"

Alex sat up and nodded.

Maggie raked the fire, kindled it and when the sticks were blazing, boiled the egg for her young brother.

Dinnertime came near and Mary had still not returned. Maggie ventured down to see if she was with Mrs Davidson. "No lassie, I've no seen her this day. She'll no be far though, maybe just at the shops."

"She's been already, for the messages are on the table. Alex had an egg for his breakfast."

Alex nodded in agreement.

"You're a proper little mother, Maggie. How old are you?"

"I'll be eleven come September."

"Och weel," said Mrs Davidson "You'll manage awa fine until Mam gets back."

Mam never got home.

Next morning Mrs Davidson suggested that Maggie and Alex were taken into some sort of care. She told the police their mother had deserted them.

Maggie would not believe this.

"She'll be lying drunk some place officer. I'm not having them in my house if she's back on the drink."

"Our Mam doesn't drink, you rotten old liar," said Maggie "How could she when you need all our money to live in your flea-ridden garret?"

Maggie was not to have the likes of her slanging off her Mam.

"You be quiet, you insolent little toe-rag. Get them out of my house at once. I should never have agreed to have them in the first place. It was only as a favour."

"It was only for the money. You greedy old miser"

The constable took hold of Maggie by the shoulders. "That's enough. You've gone too far, young lady."

"Couldn't get far enough away from her anyhow," was Maggie's final fling.

"Get your young brother and come with us."

Back to the bloody poor house she said to herself. Hope Mam hurries up and fetches us.

This time I'll be ready for them.

"Oh yes, the Chalmers children again," sneered the Superintendent. "Had to happen, just a question of time, with that drunken mother. Is she in jail again?"

"No she is not. She's just gone for a message."

"Been missing for twenty four hours, leaving the children alone," explained the constable.

"No doubt like the bad penny, she'll turn up sometime," the Superintendent quipped.

"Our Mam's not a bad penny, she's the best Mam in Glasgow. Isn't she, Alex?"

Alex nodded a favourable response.

A week passed, before Mary suffered the final indignity of a pauper's grave as her last resting place.

The board at the poor house ordered a letter be sent to Alex McMillan, the blacksmith on the Isle of Gigha, regarding the future welfare of his niece and nephew.

At the mid October meeting his reply was discussed. The blacksmith made it quite clear that at sixty years of age he did not feel he could accept the responsibility of bringing up two more children. Alex was only two; it would mean his wife Janet giving up her job as housekeeper to care for him. Maggie certainly could help but he did not feel he could meet the cost of raising three children. He would continue to keep and support Charles. The delay in replying was with much regret, however, it was because it took some time to reach this final decision.

There was only one thing to be done; Maggie would have to be boarded out with a family who would allow her to work for her keep and accept the ten pounds per annum awarded by the parochial board.

Over the four weeks in the poor house Maggie's spark had been extinguished. She was left in no doubt as to what a pauper meant. From morning to night she had scrubbed and cleaned, accepted the fact that she should be grateful to the goodness of others for the meagre diet she received.

After those four weeks she had been given clean clothes to wear. Although obviously not new, they were clean, tidy and presentable. A large luggage label was tied to her lapel. It was so close to her chin, Maggie could not read the writing. Never ask questions, she had learned, just conform and do what you are told.

The Superintendent handed her a brown paper parcel tied with a string.

"That's your change of clothes to take with you. Be sure not to lose it, for you will get no more"

Maggie grew more curious as to what was happening and where she was going. Must to be to Auntie Janet. I'll be with Charlie again.

"Right girl, come with me."

The Superintendent marched along beside Maggie. They reached the railway station.

"Stand there and don't move until I get your ticket," he ordered

Maggie's feet were rooted to the ground but her head twisted at various angles trying to read the tag tied to her.

The Superintendent came back, accompanied by a man in uniform.

"This is the guard of the train Maggie; you are to do as he says and he will deliver you at the right station. Remember, work hard, say your prayers giving thanks to your benefactors for allowing you this opportunity to grow into something better."

Maggie nodded.

Yes she might change into a brown paper parcel that would not need food or cared for.

The guard was a kindly man. He took Maggie by the hand.

"Come away with me pet. Have you been on a train before?"

Maggie shook her head.

A seat was made for her among the mailbags.

"You'll be comfy there until I get back. Don't worry"

Maggie sat without moving a muscle. I am a parcel, she decided.

All around her were boxes and packages similar to her with labels showing names and addresses, where they would be collected. She started to cry. Was this what had happened to her Alex? He would be so frightened without her. She loved her baby brother so much and even he was gone.

The train started with a jolt. The guard came back rolling up a green flag.

"Well, that's us on our way, dearie."

"When do we get to Gigha, mannie?"

"Losh lass, this is a steam train not a steam boat. Gigha is an island across the water. You need a boat to get there. This is a steam train bound for Inverness."

Maggie slumped back against the bags.

She only knew Aunt Janet, maybe she had moved to this other place. That's what it would be, yes, they had moved house a few times. They lived in New Keppoch Hill Road, then Scott Street before Maitland and Water Streets. People do move from one house to another.

The swaying of the train soon lulled Maggie to sleep. She dreamed of the two girls grabbing and scrubbing her. She could feel them pulling her shoulders.

"Waken up bairn, we are almost there. You've slept the whole journey."

Maggie sat up, grabbed her brown paper parcel that had fallen from her knee. The train was slowing down.

"You sit there until I come back for you," said the guard.

When he returned, he was accompanied by a tall man wearing moleskin trousers, a black jacket, with a coloured scarf at his throat. He had a full set of whiskers. They were snowy white as was his hair.

"So you are Maggie Chalmers," he said to her. "Well from now on you are in my care; you do what I tell you. Do you understand?"

Maggie swallowed hard then managed to say "Yes."

"That's good. My name is John McDonald but you can call me father, it will be easier for you. Could you manage that?"

"Yes, father."

"Come on then, we have a long way to go before dark."

He took Maggie's free hand; the other clutched her change of clothing.

In the yard behind the station stood John McDonald's horse and cart. He had set off from his croft early in the morning to deliver a load of peat to a distillery near Inverness. John was approaching his seventieth year, but he could still out-work many a man half his age. He stood six foot tall in his bare feet, with a back as straight as a ramrod. A God fearing man, he knelt each night to thank his maker for his health and strength to work for a full day, then sleep soundly at night, recovering from the rigours of toil.

For forty years he had been married to his wife Annie, eight years younger than he. They had two children from the union; Donald who was twenty-nine years old and Mary in her twenty-seventh year. Neither looked likely to marry.

Annie had taken one of her daft notions that if she wasn't to have grandchildren around the house, they might bring some pleasure to a poor orphan by offering a home.

John did not approve at first. It was a foolish idea. He had worked hard to provide for his own family. Annie could be so persuasive; John could not easily deny her anything. He recalled when he was a coachman at the castle, the first time he had seen Annie, the new kitchen maid. A slip of a girl at twenty she bubbled with happiness. It took him six months to ask her to walk out with him.

Not a minute of that time was wasted, for John and Annie knew and respected each other well before marrying. It was a good match. John's serious outlook on life was balanced by Annie's light-hearted, happy disposition.

He looked around to the small figure sitting behind him in the cart. How would this poor bairn change their lives? Annie would spoil her. She could feed her up. Maybe with a little roundness and filling out she would have a pretty face.

It was a stern frowning face.

"Are you warm enough, bairn?"

"Yes father," replied Maggie.

A smile crossed John's face. This Glasgow bairn had the Gaelic. Unconsciously he had asked the question in his own tongue. The bairn understood and replied naturally.

"Did you speak the Gaelic at home, Maggie?"

"Yes, father."

"Do you know anything else to say?"

"Yes, father."

John gave up. They would soon be at Culburnie. Annie would cluck around like a brooding hen. He would have to be firm with this bairn to let her understand that life was not all easy.

"Come on, jump down Maggie, here we are."

"Yes, father."

Maggie clutched the brown paper parcel and followed him into the house.

There was a big wooden table scrubbed white. On it was set plates and spoons. There was no mantelpiece, just a huge space in the wall where a peat fire burned.

Over it was a sweigh with hooks, supporting pots at various heights. Annie stood by the fire, her flowery overall protected by an apron of coarse material.

"Come away in Maggie; you look frozen bairn, come over here until I rub some warmth into your hands."

Annie took Maggie's hands into hers and pummelled them until they glowed.

"Get your boots off now until your feet are cosy."

John came back into the kitchen.

"That's the horse seen too. Is the supper ready?"

"Yes John, Donald and Mary will be in any minute."

"Are you hungry, Maggie?"

"Yes, father."

Annie looked down at the child.

"You can speak after all. I thought that the cat had got your tongue."

Maggie remained silent. She was so hungry. Would she be allowed food? Maybe if she offered thanks first she would be given something.

Yet she had been told not to speak until spoken to. What would Charlie have done? She started to cry.

"Mercy me lassie, never fear, no one will hurt you in this house," said Annie, wiping Maggie's face with the corner of her apron.

"What ails you, Maggie?" asked John.

"Please, father, I don't know what has happened to my baby brother Alex." sobbed Maggie.

"Well now, there's not much to be done about it this night, so just stop fretting right now and we'll have our supper, do you hear?"

"Yes, father."

Maggie sat by John's side at the table.

They were joined by Donald, who had been working in the fields, and Mary, home for her day off from the big house. Mary was a young edition of Annie.

After her meal of porridge, milk, oatcakes and cheese, Mary took Maggie upstairs.

The loft was divided in two by a wooden partition. Donald slept at the end nearest the stair. Mary showed her the part they would share when she was at home.

There was a brass-ended bed, covered with a patchwork quilt. A table with a jug and basin and a chair with a flowered cushion. At the bottom of the bed was a large wooden chest.

"Set your things down there, Maggie and I'll help you wash before you go to bed."

Maggie remembered the soap and scrubbing brushes. Would it happen again?

She pulled away from Mary.

"You can do it yourself, if you like" said Mary, pouring water into the bowl. She handed Maggie a small piece of soap. It had a lovely smell.

"I got that from the lady's maid where I work. Hurry up now, I'll hear your prayers before you go to bed."

Maggie took off her clothes. Mary opened the chest at the bottom of the bed.

"Here's a night dress of mine for you, until we get you one that fits."

Maggie's head protruded from a mountain of flannelette as she knelt by the side of the bed, saying her prayers.

"Thank you Lord, for those who have so generously provided for my needs, and please keep my brothers safe, and please don't let my Alex be frightened."

Mary listened in silence.

What had this poor bairn suffered?

"Right; into bed with you, get well across to the back. I'll try to be up shortly. I'll leave the candle if you promise not to touch it. Good night."

Maggie was as close to the wall as she could get.

The bed smelled of lavender.

The patchwork quilt tucked up beneath her chin. She was warm and cosy; if only she had her brothers with her.

Chapter Four

M AGGIE WAS WAKENED from a deep sleep by Mary shaking her. "It's time to get up. Put your things on and I'll take you to the byre, let you see how to milk the cow, before I leave." It was freezing. The candle flame seemed to shrink to take cover from the icy cold. "Give your face a wash, I've not got much time. It's after five and I've to be at the big house for six."

Maggie did not hinder putting on her clothes. She would dearly have loved to stay in the warmth of the sweet smelling bed that had been so soft and 'cuddled around' her body the whole night.

The pair stood by the small black cow tethered in the byre.

"Come up near, you'll never manage to reach her udders from back against the wall."

Maggie had never seen a cow before and was not too keen to become closely acquainted.

"Maggie, I've not got much time for this nonsense, come on now. I'll show you how to milk. This is to be you job from now on. I've managed since I was younger than you. Get the bucket and stool."

The cow's udder was soft and warm. Maggie soon got the hang of squeezing and pulling at the same time.

Bessie, for that was the cow's name, did not seem to mind at all.

The milk squirted and frothed into the bucket.

"Take a wee drink from the side of the pail, then pour some in that dish for the cats."

Maggie drank the milk, the froth leaving her with white whiskers. It was thick and creamy. She felt it run right down into the lower part of her belly.

Mary took Maggie to the pantry and showed her how to fill the basins for cream.

"Mam will have to teach you the rest herself. I'm away to work. See you next Thursday—my day off. Get in for your brose. Mam will be waiting."

The week passed quickly for Maggie.

She found the McDonalds kind but firm. They worked hard most of their wakening hours and expected Maggie to follow their example.

She learned in seven days that her responsibilities were to milk the cow, see to the cream for butter, turn the churn, feed the hens, collect the eggs and see that there was enough peat and sticks were stacked beside the fire to last the day.

In return Maggie had been well fed on simple country faire.

Annie had sewn a new dress for her from an old one of Mary's.

The old spirited Maggie was slowly coming to life.

She had grown fond of Donald who could make her laugh. He was unlike his father. Donald was broad and of stocky build. His once blond hair was thin on top. A round weather beaten face wrinkled up with laughter lines.

When her chores were finished Maggie ran to the field where Donald was working. She carried his 'piece' that Annie prepared. Oatcakes, cheese and a flagon of tea.

"Aye, you'll better enjoy this for next week you'll be in the school," he told her.

"The old folks were speaking about it last night. Mary's to take you to see the dominie tomorrow when she's home."

"What's a dominie Donald?" she whispered, thinking it might be someone like the poorhouse superintendent.

"He's the teacher, nothing to fear you. He's a baldy wee man; his specs are always hanging on the end of his nose. Now his nose is bright blue, wi' a drip on the end like a water spout."

"That's all right then Donald if you can fight him."

"Lassie I would never want to fight anybody. What reason would I have?"

"My Mam had to fight the police, she could lick them." Maggie boasted.

The story of that fateful day was slowly unfolded.

Donald fitted all the pieces together like a jigsaw. How Maggie had never seen her brother David again. Charlie moving to live with Aunt Janet, then Maggie's distress at not knowing what had happened to her baby brother Alex. After Maggie was tucked up asleep in bed there was a family discussion. Mary and Donald did not need much persuasion to convince their parents of their plans for Maggie's happiness.

"That's agreed then," said Donald." Tomorrow I'll go to Glasgow and see about getting the other bairn from the poor house and bringing him home."

Mary and Maggie were coming back from gathering wood when the snow started.

"This is the start of the winter already Maggie, you'll not take too badly with being at school"

"Did you like it fine Mary?" quizzed Maggie, dragging a big limb of a tree behind her.

"I wish that I'd paid more attention and been able to read and write properly"

"I can read fine Mary."

"Well then you can stick in and maybe help me. I hope Donald will get back from Glasgow safely."

"Why is he at Glasgow, that's where I come from?"

"Well I know that Maggie, you'll see for yourself what he has gone to fetch home."

Supper was past and Maggie was ready to go upstairs to her bed, when Mary told her to sit down by the fire and she could help sew some patches on the new quilt that she and Annie were making.

Maggie's head was nodding forward with sleep, the warmth of the fire and the quilt over her knees; she could not keep her eyes open. Suddenly Donald appeared standing beside the table. He carried a bundle wrapped in a coat.

"Right my little lass, come and see what I've brought in from the snow."

Maggie stood up, her legs full of pins and needles with sitting cramped for so long. She looked into the folded coat.

Sound asleep was her baby brother Alex.

That night, before climbing into bed beside her brother Alex, an excited Maggie knelt to say her prayers.

"Thank you God so much for Donald bringing my brother Alex. Thank you for those who provide for our needs. Thank you God so much for Mary, Donald and mother and father. Please God keep them safe."

Maggie was finished milking. She sat at her brose.

"Walk smartly to school and back because it's early dark and cold." said Annie.

"Yes Mam, who will look after Alex when I am at the school?"

"Oh I think I'll manage. You've done a lot of jobs to save me going out. Here's your mid-day piece. Stick in at the lessons. Off you go now. Remember back home as fast as you can."

School was two rooms. The younger children sat in the front room with the master's wife. Maggie was with four older children in the master's room. The day's lessons were no trial for Maggie. She was very quick to learn.

When she got back to the croft Annie had some hot soup for her.

Alex was toddling around the kitchen. Maggie got down on the floor to play with him.

"Come on Maggie, you have the hens to do. Bessie will need to be milked. Work must be done."

Maggie reluctantly set off for the byre.

As she milked Bessie she spoke to her as if to an old friend.

"This is good here Bessie, my new Mam is alright but I loved my own real Mam. She kissed and cuddled us and sang when she was happy. Still I've got my Alex back."

When the snow disappeared and the first spring flowers peeped through the soil, the children were completely at home at Culburnie. They had both put on weight.

Maggie gained self-confidence each day that passed. She worked in the morning before school, and then completed her chores before supper.

Over the winter nights Annie had shown Maggie how to knit. The scarf she was making for John was almost finished. The hard winter and many soakings left John with a bad cough. Annie finally convinced him that Donald should do the carting work. Alex was now John's constant companion as he worked about the place.

There was plenty to do with the ewe's lambing and crops to be sown.

Bessie was expecting a calf. John was hoping this year she would produce a bull calf. This would bring a good price at the market when it was a year old.

Maggie ran home from school. Bessie was a very special friend to her. In some ways she had been the friend that listened in those dark November days when Maggie was so down and had lost interest in her future.

It was two miles from the school to the croft. Maggie ran for a spell then walked alternately. What would be happening at home?

This was Mary's day off. She would be able to tell of all the happenings at the 'big house'. The laird and his family had moved up from London for the shooting season. Mary had promised that when the lighter nights were here she would take Maggie to see the house and gardens.

"Come on Maggie, we have news for you," said Annie as she ran into the kitchen.

"Make yourself busy, get your chores done quickly. Mary's young man is coming to supper with us."

Annie was busy trying to roll out dough, stir the numerous pots at the fire, all at one time.

Mary was busy washing Alex and putting some clean clothes on him. In his eagerness to help John, he was not particular whether it was grass, or dung he lifted, holding it close to his chest, in fear of dropping it.

"Bairn, you smell like a dung midden," Mary scolded. "You should not be lifting dirty things against your clothes."

"Helping father", said Alex.

"Donald will have to make a cart for you. That will make it easier for you to move things."

Annie was so pleased with her 'new family'.

Maggie was a hard working lass who responded well to being cared for. She was devoted to her young brother Alex.

Quite often when alone with Annie in the dairy making butter or carding the sheep's wool for spinning, Maggie would talk of her brothers Davy and Charlie.

Annie had a fair idea of the suffering of the children. She realised how much the lassie wanted to be united with her brothers.

The table was set with a white linen cloth, the blue delft dishes in their places for supper to be served. Maggie had never seen such a spread before.

John McDonald sat at the head of the table and said grace.

Mary's young man sat at her side and next to John.

The conversation was all about the big house out door staff. How James Campbell was an under-keeper on the estate.

Maggie was curious as to what "unders" he kept.

They spoke of pheasant, grouse, partridge and deer. John told of how in his younger days he had walked the hills of Glen Orrin as a stalker, of how he had brought down a royal stag. The laird of course laid claim to this feat of extraordinary skill.

Maggie enjoyed the conversation and the novelty of company; however, her eyes would not stay open despite her efforts to keep the lids parted. Alex had long since given up and was sound asleep over Donald's shoulder.

"Right then Maggie, up to bed for you," said John. ""Mary will see you bedded. James and I have business between us."

Mary tucked Maggie under the patchwork quilt then sat down on the edge of the bed.

"Will you be coming to bed now Mary?"

"No, not yet. You see James is asking father for my hand."

"He has two of his own. How could he get yours?"

"Silly lassie. He wants to marry me."

Mary could not disguise her excitement. "Will James come and live here with us?"

Mary took Maggie in her arms and kissed her. This was the first sign of true affection shown towards the child for more than a year.

The negative answer to the question distracted Maggie's attention from the meaningful act. "We will have to get a place of our own. One of the estate houses probably. You can visit as often as you like."

The banns were called in the church that Sunday. The wedding was to be six weeks later.

John set about clearing the cart shed. With Donald's help they would have it white-washed and sparkling clean for the ceilidh to follow the marriage service.

Annie was kept busy sewing dresses for herself and Maggie.

The ladies maid at the big house was making the dress Mary would wear when she became the wife of James Campbell under gamekeeper.

John dismissed from his mind the fact that his only daughter a McDonald, would take the name of the Campbell clan. Stories of the dreadful massacre in Glencoe still aroused emotions at story telling times around the peat fires in Inverness-shire.

Bessie did not wish to be left out of the excitement. In the early hours of Thursday morning she decided it was time for her calf to be born. When Maggie went to the byre she was lying down and would not rise.

Maggie ran into the kitchen. "Mam, there's something wrong, Bessie won't stand up."

"Mercy me bairn, she'll be calving and Donald's away already this morning. I'll get father. You go back and be with her."

John did not rise early since he stopped the haulage business. He did not sleep too well; the cough was more troublesome at night. Even a wee dram had lost its soothing effect.

Maggie hurried back. She found Bessie lying on her side, a large shining blood stained membrane hung from below her tail. Bessie was moaning.

John hurried across the yard, with boots unlaced, pulling his braces over his shoulders. "Oh Maggie lass, she'll need help. The calf is big for her to manage by herself."

Annie was now in the byre. "Can you help her John, Bessie is a good milker."

John was down on his knees at the cow's rear, was shaking his head. "No, the calf is almost born, the legs are lying wrong. If I could have got my hand in to put a rope round the feet we could maybe pull the calf out."

John tried to get his hand in to retrieve the calf. "No, no it's no use. I'll never manage to get my hand near."

Bessie was moaning. Her head jerked backwards and forwards. Maggie tried to calm her by rubbing her muzzle.

"She'll never manage, the calf will kill her," said John.

"I'll do it, put the rope on, if you tell me how, father."

"Its no a job for a lassie."

Maggie looked at the old man kneeling beside her. "Bessie needs help. What do I do?"

John instructed Maggie on how to put her hand and arm inside the birth canal, feel for the unborn calf's front legs, then loop the noose of the rope around the feet.

The side of Maggie's head and her cheek were against Bessie's backside as her hand disappeared into the space below her tail. Beads of sweat ran down Maggie's face. She bit her lower lip in concentration.

"That's it Father, it's on."

"You're a clever lassie Maggie; now we will pull together, steady, no jerking, a steady pull."

The calf was unwilling to leave the warmth and nourishment within its mother's belly.

The pair pulling on the rope were more determined it would and save the cow's life.

"It's moving," said John.

The hooves, tethered with the rope, appeared first followed by a beautifully formed black calf.

John pulled it round to Bessie's head. She immediately started to lick her offspring.

"Run, fetch an egg Maggie, we'll put it over your calf's throat to clear it."

"My calf, father?"

"Yes lassie, it's as much yours as Bessie's. You can think of a name for it."

Maggie ran into the kitchen where Annie gave her hot water to wash. "I'll have to get back Mam, to my calf. Father says it's mine. I can give it a name."

"Well is it a bull calf?"

Maggie realised she did not know the beast's sex. She ran back to the byre.

"Is it a bull father?"

"Aye Maggie, it's a bull, a beautiful blue-black bull."

"That's what we'll call him Father, Blue; my Dada's horse was called Blue."

John rubbed the calf with straw.

"From now on you're Maggie's calf Blue."

Maggie cheered, cuddled Bessie, the calf, then John. "Thank you Father."

The morning of the wedding, the sun shone. The kitchen was hot from hours of baking and cooking.

Mary was beautiful in her wedding outfit.

"You look like her ladyship from the big house, Mary."

"You don't look bad yourself, Mam's made a grand job of your dress."

Mary opened the chest at the bottom of the bed. She took out a small enamelled box. The box held an assortment of treasures collected over the twenty-eight years of her lifetime. Mary selected a pear shaped polished cornelian pendant on a chain. "This is for you, Maggie. I want you to keep it. My grandmother gave it to me, when I was your age."

Maggie looked at the warm reddish brown stone. "Really for me?" she questioned.

"Aye Maggie, this is the happiest day of my life, I want to share it with you. We have a happy future ahead of us."

Maggie kissed Mary on the cheek. "I think I love you next best in the World to my brothers."

Mary returned the kiss. "I love you Maggie like my young sister."

The couple left the church after the solemn ceremony, out into the bright sunlight. The bridal party was led out by the laird's piper. They walked the half-mile to the croft followed by the congregation.

The wedding party and celebration ceilidh would not be forgotten in the district for many a year. All the village celebrated.

Everyone joined in the eating, drinking, singing and dancing. No-one more so than the dominie. Thinking he was in charge of a class he took command of entertainment.

Maggie with her classmate Bathia watched from below the cart, giggling as the master became more unsteady on his feet with each drink he swallowed. The dominies wife was dancing, hoochin" and skirlin" as she reeled up and down the line of men wanting to swirl her off her feet to the music of the three fast fiddlers. Round she went like a spinning top, then broke loose and flew like a liberated bird right into the dung midden.

There she lay, winded, arms and legs apart. The enforced lie down or the smell of the dung sped up the alcohol's action. Poor woman could not stand up. She lay there laughing. The dominie staggered across to look at his life's companion.

"She's certainly landed in the shit," he laughed as he tried to pull her up. "Come away now, I'll get you home."

No amount of persuasion could get his wife on to her feet.

"How am I going to move this load of dung home?" said the laughing teacher.

Donald came forward. "Just got the thing for you dominie"

Donald was pulling the cart he had made for Alex. The dominie left, dragging his wife behind him folded into Alex's dung cart.

Maggie and Bathia rolled about at the hilarious sight. What a day it had been!

Each day that was left of Maggie's schooling brought a smile to her face, when she recalled the disaster of the teachers and the dung cart.

In the two years since Mary married John had become very frail.

He only ventured out to the seat at the door.

He missed the company of Alex, who was now in the dominies captive audience. Annie, as sprightly as ever, catered for his every need. Maggie did most of the outwork before and after school.

According to Annie's statement made numerous times daily, "We would never manage the work had the Lord never sent Maggie to us."

Alex, now school age, was able to carry out his 'own jobs'.

The haulage business kept Donald busy.

The work was so demanding that it was possible they would employ another man.

The family were to discuss this proposition at suppertime. Mary and James sat at the table facing Maggie and Donald. Annie sat opposite John at the head of the table with Alex by his side. Alex spread his bread and helped him with his meal. Though John was frail he was still the head of his own household.

Donald started in a quiet voice to explain the pressures of work to his father. "With another horse we would be able to work better hours and still do more work father."

"Aye," said John. "I can understand that but where would we get a local man we could trust to do the work?"

Donald looked across at his sister. "Well Father, we thought James might be the right person."

Annie interrupted here. "The laird would never allow it. James and Mary would lose their home."

"We've discussed that mother," said Mary. "We would have to stay here until a house in the village was empty. Maggie will be needing a place soon, so we will have her bed."

That was how it was. James and Mary moved into Culburnie. James to work the horse, Mary to look after her elderly parents.

Alex continued to share Donald's bed.

CHAPTER FIVE

MAGGIE STOOD AT the back door of the big house. She rang the doorbell. A young girl about Maggie's age, wearing a grey uniform and a rough apron, answered the call.

"I'm Maggie Chalmers, come to work in the kitchen," she told the girl.

"Come on in, Mrs McIntosh the cook is expecting you. I'm Lizzie Mckenzie the scullery maid. We're to share a room."

Maggie was ushered into the kitchen, which to her looked like an enormous hall. Under an arched alcove was a huge range. Mrs McIntosh stood between it and a large scrubbed wooden table that ran the length of the room.

The fact was, Mrs McIntosh was unmarried; her whole life had been devoted to kitchen duties and pampering the palates of the gentry. The 'Mrs' title was one of respect or if stories were to be believed, to meet the belief that one who had never married and cooked to keep a man, was of no use at all.

"Come over here until I see you lassie. You are bigger than I expected. You come well recommended by Mary Campbell. She tells me that you're a grand wee worker. They'll find it hard to manage Culburnie without your help."

Maggie said nothing; she was overawed by the size of the place used only for the preparation of food.

Above the table hung every size of copper pot imaginable. The smell of roasting beef mingled with the smell of spice.

"You'll be needing to know all about your work no doubt. Lizzie, you make a pot of tea until I get the gingerbread from the oven. Sit down Maggie. I'll be with you in a minute."

Maggie sat on a chair at the end of the table. Mary had already told her she was to be assistant to Mrs McIntosh and train to be a real cook. There was to be a concession that Maggie did not have to start as a scullery maid. She was to start right away in the kitchen.

Lizzie set down the tray with china cups and saucers. It was only cook who was allowed to eat in the kitchen. This of course avoided any confrontation in the servant's hall between the cook and housekeeper who both considered themselves head of staff.

Mrs McIntosh poured the tea.

"Help yourself to a piece of gingerbread, Maggie."

This is really like a wedding party Maggie thought, and this is what they call working.

After Mrs McIntosh went over the required work schedule for Maggie's day, her ideas changed considerably.

She was to be up for quarter to five, clean out the range, without making a mess of dust and ashes. Take a cup of tea to Mrs McIntosh for five thirty, start making the porridge that had soaked overnight, for the staff breakfast a t six. She would then assist in making breakfast for 'the family' and guests. There was mid-morning coffee, lunch, afternoon tea, high tea, dinner and then bedtime drinks, all to be prepared and served each day. The food prepared was sent to three different areas for consuming. The dining room, the nursery and the servant's hall. There was of course the occasional guest who preferred to dine in their room. This was supplied on a separate tray and served by the butler via his pantry.

Maggie was to have one evening off. She would be allowed away at lunchtime to visit her family. It was agreed she would not work on Thursday. Sunday was also considered to be a half-day with time either morning or evening to join the 'big house' staff in the family pew at the church. The housekeeper would supply Maggie with a uniform; she would keep it neat, tidy and clean. The laundry maids washed all the uniforms; no excuses would be listened too for slovenliness. Her sleeping accommodation was to be shared with Lizzie McKenzie, the scullery maid. Maggie was to remember and not be influenced by her 'sleekit' ways. She was after all to be a cook one day.

Poor Maggie was lost in what was expected of her after mid morning coffee.

She had no idea what that meant.

"Faith lassie, never look so worried. Lizzie will take you to your room. Get on your uniform and report back here as quick as you can."

Lizzie chattered all the way to the top of the house to their attic bedroom. It was through a labyrinth of back stairs and passages. "Never let yourself be seen by the gentry," ordered Lizzie. "If ever you see them coming your way, hide in a doorway or behind a curtain. The mistress does not want to see us about the house."

Maggie's logical mind could not work out the reasoning behind this strange custom. However, everything was so strange she dismissed it from her thoughts.

The bedroom was so small that if Maggie and Lizzie were in it together, one had to get on the bed so that the other could stand on the empty floor space. There was a double bed, a wooden hand chair, a small table with a basin and jug. A large hook on the back of the door where uniforms "would be hung up and not dropped on the floor."

Maggie considered if there would be room on the floor for them to lie there.

A chamber pot below the bed would be emptied by them "in turns."

One candle per month would be supplied by the housekeeper. The only natural light in the room came from a small skylight.

"Hurry up now Maggie, get changed, we don't want to get Toshie in a bad mood. This is the day that the grocer comes; he brings his message boy with him.

Have you got a lad?"

"I've got three brothers," Maggie told her.

"That's no' what I mean," said Lizzie, while helping her button up her dress and push her hair up inside her cap. "A lad of your own for a kiss and a cuddle and a bit of fun—you know what I mean."

Maggie shook her head.

"Hurry up you slow coach, you'll soon learn."

Maggie did just that.

The rush went on from early morning to late at night. The candle supplied by the housekeeper would last forever. By ten o'clock when Maggie finally finished her allocated duties, she was glad to snuff out the dancing flame and close her eyes to the darkness and sleep.

Every Thursday Maggie ran home as fast as her legs would carry her. She had already lost her natural parents and she knew that each week her father John McDonald was becoming weaker and losing his hold on life. He was now completely bedridden. He lay in the 'ben house' bed tended by Annie, Mary and the light of his life Alex.

Maggie ran into the house pulling off her shawl.

"It's so good to see you, lass," said Annie, who was sitting by the fire heating a piece of flannel. "Father's pretty low today. Maybe seeing you will brighten him up a bit. Mary is giving him a wash. Take this flannel through with you, it keeps his chest warm and stops him coughing. Away you go ben."

The thin shrunken figure propped up in the bed bore no recognisable resemblance to the proud upstanding man who met Maggie at the station years ago telling her "you are in my care now."

They had been good years for Maggie. She had to work hard but in return she'd gained so much. She had her brother Alex, mother and Mary. A job, a home and most of all she was no longer destitute and a pauper.

Maggie put her arms around the old man's neck and kissed him. "I love you John McDonald. I want to thank you for being my father."

John's bony arms pulled her close to him. "Maggie my lassie, I've to thank you. I'm a proud man and my heart bursts with pride and pleasure when I see you and Alex. It's a true saying that when you help others up the hill you get to the top yourself. Thank you and our family for getting me there. Away now and get mam to make some tea for us."

Three weeks later John McDonald was taken behind his own horse on his own cart. The horse walked slowly up the hill followed by the mourners.

Maggie and the family said "Goodbye," and left him at the top of the hill.

CHAPTER SIX

RS MCINTOSH WAS a very good teacher. She instructed her pupil in every aspect of the job, from ordering of supplies to the profitable disposal of side products.

Every Monday morning the grocer would arrive with his cart and deliver the goods ordered the previous week. There was much chatter and cups of tea between the cook and the merchant.

It took Maggie several months to work out the gratuities Mrs McIntosh enjoyed shopping at certain establishments. She had not been in service long when she found her mentor washing money and drying it by the fire. Maggie was so curious about this peculiar situation she asked for an explanation.

"Well it's the skin money, the man is dirty and I would not want to keep dirty money."

Maggie was no wiser until in bed that night she questioned Lizzie, who was a fountain of information as to all that was going on.

"Well Toshie won't let the keepers skin the rabbits and hares. She takes them with their 'jackets' on. That way she gets the money for the skins from the cadger. The keepers don't."

"Does she keep the money for herself then?"

"Of course she does. Toshie knows when she's on a good thing."

Lizzie changed the subject and prattled on about her latest 'crush'.

A new male tutor had been engaged for the laird's boys. Lizzie had seen him on one of her forbidden missions through the house.

Lizzies domain was the scullery, where she spent her days up to the elbows in hot water, cleaning pots, dishes and preparing vegetables for the kitchen.

Lizzie unlike the cook's protégé, was not allowed the privilege of eating in the kitchen, she joined the rest of the staff in the servant's hall.

All the gossip of upstairs was relayed to Maggie at night when the girls huddled together for warmth in their sleeping quarters, beneath the slates.

Toshie, as she was known behind her back, grew more dependent on Maggie as the months passed.

It was three years since Maggie first entered the kitchen. During that time she had seen Alex grow into a sturdy young lad. Mary and James had no children of their own and Donald was still unmarried.

Annie looked forward to Maggie's weekly visits with all the big house news. Annie had never been far from the croft since she married all those years ago. Gossip from the servants' hall brought back memories of her spell in service.

"You'll be getting paid soon lassie," she said. "What will you be doing with your pennies?"

Before she had even asked the question she could forecast what Maggie's answer would be.

"I'll save half of it for going to Glasgow to try and get news of my brother Davy"

Though six years had passed since those dreadful poorhouse days, they were forever in Maggie's mind. She could recall clearly the last sighting of her brother Davy being led through the door of the poorhouse superintendent's office.

Mary, busy preparing the tea joined in the conversation. "How do you think you could find him?"

Maggie stood for some time before answering, "I could go to the Mossbank School, they would have records and know where he went from there."

It was agreed that it was a good place to start. Maggie would wait for another six months' wages before venturing by train to Glasgow. She would be sixteen years old by then. Mary had suggested it might be a help to find the whereabouts of her natural grandmother Jean Fraser. Maggie turned her mind back to the day her father died, when Jean Fraser collapsed. Probably it was more than likely she would be dead by now.

Six months passed. Maggie was not free to go on her search. Toshie could not cope without her. The family had invited a large number of house guests to stay over for Christmas. To make matters worse, the elderly woman's legs were giving her problems. Over forty years of standing at the stove and kitchen table had left her with bad varicose ulcers. During the course of the day despite frequent spells sitting "to rest her weary bones", Toshie's feet became grossly swollen. She needed Maggie's help.

A feeling of excitement ran high in the servants' hall. At Christmas they were allowed to have a dance in the ballroom. This was a fashionable custom started by Prince Albert in the Royal household a number of years before. Like many other things it took a considerable time to reach Inverness-shire.

The forester had brought in a fir tree, which stood in the corner of the ballroom.

It was covered in coloured paper chains and shining glass balls. Rumour had it that her Ladyship was to attend. Maggie had only met her ladyship twice since starting at the big house. It was tradition for the lady of the house, if in residence, to hand over the six monthly wages. She was assisted by the housekeeper who read out the servants' name as she passed her Ladyship the earnings for presentation.

Maggie was no less excited than her colleagues.

Lizzie was going to be with her young man. For twelve weeks now she had been walking out with one of the under gardeners who delivered the fresh flowers and vegetables each morning. Lizzie confided that she was keen to marry and get away from the drudgery of the scullery. Unlike Maggie she had no Culburnie to visit each week nor the comfort of knowing a family did care.

Lizzie was the illegitimate daughter of a servant girl who died when she was born. Her reputed father, being the son of the owner of the house, where her mother had worked. Lizzie's old grandmother had cared for her as long as she could, then she was sent into service at the age of twelve. Since her grandmother died the only places known to Lizzie were the scullery, servants' hall and the attic bedroom.

The work in the kitchen was hectic morning to night, stuffing, roasting, stirring, frying. Toshie commanded from the chair, most of the day. Maggie now held the elevated position of bargaining with the suppliers and merchants. She had learned her trade well. Toshie's pupil was a first-class cook.

Lizzie was talking before Maggie's eyes were open.

"This is it at last Mags, the ball is tonight. If Albert Gillespie does not ask me to marry him to-night, then I will have to ask him."

Maggie tried to turn over but Lizzie pulled the cover from her head. "You'll have to get up, Toshie will not be much help, you want finished early to get ready for the ball."

Maggie pulled herself up onto her elbow. "Lizzie all I want is peace and quiet to sleep, I'll make Albert Gillespie marry you so I can have this room to myself."

"Oh, Mags would you do that please. Everybody listens to you. You are so clever, even Toshie asks what you think is right."

Maggie laughed. "Hurry up and get dressed until I can get up. We will be late and get 'hot tongue' from Toshie. I'll be going to my bed I think. I'm too tired for any ball."

The euphoric tension mounted throughout the day. Never before had there been such an event for the servants. After the dinner for the dining room was organised,

Toshie said that Maggie was free to "ready yourself for the ball."

"Will you manage by yourself Mrs McIntosh, there's still a lot to be done."

Mrs McIntosh shook the oven cloth at Maggie. "Faith lassie, I managed long before you came here, though I do sometimes wonder how, needless to say I'll need to manage again when you are not here. You must think about it yourself, the only duty as cook that I do by myself now is to go each morning at ten and discuss the menu and number of guests with her Ladyship and the Housekeeper. You do everything else. It's a kitchen of your own you'll be needing soon. I'd recommend you to anyone, so would her Ladyship."

The conversation had expanded more than Mrs McIntosh first intended. She only wanted Maggie to get off and enjoy herself with the other young staff. She never meant that the kind-hearted lassie would realise how frightened she was of losing her position and home because the pupil was better than the teacher.

When Lizzie rushed into the bedroom, Maggie, still in her kitchen whites, was sitting on the bed.

"Are you not getting ready for going then?" said Lizzie, while pulling off her shoes and stockings.

"I'd never even thought about it until tonight when Toshie spoke about it," answered Maggie in a daze.

"What do you mean, you've known for weeks," said Lizzie sitting down on the chair.

"It's not the dance I'm talking about, Lizzie. It's moving on. Toshie told me tonight, I should be in a kitchen of my own. She said her Ladyship would recommend me, so she must have spoken to her about me going."

Lizzie started to cry at the thought of losing her friend.

"What are you greetin' for? You won't be here much longer anyhow, if that Albert Gillespie has any sense he'll take you to the nearest blacksmith and make you his wife."

Lizzie wiped her nose and face on her overall. "I think he might just do that."

"Mind you Lizzie I could tell him you are not the best bed-mate to sleep with, but then again his ideas might not be that the bed is for sleeping only." They both giggled at Maggie's suggestion.

"Maggie, you could always find a place where you share the bedroom with the butler or footman."

"I might just do that."

When Thursday came for her weekly trip to Culburnie, Maggie had decided what she was to do. Of course she would tell Mary, Mam and Donald first, hoping for their approval.

After their evening meal, sitting by the fire sewing the patches on the quilt, Maggie told Annie and Mary all about the splendid occurrences at the Servants' Ball. Of how Lizzie's Albert's proclamation of their intention to marry would be called in the church on Sunday.

"She'll be leaving the big house then," said Annie trying to thread the needle in the firelight.

"So will I be leaving, Mam." Maggie told the whole story of Toshie's conversation. Mary was quick to work out that Maggie presented a threat to the older woman. "She'll no' feel safe as long as you work there lassie. Betsy McIntosh knows no other life than that kitchen. She was born in that house. Her mother was the cook before her. Her father was the laird's groom Aye, I can understand why she feels anxious while you are there."

Maggie looked at Annie. "I've never done anything wrong Mam. I've always done my best and worked hard."

Annie patted the back of Maggie's hand. She loved this lass who came to her an orphan, by a freak of nature not of her body, but her daughter to be proud of, "That's something I would never doubt," said the old woman.

"It's not always them that does best and works hard that gets rewarded for their labours. Betsy McIntosh would be the first to tell you that. Think of what would happen if her Ladyship found out it was you who does the work."

"I don't mind working hard Mam."

Annie put down her corner of the quilt. "That's part of the problem lass, the gentry do mind who does the work. They want the one who does it best for the least money in return. Betsy McIntosh knows that. She's no other place to live other than that kitchen. So, if you please her Ladyship, she' s out."

Maggie's plan was agreed. At the end of the May term, when all the country people either renewed their promises of six months work, Maggie would look for a place near Glasgow. This would make it easier for her to trace the location of her brother Davy.

Mrs McIntosh bore a feeling of guilt, when her young friend explained that "she wanted another place near Glasgow, to look for her brother." The guilt complex mingled with relief that at least another year of security was hers.

"It's not just any place you'll be going too, you're a grand cook. I'll speak to the housekeeper, she might know of something."

Maggie was busy rolling the pastry for the pies the shooters would have in their picnic at the New Year's day shoot. "I'll surely find something at the feeing market in Glasgow Green."

Mrs McIntosh stood up and banged the end of the table.

"That's not for the likes of you Maggie, you trained as my style of cook. My life's experience has been passed on to you. I'll not have you at any feeing market. If the housekeeper knows of no family needing a cook, then I'll speak to her ladyship myself. She has family around Glasgow, there's bound to be something for someone as good as you."

Over the next five months both cooks often pondered of what was in front of them could work out. Mrs McIntosh was still unsure as to whether or not she would manage without Maggie's talents and abilities. The end result would be the same. She would be replaced by someone, who would complete the hard physical demands of the job, probably cheaper for a number of years.

Maggie was promised a place in the home of her ladyship's cousin, where the cook was to be pensioned off after fifty years of loyal service. The housekeeper, over a cup of tea, explained this was not the act of consideration and charity it appeared. The family governess in her eighties was no longer able to cope. Yet being 'foster mother' to generations of family, could not be turned out homeless. A compromise situation had been found, where the gatehouse would be made home for nanny, looked after by the 'pensioned off' cook. They were a considerate family.

Maggie's doubts were not about her new position, she found herself emotionally upset at the thought of being so far away from her family. She would find it hard to afford a visit once each year, even if she was allowed time away from her kitchen. She missed Lizzie's nightly news review, despite the number of times she had wished for a bit of quiet and privacy.

Lizzie and Albert had been married, in the manse, on the second Friday in February. Maggie was a witness at the ceremony. When Albert took his vows so seriously, promising to love and cherish through sickness, health, for richer or poorer, until parted by death and thereafter pledged his troth to Lizzie, she could not stem the tears flowing freely down her cheeks.

Would she ever find this kind of love between a man and a woman? Time had dulled her memories of her mother and father. Had theirs been the kind of love that made it impossible for them to be apart?

Maggie had so often tried to reason why a mother could knowingly abandon her own flesh and blood. The instincts of the animals made them protect their young, even when in defence they would fight to the point of death. Maybe the longing to be near her brothers was love. Divided by circumstances, Alex and Charlie were both being well looked after and well provided for. Davy's unknown fate had caused her many sleepless nights. This new position in Glasgow gave her more hope of once again meeting her much longed for elder brother.

It was a more well-informed, confident young woman who sat in the carriage of the train leaving Inverness than the broken spirited orphan, who arrived there those many years earlier.

Maggie had been lucky with the caring family, chosen for her upbringing by the parochial board. Leaving Culburnie had been emotional and stressful. Annie, Mary and Alex waving until she could no longer see them in the early morning light.

Donald had comforted her throughout the journey by dog-cart. "Mind take good care of yourself in Glasgow, lass. Remember to write home often. Mam will have us fair demented until she hears you're well settled. Remember you have a home should things are not good. I've been thinking you're awful young to be away on your own."

Maggie assured her kindly foster brother that if it made him any happier she would adjust her age to twenty-two.

"Aye, that might be better," agreed Donald. "You're mature enough for folk to believe it."

Mary and Annie had already advised Maggie to be on her guard for the romantic advances by the sons of gentry. Lizzie's history had already brought home a practical lesson on the dangers of an upstairs, downstairs romance.

As the train rattled its way south, Maggie's travelling companions sat in stern silence. On either side of her were two elderly women, each occupying the window seat. Opposite them were two middle-aged men and a young girl. Maggie tried to look past the women to see the passing countryside but she felt conscious of having constantly lean forward to see clearly past their buxom figures.

"Would you like my window seat, miss?" offered the gentleman.

"Thank you sir, I would love to see as much as I can."

They exchanged positions, the man looking rather crushed between the matronly pair.

"I'm going to Glasgow to take up a new position," said Maggie, anxious to make a start to the new life ahead of her.

"You'll find Glasgow rather strange after Inverness," suggested the man sitting next to her.

"Oh no, not at all. I come from Glasgow. I was born there," she replied.

"You'll just have been working in Inverness then?" he added, trying to make conversation.

"Yes, I've been working as a cook."

Maggie feared that she might be questioned further about why she chose to be so far from home. She turned to the window and sat silently putting her thoughts together. She must start from now on keeping to herself the disasters associated with her young life at Port Dundas. In future she would not lie but if people chose to believe her family and origins were in Culburnie then so be it. She would not contradict them.

She had not thought of Port Dundas in a long time. Annie would never have allowed them to be left alone. Yet their Mam had loved them. Maggie could remember the cuddles and the kisses, laughing and singing. She could also remember the cold and hunger, how other children at school said "they stank".

How could her Mam have kept on drinking herself stupid knowing they were needing food and warmth?

"Where are we at now, miss?" asked the man.

Maggie's eyes focused on a large hoarding advertising whisky.

"Glenfiddich sir; we've reached Glenfiddich."

At Glasgow station Maggie had a porter take her trunk to a hansom cab. She instructed the driver where to take her, and then climbed inside. The superintendent had told her all those years ago to "better herself".

She would show them and find her brother into the bargain.

CHAPTER SEVEN

THE CAB DRIVER lifted her trunk and carried it through the back court of larders and cellars. Maggie was met at the back door by a middle-aged woman who introduced herself. "I'm Jessie Brown. I'm the housemaid here. Her Ladyship has asked me to see you have tea, then I'm to take you to meet her in the drawing room."

The kitchen of the Glasgow house was much smaller than she had expected, making it much more homely. The servants' hall was opposite the kitchen. It served as a sitting room-cum-dining area for the indoor staff. It was very comfortable.

Maggie and Jessie sat down at the end of the table with their tea.

"You look very young to be taking over the kitchen Mrs Chalmers, that is, compared to our last cook. She was nearly seventy."

Maggie sat her cup down on the saucer. "I'm nearly twenty-three," she lied.

"Oh, don't be offended," said Jessie, "Someone of your age will bring new ideas with you from your last place. That's what we are needing."

"How many staff are there to cook for" asked Maggie.

"Well, there's myself, I'm the housemaid, we don't have a housekeeper. Then there's Jean and Francis who work together as table maid or chambermaid, what ever is needing done. There's Elsie the scullery maid. Miss Brodie the ladies maid and Mister McLeod the master's gentleman. He's like a glorified butler. We also have help for entertaining from two of the outdoor staff's wives, the forester's wife and the gamekeeper's wife. They come in and work when needed."

The tea was finished and Maggie was ushered into the drawing room.

Her Ladyship sat in front of the window at the far end of the room. As she stood up the light from the window silhouetted her stooped slender frame. Maggie had been told that the master and the mistress were over sixty years old.

"Do come over, Mrs Chalmers. We are very glad to welcome you. Hopefully things will suit, and ours will be a long acquaintance. Do sit down."

Maggie sat nervously on the edge of the plush chair folding over the edges of her coat.

"You come with very good references. We heard from my cousin that you have been able to run the kitchen yourself when her cook was unwell at the shooting season"

Maggie just nodded. If this woman asked her age she would not be able to lie. Fortunately she had no reason to do such a thing. It was agreed that Maggie would forego her evening off in return for being off Saturday and Sunday every twelve weeks. She had requested this time off to allow her to go home to Culburnie or to search for her family.

Jessie directed Maggie to her room, which was still at the top of the house. The room was slightly bigger than the one she shared with Lizzie and had the added luxury of a window. There was not much of view, just the sky and tops of two large trees As Maggie stood staring out of the window there was a knock at the door.

"This is your trunk, Mrs Chalmers. I've brought it up for you. I'm Neil McLeod, the man about the house." Maggie thanked him.

"I hope you will be very happy here, Mrs Chalmers."

Maggie felt fit to burst out laughing at the complementary title. If only they knew she wasn't even seventeen yet. She washed and changed into her kitchen whites, then ventured down to the kitchen anxious to take on the challenge and responsibility of cooking for this household for what seemed a fantastic wage of one half guinea a week paid every six months.

The first time Maggie was due days off she stayed on working. She could not afford to go home until her wages were paid. This was no hardship to Maggie for she had three letters bringing her all the

Culburnie news; Mary was a grand letter writer. The family were well. Lizzie and Albert were having a baby early in the New Year.

Mrs McIntosh's training served Maggie well. She soon had the kitchen organised to her liking. Things had been allowed to slip by for years with her predecessors on coming age. As Mrs McIntosh had done, Maggie ordered direct from the merchants. On her half days off she went around the shops carefully noting prices and quality of goods. The tradesmen soon learned she knew value for money.

Over the months Maggie found a good friend in Neil McLeod, who knew so much about island crofting people. Originally from Islay, Neil had worked for his present master for over twenty years. Like Maggie's, Neil's age was a mystery. He had experience of so many different things. If he had ever married was unknown.

In the evenings, when the day's work was over the staff would sit by the fire in the servants hall. While Maggie was sewing a patchwork cover she would listen to Neil's Gaelic tales of how whole communities were moved off their land to make way for more sheep. The sadness of the families put on board ships for Canada and New Zealand. Maggie reasoned this was most likely what had happened to her mother's brothers from Islay. She told Neil of her grandparents on Islay and of how her aunt lived on Gigha. Although she was fond of Neil she never disclosed the sad story of her family background.

November was a cold month, with heavy falls of snow. The planned trip to Culburnie had to be put off once again. Maggie had never had money of her own before, for at Culburnie, Annie had kept her wages and bought clothes for her. After receiving her hard earned cash, Maggie put it in a purse in her trunk. Each night for a week she counted it, just to satisfy herself that it was real and belonged to her.

An expedition to the shops was planned. Maggie bought a new dress, coat, hat and dress boots. The cash was gone but one look in the mirror dispelled any regrets at being parted from the money.

When she went home to Culburnie in May, it would be in style. Annie would be so proud to see her dressed like a lady. Maggie had often thought of going back to look at Maitland Street, but was frightened someone would recognise her. She could certainly go back now for the new clothes completely changed her appearance. There was no resemblance at all to sad Maggie Chalmers, the poorhouse pauper.

Christmas was a busy but happy time.

The master and mistress were away for a holiday over the festive season. The servants' hall was decorated with holly and paper chains. He atmosphere was similar to that of a big family for each had a small gift to exchange with the other. Maggie had been busy sewing and knitting her gifts. For Neil McLeod she had knitted a scarf. For Jessie embroidered hankies. On Christmas Eve they all sat around the fire singing. Neil opened a bottle of port and gave each of them a glass. Maggie sipped hers slowly. She had always been frightened of what drink might do to her. Imprinted on her mind was the sight of her mother in a drunken stupor. That would never be her misfortune, a promise she had made to herself a long time ago.

"Come on Maggie, you sing something for us," said Neil, filling up her glass.

"Aye come on. You've got a lovely voice," said Jessie. "I've heard you singing in the kitchen."

Maggie sang her favourite song, the one that reminded her so much of her mother on the good days. "Ho ro my nut brown maiden."

Jessie clapped her hands. "This is must be a better Christmas than the gentry are having."

Maggie thought about it when she went to bed. Yes, it had been one of the happiest times of her life. She got out of bed, opened the wardrobe door. They were still there, the best clothes in the World.

The flurry and bustle of Spring-cleaning over, Maggie was preparing for her long weekend at home. With a lot of preparation Jessie had agreed that with her Ladyship's approval, Maggie would be off on Friday afternoon to Monday afternoon. Jessie would take over the kitchen duties.

Her ladyship, a kindly soul, consented without any persuasion. "You haven't been home for a year now Mrs Chalmers," she said as she handed back the menus and kitchen accounts books.

"No mam, the snow kept me from travelling. The train would get to Inverness all right. It's the journey to Culburnie that would be difficult."

"Yes, I have a cousin there but of course you already know that. She was not wrong about you. Everything she said was true. You're a grand worker, a good cook and a very dependable person indeed. Not many girls of your age would have managed. Certainly I'm pleased I gave you the opportunity."

Maggie felt her face go red from the neck upwards. This woman knew her true age. Seeing how upset she was, her ladyship tried to calm the situation. "Don't worry about it. Age means nothing if you can act out the part by doing the job of a mature experienced cook, then I'm not the one to steal the credit from you. No one knows my real age; you know, I've been telling the family for the last fifteen years that I'm sixty two."

The tension over, they both laughed. Maggie knew her job was safe as long as she gave value for money.

As the train neared Inverness Maggie became more and more excited. Would Donald be waiting at the station to drive her home? Would Annie be as sprightly after the winter? How much would Alex have grown? Would Lizzie's baby be a boy or girl?

She had not made any progress in the year tracing her brother Davy, nor their Granny Fraser. One afternoon she had gone to look for the house where Granny worked, but everything in Glasgow was changing.

Neil McLeod was her friend but so far she had not asked him to go with her to Mossbank School for fear that if he knew of her origins she would lose his respect.

She had considered writing to her Aunt Janet on Gigha to find out if her brother Charlie was well. However, she had never got over the explanation Janet did not want her, nor Alex when her mother died.

Was Charlie the lucky one?

Maggie was so pleased and happy to be going to her own family. She had a good job, fine clothes and good friends.

She could see Donald as she stepped off the train.

"Over here Maggie lass," he shouted and waved.

Maggie ran towards him, hampered with her bag of gifts and goodies. "Oh Donald, I'm so fine pleased to see you," she said, her voice wavering with emotion.

"No more so than I am. We'd better not stand here blethering though, for Mam has been making ready for days for you coming home."

"How is she Donald?"

"Well not getting about so much but interested in everyone's business as usual. She misses father for they were a long time together."

"Aye, that's true Donald. How about Mary and James. No babies for them yet?"

"No I think they've stopped thinking of it now. Alex is their one, ready made is sometimes best. Look at you Maggie. We did fine with the pair of you. Not like poor Lizzie and Albert Gillespie. Their bairn is an imbecile, it'll never be any good to man nor beast."

Maggie said how sad she was that her friend should have such a problem to cope with. She hoped it would not cause upset or offence when she visited and took the little jacket she had knitted for the baby. How good it was to be home.

Annie, Mary and Maggie sat long into the night gossiping, drinking tea, getting up to date with Maggie's news. Maggie shared Annie's bed in the ben house room. She tried to creep from the bed early to do the milking and help Mary.

After breakfast when the outside work was done Maggie set off to visit Lizzie. As she walked through the village, passing the time of day with people she knew.

"It's grand your looking, Maggie, since you've gone to Glasgow. It must be true about the Streets being paved with gold," said one of her old school friends.

The countryside was beautiful with the wild flowers in bloom, campion, blue-bells and flag irises all in rivalry for the most brilliant colour. Maggie's pace slowed down as she left the houses. Town people could never understand the magic of all this being free in the open air. No wonder her mother was so unhappy locked away all day in that room and kitchen in Maitland Street.

Maggie's reverie was abruptly ended by a tap on the shoulder. Startled, she jumped around. "You fool, you are, giving me such a fright." The words were out before Maggie even recognised whom she was talking too.

It was the Laird's son's tutor.

"I'm so sorry, it was not my intention to scare you. I just thought I recognised you. We might walk the road together. You are Maggie Chalmers are you not?"

"Yes that's right, I am," said Maggie blushing.

"I haven't seen you at the big house lately, I missed seeing you."

"I've been working in Glasgow for a year now. I'm home on holiday. I was going to see my friend Mrs Gillespie, the gardener's wife"

"I did hear they have had some bad luck with their baby. Would you tell Lizzie that I send her my best wishes?"

"I would do that if I knew your name sir, you have the advantage over me by knowing mine."

"My name is John Fraser and nothing would please me more than allowing you to get to know me better."

They were now at the gatehouse and drive leading to the big house.

"I'll leave you here, John Fraser for it would not do for me to be walking in the front avenue, a servant being seen, now would it?"

"That's just a lot of nonsense I don't agree with," answered John.

"They are only afraid that the servants will see how little brains they've got in comparison with their fortune in money."

Maggie was fascinated by this man, who spoke so openly, ridiculing his employers. "What makes you say such awful things?"

"From personal observations of course. Remember I'm there to pass on to them the experience of my learning. From reading books, there's nothing on Earth you want to know about that has not been explained or written down, somewhere."

Maggie looked at him straight into his china blue eyes. "Then tell me, how can I trace my long-lost brother?"

"How did you become separated in the first place?"

It was easy to tell John Fraser the entire story. Most of Culburnie knew of the McDonald's foster children, although their background was not common knowledge. For over an hour the couple sat together on the grass. Several times in telling the story Maggie was near to tears. John put his arm around her to comfort her.

Maggie had never experienced being noticed by a young man before. Neil McLeod, her friend, was more a father figure.

"Maggie I will have to go now," said John looking at the time on a gold watch he took from his waistcoat pocket. "If I may I would be willing to help you in your search, if it was not imposing on your privacy."

Maggie smiled. *He speaks so grand as if he knows about everything.*

"Well, yes John, that would be fine but I'm going back to Glasgow on Monday."

"Could I perhaps write to you Maggie, then if I'm free we could perhaps meet in Glasgow."

Maggie could see no harm from giving John her address. She felt flattered at the interest shown in her problem by an educated man.

As she walked to Lizzie's cottage she was more than ever convinced that her new hat and coat had changed her completely.

Poor Lizzie's circumstances brought Maggie down to earth with a bang. Lizzie was so pale and thin; her son lay in a wooden cradle crying continuously. The joy and pleasure at seeing Maggie was apparent.

"My God, Mags, you look as if you were gentry. What a difference a year has made to us both."

Maggie looked at the cradle.

"We were looking forward so much to young Albert." Lizzie broke down and started crying. "He's got water on the brain Maggie. He'll never be any better. The doctor told us his head will outgrow his body, depending on how long he lives."

What could be said that would help relieve poor Lizzie's misery? "Can I lift him and nurse him for you?"

"Aye, but be careful, there's a lump of his brain sticks out his back. No wonder he cries night and day, poor thing."

Maggie cuddled the infant close to her, humming a tune into his ear. The crying stopped. Lizzie looked amazed.

"You've always been a clever bitch, able to do things right. I'll make us a cup of tea, while he is quiet."

Maggie was sorry to hear that Albert was out working as much as possible to get away from the baby's crying and the distress at seeing his first bairn's deformed body.

Maggie told her of meeting John Fraser and walking up the road with him. Her reaction was not what Maggie expected of Lizzie.

"Oh he's certainly one for the charm and talk," she said. "Goes with his good looks and education. Tell me about your new place Mags. I wish I was back in the scullery away from this bawling."

Maggie gently put the sleeping infant in the cradle. "You don't regret marrying Albert, do you?"

Lizzie looked tired and worn out. "No. It's just things haven't been the way we thought they would be, my time is all taken up with the bairn. Much as I love Albert, he's got to take second place. Take my advice Mags, stay single until you are certain, sure things will work out right."

Maggie spent her Sunday night with Alex. He was like Charlie in lots of ways, with a keen sense of humour. He showed Maggie how to make a water gun from hollow weeds and told her how with his friends they showered the dominie with water. Maggie told him of the dancing at Mary and Jamie's wedding and how the dominie took his wife home in his dung barrow.

They both laughed.

"Maggie there's so much I don't know. Tell me about our real Mam and Dad and our brothers Davy and Charlie. Why are we not together like other families?"

Maggie's explanation was very simple but not strictly truthful. There was no need to upset Alex who was happy and secure as a McDonald in everything but name.

Monday morning and the train back to Glasgow arrived too fast for Maggie. She promised that November term would bring her home again. The summer months in the kitchen were busy ones. Making jam, preserving fruit and eggs for the winter ahead.

Neil McLeod had escorted her to Mossvale School in search of Davy. It was an upsetting disappointing journey home for they were told Davy was now living in New Zealand.

"I'll never see him again, Neil," said Maggie. "There's no way he even knows where I am."

Neil could say so little to make Maggie's disappointment easier.

"You've got your brother Alex for yourself. Davy and Charlie don't even have that, so at the end of the day you are the lucky pair."

Maggie agreed, he was right.

John Fraser wrote to Maggie twice. The second letter said he would be in Glasgow to buy books, the last week of November. He would consider it a pleasure to escort Maggie home to Culburnie.

John met Maggie at the station. They went for tea and cakes before setting out on the journey to Inverness. The train was not busy. They got into an empty carriage. "Close the door and let the place heat up," said John, adjusting the heating control above the seat. Maggie put her hat on the rack above, beside her bag. "That's it, make yourself comfortable, we've quite a bit to go," he said sitting down next to her.

The train left the station on time at three o'clock. It was already getting dark. The carriage was quite warm. John went across and pulled down the blinds. "No point in sitting staring out into the darkness. We'll keep the heat in better with the blinds down. Glass and cold cause condensation."

Maggie could not keep her eyes off him. He was so good-looking and very masterful.

"You know Maggie, I've looked forward to being alone with you for months now. Tell me, how are you getting along with the search for you brother?"

Maggie told of her disappointment t finding out how Davy had left the industrial school and went to New Zealand. "It's so far away. I've no chance of ever seeing him again." Tears ran down her cheeks before the sobbing racked her whole body.

John took a clean handkerchief from his breast pocket. "Don't cry sweetheart. It upsets me to see you so unhappy." John put his arms around her and held her close to him. "You are so beautiful. Did you know that?"

Maggie shook her head.

John dabbed her cheeks dry with his folded handkerchief. "You need a man to love you and care for you."

This was a new experience for Maggie. She was flattered by the young man's attentions.

"I used to watch you at Culburnie. You were the finest looking girl there."

"I never saw you there then for you never spoke to me," she replied.

"You know yourself how difficult it is to meet anyone from downstairs Maggie. I've come all this way to Glasgow, just to be with you." He kissed her on the cheek.

Maggie knew she should not allow him to go on but deep down she did not want him to stop. As the train thundered on through the darkness, John's advances and sweet talk had Maggie convinced that he was deeply in love with her. She wanted this young man so much to be her protector and guide through life. If he really loved her then that's what the future would hold a life for them together. Maggie gave herself to John to seal their bargain of true love to each other.

By the time the train reached Inverness, Maggie had started to worry about what had happened between them. John assured her it was their secret "A beautiful bond between them"

Donald was waiting to take Maggie home. With the cold weather Maggie spent most of her two days indoors. Annie had a bad cold. Maggie noticed that she was becoming very frail. "You'll have to take things easier Mam," she told her.

"Lord lass, if I take things any easier I'll fall over. Hard work never killed anyone yet. It's an active life that keeps you going."

Maggie did not manage to visit Lizzie but according to Mary the baby was still alive, needing constant attention all of its mother's waking hours.

Maggie was not her usual bright self for she still had feelings of guilt at what took place in the carriage. John was right; it was a special thing between two people in love. John had said he loved her.

Back in Glasgow the kitchen work was hectic. The family were to spend Christmas at home with the children and grand children.

Maggie cooked and baked from morning to night in preparation. On Christmas Eve there was not the same feeling of fun. The staff could not relax with the family in residence. They were all tired. Maggie was disappointed, she thought John would send a card or write to her. After all he did love her.

Neil opened the port and gave them all a drink, but it was not a party atmosphere. Maggie was glad to get to bed.

The last week in January, Maggie wrote to John telling him how much she missed him, how she hoped he was well, as he had not written as promised. She anxiously waited for his reply.

The winter seemed to be extra cold. Maggie felt shivery. Jessie had noticed she was not her usual self. "You look as if you are coming down with something. You'd be wise to spend your afternoon off in your bed, instead of trailing round the shops," she ordered.

Maggie was glad to lie between the blankets in the privacy of her room. She was quite sure of what was wrong with her. She was eight weeks past her time. There was only one conclusion, but what was she to do.

The smell of food and cooking made her feel sick. Yet away from the kitchen alone in her room her tormented mind still brought on the sickly feeling. A knock at the door made her jump.

"It's me, Maggie. Neil. I've brought you up a cup of tea. Can I come in?"

Maggie told him it was all right.

Neil sat on the edge of the bed, while Maggie drank her tea.

"If you are not any better tomorrow maybe we should send for the doctor," he announced.

"Look Neil, I'm fine, no need to bother with doctors. Tomorrow I'll be in my kitchen as normal."

Maggie lay half the night planning what she would do. She would work until payday. When she went home at the end of May she would not come back. Hopefully she would be able to hide her condition until then. John would stand by her when she told him. He would go with her when she told her family.

When no reply to her letters came from John by the end of March, Maggie knew that something was wrong. She was finding it difficult to disguise her increasing waistline. She was sixteen weeks on now by her calculations. The baby was due to be born after the middle of August.

Chapter Eight

NEVER BEFORE HAD the month of May taken so long to pass. At last the twenty-eighth arrived bringing with it Maggie's six months pay. The money saved from the sale of jam jars, lemonade bottles and rabbit skins added to her worldly wealth.

The train journey seemed to be the fastest ever. Maggie tried to put things right as to what she would tell Mam, Mary and Donald. There was no way of dressing it up. The straight truth was the simplest way. Perhaps it would be the end of Culburnie as her home.

She would go tomorrow and see John and ask why he had not answered her letters. He must be ill. There would be some good reason for his silence. John loved her, he told her so. Their special secret, a token of their love was wriggling and moving below Maggie's heart.

As the train pulled into the station platform, Maggie could see Donald standing waiting. She swallowed hard, a sickly feeling made her feel dizzy.

"Inverness," shouted the guard. A young man in the carriage lifted down Maggie's bag from the luggage rack. She had left her trunk back at the house in Glasgow. She would send for it after everything was settled. John would most likely collect it before they got married. Maggie stepped down from the train, her feet felt as though they were on cotton wool. Her head was spinning. Donald was coming towards her.

"I'm so glad you're home lass."

Maggie knew no more until she came round in the stationmaster's office.

"Just lie still now, the doctor's on his way," said the elderly stationmaster complete with top hat, he'd forgotten to remove in the excitement of the young woman's collapse, as she got off the train.

Donald looked all flustered and red in the face. "Stay still until the doctor sees you Maggie. I thought you were dead lying there so pale and white." He kissed her forehead.

"Oh Donald, I wish I was dead instead of living here like this."

"Don't say such a thing. Whatever is wrong with you, we'll get you better and on your feet in no time. Mam knows all natures cures for any illness."

"It's too late now Donald, for a cure for what I've got. I'll just need to see it through to the end."

Maggie was crying and Donald was fighting hard to keep back the tears.

"For God's sake lassie, what ails you? What fatal disease have you got? I love you as my young sister." He took Maggie's hand in his.

"Donald, I'm going to have a baby."

Donald let go of the hand as if it had suddenly turned red hot and burned him. "What dirty bugger did this to you? I'll kill him with my bare hands."

The doctor examined Maggie. He assumed that Donald was her husband and addressed his findings to him.

"She's a fine healthy young woman, the baby is alright, no harm done by wearing those corsets too tight. No more travelling, get her home to bed. A day or two's rest and she will be as right as rain." Donald paid the five shillings consultation fee and they left for Culburnie.

Donald was silent for a long time then he asked, "Is the man McLeod the bairn's father?"

Maggie assured him that he was not, that their relationship was similar to a father and daughter. She decided it best to keep her lover's name to herself until everything was settled.

At least she was saved the bother of trying to explain her condition by herself, for Donald told Mam the minute they got into the house.

Annie took Maggie in her arms. "Maggie my lassie, I thought you had learned enough sense to avoid something like this. Nothing is ever easy for you. Who's the man that's responsible?"

Maggie sat down on the hearth stool. "I'm frightened to say Mam. Donald is so angry he's going to kill him."

"Lassie, I canna' blame him, we're so proud of what you've turned out to be . . . . Now he's tainted our pleasure."

"But Mam, he loves me, he's told me. When I see him tomorrow, then I know we will get married."

Annie and Donald exchanged looks.

"It's somebody local then, not someone from Glasgow?"

Maggie realised she'd made a blunder in what she said.

Donald looked her full in the face. "It can only be one of two men, Maggie. Albert Gillespie or that mealie-mouthed pansy from the big house that teaches the laird's sons."

Maggie jumped up. "Leave him alone Donald. I love him."

Donald turned towards the door. "I'll teach him to keep his flies buttoned, he'll no be able to father any more bairns by the time I'm finished with him." He banged the door as he left.

Maggie rose to go after him.

"Let him be Maggie. It needs a man to sort out this mess you've got your self into. Put the kettle on. Mary, James and Alex will be back soon. They've been away to see about Alex's schooling. There's a chance he might get a bursary to stay on."

In the past few months Maggie had never given any thought to her brothers, her own ever-growing problem kept her mind preoccupied night and day. Maggie's state of nervous tension became worse when Donald was still not back after two hours.

Neither were the rest of the family returned home.

"Do you think that Donald has killed him, Mam?"

"Lassie when you are as old as I am you never try to foretell what another human being might do. Take you for instance. I never dreamed that you would be taken by a man until the minister had first joined you in marriage first.

"John will marry me Mam, I know he will."

The old woman sat staring into the fire as if the answer was to be found there. "That's something we will need to see lass, time will tell as sure as the bairn's to be born, it will come in its own time."

It was dark when Donald got back, almost as black as his mood.

Annie was the first to speak as he marched into the candle lit room. "Well what have you been up too until this hour? You smell of whisky."

Donald sat down by the fire. "Where's Maggie?"

"I sent her to bed. If she had got any more excited she'd have had the bairn the night," said Annie.

"Well Mother, that might not have been a bad thing, for what I've learned this evening is not good at all."

"What are you trying to say Donald?" quizzed Annie.

"Well Mother, I did go after the teacher mannie but he's gone, frightened for his life and he's never heard of me yet."

"Who's he frightened of then to run away?"

"Albert Gillespie, Mother. You see Lizzie has gone off the head because of the idiot bairn they've got. In her madness she told Albert that he's not the real bairn's father. That fancy talking teacher had been at Lizzie before and after she married Albert."

"My God Donald. What kind of bairn is our poor Maggie carrying?"

"Lord knows mother, but I'll find him and he'll pay dearly for his moment of pleasure with our Maggie. One thing for sure, maggie will never be his wife. I'll damned well see to that."

Mary, James and Alex came breezing into the kitchen. "We've had supper at the dominies Mam. Looks as if Alex is going to bring us a prize for all his hard work and brains," boasted Mary.

"Get away to your bed Alex, you're not too clever yet to do as you are told.

"I know that Mam, but where's Maggie?"

"She's away to her bed laddie, you'll see her in the morning. She's brought a surprise as well."

"Is it a reward for her hard work and brains Mam?" asked Alex not wanting his moment of glory to be out matched by his elder sister.

"Well she's worked hard enough laddie, more than most, in this case her brain has been over ruled by her heart. Just how much pleasure the prize she's got will take a lifetime to tell. Now get away to your bed when you are told."

The adult family sat most of the night discussing their problem and how it could be solved. Annie wished that John had still been alive; he would have known what to do. Yet she would not have wanted him to see his Maggie shamed as she was. Donald promised to bid his mother's warning to leave John Fraser well alone to Albert Gillespie, whose wrath needed satisfaction if anything of his marriage to Lizzie was to survive.

Mary and James willingly agreed that if Maggie approved they would bring up the bairn as their own. As Annie put it to them "God works in mysterious ways" this bairn was maybe meant for you. Just as your father and I were meant for Maggie and Alex. Every bairn brings its own way and the joy, pride and pleasure, are yours in return for its safekeeping. We've let Maggie down by not warning her enough about the wily ways some men have to meet their needs for pleasure. We'll help by bringing up the bairn. God willing.

Maggie wrote to Glasgow saying she was unwell having collapsed when getting off the train. She had been ordered by the doctor to rest. Her trunk was sent home to her by train. A temporary cook would have to manage until Maggie was well enough to return to her kitchen. This news gave Maggie quite a boost. She found it difficult to accept that Mary and James would take on the responsibility of her child.

What if it was an imbecile like Lizzie Gillespie's child?

That in itself was a shock, which in an odd way helped her to overcome John Fraser's disappearance.

It would probably never have worked out anyhow. John's fancy habits and learning would never have balanced with her down to earth ways. She tried to tell herself those things but the hurt was there just the same.

Maggie felt abandoned again. How often in her life was this to happen?

Annie and Mary were so good and kind.

Annie kept plying her with raspberry leaf tea.

"It will calm your nerves and make the bairn's birth much easier on you both." Mary was already making binders and gowns. She was as excited as a young pregnant girl.

Poor Maggie could feel nothing about the baby's birth to look forward too at all. She would be glad when it was all over. Probably for her wickedness God would punish her by making her baby abnormal.

What would Mary do then? She had said that whatever happened the bairn would be hers to love and care for.

Donald was busy in the shed making a cradle. He was so caring and gentle. He wanted Maggie to have the best of attention by the doctor and local midwife.

Annie was for none of it. She would see to her "own bairn", when the time came.

It was a warm dry summer. Maggie helped about the house and croft as best she could. Annie kept a close watch on her condition.

"You'll not be long now lass, you've dropped quite a bit in the past few days. Next week at this time we should know if it's a boy or a girl.'

As usual the old woman was right. Exactly seven nights later Maggie was wakened by the bed feeling soaked.

What am I coming to now? She thought.

Annie got up from lying asleep beside her. "Lassie, have you no got pains yet? That's the waters broken."

"No Mam, I've no pains. I didn't know I was wetting the bed."

"Just lie where you are until I get dressed and tell Mary that the bairn's on its way."

Annie's raspberry leaf tea could have played some part in Maggie's easy labour. At seven in the morning she gave birth to a baby girl.

"Is she alright Mam? Has she got everything?"

Annie handed Maggie her baby. "She's perfect in every way, lovely black curls and all."

Maggie looked at the tiny wrinkled face. "Oh Mam, she's beautiful."

"What are you going to call her then?"

Maggie looked at her daughter. "Do you think Mary would mind if we called her Annie?"

"Let's get her in and ask her."

Mary was full of emotion when she held the precious bundle. This was the nearest she would ever get to having given birth to a child of her own.

"Maggie this must be one of the happiest moments of my life. Look at her Goes to prove that good always wins through in the end. Despite how much evil is involved. We will call her Margaret, a grand name for a lady in the making."

Annie and Maggie offered up no argument.

Mary was so deliriously happy with her child. During the four weeks following Margaret's birth, Maggie returned to her normal healthy self. She had written to say she was now fit to take up her position again, if possible.

It was a difficult parting from Culburnie, but Maggie knew she must go back to work to earn her keep. James and Mary were to provide for all Margaret's needs, which in some ways was to her a blessing.

Nothing had been heard of John Fraser.

Lizzie and Albert had patched up their marriage and once again Lizzie was expecting a child.

Alex was helping James and Donald with the haulage business. Donald was away from home less. He was walking out with a young housemaid from the big house. Seeing his sister so much with Margaret made him realise that before long he would be too old for a wife and family of his own. This pleased Annie. She wanted to see her son settled before she joined John.

This reunion came quite suddenly one frosty November morning. Annie was coming from the byre with two buckets of milk. Whether it was the ice that made her slip or the economy of wearing Donald's old boots for out-side work, no one knew.

The doctor said her hip was broken.

Mary's guilt was hard to bear. She had allowed Annie to do the milking while she persevered feeding Margaret who was reluctant to accept anything other than mother's milk.

Maggie's two days off were extended to three to allow her to attend the funeral and pay her respects to her Mam.

When Maggie returned to Glasgow on the Monday morning she knew that the end of her days of Culburnie as home were near. After the funeral Mary and James told her they were no longer tied to the croft with Annie gone.

Donald was planning to bring his own wife home to his place for the croft was Donald's by right.

Mary and James would need a new home of their own to bring up Margaret and Alex if he wished to go with them. They had thought of a gamekeeper's job with a house but James was anxious to take up one of the resettlement schemes and emigrate to Canada. He had a cousin there, who wrote saying there was a fortune to be made for those prepared to work. No one could deny that Mary and James were prepared to toil most of the hours of each day that God gave them. At least they would write and give Maggie some news of Alex and Margaret.

Christmas was, as ever, a busy time in the kitchen. The gentry were away and the servants' hall party was a jolly affair.

The normal exchanging of gifts took place.

Maggie's mind was not with her friends and colleagues. She was thinking of wee Margaret. This would be her first and probably her last Christmas in Scotland.

Donald was to marry in the spring, when his sister and family were leaving for Canada. Maggie did not feel she could ask for more time off to attend the wedding and farewell party, yet she longed to hold her baby once again.

"Come on Maggie, cheer up. Sing us a song," said Neil McLeod.

"I can't do that; I am so unhappy Neil," she replied as she got up and rushed from the servants hall.

Some ten minutes later, Neil knocked on Maggie's bedroom door. "Can I come in please?"

Maggie sat up on the bed and wiped her face.

"I'm alright Neil, but you can come in."

Neil had a whisky bottle and two glasses with him.

"Lassie what can I say to you? You've lost your family and the woman that was mother to you."

He poured some spirit into the glasses.

"Here, take this wee dram with me. I've never told you before but like you I'm very much on my own."

Maggie took the drink and looked into the amber liquid.

"You are a good friend Neil," said Maggie sniffing the aroma.

"Aye lassie, that's a real whisky smell, peat stained water and barley mash right from an Islay distillery."

Maggie sipped from her glass. It was as if she was drinking brown velvet, if that was possible.

"You know Maggie, you are as if you were a daughter to me. I hate to see you so unhappy."

Maggie had to bite her tongue to stop herself from telling of her need to hold her baby.

"Oh I'll be alright shortly Neil. Since Mam died Mary and James are going to Canada and taking my brother Alex with them."

"Why don't you go to Canada as well then?"

Maggie had never considered this option. There would be a need for good cooks in Canada.

Neil poured her another measure of the amber liquid. "You could always visit your Aunt in Gigha and see your other brother," he suggested.

"She did not want Alex nor me before, so why do you think she'd want to see me now?"

"Well you've never given her the chance to explain why you couldn't have gone to stay with her."

The whisky made Maggie feel more relaxed than she had felt for weeks. "Yes, I suppose as usual Neil, you are right, I think she should be given the chance."

"You could always write and enquire after your brother."

Maggie looked puzzled, "Who knows what sort of man Charlie will be? He must be about nineteen now."

"Well there's one way to find out, write." Neil got up off the chair. "I'm away downstairs again. Are you coming to join the others? They know you miss your family at Culburnie."

"Yes I'll come. Thank you Neil for being such a true friend and caring for me."

What did this clever man know of her family? Had he worked out her secret?

Gentleman that he was, he would never say.

They entered the servants' hall hand in hand.

"Here's our lady with the singing voice, the one we need so much."

"Come on Maggie we are all waiting for you," her friends cried in unison.

Life's not really so bad she decided, as she joined in the merrymaking.

The winter was long and hard.

Maggie never managed north to Culburnie for the wedding nor the farewell party for Mary and James who were bound for Ottawa in Canada. James had been offered a post as gardener handyman by one of the 'big house' kin. There was a cottage for them with prospects of work for Alex.

Perhaps it was for the best, she never managed home to say goodbye. It would be most painful to leave Mary, James and Alex, but the thought of her child being taken from her arms never to be seen again was a torment she could not have willingly faced.

CHAPTER NINE

THE FOURTEENTH OF April brought Maggie two letters. One was a farewell message from Alex before embarking, with promises to keep her up to date with their progress of their life in a new land.

The second was from Aunt Janet. Charlie was no longer living on Gigha. He was now at sea in the Merchant Navy. Uncle Alex had died in the winter of 1896. He had been in poor health for some time before that, although Charlie carried on with most of the smiddy work during Uncle Alex's illness. Unfortunately at the age of fifteen he could not carry on the business. Janet had moved from the smiddy croft to an estate house at Woodside. She was still housekeeper at the big house. Like most young men on Gigha, Charlie had the choice of leaving the island to find work either in a city or at sea. Janet had last heard from him when he was in New York.

Maggie read the letter twice, it was so strange to think that those with the same parentage and blood link could be scattered world-wide, when back in Inverness there were families who never moved more than five miles from their birthplace in seventy years of life.

Aunt Janet had invited Maggie to visit her, she wanted to meet her niece and hear how life had treated her over the years since she was orphaned. It did not seem over ten years yet so many things had happened to mould her into the person she was.

To meet her mother's sister again after years was not a chance to be missed. There would be so many questions answered about her family background.

At twenty years old Maggie still shuddered at the thought of the poor house and being called a pauper. The experience had made her very tolerant and generous to those who had fallen on bad times. No tinker or beggar ever left the back door without a piece or tasty bite of some description with the blessing of the young cook.

That night Maggie sent off her reply. She would visit Gigha on her first weekend off duty. It was a long journey but she was determined to make the effort.

Maggie sang to herself as she worked about the kitchen. Neil McLeod was quick to mention that she looked much happier.

It would cost quite a bit for the boat from the Broomielaw to Tarbert in Argyll, then steamer to Gigha, but Maggie was determined to meet again with her mother's sister, who as far as she knew, the only relation left in Scotland.

She tried hard to recall what Janet had looked like all those years ago, when she visited them in the attic room at Water Street. She found it difficult now even to remember what her father, mother and brothers were like.

The days and weeks went by until payday, then at last the day dawned when Maggie set off for the Broomielaw. It was beautiful weather for the start of June. Wearing her best clothes, hat and boots, Maggie watched from the stateroom as they sailed down the Clyde. The scenery was magnificent as the sun shone on the riverbanks.

What had Davy thought, sailing away with no knowledge of the future nor the whereabouts of his family?

There was James and Mary and Alex away to an unknown life in Canada. Margaret would soon be one year old.

Maggie wearied for her baby despite the circumstances of her conception. She ached to have part of what was her back.

John Fraser had disappeared completely. News from Culburnie said that he was away to South Africa to fight the Boers. Maggie felt some relief at the fact none of her brothers were there where the conflict between British and Dutch settlers had developed into civil war.

The sea became choppy as the ship turned towards Campbeltown. Maggie wished the journey were over. The movement of the steamer, the excitement of travelling and the anxiety of the meeting with her Aunt were not a good combination.

Would she tell Aunt Janet of Margaret's existence?

There was no reason to tell. How could Janet find out? Deception and lies did not come easy to Maggie they were not part of her 'make up'. She would play it by ear. There were so many other subjects for discussion.

The steamer sailed on, up Loch Fyne towards Tarbert, past Arran and Tighnabruich. It was late afternoon when they finally tied up against Tarbert jetty. There was time for a welcome cup of tea. Maggie was fascinated by the fishing yawls tied up side by side at the quay. The air smelled of fish, wood and peat smoke. Outside the Inn stood a horse drawn brake, ready to take the passengers to the West Loch, to board the paddle steamer 'Pioneer' on her journey to the Isles of Jura and Islay.

There was no harbour for passenger to disembark on Gigha. The people wishing to stand on God's Isle, as it had been named by the Norse, did so by jumping from the steamer into a fishing cobble, rowed out from the shore by the island's men folk. Maggie was not looking forward to this at all.

It was six in the evening when 'Pioneer' drew level with the cairn at the north end of Gigha. Maggie was tired. She had been travelling for twelve hours.

The fashionable clothing was not the best attire for jumping down eight feet into the bottom of a constantly moving fishing cobble, but Maggie made it clutching on to her hat.

The small vessel was awash with seawater from the choppy waves, and Maggie's coat and dress were soaked around the hemline. She tried to wring out the water and folded them over her knees.

"You'll be the grand lady from Glasgow visiting the blacksmith's widow," said the man on the oars speaking in hesitant English.

Neil had told Maggie of how so many of the island people had no wish to talk anything other than Gaelic although it was now compulsory to teach English in the schools.

Neil had taught Maggie so much, she would forever be so grateful for his friendship. The boat had now manoeuvred its way through the rocks and two hundred yards of seething water to the shore. As Maggie stepped onto the rocky beach she could see her Aunt waiting up on the grassy bank. What stories and secrets would they exchange over the next forty-eight hours?

When Maggie left for Glasgow on Monday morning they would surely know a bit more about each other.

Janet McMillan was a sober, down to earth person, haunted until the day she would die by the thought of being unable to offer a home to her sister Mary's children. She would never be able to understand how Mary given God's gift of bairns, took to the devil's road by drowning herself at a time when the wee ones needed her so much. Janet remembered so well, the nights that she and Alex tortured themselves with remorse at being unable to give Maggie and young Alex a home.

Poor man, Alex was unwell, Janet remembered how her husband was prematurely old at that time. Bringing Charlie to help had made a difference at first, bur Alex grew more senile each week that passed.

The doctor had tried to explain to Janet that despite her husband having lived for fifty-five years, his body, through hard work, was that of an eighty-five year old.

Charlie had been a blessing those last months, when Alex could not make any sense at all. Turning night into day, hammering away in the smiddy in the early hours, yet having no idea what he was making. Physically his body was still very strong but his poor brain was completely gone. Janet was at times frightened to approach him foe fear he would not recognise her and lash out with a heavy hammer. Somehow Charlie was able to persuade his uncle to go to bed, Then there were the other times when he would be quite lucid and tell Janet of his love for her and his plans for Charlie and their future.

Janet hoped that Maggie would understand that it was not lack of feeling for her that she had been unable to take them into her home, but the fear of what sort of unsure future she had to offer. It had been hard enough making ends meet those last years.

Life was easier now. Charlie sent her money sometimes to help.

"Come away lass, it' fine pleased I am to see you," said Janet before kissing her niece's cheek. "You look very grand with your expensive clothes."

Maggie looked at her Aunt dressed in plain homespun material with a knitted shawl around her shoulders.

"How are you Aunt Janet?" was all Maggie managed to say.

Was this what her mother would have looked like if she had been alive? Janet would be over fifty now, yet she looked the type of woman who was ageless between seven and seventy.

"We'll need to get going for it's five miles walk to Woodside at the south end of the island."

There was a cloudy haze over the sun but the soft breeze was warm on Maggie's cheek. As they walked along at a good pace, Janet showed Maggie the places where Charlie had swam as a boy. The school where he had joined the other island children in daily lessons before starting work at the anvil. Past the church, then smiddy croft that had been her home for so many years.

It was nearly eight o'clock when at last they reached Janet's cottage.

When Maggie sat down by the fire she could barely keep her eyes open.

It was a cosy room, a highly polished dresser and table almost filled the room. Two wooden chairs with velvet cushions sat one each side of the fire. China knickknacks and ornaments along with red geraniums in pots made it feel so welcoming.

"Aye it has been a long day for you from five in the morning to nine at night. No doubt you are used to that, working as a cook." Janet had just finished clearing after their meal and sat opposite Maggie at the fire.

"Do you ever hear of your brother Davy?"

Maggie told her Aunt how she had gone to Mossbank School and how she believed that Davy was probably near to Janet's brothers in New Zealand.

"You know Maggie, once a family is split up they very seldom keep in touch. It must be over thirty years since my brothers left Islay for a life in New Zealand. You mother and I came here as girls to work. It's only across the sound yet in over forty years I would have been as well in New Zealand for I have never been home. Not even when my father and mother died."

"My mother was never hame either before she died" said Maggie.

"It was all so unnecessary you know. Your mother was always impulsive. Never thought things through. I still cannot understand why she did it, why she took to drink. So irresponsible. For God's sake Maggie if you are ever blessed with children look after them well. They are put into you care by God to love and cherish."

Maggie could not hear what Janet was saying; the anxiety, fatigue and emotional stress all together were too much.

Maggie burst into hysterical sobs. "I've given my baby away Janet. I've betrayed God's trust."

"What baby are you talking of? Wheesht lassie, what a state to get in, calm down. You'll have the old man next door thinking I'm attacking you."

By morning Janet knew all the sadness, pleasures, kindness and disasters of her young niece's life. They needed each other more than ever. Janet recognised herself so much in this daughter of her sister. She was hard working, a lass who had stood on her own most of her life. She tried so hard to get ahead, yet through being kind and considerate to others always run into difficulties. Janet promised herself she would try to make up to Maggie for those years of family abandonment.

On Sunday they went to church together. Janet took Maggie up to Achamore House; the family were not in residence. Janet showed Maggie the laundry where as a girl her mother had started work. They strolled through the gardens where imported exotic flowers bloomed.

"That's what happens to families who start off anew in fresh soil. They blossom Maggie. You should save your pennies and go to Canada, be near to your baby and brother."

"Do you think I would get work there?"

"Well if you are half as good a cook as hold down a job for about seven years, I would think so."

When Maggie left for Glasgow on Monday morning her mind was made up. She would save her fare for Canada.

Neil was anxious to hear all Maggie's news of her visit to her Aunt. "Did you learn a lot about your brother Charlie?" he asked as they sat at the kitchen table.

"He's away in America with the Merchant Navy, but my aunt is to tell him of my visit next time she writes, or better still, when he goes home to Gigha, she will let me know in advance so that I can visit."

Neil looked at Maggie, her young face flushed with working all afternoon at the range and oven. She was a beautiful young woman. He knew that he loved her dearly. "Things are beginning to be much better for you Maggie. You only have to make contact with your brother Davy now and things will all come together."

Maggie filled up his teacup. "I don't know so much about that Neil, I've made up my mind that will never happen. From now on I'm to save up my money to go to Canada to join my family."

Neil almost dropped his cup. "What makes you think that things are better there Maggie?"

"Well at least I would be with my folks who care."

"Oh Maggie lassie I care about you more than you will ever know. You don't have to go to Canada to find someone who loves you."

Maggie was momentarily stuck for words. Her friend Neil who was so much a father figure to her, expressing his love. "Oh Neil, I'm so fond of you my dear, dear friend, but I do need to be with my family in Canada."

"What about me Maggie? You must know I cannot imagine life without seeing you."

Maggie stood up and started to clear the tea things.

"Well Neil, you'll see me for a long time yet, for I'll need to save my fare before I go."

Neil took Maggie's hand and pulled her close to him. "I mean it Maggie I love you. The thought of losing you is more than I could bear. I know there's a difference in our ages, but I love you so much and want to care for you and protect you. Marry me Maggie, give me the honour and privilege of being you husband."

Maggie was taken completely by surprise. "Oh Neil, please don't think badly of me, you are such a good man. I do care so much for you; life for me is such a tangle meantime. I'm not sure what I want, I certainly could not settle down to marriage yet. There's so many things I have to sort out first."

Neil looked down at the table as she brushed away the crumbs. "Don't brush me aside like the debris Maggie. I mean it, I love you."

Maggie looked right into his eyes. "Neil, I would never hurt you. In my own way I love you dearly. I'm just not ready to marry. You would look after me so well, in the future, as you have done in the past. The time is just not right, yet."

Neil put his arms around her. "Then it's not a definite no?"

"Just a request for time to think where I go from here please."

October brought a letter from Janet with tragic news. Charlie had been ashore in New York with his friend John McNeill from Gigha. John was the son of Janet's sister-in-law Annie. The lads had been walking back to their ship in the harbour after sight seeing when they were attacked and robbed. Both men had been stabbed several times and died from their injuries. Janet's message was brief but pleaded with Maggie to join her on Gigha.

Neil found Maggie sitting at the kitchen table, letter in hand staring into space. "What's wrong lass, is things at Culburnie causing problems?"

She didn't answer at first, tears started to trickle down her cheeks. "Oh Neil, I'll never see my brother Charlie again," she sobbed and handed the note to him. "I've been awake for nights thinking of all the things I would say to him. The daft things he did when we were wee. The black days in Maitland Street and Water Street. Charlie could always make things seem brighter somehow. Now he's dead, killed in a foreign land. What is it about my family? Things just never work out for us. Do you think God has forsaken me or is he punishing me?"

"Maggie, I don't think this is anything to do with you or your family. It's just life as it goes on. Are you going to Gigha? Your Aunt needs you. She's lost the boy she brought up as her son; she's lost her nephew. She needs you her only niece to be with her."

Maggie wiped her face and put the kettle on for tea. "I suppose you are right, but Neil I haven't got the time off to go."

"Never worry, I'll speak to the Master or Mistress. You have your tea, then make arrangements to go tomorrow."

Neil busied about the kitchen checking that Maggie was coping with her grief. After their evening meal Maggie did not sit in the servants' hall with her friends, she went up to her bedroom to prepare for the trip to Gigha. As she selected items from the drawers she saw the pendent given to her by Mary on her wedding day. It was such a happy time then but they were all so far away now.

Maggie felt so alone. Her family all away, not even her baby left with her. She started to cry, softly at first then loud uncontrolled sobbing.

Neil McLeod could hear the crying as she reached the top of the stairs. He ran along the corridors to Maggie's room.

"There, there lassie, it will be all right. I promise you." He took her in his arms and held her close to him.

"It won't be alright. It never is. Things go on for a wee while, then anything I care for is taken away from me. Why am I punished? Why am I never allowed to love other people?"

Maggie was almost hysterical by now. Neil sat her down on her bed.

"Maggie lass, you know I love you and want to look after you. Nothing would ever part us if that is what you want?'

She looked at Neil. "Yes I know that Neil, but I'm frightened that you would be taken from me as well."

"Wild horses wouldn't drag me away if you needed me."

"Oh my poor brother Charlie's dead in America, Davy on the other side of the World, alone like me, and Alex in Canada with my poor baby."

Neil made no comment about the baby. He felt it best not explain meantime that he, and her friends, had known all along the reason for her absence from work.

"Lassie, you're not the only one that feels alone. Like you I've had to work hard for survival. Like you I was born into service. Every day running, tending the needs of my so-called betters. No better than me at all. My father was supposedly better class. Lord and masters of a big estate on Islay. My mother just a servant lassie. Oh he said he loved her, even wanted to marry, but his family forbade him. He was sent away to the Bahamas. My mother was sacked and left to tend for herself and unborn bairn. My father married eventually, and then took over his rightful inheritance. As his natural first born and only son the same inheritance should be mine, but no, I'm illegitimate and not recognised by law. We all have our crosses to bear Maggie, we all feel alone at times. You'll always have me."

Maggie kissed Neil's cheek.

He was a good man. As she lay on the bed Neil moved his body next to her, cradling her head on his shoulder.

"Never fear lass, I'll wait until you are ready for me. I've waited a lifetime for you, I can be patient yet. Just try and compose yourself. I won't leave you."

Maggie dosed off to sleep, safe and secure in Neil's arms.

The journey to Gigha was a far different trip in June. The high winds and rough sea made her sea sick. The ship rolled backwards and forwards hitting each wave. By the time she reached Tarbert Maggie wished she had never set off. It would be dark by the time she reached the island, weather permitting. She tried to coax her stomach to accept some warm sweet tea before boarding the Pioneer. When she finally reached Woodside, Maggie was exhausted. The gale force wind almost lifted her off her feet as she tramped the island road. Sheets of rain seemed to run before the wind, soaking her to the skin.

The once cheery room was dark, the peat fire dull. Janet sat staring at the embers.

"Who is it come at this hour?" she asked.

"It's Maggie. What are you sitting in the dark for?"

"Oh, thank God you are here. You have come to me."

Maggie lit the lamp then put more peat on the fire. "I'll make us some tea. What have you had to eat to-day Janet?" asked Maggie.

"Oh, I had some oatcakes and cheese at dinner time. I've no notion to be eating at all."

"That won't do any of us any good at all if you fall ill."

Maggie put the kettle over the fire. "Life must go on Aunt Janet. We have each other to care for."

Janet took Maggie's hand. "That's true lass, it just seems to me though that there's no reason for my living. My family are no more. All I've got is my work. It's so pointless working to keep alive waiting for death to take me."

"You've got to stop thinking that kind of nonsense. Surely the future has something better for us."

Maggie poured the water into the teapot.

"Hopefully I'll marry some day and have children for you to share."

"I suppose that's right Maggie; don't make the mistake of marrying a man older than yourself. Look what happened to me, I married Alex for a home of my own and security. With no real love. There was little chance of bairns. I got to love him though and we both loved Charlie. He was our laddie."

"Oh Janet there's nothing we can do about that now. He's laid at rest with no more suffering."

"That's part of the problem. He's not here at home in the graveyard at Kilchattan beside Alex."

Maggie tried hard to console her Aunt. Eventually she persuaded her to go to bed. Tired as she was Maggie slept little. The rain battered on the corrugated tin of the cottage half the night.

It was a fine dry morning. After breakfast, when the house was tidied Maggie coaxed her Aunt into taking a walk in the fresh air.

"We'll walk up the hill to the graveyard and pay our respects."

The sun shone and a soft warm wind made walking so pleasant. It was unbelievable that the previous night the storm had been so fierce.

Gigha was a beautiful place to stay thought Maggie. Little wonder her mother had been so unhappy in the Glasgow tenements.

"Tell me about my mother. What was she like when she was young?" asked Maggie as they walked along.

"Mary was a happy girl. When we were young she loved to run barefoot along the shore. She was never still for two minutes. Laughing, joking and singing. She was always so happy. Everybody enjoyed her company."

"Sounds a bit like Charlie."

Maggie could have cut her tongue off as the words slipped out, for fear of starting Janet off crying again.

"Yes, Charlie was like your mother in lots of ways. Neither of them had a natural end to life."

"Tell me some of the things she did to make you laugh."

Janet was quiet for a while, then she said, "Och, it was all so long ago. She was wicked though. I remember this family who moved near us from Ireland. The woman was a bit scatter brained and kept on about water kelpies and goblins. Your mother and some others waited for her one night, when she was bringing her cow back from the hill. Mary, in the half-light, jumped up behind a gorse bush, with a sheet over her head, wailing and shouting like a banshee. Poor Bridget, I think that was her name, stopped in her tracks shouting ""Holy Mother of God, save me. Mary, blessed Mary full of grace, where are you? Well your mother popped around from the far end of the ditch."

"Can I help you Bridget?" she said.

"We called her the Blessed Mary for weeks after." Janet laughed. "Aye they were good times.

Maggie assured her they would come again.

The days flew by and it was time for Maggie to return to Glasgow. The week had given both of them a chance to share their grief. Time also created a bond between them Maggie knew she could not go to Canada and leave her aunt alone. Margaret would have to be left in the safe keeping of her foster parents meantime.

CHAPTER TEN

MAGGIE WORKED ON for four months. She decided that she could not afford to visit Janet every weekend off. Not only was the cost of the journey restrictive, the fatigue after travelling stayed with her for days afterwards.

She chose to remain in Glasgow. Neil had offered to take her to a Highlander's night with singing, dancing and story telling. Maggie had never been to such an occasion since leaving Culburnie. Ceilidh was part of the Inverness way of life. They set off after the household evening meal was served. Neil looked really smart in his kilt and tweed jacket. Maggie had on her best black dress. She wore her cornelian pendant.

"Tell me Maggie, what would your clan be should anyone ask?"

"I've never thought about it much. My mother's name was McKinnon, her mother's name was Mclellan, my father's name was Chalmers and his mother's was Fraser. I suppose I must be the gathering of the clans personified."

It was a marvellous evening. Maggie enjoyed dancing the reels, the Gaelic singing of love and island homes echoed through her head as she walked home hand in hand with Neil.

"What a wonderful night, I wished it would have gone on for ever. Thank you my Highland gentleman."

Maggie kissed Neil on the neck.

"You know I just want to make your whole life happy."

They had both had their fair share of drams of the best malt whisky.

"I know you do Neil. You've looked after me for years. I love you dearly, I just cannot imagine what life would be without you."

"Does this mean Maggie, my darling, that you are ready to marry me?"

"What I'm trying to say Neil is that I love you as an older brother or an uncle." They both stopped under a gas lamp.

"Does this mean you will never marry me Maggie?"

"I'm not the right wife for you Neil. You are a good man; you'll be a fine husband for the right woman. There's so much about me you don't know."

"Look lassie, if it's your baby, we could bring it up as our own."

Maggie was stunned. "How do you know about Margaret?"

"I've seen a fair bit of life, it's not the first time someone in service has gone home with an illness lasting three or four months. We worked it out."

"How do you mean we?" her voice was getting louder.

"The rest of the staff and myself."

Maggie was now shouting. "Does that mean everyone knows I've given my baby away?"

"Come on now, calm down, we are your friends, we know you, we know that you would do what you could manage. We all have to face hardships, but you've had more than your share. Your father, mother and brothers all gone, then a baby with no man. I want to save you from worry. Your friends like you because of the hard working person you are Maggie, regardless of all the knocks life has given you. You are a true Highland lady, and we love you."

"Neil let's get home. I just want to get to my bed to be alone and try to think out what I'm going to do in the future"

"Am I to be part of it Maggie?"

"Neil I am so mixed up. I'm trying to find my brother Davy, look after my Aunt Janet on Gigha, visit my step brother Donald at Culburnie, save up money to go to Canada to my daughter Margaret and brother Alex. What a mess. I'm never going to sort it out. Yes I love you but not as your wife. I'm selfish I want to find my relations first before I start a family of my own. It's important to me. I have to find out who I am."

"Maggie you are young, there's so much ahead of you. I can understand how you feel about you responsibilities but remember you can only live one life. Your brothers are the same. You do the best you can and make the most of the gift of living. What you ask maybe impossible. If your brothers are as dedicated to be a united family as you, then it's certain you will be together someday. With your determination you'll be with your daughter before long."

"Do you think so Neil?"

"Maggie you will manage anything you put your mind to."

"Will you always be my friend Neil? I want that so much."

"Lassie you have already heard how much I feel for you. I'll always be there near you waiting.

"Come on then or everybody, including her ladyship will be waiting for their breakfast if we sleep on."

Donald's wife expecting a baby prompted a visit from Maggie. It was good to be back on the train bound for Inverness.

How would she find her old friend Lizzie Gillespie? Would her new baby be a boy or a girl?

Thoughts of Lizzie's first born turned her to thinking about John Fraser and her daughter Margaret. Maggie had often reproached herself for being so taken in by John's sweet talk. It definitely would not happen again. She had made up her mind. Perhaps she would never marry if the right man never came along.

Neil McLeod would never accept that she would not marry him. He was such a dear, dependable friend. Since their conversation, their relationship became even closer. Neil encouraged her to write to Mary asking for details on Margaret and Alex's progress. Aunt Janet was picking up the threads of her life and seemed to be coping.

The train pulled into the station. There he was, waiting for her as he had done in the past, Donald McDonald. "Lord lassie, you are looking more beautiful than ever," he greeted her.

"Yes and being an expectant father looks as if it agrees with you," replied Maggie.

"Aye lassie, things have turned around a bit. Mind you I don't think I'll throw myself down on the platform to draw attention to myself, like someone I know."

Maggie could feel her face turning scarlet.

"I didn't mean to upset you Maggie," said Donald who was now embarrassed. "I meant it as a joke."

"That's alright Donald, I'll never get over just how stupid I was about the whole thing."

"Aye, it must have been an awful thought for you to come home with news of that kind."

Maggie looked at her foster brother, he was a handsome man and marriage obviously agreed with him.

"Well. Tell me, how long have we to wait for the next generation of McDonalds?"

"The doctor said Agnes is fine and the bairn could arrive any time now."

"Well you big silly lump, what are we hanging about here for?. Let's get away to Culburnie. Young John McDonald won't wait for anybody if he's like his grandfather."

Maggie linked into Donald's arm as they crossed the station yard to the waiting horse and trap.

"It's just like old times Donald. I'm so happy to be going home to Culburnie."

Maggie liked Agnes. She was just the same type of person as Annie McDonald. A cheery bright girl who kept herself busy in the kitchen. The house seemed brighter. Agnes had made a few changes for the better. What had been a bedroom for John and Annie was now the parlour, with a polished table, velvet chairs and a large gilt framed picture on the wall, bright flowered curtains and cushions. It was a lovely room.

"Donald's so good to me, you know Maggie. I really feel quite spoiled."

"You're just right for him Agnes, he's a hard working man who deserves the best and with you and the baby, he's well rewarded." Maggie helped clear the supper dishes.

"Do you think your father and mother would have approved of the changes I've made?" asked Agnes.

"I'll tell you one thing for sure, the town of Inverness would not have been big enough to hold them with stories of their grandchild."

Agnes looked down at the basin and never lifted her eyes to meet Maggie's. "Of course Donald's Mam had a wee while of your wee lass to herself, that must have pleased her."

Maggie thought for a while. "I suppose so in some ways, but Margaret's birth was nothing to be proud of nor was there a drop of McDonalds blood to call her theirs. You'll have all those things to be proud of Agnes, enjoy them. It's a rare gift to be sure."

Maggie slept in what was to be the baby's place, Donald's old part of the attic. Where Maggie and Mary had shared was now a bedroom, complete with window. The baby decided it was not ready to put in an appearance.

They were a few happy days at home. Maggie visited her old friend Lizzie. Albert was now the head gardener for the estate. He looked quite grand with his black suit, waistcoat, bowler hat and polished brown leather leggings. Their little girl made up for all the sadness and despair brought to them by the birth and death of Lizzie's first born.

She never really changed. Lizzie chattered on about old times. "Remember how strict old Toshie was—"Get those vegetables washed properly, Lizzie, while you're at it a drop of water wouldn't go amiss on your neck my lass," she mimicked.

"Should she have guessed I washed them both in the same water that would have sent her frothing at the mouth."

Laughter at the thought of bygone happenings brought tears to there eyes.

Maggie giggled herself, thinking back to when they started in service.

"Remember the time she sent you out to the laundry with the dusters?" said Maggie.

They both burst out laughing.

"God I do that, I'm sure if I'd had a home or any place to go I would have got the sack."

"See those filthy rags girl, get out to the laundry with them, put them in the boiler. I did just that."

Maggie dried her cheeks with her handerkerchief. "You stupid bitch, she meant you to put them in the boiler fire, not in beside the white washing."

"Remember the laird's long drawers were greenish blue, her ladyship's combinations looked as if she'd shitten on the back flaps."

"Oh yes and what about the time when she knew you had hidden the rabbit skins to sell yourself?"

Lizzie giggled, waving her arms and beckoning with a curled index finger.

"Come here girl, I had several lovely rabbit skins that I peeled off myself and hung them in the out house. Do you know anything about them Lizzie?"

"Oh no Mrs McIntosh, I don't need them, Maggie knitted a cardigan for me for when it's cold, you can borrow it if you feel chilly."

Maggie looked at Lizzie who was so happy and contented now. "We were frightened to laugh then Lizzie, not a penny to our names and frightened we would be turned out."

"Well we've certainly made up for it today. It's been so good spending time with you Mags. You've always been a tonic I feel the benefit from. Visit oftener, you are such a good friend to have."

On the train journey home Maggie did wonder if things were very much different from the insecurity of those early days. She would have to think seriously about her future. Perhaps she'd end up after years of being in service like Aunt Janet or Granny Fraser.

Her arrival back at Glasgow and the house soon put such thoughts from her mind. A letter from Janet was waiting for her. The news was unbelievable. Her brother Davy had written to Gigha to the laird making enquiries as to the whereabouts of his aunt and uncle. There were little details in the letter but an address for information to be sent back to him in Dunedin, New Zealand. Janet had passed on the details to allow Maggie to contact her brother.

Maggie could not control her emotions. She laughed and cried alternatively. "Neil, I'm going to be in touch with Davy again, I never thought it possible. I'll have to write to Canada and tell Alex that Davy's alive and well. I'll have to explain to Davy about Charlie being murdered. What a pity we could not all have been able to be in contact again."

Neil was so happy for her. "I told you some day it would all work out right.

Didn't I say that?"

Maggie agreed he had. It had been such a lovely weekend too, home at Culburnie. She felt so happy that things were going in her favour, for a change.

It took Maggie three evenings and many attempts to write all her news in letter form for her brother. It was not easy to remember the events of fourteen years and commit the memories to paper.

Would Davy even know that their mother was dead? Probably not. Maggie had to work out that by the time her letter reached Davy and he replied to her it would take about four months to exchange information. She decided to put that time to good use. She would join the library and read all she could about New Zealand, where Davy now had his home.

The trip to the library was most eventful. As she sat 'up top' on the tram she could see the streets were extra busy with people. Maggie spoke to the woman who sat opposite he.

"Is there something special happening? There's so many people about at this time."

"Have you not seen the papers? Mafeking has been relieved—Good news is it not?"

Maggie agreed it was good. She sat quietly trying to work out who Mafeking was and what had given him so much relief that Glasgow people were interested. Most likely some of the Royals married to some of Victoria and Albert's children.

Maggie realised that outside of her own little domain in the kitchen, Culburnie and Gigha, worldwide happenings were a mystery to her. When she returned home Neil would be able to tell her how this foreign king had got relief.

The library was deserted. The young assistant was very helpful advising Maggie on books about New Zealand and Canada. She was determined to increase her knowledge of the other lands that were her brother's homes.

Back at the house the servants' hall was buzzing with the 'war news'. Neil was explaining to the women "our troops will be coming home victorious".

Maggie's thoughts went to John Fraser for the first time in months. Would he be alive? Would he go back to Culburnie?

Perhaps he would get in touch with her. She did not know if she could cope if he did.

Maggie was kept busy during the days but at night she was engrossed with her books. Neil borrowed them from her and they discussed what they had learned from their reading.

Neil invited Maggie to accompany him to another meeting at the Highland Society. She was eagerly looking forward to the occasion.

Maggie now had so many things bringing her pleasure. Alex wrote long letters from Canada telling her of their life.

Margaret was toddling around and starting to say a few words.

Davy had sent a long letter from New Zealand. He felt so alone and deserted when first sent to the industrial school. Someone had told him at the time that their mother no longer wanted him at home, as she could not cope with him. Davy never believed this to be true. He had worked hard at the school and left with a good knowledge of mechanical engineering. Davy was unsure as to how his uncles had managed to trace him but Donald and John McKinnon, who had emigrated to New Zealand from Islay, wrote to Glasgow Corporation accepting responsibility for his upbringing.

The McKinnons were not wealthy but shared their home with Davy. With his engineering skills he had no difficulty in finding work at the new hydroelectric schemes. He lived most of the time in the work camps.

Davy was very keen to arrange for Maggie and Alex to join him in New Zealand where they could set up home together. Maggie knew this would not be. Too many years had passed and too many of life's happenings made it impossible to be a united family again.

It made Maggie feel happy that her older brother wanted to care for and protect her. She knew Davy was to write to Alex and aunt Janet. Family links and contacts were again re-established.

Maggie thanked God for answering her many years of prayers to find her brother Davy.

CHAPTER ELEVEN

O VER THE WINTER months regular letters kept Maggie in
touch with her family in Canada, New Zealand, Gigha
and Culburnie. This gave her a feeling of belonging. She
became a steady attendee at the Highland Society accompanied by
Neil McLeod. At the meetings they became very friendly with other
couples who invited them to visit their homes. Maggie felt accepted
for what she was, never before in her life had she been so happy.

The Society evenings were normally singing and dancing or some
form of musical entertainment. Maggie developed quite talent for
dancing. Light on her feet with a good sense of rhythm she would
never sit down all evening. The singing in Gaelic reminded her of her
mother, yet it all seemed so long ago.

Maggie was twenty-four years old on her next birthday. She was
a beautiful young woman. Years of working in service had taught her
to be well spoken and knowledgeable of all the social graces. She was
indeed a lovely Lowland Maiden.

The half-day visit to the shops now included a visit to her friend
Tibby Grant, whom she met at the society. Tibby was the cook for
another grand family who lived near Kelvinside. They would have
afternoon tea together and swap bits of gossip. Tibby was courting
a Glasgow policeman, John McLeod from Islay. After meeting at the
Highland Society, they had been company for over a year.

Maggie was always anxious to hear any developments in the
romance. It reminded her of the days she listened to Lizzie Gillespie's
ramblings on her latest boy friends. Tibby was arranging to have a
birthday party in the servants' quarters. She had invited Maggie and
Neil with several other couples they knew. Maggie was quite excited

about the party because she was sure that Tibby and John would declare their intention of marriage. It had even crossed her mind that both she and Neil would be asked as the official witnesses, bridesmaid and best man. It would be a very different occasion from when she witnessed Lizzie and Albert' wedding. Yet they were still together with two grand bairns. Donald had a fine son John. Maggie was often deep in thoughts of what the future held for her.

Would she ever marry and have another child? Would she marry Neil McLeod? Certainly she would have a secure future but her feelings were not that of a lover, more of a father. Maggie wanted a husband to love and cherish and pledge his troth until death do them part. She thought of that far-gone day when she cried at the marriage of Albert and Lizzie.

Janet wanted Maggie to visit. She had written her asking if it would be possible for her to go and stay for a day or two. They would really give Maggie time to relax and think.

It was September when she found herself walking towards Woodside. Janet welcomed her like a daughter.

"Come on in my lass. I'm so pleased you have come home."

How Maggie would have loved to hear those words thirteen years earlier. No one had any control over the past, only the future was within her control.

The week passed very quickly. Gigha was an island of paradise. The families were all related and known to each other. Maggie was accepted as a member of that family. Life on the island was unhurried, yet no islander could be accused of being lazy.

Contrary to mainland life, nothing was done by the clock. Work went on if and when the operative was ready. Maggie loved nothing better than to help in the fields or on the shore collecting seaweed.

The men made most of their income from fishing for lobsters. Maggie even became an expert at baiting the creels of her 'cousins' the McNeills. In return she could spend the evenings by the peat fire listening to their stories of days long gone. How the Norse seamen came to Gigha and found its natural moorings and anchorage. The Norsemen found the climate mild and warm. The volcanic soil made it ideal for growing.

There was also the story of the small offshore island of Cara and how a brownie or fairy lived there. The island had been visited by St

Columba, on his way from Ireland to spread the story of Jesus. The ruined chapel still remained on the islelet. For the solitary family who lived on Cara, life was hard and lonely.

Maggie dreamed of how she would manage to cope, with a good husband, working together, life on Cara would be ideal. She sat on the soft grass looking out over the Sound to the Kintyre coast, contemplating the joys of bringing up children on the island.

If only Janet had been able to give them all a home, life could have been so different. She soon reasoned that the experiences in life developed the personality. After all her way of living was not so bad now. Next week she would be back with her friends in Glasgow preparing for Tibby and John's wedding.

Janet seemed closer to Maggie each visit. They enjoyed each other's company. Janet still spent most of the day at the big house carrying out her house keeping duties, leaving Maggie plenty of time to herself. When together they talked of the past and the future.

The last night of Maggie's holiday they sat out in the garden watching the sun set over Islay.

"It's such a beautiful sight Janet, everything seems so calm and peaceful."

"I suppose it does, but the sun rises and sets everyday despite what is happening."

"I'll always be able to remember what it's like I'll tell my children."

Janet looked at Maggie. "Tell me when are you thinking of having them?"

"When I meet the right man to be a good father to them, Janet. It's no use marrying unless you are both to gain something from the marriage."

"What makes you such an expert Maggie?"

"I've thought about it a lot. Neil McLeod has asked me to be his wife many times. He would give me a good secure life. I'd be well looked after. Something many women would welcome but I think there has to be something more."

"What sort of thing are you looking for lassie? Your mother and father thought they had something special. Life in the city soon put paid to that."

Maggie quickly sprung to the defence of her long lost parents. "They loved each other. For all her faults my mother loved my father. That's the kind of love I want from the man I marry."

"Well lassie," said Janet. "I hope you are lucky when you find the kind of love, don't be like your mother and let it go sour."

Maggie rose from the seat and went into the house. Janet followed.

"You have no need to huff Maggie. I'm only speaking the truth. Your mother was never much help to David with her girning on about wanting back to Islay.

She just could not accept she had to stay where he found work. There was no work on Islay; otherwise we would not have left. You must settle where your man finds work to provide for your family. What does your young man work at?"

"I've no young man Janet, I'd rather be on my own, if the right one is not there for me."

"I suppose time will tell, I'll just hope that I'm here to see your bairns."

When Janet waved goodbye to Maggie at the ferryboat she knew it would probably be the spring before she returned.

Back in Glasgow Maggie was preparing for Tibby's wedding in October. It was to be the same week as her twenty-fifth birthday. Although she had been asked to be the bridesmaid, it was a friend of John McLeod that was to stand for him. Maggie baked and iced a grand cake. There was to be a celebration party in the servants' quarters where Tibby was the cook.

She took great care in grooming her hair. The dress, coat and hat, bought for the occasion were very smart. A cab called for her before picking up Tibby, the bride. The marriage service was to be held in the vestry of the church at Maryhill.

Tibby looked beautiful in a French navy suit, topped off with a black leghorn straw hat. She was so nervous and excited. "What if John is not there, Maggie? What if he has changed his mind?"

Maggie soon calmed her down. "Of course everything will go just right. The best man will see that he is there. Who is the best man Tibby?"

Tibby straightened her hat, smoothed the fingers of her gloves for the twentieth time.

"It's James Chisholm. He's John's beat partner. He has not been long in the force but they've become very good friends. He was in the army fighting the Boers and came home from Africa recently," she answered.

The service was simple and short. Afterwards the bridal couple left in a hansom cab to return to the party. Maggie was left to share another cab with James Chisholm. He was a very handsome young man. Well over six feet tall, blond, with a fair complexion and very stunning bright blue eyes. "I hope you don't mind having to partner me Maggie?" he said." I think it's best that they start off their married life together alone, for the first half hour at least. Forgive me for addressing you as Maggie, but I don't know your surname."

Maggie could hardly answer; she was so fascinated by this good-looking man with magnetic eyes. "I'm Maggie Chalmers," she stammered.

"Do you wish me to call you Miss Chalmers or Maggie?" he asked.

"Maggie is just fine, everybody knows me as that. Only her ladyship calls me Mrs Chalmers."

"I'm sorry, I did not know you were married. I would have never taken the liberty of calling you by your Christian name had I known. Please accept my apologies madam."

Maggie laughed. He was so correct and formal. "I'm not married at all. It's just a title that goes with the job of being head cook."

"Thank goodness I've not upset you. I'm Jim Chisholm, I hope you will call me Jim and we will be good friends."

The party was a great success. Jim toasted the bride and groom and complimented the bridesmaid. He then kept the evening's fun going by announcing each dance and encouraging the company to sing. Neil McLeod told him Maggie had a fine voice. She sang as never before to impress Jim Chisholm.

Towards the end of the evening Neil danced with Maggie. "Lassie you look so radiant. I've never seen you so happy."

"Och it's been a grand day Neil. Tibby and John are a well-matched couple don't you think?" said Maggie.

Neil held her close while they danced. "They are not the only well matched couple here tonight. I've watched how the other young bobby looks at you and you at him Maggie."

"What a blether you are Neil McLeod, we are only carrying out our official duties."

Neil chuckled. "Well I'll wait and see lassie. He's a fine young man. What chance has an old dodder like me?"

Maggie kissed his forehead. "Neil McLeod, you own part of my heart that no man will ever reach. I never met the young man until today."

Neil in turn laughed. "Aye but I don't think this will be the last time you'll be seeing him."

Neil's prediction was correct. Over the next two months Jim, as Maggie got to call him, was a frequent visitor to the servants' hall. When they had time off together he took Maggie out. They walked in the parks, visited Tibby and John in the new home they had set up together.

Jim gradually told Maggie of his family background. How he had been born near Forfar in Angus. His family all lived in that area except his brother William who lived in Milngavie. Jim had worked as a farm servant until he joined the Scots Guards in the spring of 1899. He felt the farming life allowed him no room 'to better himself'. Jim was very keen and ambitious; he wanted to break away from the everyday drudgery that being 'hired' to a farmer entailed. His years in the army had certainly given him a change of experience. He had fought in the South African campaigns against the Boers.

Maggie told him of the night she had gone to the library, when the crowds were celebrating the Mafeking relief. She told him how she believed it to be a person."

Jim was amused by her story. "I've got a picture at home with my kit which shows the regiment marching through Mafeking." He promised Maggie that someday she would see it.

Maggie told him part of the story of how she was orphaned and separated from her brothers.

The time they spent together was never long enough. Jim was so good looking; Maggie's eyes could not leave him. He was so polite and correct.

Neil McLeod would spend time chatting with him until Maggie finished work. "He's a good man." Neil told Maggie. "I knew you would see more of each other."

"You're not match-making now are you? Needing rid of me?" she teased.

"Lassie it does my heart good to see you so happy that is all," he answered.

The plans for Christmas were underway. Jim had been invited to share the meal and party at the servants' hall.

Davy sent Maggie a present of a brooch. She thought it was the most beautiful thing she had ever seen. It had a centrepiece of blue-greenish stone, which changed colour with the light. Davy said it was a small piece of New Zealand to bring them closer together.

Janet seemed to be kept busy. She wrote regularly telling of all the island news. Maggie had still not told her of her friendship with Jim Chisholm.

At Culburnie the haulage business was prospering. Donald was kept busy about the place with directing the workers and keeping the paper work up to date. This gave him plenty of time to spend with his son John. Maggie would have to visit as soon as the good weather came for they were never ended inviting her to come home. Donald seemed to miss the company of his sister Mary and her family and his stepsister Maggie.

Life in Canada sounded grand according to Alex's letters. People were not judged by who they were; it was what they could achieve and how they worked that mattered. Certainly if work was the gauge, then Maggie knew her family would succeed.

Christmas day was one Maggie would never forget. After the part when the singing and dancing was over, Maggie and Jim sat alone by the fire.

"You look tired Maggie, it's been a long working day for you," said Jim, lifting her feet up on to a stool.

"It's a day I never want to end Jim, I'm so happy. So much so that I sometimes wonder if I'm dreaming."

"It's been a good day for me as well you know. Christmas has never been anything to me before."

"Why not?" asked Maggie.

"Well when I was young it was just another ordinary working day, with beasts to be fed and work to be done. Where I come from Hogmanay is celebrated, but that's all. It's not a holiday. It's been the same in the army, away in the African bush, the Zulus never heard of Christmas."

"They've heard of big Jim Chisholm though."

"Too true they have." Jim was laughing. "At Christmas I fell into an animal trap they had made. Well the buggers stood around the edge of the pit and showered me with boulders. I'd hurt my heel falling down, but if I'd been able to get hold of them I'd have given them Christmas."

"Well you are safe enough here with me," said Maggie.

Jim sat down beside her and put his arm around her shoulders. "I'm not just so sure how safe you are though Maggie", he said before kissing her.

Maggie's heart was pounding as though it would burst from her breast. Not since that afternoon in the train with John Fraser had she been so roused by a man. "I hope I'm safe with you Jim. I trust you to be the gentleman I believe you to be."

"Maggie. I'm no gentleman, I have all the urges natural to any man who is close to a beautiful woman like you."

"It's not right we should be getting ourselves like this Jim, I'll make you a cup of tea before you go home."

"Maggie I don't want to go home, I want to stay here with you."

"Don't be difficult Jim; you know that's not possible.

"Do you want me to stay Maggie?"

She hurried through to the kitchen so that Jim could not see her face. Yes, she wanted him to stay; she wanted to be near him always.

The lesson learned from John Fraser kept her from admitting her desire.

She carried the tea tray back.

Jim was lying back in the chair with his eyes closed.

"Are you asleep Jim?"

"No I'm just thinking how it would be if this was our home, the pair of us together alone. Maggie, I'm twenty nine years old, with very little to offer you but will you marry me?"

Maggie had so much wanted to hear those words from Jim but she was not prepared for them. "Oh Jim I don't know what to say."

"Try saying yes, then we can take it from there," he told her.

Maggie poured the tea into the cups and handed one to Jim.

"I'd be good to you Maggie. I can work beside any man. I'll save for us to set up a home. I just want us to be together."

Maggie wanted to laugh, sing, cry, dance all at the same time.

Jim, her Jim, now wanted her to be his wife. "Yes Jim. I'll marry you." The words came out in a quiet whisper.

Jim stood up, his huge frame dwarfing Maggie's slim figure. "Am I allowed a kiss to seal the bargain or would that be going too far?"

Maggie kissed him. She knew that if the kiss developed into anything else she could not help herself. Jim was to be her husband, partner for life, father of their unborn children.

Jim returned to his lodgings in the early hours of the morning. He was on duty at six. He would see the sergeant about any extra duties he could work. The sooner he saved up enough to set up home the better. He could not leave Maggie alone much longer. It was time to settle down anyhow. He would be thirty on his next birthday, Maggie twenty-five.

After breakfast Maggie told Neil that she was to marry Jim. It was not easy for she did not want to hurt the feelings of her dear friend.

"I knew that you were right for each other. Congratulations, and the best of luck to you both." He kissed her cheek then hurried from the kitchen for fear that Maggie would know how much her news upset him.

She wrote to Janet and her brothers, telling of her plans.

Jim discussed with Maggie how long it would take them to save money for furnishings. They settled that they would marry late autumn the following year. That would allow them time to find a home. Jim did not want his wife to work. A house near the police station would suit them best. Despite the restrictions on spending they both agreed it was necessary to visit Gigha and also be able to meet Jim's family in Brechin, where their father had settled.

They set off for Gigha at the end of May when Maggie received her wages. It was lovely weather and the island was at its best. Maggie was so proud. Jim was so good looking and had travelled abroad; he could speak on so many different things.

Janet was most impressed by his appearance and impeccable manners. She agreed that if she were 'well enough' she would attend the wedding. It pleased Maggie that at least one member of her family would be there.

The visit to Jim's family was in the first week of September. Maggie was very apprehensive about going. "What if they don't like me?" she said.

Jim told her not to be stupid. It would make no difference at all. They were getting married to each other, not the family. The week of the Brechin visit they had managed to find a two-roomed house to rent in Earlston Avenue. Jim was to paper and paint it for October, when they planned to marry. They visited the salerooms looking for bargains of second hand furniture. Maggie had an eye for good pieces.

She thought of what Jim had said. It was silly worrying about relatives, after all they would be so happy together.

It surprised her to discover Jim's family were most self conscious at meeting her.

His father was a kindly old man, who had been a widower for years. He lived alone near his daughters Helen, known as Nellie from a young age, and Isabella, who both helped him with his house keeping.

Nellie was married with four children. Life was hard for them with very little money. Isabella lived in the country in a 'tied' farm cottage. Her husband worked on the land. She had young children to care for. They were hard working people but not like the folk from Gigha or Culburnie. They seemed a dour lot, but then maybe they never had much to laugh about.

Maggie was glad that they were to settle in Glasgow where she felt she belonged. Time just flew past. All the free hours they had away from work were spent making their home ready. Maggie never had more than a few hours each week. Her cooking duties kept her busy from early morning to late evening. Jim did his best to get things in order. Money was hard to come by for furnishings. Maggie liked the best. Jim had moved into their home to save paying lodgings. Maggie tried to see he was kept supplied with cooked meals.

The wedding arrangements were finalised. The last week of November the ceremony was to take place at Barony parish Church.

The minister there had agreed to marry them Tibby and John were to be the witnesses. Neil had agreed to 'give Maggie away'. The only extravagance she allowed herself was a new dress and hat. Nothing was to spoil the day that she became Jim's wife.

Janet sent a gift of blankets from Gigha. The cold windy days of November made it impossible for her to cross to the mainland for the celebrations. Davy sent her five pounds to buy something they needed. They both agreed on a brass-ended bed.

Maggie giggled at the thought of them sharing it. She was so happy at the thought of having things in a home that belonged to her. Since those far-gone days in Maitland Street she had always shared or used other people's homes or belongings.

Her Ladyship gave them a gift of a magnificent dinner service and a set of toddy ladles. Very grand, but not much use to a working class couple setting up a home.

CHAPTER TWELVE

"I NOW DECLARE YOU to be husband and wife. What God has joined together let no man put asunder." The words of the minister echoed through Maggie's head. Jim kissed her lightly on the cheek. "I love you Mrs Chisholm," he whispered.

Neil McLeod was the first to congratulate them.

"May all your blessings be little ones," he said. He shook Jim's hand. "I hope that in years to come Jim, I can still remain a friend to you both."

The reception back in the servants' hall was a grand affair. Her ladyship despite her frail condition put in an appearance to wish the happy couple good luck in the future. She hoped Maggie would keep in touch as she was looked upon as being of her 'family'.

Maggie thought it had taken her a long time to work out how she would be missed. Nothing was going to spoil her day. When the party was at its height, Jim whispered to Maggie, "Come on lass, I think it's time we went to our own home."

How wonderful those words 'our own home' sounded. They had two days by themselves before Jim went on duty again.

"I really feel like gentry," said Maggie sitting up in bed on the Saturday morning. "It's after nine o'clock. I don't think I have ever been in bed so late."

Jim turned back from where he was pulling on his trousers at the bedside. "Would you like me to come back beside you again? We can miss breakfast for something better."

He was all hers to have and to hold. Maggie would never understand how someone so wonderful as Jim wanted her for a wife.

Never before had she had time to spend by herself, doing as she pleased. She took extra care preparing the evening meal. By four o'clock she was wearying for Jim to return home. When it was after half past six, Maggie was anxious what was keeping her husband. After seven she heard his key in the lock.

"Oh Jim, where have you been, I thought something had happened to you?"

Jim appeared red in the face. "It's alright lass, some of the lads and I went for a celebration dram after the end of the shift."

Maggie reckoned it had been a good celebration for Jim appeared to be very merry.

"Never mind the dinner Maggie, come on let's have a walk over to see Tibby and John."

"Let's have our meal first, it's all prepared. We can go out once we have eaten."

Maggie had made a full dinner with soup, main course and sweet. Once Jim had finished eating he sat down beside the fire and fell fast asleep. Maggie sat watching him. He must have enjoyed the company of his friends. They would have to be careful with their pennies. She knew that she had overspent on the food, but it was their first meal together when Jim returned from work. They could certainly could not to afford money to spend on drinking. It was only hisfriends celebrating their marriage after all. Maggie could not get Jim wakened. After hours of sitting watching him asleep she went to bed alone.

Jim was full of remorse at having spoiled their evening together. "I wanted to take you out and show you off in front of the lads Maggie," he tried to explain. "We could have gone for a drink before going to Tibby and John."

Maggie looked at him in surprise. "Jim I've never been drinking in a public house and I certainly don't think I want to start now. What's more, we really don't have money to spend on drinking."

Jim looked sheepish. "Maggie we cannot just live like hermits. There has to be more to life than working, sleeping and eating. God knows, I spent over three years in Africa fighting for people's rights, I want my wife to have some enjoyment from life."

Maggie cuddled up to him. "I'm sorry Jim for upsetting you. I suppose it's because I've always had to save every penny towards my future."

Jim kissed her. "Aye, lassie, you've had a hard life but I'm with you now to look after you. Away and put your hat on and we'll go round to John and Tibby tonight."

They had a fine evening with their friends. Long after Jim had fallen asleep Maggie lay in bed in his arms thinking of how she must try to change her way of living. She loved him so much; he might turn against her if she nagged him about money. Lying midway between consciousness and sleep, a vision of her father and mother flashed before her eyes. She could see her father slapping her mother's face in attempts to waken her from her drunken stupor. Her father shouting "There's no food in the house for the bairns and you've spent my wages on drink."

Maggie made a solemn promise to herself that never would she waste money buying alcohol. She thought of how this could affect Jim but reasoned that he was entitled to some of his wages to himself. What he did with his 'own money' was his own affair.

By the end of January Maggie thought she was pregnant. She considered it wise that until she was certain she would keep the news to herself. During the day when she was alone she worried how this might change the relationship between them. How long could she safely cope with his nightly lovemaking. Maggie had heard of how at times like this men turned their attention to other women to serve their needs. She could not even think of how she would face such a situation.

How would they manage to afford what baby's needed? Already in their few weeks of marriage, Maggie realised that the lifestyle they could afford on Jim's wages was precious little more than an existence. However, her Jim still insisted that he did not want his wife to work. Her place was in the home.

When alone the thoughts tortured her, to the point where Jim came home to find her sitting sobbing by the fire. It was obvious she had been distressed for a considerable length of time.

"Maggie lassie, what's wrong? Are you ill or something?" He held her close to comfort her.

"Oh Jim I'm going to have a baby, you won't love me any more and we cannot afford to keep it."

Jim lovingly tilted her face towards her own. "Lassie that's the best news I've heard in my life. Stop loving you—what nonsense. I'll love you even more. How do you mean we cannot afford to keep it? I'm the bairn's father Maggie. I'll see it's provided for. Come on let's go and tell somebody."

"I'm not fit to be seen by anybody like this," she started to cry. I haven't anything for your tea. I was so worried about not managing to keep the baby."

Jim placed his hands on Maggie's shoulders, turned her round to face him. "We agreed that happened before I met you was in the past. What ever 'the thing' was that fathered your daughter was not a man. No real man could turn his back on his bairn. I've had to wait a long time for mine. I'll get a spare-time job for extra money. Lassie, you've made me the happiest man on earth. Now stop the worrying or we are going to lose the baby."

"Jim you're such a wonderful man. I love you more than you'll ever know. We'll go round and tell Neil McLeod first, we'll be sure of a cup of tea and something to eat there."

Neil McLeod was pleased to see them both. Life for him had not been going very well. The cook who replaced Maggie did not fit in, with the rest of the staff. Her ladyship was unwell and had taken to her bed. This gave rise to a feeling of doom and gloom, in the servants hall.

What would happen to their jobs and living quarters should her ladyship die?

As they walked back to Earlston Avenue they decided that there were people much worse off than them. Jim was whistling away as they marched along. He never forgot he had been a soldier.

"I'm still on the reserve you know. They cannot do without lads like me. If any war broke out I'd be the first to go."

"Surely not now Jim, you're married with a home and family."

"That would not matter Maggie. In times of war if your Queen needs you, then you've got to go."

Maggie decided that the malt whisky Neil had given him to celebrate the New Year and the baby was making him blether. She decided not to even think of Jim being taken from her.

Jim was as good as his word, when on his days off duty he took on a job with the corporation driving a horse drawn street sweeper. Maggie knew that Jim would be sacked from the police if it were known he had two jobs. The extra money was very handy. It allowed them to live a little. Jim took Maggie to the theatre and to see a musical show.

Janet was delighted to know that the baby was to be born. In a long letter to Maggie she explained how empty her been without children. She invited them both to spend time on Gigha as she enjoyed company. There was little enough time for them to be together. Jim rushed home from finishing one job to start another.

By the end of August both were showing signs of strain. Maggie spent most of her waking hours alone. Jim, by the time he reached home, was so tired he fell into bed. The pregnancy was not an easy one. Maggie was finding it increasingly difficult to get about. Circumstances caused her to spend a lot of time inside the house. Sitting for hours resulted in her feet and legs swelling.

"I'm so wearied to have it all over with," she said as they sat having their meal together.

"Four weeks more lass, it will all be worth it."

"It's the waiting that's the worst. If the baby were here I'd have company. I'm worried I 'start' when you're working."

"We've been over all that Maggie. Get one of the neighbours to leave a message at the station. I'll be home as fast as I can. If I'm working on the streets, one of the beat lads will pass on the message. You are such a worrier."

Maggie knew this was true. Jim got annoyed with her at times. He did his best trying to provide for them by working long hours, he could not be with her at the same time.

Tibby was visiting for an afternoon chat when the pains started. She helped Maggie into bed and hurried for Mrs McLaren the 'howdie' wife. She then went off in search of Jim.

Despite being a second baby it was a long difficult labour. Mrs McLaren told Jim, "I usually manage fine by myself son, but I think you should have the doctor see your wife. The bairn is lying wrong; it's to be born feet first. I've tried to turn it. Your wife is exhausted, only the doctor can help her now."

Maggie drifted between levels of awareness, the pain at times felt as though her body was being wrenched apart. "Help me Mam," she muttered, visions of both Mary and Annie appeared to her.

"For God's sake help me one of you." She pleaded to the imaginary figures. Mrs McLaren tried to hold her down on the bed.

"The doctor will be her soon. Try to lie still until your husband gets back with him."

"Get my Mam Jim," Maggie shouted. "I want my Mam."

From somewhere Maggie could hear music. It was her mam singing "Ho ro my nut brown maiden."

There she was with Annie. "Drink up the raspberry leaf tea, you'll be fine then,' Annie said.

"I'll be fine now that you're here," said Maggie and lay back on the pillows.

"Hurry doctor, she's collapsed," Mrs McLaren told the doctor. "I'm fearing for the pair of them now."

"Come on Maggie lass, waken up and see our son," Jim shouted, as though he was shouting down a long tunnel.

"Where's Mam and Annie?'

Jim looked at the doctor.

"She's a bit muddled. It's been a hard time for her. Come on, Mrs Chisholm you've got a lovely boy. It's all over now."

It was just the beginning. Young James Chisholm was beautiful baby with a mass of dark curls. Jim paraded about the room carrying the tiny infant the size of one of his massive hands.

"You're a lovely wee chap, like your mother. Stop crying and let her rest, I'll have to get away to work now." Mrs McLaren took charge of the infant.

"Your wife will be fine by the time you get home. Bring a wee drappie with you and we'll wet the bairn's head."

Jim celebrated the birth of his son with numerous drams before Jim McLeod helped him home. Maggie, tired and pale, sat up in bed waiting.

"He's just had a few drinks Maggie, to get over the worry then the excitement. He'll be fine when he wakens up. How are you lass?"

Maggie held back the tears of disappointment and embarrassment at seeing her husband drunk. "That's alright John, I understand. Jim's tired. He works hard. I'm fine. I'll be up and about in no time."

"He's a grand bairn, I'll send Tibby around to see him. Anything that you're needing?"

"No John, I'm fine," she lied holding the tears at bay.

Jim lay in the chair snoring. Maggie lay in bed crying with the baby in her arms.

"I just wanted your company for a wee while Jim, just to share our son together," she sobbed, her tears falling on the baby's face.

Eventually she drifted into an exhausted sleep.

James was a good baby and demanded little attention. Maggie was soon on her feet again. It would be a long time before in her heart she could forgive her husband for deserting her in her hour of need.

On the surface life returned to its normal routine. Maggie was, however, aware that often, when he returned form working, Jim's breath had the smell of drink.

"There's nothing wrong with a refreshment at the end of a days toil lassie," was his answer to Maggie's queries about its origin.

When James was twelve weeks old she suspected that she was expecting another bairn.

"How can that be Maggie? James is not four months old."

"You of all people should know the reason why Jim Chisholm, for you're the only man in my life."

"Lord knows Maggie that's not what I was meaning you to think. Its just we could have done with a bit of time before the next one. Are you sure?"

"I'm almost certain, I've been sick in the mornings now for a month."

"I'd never noticed lassie but then I'm always away working. Well not to worry, the bairn will make a way for itself when it comes. We will manage."

She knew deep down that she would. She also knew in her heart that it would not be the last bairn she would carry for Jim Chisholm, he was a marvellous lover. Maggie could feel so angry at his behaviour when he was away from her, but when they were together she could not resist or deny anything.

Letters from Alex were full of news from the family. Margaret was quite a lovely little girl who, according to Alex, never stopped chattering. Alex did not seem so secure as before making contact with his brother Davy. From what he said Maggie thought it was only a question of time before the brothers would be together in New Zealand. This idea did nothing to help Maggie's depressed state of mind. It made her feel even more cut off and alone.

During one of her black moods Neil McLeod visited her at home. Poor Neil was there to say goodbye before leaving for Islay to take over his grandfather's croft. Her Ladyship had died and the house was to be closed until a buyer could be found. The staff was dismissed with the bonus of a week's extra pay in lieu of notice.

"I've had enough of life running serving others Maggie, you were lucky and got out." He sat with James on his knee. "Yes, things are certainly going well for you at last. You'll tell Jim I'm sorry that I missed him. He's a good man."

Maggie did not bother even to answer. She lifted the kettle from the fire and filled the teapot. "He's on duty until after six tonight. He's been working around the docks area lately."

Neil looked at Maggie. "That's where you were brought up was it not?"

"Aye Neil, that was a long time ago. I've never really had the courage to go back and look at where we stayed in Maitland Street."

"It's strange lass but I know the feeling. Here's me going back to Islay after more than thirty years, trying to imagine what it was like there when I left."

"One thing for sure Neil, you'll be working for yourself, so it will be a big success."

"I'll give it a good try anyhow. Jim, you and the bairn can visit, that way I'll be sure of at least one well cooked meal."

"I'm afraid that won't be this year now I'm expecting another bairn."

"Oh, Maggie I hope its a lassie for you this time, a sister for young James."

After he left Maggie felt uplifted by having company. It would be good if the bairn were a girl. Jim would have to change from telling about "My braw son."

It was past nine o'clock when Jim finally came home. He had drunk enough to make him argumentative. "Did your loyal friend not want you to go to Islay with him?"

Maggie never looked at him; she sat at the table slowly spreading butter on to bread.

"Did he not want you, with my son? He could never manage to father such a lad, eh? Another one in your belly too. Did you tell him of that? No he would not be fit to sire you and work night and day to stop your whining and girning about money."

Maggie had learned that when he was in this frame of mind Jim was best left to have his say uninterrupted.

"It takes a man like me to meet your needs Maggie. You need a real man eh? Not a half baked flunkie that's an apology for a man."

She got up from sitting at the table.

"Not want the company of a good man now?"

Maggie looked him straight in the eye. "If you don't mind I'm away to bed for it's been a long day alone here with the bairn."

"That's quite correct lassie, just you get undressed and I'll come and give you company, that's sure to make you feel wanted, satisfied and contented."

He left the house before six in the morning. Maggie went back to bed. It was so good to lie relaxing without fear of moving and waking Jim. It was always the same if he'd insulted her when drunk, the apologies and begging forgiveness ended with more sexual demands.

Maggie felt exhausted both mentally and physically. What could she do to get them from this rut that seemed to grow deeper each day that passed?

Janet wrote that she could no longer wait for them to bring her nephew James to Gigha. She would come and visit them in Glasgow. This was just what Maggie needed.

Jim read the letter as he sat eating his evening meal. "We will have to get the bedroom ready now. We cannot have Janet thinking I don't look after my family."

"She would never think that Jim, you work hard, we just never get time together to enjoy life. Still, there are others worse off. This morning when I was shopping there was a family evicted from their home across the street."

"Aye that's what happens when there's no work for men. Every day I see queues of men fighting for a day's casual work at the docks. Its high time the government realised a man deserves to have the right of a days pay for a days work."

"It was the poor bairns clinging to their mother and granny, with no where to go."

Maggie was obviously upset by what she had seen.

"Well we aren't at that stage yet, are we lass? Your aunt will have a bed to sleep on when she visits."

"You are a good man Jim."

At times like this Maggie was so proud of her Jim, if only he could keep away from drink life would be so much happier.

They managed to buy a bed cheaply at a warrant sale. Many Glasgow families were leaving Scotland to settle in America where there were opportunities for work. The shipyards were laying off men, with no orders for ships on their books. The few belongings collected over the years were sold to provide a little cash for their passage to a new life.

Maggie and Jim discussed the possibility of them emigrating. Jim was not in favour at all. He believed that Scotland had enough to offer him in life. The years spent in the veldts of South Africa fighting Dutch settlers influenced his decision. Jim reckoned that in America or other countries where international immigration was encouraged there would always be racial prejudice.

Nothing Maggie could say would persuade him otherwise.

It was mid July when Janet finally arrived in Glasgow. The heat was tremendous. Janet looked tired from the long journey. Maggie met her at the Broomielaw as she disembarked from McBrayne's steamer. Jim was on duty but had promised faithfully to come straight home at the end of the shift.

Young James was everything wonderful to Janet. As they sat having a cup of tea, James lay across Janet's lap, kicking and gurgling. "I'm so pleased to be here Maggie. You know I never thought I would ever nurse the next generation of McKinnons."

"He's a Chisholm Janet, he's Jim's son," answered Maggie. "I know that lassie, but he's the first bairn I've known in our family for over fifty years."

"Surely not Janet, there must have been others before now."

"Well lassie I'm fifty-nine and apart from you and your brothers I've never seen any family bairns. You were all a bit past this stage before I saw any of you," she explained.

"Tell me something of the McKinnons Janet, there's so little I know of my background, what happened to our grandmother and grandfather?"

"I suppose it's quite a story. The McKinnons farmed at Tormisdale for generations back. My father's father and brothers all lived from the working of the same land. Your grandfather Charles McKinnon was a big strong man, my mother Margaret, that you are named after, was his second wife. She married when my father was fifty seven years old."

"That's about your age now Janet," said Maggie quickly thinking would Jim's sexual demands on her go on until he was sixty. "He must have been an old man when you were born?"

"That's right Maggie, he was sixty-four when my brother John was born."

"What happened to your brothers then? Mam used to tell us stories but with no disrespect she must have blethered a lot when she had too much to drink."

"Aye Maggie, that's something I'll never understand about her. Leaving me, with what she did, on my conscience."

"Tell me about your family?" said Maggie trying to avoid another lecture on the inadequacy of her mother. "What happened to them?"

"Right, my elder brother Donald went away to New Zealand. There was no point in him staying on Islay for the family from father's first marriage had prior claim to anything that was heritable. There was your mother who went into service with me when we were young. Only God knows what took her on the road to sin and destruction. My brother John is a merchant seaman. Last I heard he had a house in Portnahaven for his leaves ashore. He never married."

Maggie was curious about news of those unknown relatives. "Do you keep in touch with them Janet?"

"Well lassie it's been such a long time, you see. It's over forty five years since I left home."

"What about your mother and father then?"

"My father died when I was about eight years old. Mother was left to bring the four of us up best she could."

"But Mam wrote to her mother and father about the time my father was drowned, asking if there was work and a home for us on Islay." Maggie quizzed with puzzled excitement.

"All I can say is she must have been wrong in the head at that time then, for she knew that mother had a hard time providing for us."

"But my mam told us we could live there beside grandmother and grandfather."

"Maggie your mother must have lived in a fantasy world. My mother did not even have a home of her home. She lived with the widower of my dead sister, helping to bring up their nine children. When you were left orphans in 1889; my mother already had enough to cope with for a woman in her seventies."

"What happened to her then?"

Tears began to trickle down the older woman's cheeks. "That's another thing on my conscience lassie, I'm not sure what exactly happened but after a very long life of bringing up bairns of her own she was no longer fit to cope. Age took its toll, she went wrong in the head. Around 1893 she was taken to an asylum in Lochgilphead on the mainland and died there. I didn't know at the time. I was so preoccupied with Alex and Charlie."

"You can't blame yourself, Janet. If no-one let you know. How could you be responsible?"

Janet blew her nose and wiped her face.

"That's true lass, but you should look after her mother."

"That's a good sentiment Janet, if you get the chance."

As Maggie prepared the evening meal for when Jim would be home, she thought of what Janet had told her. It was the answer to so many questions—why the family had allowed them to be fostered and not cared for by their own. Her poor grandmother dying among strangers away from the land she'd known all her life.

Poor Janet's life had not been easy for her either. Maggie looked around from where she stood by the window. Janet sat nodding asleep, with James still on her knee, the kettle singing on the hob. Yes she would make a fine grandmother.

Maggie shook her gently. "Janet, I've something to tell you before Jim gets in. I'm going to have another baby soon. If it's a girl we'll name it after you."

Janet sat straight up in the chair. "That would be so nice, lass. If it's a boy would you call it Charlie after our laddie?"

Maggie would not immediately agree. "I'll see what Jim says but I'm sure it will be alright."

The few days visit did them all good. Jim was on his best behaviour. Not once did he even have the smell of having been drinking. Maggie and Janet visited the shops. James was given many gifts by his adoring aunt, before she left to go home to Gigha.

Janet gave Maggie five gold sovereigns. "Keep this money lass so that when my new bairn arrives you can all come visit me at home. Promise you'll do that now, I want everyone at home to see my bairns."

Maggie agreed to keep the promise.

CHAPTER THIRTEEN

CHARLES CHISHOLM WAS born at the end of November. He was a chubby little fellow with fine fairish down covering his head. It had been an easy birth. Jim was at home in the early morning when the pains first started. He was very concerned and attentive. He ran to fetch the howdie wife then dressed and fed James. "I'll just take the bairn across to Tibby and come straight back in case you need me here lass," he said.

True to his word he was there in the house when his second son made his appearance into the world. Maggie was so happy that everything had gone so well. At last it seemed Jim had settled down to the responsibilities of marriage and being a father.

A long letter arrived from Davy. Life in New Zealand was good for him. He enclosed money for Christmas for Maggie and her family. It would probably be Easter before he got news of the birth of his nephew Charlie. Maggie considered how he would accept the child being named after their brother.

News from Canada was good. Alex and James were never short of work. Mary had managed to set up a comfortable home for them. Margaret was quite a little lady. She attended dancing classes and was fast becoming quite a celebrity. All this good news filtered through to Janet on Gigha. Her letter to Maggie expressed gratitude for respecting her wish in naming the baby. Janet enclosed a good luck penny for Charlie and money for a 'little something' for your Christmas.

"This is going to be a grand end to the year, Jim," Maggie said as they sat by the fire.

"It's not before time, we should have some return from life for all the hard work we've put into living."

Maggie sat down on his knee. "I wouldn't say we've not had enjoyment from living, would you? Like everything else, you pay the price."

"Don't wind me up lassie, we cannot afford any more bairns for a long time yet."

"You know fine Jim Chisholm I can love you the person without needing to make bairns."

"Aye, that's what you say but I cannot help myself when you are so close. Regardless of the horrible things I say through drink, Maggie Chisholm, I love you with all my heart. Never forget that, I just cannot imagine life without you."

Maggie kissed him on the forehead. "I'll never leave you Jim, it's just that I weary so much when you are working. I don't make friends easily, like to keep to myself."

Jim took her hand in his. "With two bairns there's not to be enough hours in the day for either of us to weary. We'll both need to work to give our bairns the best."

"That's very true Jim, we're at the start of the New Year soon, we'll both do our best to get on for the sake of the boys. I'll try to get them out for the air everyday, when you're at work. It's a pity you have to work at two jobs and miss the bairns during the day."

"Maybe things will change Maggie, if I get promotion then I can give up the job with the street sweeper."

Maggie was quite excited; she was going out for the evening at the Highland Society with Tibby. It was the first function she had attended since marrying. Jim was to look after the boys for the evening. Since Charlie was born he had been very helpful and caring towards Maggie, hurrying home from work without stopping for a drink. Proudly he had given her the money he had saved to buy something new to wear to the Highland. It was after seven when they left.

Jim sat by the fire smoking his pipe. The children were both asleep and settled for the night.

"I'll be back for ten Jim, before Charlie needs fed," Maggie promised.

Maggie felt it strange without her husband. Tibby was a good friend but flirted unashamedly with all the men. Despite the music, dancing and good company Maggie was glad when the hands of the clock approached ten and she could hurry home to her family.

As she walked smartly through the gas-lit streets she realised that her longing for company and freedom from housework had no foundation at all. Her life was with Jim and the family at her home.

The boys were still asleep in bed, Jim was still sitting in the chair by the fire which was almost burned out. "Lord lass I never meant to sleep. I was to have the kettle boiled for you. I'm really sorry, the bairns have never wakened." He got up and put some dry sticks on the fire to boil the kettle.

"Did you have a good evening?"

Maggie was taking off her new dress, "It was alright I suppose. If I was truthful then I would admit now I would have enjoyed an evening here with you."

"Is that why you are in such a hurry to get your clothes off?"

Maggie winked, then mischievously answered, "I missed you as you well know."

Jim was keen to be promoted to police sergeant. The extra money would make such a difference to their lives. He had been promoted sergeant in the field when fighting in the Boer war. He explained to Maggie this was an honour for bravery awarded by the Queen, which could not be taken from him. If ever he was recalled to serve with the Guards regiment his rank would be restored. If only it was recognised by the police commissioners, he could give up the extra work. With so many men idle, Jim did have feelings of guilt about keeping someone else on the dole; however, they needed the money to survive.

John McLeod knocked on the door before entering. "Maggie, I've come on ahead to warn you. Jim had an accident; he's going to be alright though."

Maggie was washing the floor. She wiped her hands on the rough apron then stood up. "What's happened? Is he hurt? Where is he, John?"

"Put the kettle on for some tea, he'll be here shortly. He's at the police station just now."

"But he's not on duty until afternoon," Maggie interrupted.

"Aye that's right, but Jim had a mishap with the road sweeper you see, and the police were involved."

"Oh my God, John, he'll lose his job. Is he badly hurt?" Maggie asked fighting back the tears.

"Just a few scrapes and bruises, nothing serious, but he'll not take lightly to being sacked," John said as he prepared the tea.

"Sit down Maggie before you drop down." Maggie sat on the chair her body shaking from head to toe.

"Surely they just cannot give him the sack for an accident. What happened anyhow?"

John started to explain. "Jim had a drink with one of the lads going off night shift. His wife just had a bairn. He had a good dram then set off with the horse and brush; he must have nodded asleep and fell behind the horse in front of the brush, it went over him, he's a bit scratched, that's all. Some women who clean the bank saw it happen and reported it. For anybody that wasn't a bobby it would not have mattered but you know yourself Jim should not have been working. I'm sorry."

Maggie tried to think straight. "Is Jim really all right? He's not badly hurt? I wish he would hurry. Look after the bairns John, I must go to him."

John sat her down again. "Maggie keep calm; he'll be here shortly. It's losing his job, that's the biggest loss of face, not the few scratches, they'll heal."

Maggie's voice had anger in it. "He should never have been drinking in the first place. It never would have happened." She was almost hysterical.

"Come on now that's enough Maggie. Jim fell asleep because he was tired. He does the work of two men. So he had a dram, the first for months. Be patient with him, remember he has to live with himself."

All Maggie's anger left her when two hours later Jim came home. His face, neck and arms were torn and scratched. He was limping badly. "A fine mess I've made of myself, Maggie. What will we do now?" he asked her. The two hours time alone to think made her aware how fortunate Jim was to be alive. At least they were together to face whatever the future had in store.

The following day brought no comfort nor joy. As they both knew, Jim was instantly dismissed from the Force. The blow was even worse when the Council decided he was not a responsible person to be in charge of the horse drawn street sweeper. "Never fear Maggie, I'll manage to get some sort of work. I promise you."

Poor Maggie felt so sorry for her Jim, yet in her heart blamed him for the state of distress they were in. "Oh I know you will Jim. I could always look for some kind of cleaning or washing work until you get settled,"

Jim rose from the chair by the table. "I'll not have you even think of it Maggie," his voice was raised in anger. "No woman, least of all my wife will have to provide for my family. I'll get something, just you see." He started putting on his boots.

"Jim you are in no fit state to go out yet, calm down. I did not mean to offend you. I was trying to be helpful and save you worrying."

"That may be lass, but nobody will come knocking at the door with money. More likely asking for it. I'll not be hanging about idle for long. When I come home hopefully somebody will have given me work."

The bairns seemed to know that there was a crisis for they were no problem all day.

Maggie's mind ran riot trying to figure where their future lay. She accepted that Jim had pushed himself to the limit working both jobs, that his struggle to provide, forced them into an existence rather than living. Was this the situation that her mother and father faced all those years ago in Maitland Street? The despair and hopelessness of trying to 'better things' yet no chance at all of ever finding the means.

Maggie decided her happiest years had been at Culburnie where there was always work from dawn to dusk but at the same time good substantial plain feeding and a warm fire to return to at the end of a hard day's toil.

Maybe that was the answer, Jim should return to farm work where people's sense of value differed from the towns. There wouldn't be the same opportunity for Jim to frequent the places that sold drink. Good fresh air for the boys. It's strange she thought, how life goes the full circle, her mother and father must have had the same ideas when they decided to make a change and move to Islay. Maggie wondered just how different things would have been for her had fate not dealt that severe blow at the Forth and Clyde canal.

We will have to sort this out by ourselves somehow.

If only she had someone to go to for advice, John and Annie McDonald, Neil McLeod, her brothers, Davy and Alex, but no, they were all separated from her.

Jim's family found it difficult enough to make provision for themselves. Aunt Janet was in her sixties now and finding it difficult to cope with her housekeeping duties. She might be able to help. Maggie would write to her anyhow.

Jim got home after seven. He was tired and limping badly, but despite the scars and bruising he managed to give her a smile.

"I've managed to get fixed up, Maggie." He put his arm around her waist. "Things are not so bad. I've got a start as a doorman at one of the big wine merchant's warehouses."

Maggie helped him off with his jacket and his boots. "What sort of work is that, Jim?"

"It's a sort of watchman, keeping an eye on who comes and goes, with what. The money isn't much but it's better than nothing."

Maggie quickly agreed. She could not dash his spirits when he was so pleased at finding work. Maggie lay awake in bed thinking of how Jim would cope with working where he had easy access to drink. Maybe the accident had taught him a lesson, only time would tell. They still had the sovereigns saved that Janet gave them to pay the fares to visit Gigha. The money for Christmas was with it in the velvet pouch beside the cornelian pendant and brooch from Davy. She would keep them for as long as she could. When the time was right she would 'sow the seed' in Jim's mind how it might be a good idea to move away from Glasgow, back to the country.

The new job certainly gave Jim more time at home in the evenings, with Maggie and the boys. Each night he was home just after six o'clock. He started at six each morning when the carters delivered the barrels from the docks. It was a busy day trying to keep check on the loads as they came and left. Not the sort of work Jim enjoyed for he found that after a week he was bored.

"I'm not the kind for tallying up loads Maggie, and snooping to see if the carter has managed to get a drink, but I suppose until something else comes along then I'll have to stick with it."

"Yes Jim, it's not the work I could see you in, the farming would be more in your line. All the hard physical work in the fresh air. Plenty tatties and meal."

"I suppose that is true lassie, but I tried it and could see no future for myself."

Maggie put down her mending, checked that the bairns were asleep, then sat beside Jim at the fire.

"There's not much future here either, the fresh country air would be grand for Jimmy and Charlie."

"I agree with you that Glasgow's not the best place for the bairns, but there should be some prospects of improving yourself with all that goes on here."

"Well we've tried Jim, it hasn't got us far has it? Two bairns, two part furnished rooms in a tenement, you working yourself to an early grave trying to keep us together."

Jim leaned forward and stroked her hair.

"Oh Maggie, I've failed you lass, this isn't what I wanted for us."

"I know that Jim. We've got to try to make changes for the future ourselves. A long time ago I was told to keep trying to 'better myself'. We are never to achieve much here with no job prospects, little money and everybody around us the same. We aren't wrong to want what is best for the boys are we?"

"I expect you are right Maggie, we'll have to think to the future."

The howling March winds kept Maggie and the boys prisoners indoors. It had been difficult to get something for their evening meal. Maggie stewed some liver, the cheapest the butcher had on offer. Changed days she thought from roasting whole haunches of venison and beef for the gentry. Cooking two slices of offal for a hard working man. Jim was quite cheery when he got home. He played with the boys while Maggie served up their food. They sat at the table, Jim with Charlie on his knee. He looked at his plate.

"Lord lassie, what's this you're giving me now?"

Maggie moved her portion about the plate with her fork. "It's liver stewed with onions, very good for you. All that we could afford from the butcher on a Thursday."

Jim pushed the plate away from him. "God knows we haven't much but I'm damned if I'll eat cow's guts like a farmyard dog."

Maggie picked a piece from her fork and chewed it. "It's really very tasty, the gentry eat it all the time."

Jim rose and put Charlie on the bed. "We all know what rubbish they eat, rotten game hung for weeks, snails, frogs legs, they'd eat shite if it arrived on a silver platter. Not me. I was brought up on tatties and meal and that'll be good enough for my sons."

"Where are we going to get that Jim, with nothing to pay for it?"

"I'm going back to work on the land. It's part of the fee to get meal, milk and tatties. We won't go hungry."

Maggie's seeds had flourished and she was about to harvest the crop.

"Where's the farm work around Glasgow, Jim?"

Jim poured himself some tea, dipped a piece of bread in it and gave it to Jimmy.

"We will have to move away from here; probably back to Brechin, where I know the farms."

The decision was made; Jim even surprised himself. Days of uncertainty brought to a definite conclusion by two slices of liver.

Once the idea was accepted Maggie and Jim could not wait to move into action. The best time to 'flit' would be before the May term when all farm folk made their bargains to work for six months at a place. Jim wrote to his father of his intentions, also asking him to find them a place to stay. The money saved for an emergency would pay for their belongings to be taken by train to Brechin.

The few weeks preparing went past quickly. The thought of a fresh start made Maggie and Jim as happy as the early days of their marriage. The work at the wine warehouse seemed less tedious, at least bearable with the thought the end of it was in sight.

Maggie was kept busy packing, all the household goods and bedding packed into tea chests, with the dinner set gifted by her ladyship as a wedding present.

The brass bed, table, chairs and packing cases, were all lifted by the carter into a horse drawn rail wagon. This was the easiest method of moving their goods from one district to another.

Maggie the boys and Jim would travel by rail to Brechin. Hopefully the wagon with their belongings would follow and be delivered in less than a week.

Jim's father had not been idle; he managed to rent for them a house at the Southport. Three rooms, one very small that would do the boys. In his letter telling them of his house hunting success, he told of how much he was looking forward to enjoying the company of his grandsons.

Tibby and John McLeod saw them off at the station. "Now remember we will be to see you as soon as you are settled," said John.

"Aye it's a good move you are making. Things are bound to get worse here. We might follow your example, before long."

"Would you go back to Islay, John?"

"There wouldn't be much point for there's even less work there to support a man and his family. No, I think I'd choose America or Australia."

Tibby looked surprised. "You've never mentioned this to me, John."

John looked her in the eye. "I've been thinking of it since Jim had the accident. There's no justice in this country where a man is sacked for having two jobs to support his wife and bairns. No doubt you will both succeed where there's a chance of work."

Jim was fond of his friend John, yet he knew that his promise of visiting would never take place.

"We'll look forward to having you and Tibby at Brechin, there might even be a little McLeod by then."

The men shook hands; Tibby hugged and kissed Maggie as they boarded the train. Another stepping-stone of life passed hopefully on to a brighter future.

Chapter Fourteen

1908

Brechin was so different from the hustle of Glasgow. Nestling between the braes of Angus, with the river Southesk winding its way past castles and Cathedral. The river provided water power, for the many small industries. Despite being a country town there was plenty of work on offer in the linen weaving and spinning mills. The bleachfield was kept busy with the factories also many independent hand loom weavers. There were also two distilleries keeping up the tradition of Angus Glens whisky being the finest. The Excise men having put paid to the mountain stills, the capitalists were realising on the local skills. Brechin was an ancient city by right of Charter from King David the second and by right of being a Cathedral City.

Jim's father, no longer able for work, lived in a single-end in Bothers Close off the High Street. As was the custom these pends or closes ran off the main thoroughfare to avoid paying tax on houses fronting the main streets, causing the narrowest or gable end of the dwelling house to face the street. He lived midway up the steep hill, near where the Market Cross had stood many years before.

Where Jim and Maggie were to set up their new home was at the Southport.

The entrance to the upstairs flat was through a close from the High Street, There was a kitchen living area, with one large and one small bedroom. In the kitchen window was a cast iron sink, with a tap and running water. The window overlooked a small drying green that was behind the communal washhouse. There was also a second window on the opposite side of the room, which overlooked the main street.

"The bairns will get out to play at the back door Jim if you can put up a gate."

Jim stood so forlorn looking down at the floor. "Aye with no work I'll have plenty of time to do that."

She was to have no self pity speech from Jim, spoil her pleasure of thoughts of a happy future. She took Jim's hands in hers. "These hands are big enough to provide for your family. No one could deny you have the ability to do the work of two men. You are a brave and courageous man, honoured by the Queen for acts of bravery. What's more you're the man I love and I'm proud to be your wife."

Jim pulled Maggie close in his arms. "God knows I don't deserve you Maggie/ I do love you. I always mean to do the right thing, it's just at times I wonder to myself where all my efforts are leading."

The pair stood close together in the bare empty room. Maggie knew Jim felt embarrassed returning to Brechin and his family after being dismissed from the Police. It had been a different home coming from South Africa years before.

Maggie broke the silence. "This is our chance and I know this is the right place for us. You can see some of the farmers foe work. I'll stay here a wee while. Tomorrow the furniture will be delivered from the station. The bairns will be fine with your father for another half hour."

"I suppose you know best lassie. I'll just toe the line and start again."

"Off you go. I'll get back up the street myself. Best of luck."

Maggie walked about the empty rooms looking out the windows, running the water from the tap. She examined the range. "Aye Toshie would have been screaming if she saw you," she said to herself. "Black lead, emery cloth and elbow grease and you'll be beautiful."

It was after seven when Jim got back to his father's home, where they were to spend the night. Maggie was anxious as to whether or not he would have been drinking. He was flushed and excited but she could not detect any smell of whisky.

"I've got a job at Burghill at the neep thinning." "That's good news laddie," said Jim's father who was sitting by the fire with Charlie on his knee.

"How far away is it Jim?" asked Maggie.

"It's only a good fifteen minutes walk from the Southport."

Maggie clapped her hands. "I knew you'd get something."

Jim was pleased with himself. "The job's not permanent but at least it's a start. I said I wouldn't be staying in the bothy, I'd live at home."

Maggie stopped laughing and clapping. It had never crossed her mind that Jim might have to live away from home, to find paid employment.

"Oh Jim, I'm so glad you've been clever enough to find work so early."

Jim left the house at six the next morning. Maggie watched him as he marched down Bridge Street. He was a handsome figure of a man. She unpacked the remaining belongings, made the place tidy. It was a fine morning. She took the boys out for a walk down to River Street. She watched the swans and their cygnets foraging for food in the weeds at the water's edge. This is almost as peaceful as Gigha, she thought. She would have to write to her family and bring them up to date with events. No need to go into detail. She would just tell them they'd moved for something better.

In the afternoon she went around the shops to see where she could get something for Jim's evening meal. She felt like a bride on her honeymoon again. Jim arrived home after six, burned with the sun and wind.

"Well how was it Jim?" said Maggie as she unlaced his boots.

"Just as thinning neeps would be lassie, row after row. My bloody hands are blistered." Jim showed her his palms.

"They'll soon harden up again to farm work, a good rub with a bit sheep's wool would help them. The oil from the fleece is good for skin."

Jim looked at Maggie and laughed "Lord lassie, for someone who is a cook you never fail to amaze me with your ideas."

Maggie was hurt by Jim's remark and answered back sharply. "I've done all kinds of farm work Jim Chisholm. I was brought up on a croft, you know that fine."

"Aye fine that lassie, but have you got sheep here until I pull a bit off its coat for my hands?" They both laughed.

"You can be so smart sometimes Jim."

"Aye and you can always bring me back down to earth. Let's see what you've got to eat."

After eating their meal, Jim sat by the fire nodding asleep. Maggie wondered how long it would be before he visited the two public bars in full view of the front window. Life had certainly changed for the better.

Jim was happy working on the farm. He was kept on to work at the hay making and then the harvest.

Three months and he had never shown any desire to take strong drink. Maggie was so happy. Jimmy and Charlie were thriving in the good fresh air.

Jim's father spent time with the boys allowing Maggie the opportunity to improve the house with fresh wallpaper and paint. She bought bright coloured material and made curtains. By the now gleaming range was a rug made from bright coloured rags. The end result of her labours made Maggie feel so proud. Letters had arrived from her family wishing them success in their new home.

Maggie was walking out with the boys each day. She acknowledged the willingness of her neighbours to be friendly, but never allowed herself to join in the gossiping.

"Why don't you stop and have a bit news with them?" Jim asked her.

"Well Jim I've never been one for gloating about other's misfortunes. From past experience I've learned that when women talk together it ends up with some poor soul's character being pulled apart. Probably with time each others. I've learned to stay clear," she explained.

"I suppose maybe you are correct, but look what good friends you found in John and Tibby."

"Yes they were friends Jim, but I prefer to keep myself to myself, then the least number of people are likely to know your business."

"Suit yourself lassie, I'm sure we will manage fine as we are."

Summer turned to autumn, although Jim was still working at Burghill the end of the harvest was in sight. Once the potatoes were lifted then he thought he would have to look for another job. The cottared folk would be kept on until the end of November, when all farm workers made their bargain for six months work in return for meal, milk tatties and accommodation.

The feein' market was a big day in the town. The farmers would congregate around the middle of the High Street where the Market Cross had been. The farm workers made their approach asking foe work. Once a bargain was agreed then the men went off to celebrate with a drink. For many of the young farm lads this was their only chance to visit the town and they made the most of their day of freedom. Bonnets on the side of their heads, decorated with straw ornaments they paraded up and down the street.

Maggie enjoyed watching all the merrymaking and activity from the window. "Watch for your dad, Jimmy. He'll be in soon to tell us if he's fixed up with a job."

Maggie sounded confident enough telling Jimmy but in her heart she worried what would happen if Jim started drinking again. The concern was unnecessary for Jim came striding down the street. Being taller and broader than most men he was easy to see coming down past the Mill Stairs.

"Dad looks pleased with himself Jimmy, he's surely found a place. I'd best make something for him to eat."

Jim had not let her down Proudly he handed her the five shillings feeing money given to him by the farmer. "I never bothered with the dram Maggie, the money will be more use to you."

"I'm so pleased you've got fixed up, which farm is it?" she said fearful that it was not within walking distance and Jim would have to live in the bothy.

"It's at Little Haughmuir just a mile out the Forfar road. I'll be able to walk it in about twenty minutes."

"Things are certainly working out for us thanks to your hard work. What kind of job are you to do? Are you to be working with the horses?"

"Aye and that'll mean an early start for half past five to feed the beasts before yoking time. I'm sure I'll come to some arrangement with the other lads. I'll have to see to the beasts on Sundays when it's my turn."

"Maybe it would be easier Jim if we moved to a cottar house."

"Maggie I've told you before, I'd never be tied down in a house that went with the job. Think of it, I'd just need to get the sack and we'd have no roof over our heads. I thought you were happy here."

Maggie was flustered; she had upset him and all so well meaning. "Jim, don't be like that, this is the home I've always wanted. I just thought it's not to be easy for you away from five in the morning to after six at night. All that walking to and fro."

"Never worry about me walking. I've marched for miles in the army. I'll be fine knowing that there's always a roof over my head regardless of the farmer's moods and fancies."

Alex wrote to Maggie before Christmas. He was glad they had made a move to better things. He told of how in the spring he was to join Davy in New Zealand. Maggie received the news with mixed feelings. It would be good for Davy to have 'someone of his own', with him. Alex had been with Margaret since she was born; now he was to leave her with Mary in Canada. Her brothers would be together, leaving both her and Margaret apart on their own.

Although now mother of two sons, Maggie still thought of her first child. Her heart pounded at the memory of the last day she saw her at Culburnie. Would she look like Jimmy and Charlie? How or when would she explain to them that they had a half sister far across the sea? Would Margaret ever understand how much Maggie wanted to have her with her, even though she had a good life with her foster parents?

Her thoughts of Culburnie jogged her mind that she had never let Donald know they were living away from Glasgow. She would find time to write before the New Year. Maggie was certain that Jim would have made a great success of the croft for he was an able worker. Perhaps one day they would aspire to a place of their own. Maggie knew she could work hard, like Annie McDonald, have a cow, sheep and hens. She would even spin wool for knitting jerseys for the boys.

She was happy in her own little house in the meantime.

Maggie and Jim made several visits to the homes of his sisters, Maggie felt it quite a strain for they did not seem to accept her as family. They were good hard working farm folk, whose broad accent highlighted Maggie's soft lilting highland voice. Isabella was never finished washing, cooking and cleaning her bairns. There were five already and another on the way. They had moved house at the term day to a farm well off the main road. It was too far for them to visit now.

At the end of December the weather was bad. There had been three continuous days of snow and wind. Jim had struggled out each day to the farm, arriving back at night with his clothes soaked to the skin. Maggie has his clean flannel shirt drying on the screen by the fire.

Jimmy and Charlie were occupied watching the people struggling through the drifts to get back to work at the factory after their dinner.

Maggie went to put more coal on the fire intending that she would make a few girdle scones for tea. As she lifted the coal bucket she felt a wave of nausea rise from her stomach. Dizziness made her reach for the drying clothes. As she fell to the floor the screen tipped over on to the fire. The boys began to scream. Jimmy ran forward.

"Get up Mam, are you hurt?"

Maggie could hear him but could not answer.

Jim's father was shouting up the stairs. "Anybody in today? Here's granddad coming."

When he entered the living room he was startled for a moment at what he found. "For God's sake Maggie lass, are you alright? The shirts are on fire."

He quickly gathered the burning washing, threw it into the sink under running water. He helped Maggie on to the wooden armchair.

"What's wrong lass, did you fall? Is anything broken?"

"I'll be alright in a minute, Father."

"Will I get a woman neighbour in?" the old man asked, thinking that the problem was not for divulging to a man.

"No don't upset yourself, I'll be fine. I've been like this before."

Jim's father had started to fill the kettle. "Is it to be a cup of tea to celebrate then lass, I'll look for a girl this time."

The thought of a girl boosted Maggie's low spirits, she felt so tired and listless. Maybe the fainting attack was a sign she was carrying a female. After all she had fainted at about the same stage when she was carrying Margaret.

"What am I to do with Jim's working shirts?" she said trying to see the extent of the damage.

"Just tell him you are all lucky not to have been burned to death. I'm glad I made the struggle down the street in the snow to see you. I just had to get out a while. I felt imprisoned by the weather."

Maggie was now fully recovered. "It's a miracle you got here when you did. Jim will be so grateful to you. Thank you."

The boys were climbing all over their grandfather. Charlie had taken his bonnet and had it on his own head back to front.

"I never had much time to spend with my own bairns you know, I was always working. Jim and I never really got to know each other as a father and son should, I enjoy the company of his laddies though." He was on his knees by this time crawling about the floor with Jimmy on his back. "You'll make a fine horseman yet my bairn."

Maggie was very fond of this lonely old man. Jim never had much to say to his father when in each other's company.

"Maybe you'll want to try something better like your father," he said to Jimmy.

"I'll be the horseman granddad," he said, pulling at the collar of his grandfather's jacket.

"Jim should have had a farm of his own to work, he wants to work for himself, not for other people, that's what bothers him," Maggie explained.

"Aye, I suppose that's him alright, but we seldom get what we want in life, even if we got rewarded for our labours more fairly." The old man looked Maggie straight in the eye.

"You are happy with him?"

Maggie turned away. "Of course I'm happy. Jim's a good man and a good father."

She walked across and had a look at the shirts in the sink. "He works hard to provide for us, Father."

"I'm sure he does; it's just that you are such a gentle, well bred lassie that sometimes I wonder what you see in a big rough devil like my son Jim. Mind you I'm eternally grateful that you married and made a decent home for him."

"I think you are getting a bit muddled in your old age, thinking of me as a well bred lady, I've had to work hard all my life just to survive."

"Well I don't want you working too hard from now on so that my grandchild can survive. Take care of yourself, I'll try to take the young lads off your hands now and again."

He was true to his word and most days would walk out with the boys or keep them occupied while Maggie rested.

By mid March Maggie was finding it difficult to cope. It was Sunday morning. Jim had told her to stay in bed when he was off work. Maggie was feeling too unwell to argue.

"I don't know what's wrong Jim, I've no energy at all. The bairn is lively enough, never stop moving, keeps me awake at night."

Jim was trying to tidy up the fireplace. "I've made up my mind we will have the doctor in to see you tomorrow. He'll have to see you before the birth anyhow."

Maggie was not keen on this proposal. "Where's the money to pay for the doctor coming from?" she asked.

"Oh there'll be the feein' money in May. I can sell some of our tatties and meal. We can manage on less. You are seeing the doctor and that is that."

Jim was at work the next day when the doctor visited and examined Maggie. "You've quite a bundle of trouble there, lass," he said after the examination. "It's twins you are carrying."

Maggie gasped "Two bairns, no wonder I'm tired."

The doctor sat down on the bed. "You'll have to be very good to yourself, you are run down feeding those two," he said as he patted her belly. "You'll need plenty of fresh air, good food and rest if the things are to work out."

"Oh they will be alright doctor," said Maggie excitedly. "Jim will be thrilled at the thought of us having twins."

The doctor was amused by her enthusiasm. "Aye, he had the best part of them."

"What if it's two girls?" said Maggie as Jim lay beside her in bed.

"That would be fine, just balance things out against Jimmy and Charlie."

"What would you wish for Jim?" said Maggie trying to ease herself into a comfortable position.

"I don't really mind Maggie if the bairns are alright. I'm more worried about how we will manage to provide for them."

"You've got a steady job now, we will manage fine."

"I sometimes wish I had stayed in the army, I would have been better off,' he lay quiet for a minute then put his arm around her.

"I wouldn't you know, for if I'd never left the army I wouldn't have met you. You're the best thing that ever happened to me Maggie."

Spring was so long in arriving and by the time the weather improved Maggie was not fit to walk far. She would be glad when the twins were born at the end of April.

Everyday the boys spent time with their grandfather. They would go for walks down the path from the back braes, along the path by the 'skinner's burn', past the back gate of the castle to the Inch.

The paper mill by the river was not busy and the men stopped to talk to the old man and the boys. They played throwing stones into the water.

"You'll frighten the salmon," said their grandfather, "The men of River Street will be after you for that."

"Why?" asked Jimmy.

"Well they won't be able to catch them."

The main hobby of the male population was poaching fish. The old man knew that many of the families' only means of income was their ill gotten gains. Perhaps Jim was right in thinking it was wrong that the 'moneyed class' could claim by their birthright the very fish in the rivers and the sea.

The trio slowly wandered past the Meiklemill and up the Pathie.

"Come on bairns when we get to the top of the brae I'll buy you something from the sweetie tray in shoppie Jocks."

By the time they got to the top of Bridge Street they were all tired and ready for a sit down.

"Hurry up bairns, if we are lucky Mam will have a fly cup of tea ready for us."

Maggie had much more than making tea on her mind. She had been scrubbing down the stairs when the pains started. She knew that she would have to get help. There was so little time between the contractions. Her twins were in a desperate hurry to make their entry into the world.

Maggie took off the jute apron she was wearing and started to walk slowly to the cottage down the back where Bridget McMahon lived. Maggie was sure she would come to her assistance. Bridget was a good Catholic and had nine children to prove it. Slowly Maggie walked past the wash house, hanging on to the wall for support.

"Oh please God let her be in for I'll never manage back by myself."

As she turned the corner of the cottage she could see Bridget in the garden planting potatoes. "Hello Mrs Chisholm, it's a fine day to be sure."

Maggie stood her back against the wall, the searing pain racking her body cutting off any words she tried to utter with short gasps. Bridget ran towards her.

"Holy mother of Jesus, you've started, by the looks of it almost finished. Hang on to me and I'll get you back to bed."

Mrs McMahon was a strong woman with years of hard work in the fields; it gave her no bother to half carry Maggie back home. The stairs proved a problem but eventually they made it to the top. "Now my pretty colleen, undress and into bed with you. I'll get some water boiled."

Bridget stoked up the fire, filled the two big cast iron kettles and put them over the flames to heat.

"Now my fine lass, lets be having a look at you. See what the little stranger is doing."

Maggie was relieved to be back in bed, in her own home. She felt safe and secure with this woman, who until a few minutes ago had only exchanged polite pleasantries. "It's twins I'm expecting, they weren't due for another three weeks."

Bridget helped her take off the last of her clothes. "I'm sure no one told them of that arrangement. They want to be here to celebrate St Patrick's Day with their aunt Bridget. Where's your man and the bairns Mrs Chisholm?"

Maggie could not answer at first; she hung on to Bridget's hands. "I'm grateful for your help, Jim is at work, and the bairns are out with their grandfather. You won't leave me will you?"

Maggie seldom found herself in the position where he was dependent on other people. "I was to get help from Jim's sister but there's not time to get her here."

Bridie wiped Maggie's forehead with a cold damp cloth. "Never fear my bairn, I'll be with you. Many's a time I've brought the wee ones into life's struggle, safe and sound," she went on, "Never two at a time though, but between us we'll manage fine. You do your bit and I'll get the clothes aired. Where do you have them?"

In less than an hour, Donald and George Chisholm were born. They were both very tiny babies. Bridie put them on a pillow covered with a blanket in the washing basket, beside the fire.

"You'll best rest now my pretty, it's a grand job you've done. I'll away get a message for the doctor to come. I'll be back in five minutes no more.

Maggie nodded her head in reply; she was exhausted. "Aye it's a fine surprise your man will get when he comes home."

Jim's father could not believe his eyes when he entered the room. "Mercy sake Maggie, I never know what I'm going to find at the fireplace of this house. I'm better pleased with this surprise than Jim's sark tail on fire though."

Maggie lay back on the pillows with her eyes closed she was so tired; if only they would let her sleep.

"Come on Maggie lass you'll have to sit up and try and feed the bairns. They are tiny wee lads and need you." It was Jim speaking.

"Thank goodness you're home to see Jimmy and Charlie.'

"Come on lass they are both fine with my father. It's you and our two new sons I'm worrying over. Try and take this soup. The doctor said you'll need a lot of nourishing food if you're to feed two laddies."

"What doctor are you speaking about Jim? It was Mrs McMahon that helped me," answered a puzzled Maggie.

"That was two days ago lass, the doctors been in at least four times, you've had a bad time. The bairns are no little they are very weak. Bridie McMahon has been a grand friend. She's been out and in, night and day. She's away home to make something for her lassie's tea. It' nearly six o'clock they'll be home any minute."

Maggie sat up and took the cup of tea. "Am I going off my head Jim, I don't remember anything since I tried to get Mrs McMahon for help."

Jim sat on the edge of the bed. "No you're fine now Maggie, the doctor assures me you will be fine."

Maggie sipped the soup. "Let me see our bairns Jim. I don't know what they look like."

Jim took her and said "They really are small lass, the doctor's surprised they are still hanging on to life."

Maggie let out a wail. "I can't lose them Jim, bring them to me. Oh my bairns."

Gently Jim lifted the washing basket to the side of the bed. Two tiny figures were side by side under the covers. The babies were just the size of their father's hand.

"They don't weigh six pounds between them Maggie, that's three pounds less than what Jimmy and Charlie were when they were born."

Maggie leaned over the side of the bed. "Give me them up here, see if they'll take the breast."

George Chisholm died during the third night of his short life. Maggie was grief-stricken but tried to concentrate on keeping her strength to feed the other baby. For two weeks it seemed that the battle for survival was being won, when Jim found his youngest son dead before going out in the morning to work.

Maggie was too weak to attend the burial of her babies. Bride was with her when the men attended the funerals. "Come on now Maggie, you'll have to stop grieving, you've two bairns alive and healthy that need you. It's nearly four weeks since you were out of the house for a breath of fresh air."

The two women had become very close friends. Bridie had told Maggie of how there family had come over from Ireland to find work. They had nothing but the clothes they stood up in, when they arrived in Dundee.

Both she and her husband took work in a spinning mill, leaving their two youngest children to fend for themselves and go to school. The three older ones had to work in the spinning mill. After two years and another child they found life in the city to be unbearable. Birdie's husband had worked on the land most of his life, so they looked for a farm worker's job. They were lucky and with their three youngest children moved into a cottar house near Forfar. The older children stayed on in Dundee working in the mills. Things were good for them for a few years. Bridie had three more children and they moved around the Angus farm towns. Then tragedy struck its blow. Birdie's husband was killed when a bull broke loose and trampled him to death. The farmer asked her to be out of the cottage by the end of the week, as he needed it for the newly appointed cattleman. Bridie tried to reason with the farmer, by insisting her husband had been killed doing his job and how she deserved better treatment. It was a waste of time for the farmer then implied it was his own fault that the beast turned wild and killed him.

The Saturday following her husband's death found Bridie and five of her children homeless.

Being Irish they could not claim any Parish relief. With what belongings they could carry they made their way to Brechin, the nearest town. After a week in the poors' house, Bridie managed to get enough money from her children working in Dundee, to rent the cottage they now lived in. Bridie had been in Brechin for twelve years and in that time had worked at the local farms doing all kinds of outdoor work.

It was difficult to gauge how old she would be, but Maggie reckoned she was at least fifty years of age. The frankness about her life story stirred up bitter memories in Maggie's mind.

The day that she and her brothers were taken to the poors' house.

The governor, leaving her unaccompanied on the train to Inverness to face an uncertain future alone at only ten years old. She would have to pull herself together for no child of hers would face such hardship. She was lucky to have a good husband and boys to care for.

Jim was right; their home was secure as long as they paid the rent. No farmer could turn them out into the street because another worker needed their home.

CHAPTER FIFTEEN

THE SUMMER CAME and went, the time leaving Maggie with thoughts of how she would have managed the twins. She felt so weak yet each day she tried to tell herself she was stronger. Jim gave her all the help he could but working from five o'clock in the morning to either six or seven at night left him little time for more than eating and sleeping.

Saturday evenings and Sundays were the only occasions they had to spend together as a family. Jim's father was a regular churchgoer and tried hard to persuade Maggie and Jim to attend the services in the Cathedral with him.

Maggie had mixed feelings about God and the church, probably fostered by ideals passed on from her mother. She accepted that she was married in the church, yet found no reason to have their children baptised.

This caused Jim's father a great deal of concern, however he hoped Maggie 'could be won over to do the right thing.' He had long since given up on Jim, who went in the opposite direction to any suggestions made by his father.

In the good weather Sunday was spent walking in the country or listening to the brass band playing in the public park. Maggie loved to walk past the big houses that had been built up Latch Road. Sometimes Jim would take the boys with him to feed his horses on the farm, then meet Maggie and they would walk past the castle kennels, over the bridge at Stannochy farm, then past Burghill farm where Jim had worked. As they walked along the side of the castle wall their conversation normally turned to how life could be so unfair. Why because of one's parentage, wealth or poverty was your right?

Maggie had a letter from her brothers in New Zealand, telling of how grateful they were to be reunited. Davy made it all sound so wonderful and suggested that she and Jim should think of emigrating.

"Aye, it might be alright but we would need money for our passage there, Maggie. It's six weeks on the boat, not like going to Montrose or Glasgow."

Maggie could detect that it would take time to win Jim over to the idea.

"We cannot move away now and leave my father, he's so dependent on you and needs the laddies company to keep him going.'

Maggie agreed that Jim was right in his thinking. She carried on without talking, washing the supper dishes.

Jim sat reading the Brechin Advertiser, his paper of the week's local news. After ten minutes of uncomfortable silence Jim folded his paper.

"Come on lass, be fair, we neither have the money nor are we free to go."

Maggie hung the towel on the brass rail under the mantelpiece. "Och, I'm sorry Jim, I know you are right. It's just that most of my life I've tried to meet my brothers, all that's left of my family. It's something to look forward too even that someday we might go and I'll be with them."

Jim pulled her down to sit on his knee. "You've got me here and Jimmy and Charlie. My father is in and out every day, 'Never had so much to live for, for years' or so he says. Yet you aren't happy. We haven't the money to go, so what am I to do with you?"

Maggie knew that Jim was right. "I suppose I'm being selfish in what I want. I've not got over losing the twins yet, it seems everything I look forward too turns sour. Maybe it's just as well we forget it meantime." Jim held Maggie close to him.

"They were my sons too you know, part of me died with them. Often when I'm working in the fields I think that maybe I was to blame for them dying. You were so poorly all the time you carried them, yet I can't work any more than I do now Maggie. You get all my wages, I've never taken a drink since that mess in Glasgow."

Maggie kissed him on the cheek. "I'm sorry Jim for being so ungrateful and unfeeling. I know you do all you can. We love each other and we are together. That's all that matters."

St Patrick's day Maggie knew she was carrying another child. The year had passed so quickly but still left her sad with memories of her twins. Would this pregnancy be another disaster?

Jimmy would be starting school after the summer, a big adventure he looked forward too.

"Will Charlie have to play by himself when I'm learning to read?" he asked.

"Maybe we can get another baby for him to play with if you like."

Charlie did not want to be left out of the planning. "Could I not get a dog instead Mam? Granddad would walk it with me," he smirked. "Of course you'll be sitting in the class Jimmy."

The boys were good company for each other, just like her brothers. Even their natures were similar. Jimmy was a good helpful little fellow, with Charlie forever being up to some mischief.

Jimmy seemed impressed with his brother's proposal

"Will we get a dog Mam?" he asked.

"You'll better ask Dad when he gets home at night. I just don't know."

Maggie never liked to refuse them anything and found it easier to pass on impossible requests for Jim's refusal. Like it or not it was definitely another baby they would be getting.

"Plenty of nourishing food, exercise and fresh air, then everything will be fine, Mrs Chisholm," the doctor told her after his examination. Jim had insisted that Maggie be seen by him to avoid any problems or things going wrong again.

"I tell you everything is fine this time."

Maggie told Jim as they sat together on the doorstep. Jim enjoyed sitting in the evening sun smoking his pipe. "Maybe we'll get a lassie this time to please my father, he's getting pretty done now. I see him looking older. Have you noticed Maggie?"

She moved the cushion she was sitting on to a more comfortable position then started knitting again before answering. "Yes I have, in fact to be honest Jim I don't feel happy about him taking the bairns out walking now. Jimmy was telling me that Charlie runs away and hides from them. They had been passing the paper mill and Charlie ran away. A workman found him hanging over the edge of the wall at the Lido. The river was running high Jim, Charlie could have been washed away."

"When did this happen?" he snapped at her.

"Look it was last week, I knew how you would be about it, I don't want you mentioning it to your father. He was really upset when I spoke to him about it after Jimmy told me. I don't think you father is well. He was telling me he's so forgetful now. It worries him, some mornings he doesn't remember how to make a cup of tea or what to do to light the fire."

"Stupid old devil, of course he knows, he's done it all his life. He's just feeling sorry for himself."

Maggie stopped him. "That's not true Jim. I've noticed lately that he's not as tidy as he used to be. If you bothered to look in on him at home sometimes you'd notice the place is a mess."

Jim stood up. "Do you want me to be a bloody housemaid now and clean his house?"

Maggie rose to her feet. "I just knew you would fly off the handle, that's why I never told you before. Jim, your father is old and done and needing looked after, that's what I'm trying to say."

"Well what do you want me to do about it? We don't have room for him to live here."

Maggie picked up the cushion, then slowly went up the stairs.

Jim had calmed down by the time he joined her in the living room.

"Well Maggie, what are we to do? Another bairn with what we've got is as much as we can manage."

Maggie knew that this was true. "I'm just trying to say we will have to return some of the help we've had from your father. He's a good man, Jim, as you yourself said he needs us now. In a way I hope you know how lucky you are to have your father. Until we got married I had nobody of my own to care for at all. I just want to show him how we feel and care for him.'

Jim clattered about the room preparing his working boots and clothes in readiness for the morning. Eventually he sat down by the fire. "I suppose you think I don't care but it's not easy for me to admit my father cannot cope. He's always thought of me as a young lad, telling me what to do and so on. I have noticed a difference in him but didn't want to admit it. You'll just have to try and go walking with them. If you stop letting him have the bairns now he'll feel worse."

Maggie agreed that she would try to go with them. The walking each day kept Maggie fit. She blossomed with her pregnancy.

"Sure it's a fine baby you'll be carrying this time Maggie," said Bridie as they met in the close.

"I'm hoping you'll manage to be with me again when the time comes," said Maggie.

Bridie put her arms around Maggie's shoulders. "Of course I'll be with you, I'll be praying to the blessed virgin for an easy time for you. Remember not to be doing too much lifting. Take care of yourself."

Maggie was quick to reply, "Just the way you take things easy yourself."

"To be sure lass that's what I'm doing, now the family are all earning I'm able to enjoy a few things," she lifted the dish towel covering the basket on her arm to show Maggie it's contents. A half bottle of whisky and the People's Friend.

"I'm away now to put my feet up by the fire and enjoy a little drop of the craitur forbye."

Maggie leaned forward and pulled the cover back over the basket. "You are a tonic to me Bridie, you are always so happy and contented with your lot."

Bridie moved closer as she was about to whisper in Maggie's ear. "Let me tell you lass, in my time there have been days when I had not a penny in the world, no roof over the heads of myself and the poor wee ones. To imagine that I'd be settled in a warm home, with food to eat and a wee drop to warm my old bones, was beyond my wildest dreams.'

"You deserve your comfort Bridie, you're a good hard working woman," Maggie reassured her.

"To be sure that's nothing to do with it Maggie. Work doesn't always mean wealth and contentment. Some people are never happy, always after more and more for themselves regardless of whether or not it will make them happier. I'd be even happier with life if my poor man had been spared to share it with me. However, we cannot change these things. I'll away now. Come by for a wee cup of tea and a blether."

Maggie agreed she would then went on her way up the High Street, to fetch some butter from the Maypole. Old habits died hard, for the Co-operative Store was almost next to the close where they lived, yet Maggie preferred to shop where quality counted. The boys ran ahead.

"Come on Mam, we'll see if granddad is in. As they went upstairs Maggie could detect a peculiar smell. She bolted ahead to get to the door first. "It's me Maggie," she shouted as she entered the room Jim's father was on his knees by the fireplace. "Come away in, I'm just tidying up before moving to the new place," he said adding more papers and what looked like old clothes on to the fire.

"Are you moving house then?" asked a puzzled Maggie.

"Aye I am that, it's time for another job. I've been idle long enough I've got over Margaret dying now so I'll be going back to the gamekeeping."

The boys were jumping up and down on a rocking chair. "Make less noise you two," she said. "I'm going to make a cup of tea for granddad."

She turned to the old man "Have you eaten anything at all today?"

"Of course I have, my mother always sees to it I have a good breakfast of brose and milk at the start of the day."

Maggie realised that her first instincts were correct. Jim's father had 'gone funny'. He seemed to be unaware of time or place. "Tell me about Margaret dying? Who was she?" she asked. "You know fine, she was my wife, poor lassie, suffered so much before God took her away." Maggie busied herself with washing the cups and preparing the tea.

Jim's mother had been called Betsy; what was the old man on about? She could not leave him in such a state. "Come on let's have a cup of tea, then I'll help you get tidied up."

"You are a good lassie Maggie, I often think you're better than my own." "Now you can't say that father for they are always busy and can't manage to see you as often as I can."

He seemed more rational again.

"I suppose you are right but I'll need to get work, this is no use shut up all day with nothing to do."

"Sit down and drink your tea. Stop that noise you bairns, you'll give granddad a sore head."

The old man sat down at the table.

"I feel wrong in the head Maggie, everything is so mixed up. Maybe if Jim was home from the war I wouldn't worry so much."

Maggie said nothing. What was she to do? It was obvious that Jim's father was far from well. "Jim will be here at night. Don't you remember, I'm his wife, we live at the Southport now with Jimmy and Charlie."

The old man looked at the boys. "I suppose that's right Maggie, it's just that I sit alone thinking about things in the past, then it gets mixed up with the everyday things. Will Jim be here at night?"

Maggie tidied the house; the boys were playing out the back. "I'll have to go home now and get Jim's supper ready, you'll be fine until he comes to see you," she told him.

"I'm grateful to you lassie sitting watching you work about the place. I've enjoyed the bairns running out and in. The best of life is when you are young and the bairns are little. You never think that at the time though."

"I suppose you are right Father. Now I'll away home, I'll see you tomorrow. Jim will bring some soup for you later."

Maggie collected the boys from the back garden. "You'd no business throwing stones on the roof of granddad's shed," she scolded. "You could have broken something or hurt yourselves. Hurry down the street now for dad will soon be home, that's the eight o'clock bells ringing."

The days never seemed long enough for all that had to be done, yet Maggie's health stood up to all the work she had to do. Each morning she visited Jim's father who seemed to have good days and bad days. He was always pleased to see her and enjoyed their long walks. Jim tried to go each night before bedtime to check that all was well with his father.

"We never have a minute to ourselves these days," said Jim as he got into bed. "I suppose it will be worse when the wee one arrives."

Maggie was sitting up in bed brushing her hair loose. "That should be any day. I feel so well this time I'm sure there will be no bother. Well, apart from how we'll manage your father for a week or two.'

Jim lay back on the pillows his arms behind his head "I'll have to get Helen or Isabella to take him with them until we are able to manage again."

Maggie stopped brushing. "He won't like moving out of his house, that will make him more muddled, but I suppose there's nothing else we can do."

Jessie Chisholm was born on a bright October morning. Her entry into the world caused little upset or pain.

"I think we'd better fetch Bridie."

At half past five Jessie was born a beautiful dark haired little girl. Maggie looked at her and found the resemblance to her first daughter remarkable

"Is she not beautiful?" said Bridie as if she had manufactured the child herself Jim lifted his daughter from the bed. "My father will be so pleased with you bonnie lass, he never forgive us for not calling you Margaret though."

They had agreed that if it was a girl she would be named after aunt Janet. Jessie was 'the proper way' of saying it. Jim assured Maggie that no one knew of Maggie's daughter Margaret; they would give no reason for their choice of name.

Jessie was six weeks old before she made the acquaintance of her grandfather.

"What a lovely lassie she is Maggie" he said as he held her close to his chest.

"I couldn't wait for the term day for Isabella to bring me back to Brechin. Her bairns are a hardy lot, not so genteel as Jim's and yours. This wee lass is perfect."

Jessie yawned and stretched just to add to his delight.

"We are glad you are home again Father, we've missed you." Maggie kissed his cheek. "The boys have asked every day when you would be here to take them for a walk."

"I haven't been walking so much lately. The cold weather kept me by the fire."

Maggie nodded in acceptance of what he was saying "The winter seems to be upon us so suddenly. You'll have to take care of yourself now Jimmy is at the school anyhow and Charlie will start at Easter."

The old man sat humming and diddling to his grand daughter. "Never mind my bonnie lass, we'll soon be walking past the ladeside."

Maggie took the sleeping infant from him. "You'll need to wait a wee while yet for that Father, in the meantime you can nurse her here in the house."

Janet was delighted with the news of the arrival of her grandniece. In a letter to Maggie she said she could not wait for better weather in the spring when she hoped the family would visit Gigha.

Davy and Alex were both writing to their aunt telling her of their progress in New Zealand. Janet also said in her letter of though it had taken many years, she felt family ties with her sister Mary's children. Maggie found it a long time since she was described as a child. She would be thirty-four her next birthday. How could anyone be close to a family half a world apart?

Maggie decided she would have to try and do the impossible, by saving for the journey to visit Janet with the children. Jim would not be able to stop working and he could just manage his father for a few days.

The days and weeks went past so quickly. Maggie cooked, cleaned and tackled the never-ending bundle of washing. Jessie was happy and contented child, who slept once she was fed. The boys enjoyed the school. This gave Maggie time to check on Jim's father when she shopped up the High Street in the morning. He was becoming more mentally confused and unsteady on his feet. Fortunately he never ventured from the house except to go out to the back garden and the lavatory. There were times when these expeditions proved to be a disaster, adding more laundry to Maggie's daily load.

"I'm not going to get to visit Janet yet." Maggie said to Jim as they followed the route of their Sunday walk.

"You know fine that I'll manage father and we can sell some of the feein' arrals to get you fare. Bridie will buy some tatties and meal."

"I'm sure she will Jim but I'll still not be able to go, you see I'm expecting another bairn probably about the May term."

"Lassie that'll be four we'll have."

"Oh I can count that fine Jim, we'll have to count our pennies though to provide for them."

Jim marched on ahead of Maggie and the bairns, stunned by the news. Eventually he stopped, allowing them to catch up on him.

"You'll manage lass, you always do." He took her hand. "That'll make up for the two we lost, eh?"

Maggie squeezed his hand. "Yes Jim, I suppose it will." She realised how much losing the twins had really meant to this man she loved so much.

A s they walked home hand in hand Jim told Maggie how he wished he had never left the Guards, they would have been much better off living on a sergeants pay.

"But Jim, we would not have been together if you were in the army," said Maggie.

"Aye and you wouldn't be in this state I've got you in now," said Jim. "Four bairns and a little money and coping with my daft old father into the bargain."

The boys were wandering on ahead pulling the tops of the dandelions at the roadside.

"You don't have much faith in me as a wife, do you Jim?" she asked.

"I've every faith in you, but what I wanted for us when we got married is not this life we have now. I wanted better things for us and the bairns. We must exist by working all the hours of the day. We eat plain fare, tatties, meal and milk. You a trained cook, spend your time washing, trauchling with the bairns and a daft demented old man."

"Stop it, Jim Chisholm, you've gone far enough. I've never grumbled about our life together. We are a family together. That's how it should be. Look at Jimmy and Charlie playing as brothers, I've never seen mine since I was a little older than them. I would have been so proud to look after my old father given the chance, but never even got to know him, so yours is the next best thing. Of course I'll manage, I've faced a lot more than minding bairns in my lifetime, in fact I've longed to hold one in my arms Many's a night as I sobbed my self to sleep."

Jim stopped and looked at her.

"I'm sorry lass, I just want a better life for you, that's all."

Maggie kept on walking. Now that she was angry she knew she would probably say the wrong thing. If Jim had done the 'right thing', in Glasgow and still been in the Police then things might have been better. She could not say that to him though for Maggie would never knowingly hurt anyone.

Later that evening, once the bairns were asleep, when they sat by the fire, Jim said, "You never talked much about your mother and father Maggie."

She kept her eyes on her mending.

"I suppose that's because I don't remember much about them.

"It's all so long ago."

She knew in her heart this was not completely truthful but it always saved the heartache of telling the sad tale of drink and deprivation that had marred her childhood.

"What's the first thing you remember then?"

Maggie thought for a while.

"I suppose Culburnie and the family there. Then the wedding when the dominie and his wife were drunk and she fell in the dung." She laughed. "Och my life hasn't been all doom and gloom"

"Just since you married me," Jim got in quickly.

"I wish you'd stop it. I told you this afternoon. What's got you so fed up?"

Jim rubbed his face with his big calloused hands. "I suppose it's just the same routine, work ever day, boring with no prospect of any change to be seen in the future. It took a war to get me away from the land before. That's what we need again to give me a change."

"That would be the answer, leave me with your father and the bairns. Stop this conversation before we say too much. Let's get away to bed."

Maggie stood up and started untying her print crossover apron. Jim rose and grabbed her round the waist.

"Come on lass, you're right. It hasn't been all doom and gloom, we've had some grand times together, eh."

Maggie pretended to punch him on the chin. "Aye and all those bairns to prove it."

Chapter Sixteen

THE WINTER WAS long and hard. Jim found it difficult to get through the snow to the farm some mornings. Maggie struggled every day with the bairns up the High Street to Bothers Close to check on her father in law. There were good and bad days, however, his condition was worsening. Maggie tried to keep the home tidy and Jim's father clean. It was a hard job, for sometimes she would have two changes of clothing and bedding to wash. Her whole life seemed to revolve around the washtub and the boiler.

"Come on Father, you'll have to get up and put on your breeks. The bairns are here; they can't see you going around bare naked," she leaned forward to help the old man from the bed.

"Oh, lassie just let me be. I want to lie here in the warm."

"Come on look your bed is soaking. I'm not able to lift you now."

The old man was quite frail never having been out in the fresh air for months.

"Lord lassie, I'm about done, just let me be. Sooner I'm out of this world the better. You've enough bairns without me," he moved forward and took her hand. It was one of the good days when he was aware of his surroundings.

"None of that nonsense, it will soon be the bonnie days again and we'll get out walking down the Pathie and along River Street."

He got his legs over the side of the bed. "Nae chance o' that Maggie, I'll be going up Southesk Street and across the bridge to the cemetery."

Maggie sat by the fire. The boys were in bed and Jessie was asleep in the cradle. Jim will soon be home, she thought as she stirred the soup in the pot on the hob of the grate. She took the letter from the pocket of her apron, the words she already knew by heart, but it brought her much joy to learn that her brothers were prospering and both well.

As she faced her daily drudgery she often dreamed of what life would be like for Jim and her in Canada or New Zealand. Neither of them was afraid to work. Jim was a big strong man who never shirked at hard labour, yet despite his desperate efforts could only earn enough for their survival. It seemed from her brother's news that things were different in the so-called 'new countries'. No class distinction, the people who worked hardest, gained most.

Maggie smiled to herself; they would be millionaires. Even a place of their own with a 'wee bit of ground' to work. Her thoughts had followed this line many times. She could not even think of working herself for carrying bairns. Another month and another would be born. They were better off than most families who lived nearby.

The people in the adjoining streets, bridge Street and Union Street were mainly linen weaving factory workers. Long hours, many bairns and low wages kept them in an impoverished state. No tatties, meal and daily fresh milk for them

She decided that all things considered they were better off.

Jim was cold and tired as he climbed the stairs. "Thank God I'm home Maggie, it's been a long day." He sat down and untied the laces of his heavy working boots. "Lord the straw inside them is wet like dung. Good job tomorrow is Saturday to fill them up fresh."

This old farming custom had puzzled Maggie when she first learned of it. Jim assured her it was grand for the feet, when walking about fourteen hours each day.

"My hands are sore and chapped. We've been gathering stones, since seven this morning. The wind has never let down all day." He went to the sink to wash.

"I'll lift your soup, it will be fine for supping when you are ready," said Maggie as she laid down clean socks for him.

"Aye that's grand lass, those poor bothy lads that are away tae that cold comfort of an out fire and a plate of cold porridge. Little wonder they envy me."

Maggie smiled as she poured the water into the teapot. "Yes Jim, we could be worse off. There's a lot we have to be thankful for."

Maggie was wakened by the sound of banging on the door. "Jim, see who it is before the bairns are all awake. I'll see to Jimmy, he's already crying."

Jim jumped from the bed, lit the gas mantle and pulled on his trousers. "Alright I'm coming," he shouted, running down the stairs. He stubbed his toe against the outside door.

"Hang on, it's dark, let me get the door open," he shouted.

"James Chisholm is that you?" boomed out at him across the black dark void.

"It's the police, we want to speak to you about your father. Can we come in?"

Jim pulled his braces over his shoulders. "You had better come in. What has happened to him now? Is he alright?"

The two burly figures were following him upstairs. Maggie stood by the blackened fire, a shawl over her shoulders and nightdress.

"It's something about my father lass, the bobbies are here." He turned to face them.

"He's not dead is he?"

The older of the two officers stepped forward. "No lad, he's not dead but he could well have been. His house is burned out."

Maggie wailed. "Oh no, we knew he wasn't safe on his own but what could we do? Where is he?"

Jim put his arm around Maggie.

"Is he hurt at all? Tell me."

"No, he's not injured but we've taken him to the Infirmary just to make sure. Maybe you had better put the kettle on Mrs Chisholm for we have a few questions we want to ask." Jim looked awkward standing wearing only his trousers.

"I'll just put on my shirt," he pulled it from the back of the chair, where the young bobby was leaning.

"What time is it now?" asked Jim. "We were sound asleep when you came to the door."

"It's just about three o'clock, no sleep for us, your father seen to it we were kept busy.'

It was after four o'clock when Jim and Maggie were left alone. She started to cry. "Your poor old father, he might have been dead."

Jim was shaken by the facts of the night's events. "Lassie he might have been better away than what's in front of him. Sent to the asylum and nothing we can do about it."

"Jim what if other folk and bairns had been killed because of him, what would folk say? What will they think of him being certified?"

"Look Maggie I'm damned if I care about other folk, even my own family. If the doctors say he's in the asylum that's it. We could not have gone on running up to look after him. We'll have another bairn next month and you know fine that he's been a worry." Maggie started to go back to bed.

"We'll just have to visit him as often as we can. Imagine him walking about the street in his shirt-tail and bare feet. Yesterday he would not even stand up out of the chair for me."

Jim shook his head. "Aye he's quite a man. Telling the bobbies he was burning the heather for new growth to feed the game. He must have set the rug on fire first."

"Probably we'll never know. Maybe we can see him at the Infirmary before they take him to Sunnyside. Oh Jim what are we going to tell Jimmy and Charlie? They love their granddad so much."

Jim got into bed beside her. "I just don't know lassie. I've seen something like this coming for so long, yet I still don't know what to do. We will just have to tell them he's died for it's unlikely that they'll ever see him again. Now let me get an hour's sleep before I go to work."

Maggie lay quiet; she was aware that Jim was awake but left him with his own private thoughts. Poor Jim, his father's fate's like the living dead. She herself loved the old man who had been as good as a father to her. Life had not been easy for him either. Maggie had often sat with him listening to the stories of his life. Born on a croft near Laurencekirk, his start in working life as a gamekeeper on a large estate near Rescobie. How he married young to a lovely young girl from Forfar named Margaret, they had one son before she was struck down by a weeping growth on her spine, which kept her bedridden for two years before death released her from constant pain. A second marriage to Jim's mother, then the lonely years as a widower. At least it seemed he got some pleasure from his grandchildren. Maggie promised herself that somehow she would manage to visit him in the asylum at Hillside near Montrose. She could get the train part of the way and then walk the rest of the seven miles.

Early in May, Maggie's daughter Mary was born. She was a lovely baby, so like her father. Fair as the others were dark. She was big for a girl and fed and slept well. The extra work of an infant did not tire Maggie as much as she had anticipated. Despite the feelings of guilt about her father in law, she was free from the worry his care involved.

Jim kept busy at work, the haymaking and harvest. He planned to try and buy a second hand bicycle. It would save him walking to and from work at the farm each day. He told Maggie how he would be able to use it to visit his father for it was nearly five months since he had been taken away for his own safety.

They both felt guilty at not visiting in that time but with the bairns and work there was no opportunity. Jim would have a free day come the feeing time and with a bicycle a means of transport to make the journey.

The savings were needed for other things more necessary than transport for by the end of August Maggie had 'fallen' with another bairn.

Bridie was the first to hear of the news.

"You certainly haven't wasted much time lassie," she told Maggie. "Jessie won't be two until October and Mary is only three months, this other one should be born the end of April. It's time that Jim was giving you a chance to more than make and carry bairns."

Maggie was annoyed at her friend's criticism. "I'll manage fine Bridie, you managed with your family, did you not?" she challenged.

"That's right Maggie, but I'm older now and know things could have been easier, believe me. Jim should try staying away from you for a while after the next one is born."

Little did Maggie know how often these words would return to her in the days ahead.

Jim's father died two days after Jessie's second birthday. The bobbies once again came to the door with the bad news. The combined feelings of grief, guilt of abandoning his father sent Jim into depression. For the first time since leaving Glasgow he took strong drink.

Maggie, with Jim's sisters, prepared a meal for the men returning from the burial. Jim had bought some whisky for the men and sherry for the women. "His father would be given a respectable send off."

The women sat by the window watching the street for the men's return.

"They'll go to the pub first," said Helen.

"You can watch which one then," said Isabella.

"You'll be able to watch any of three, Southport, Eagle or City Royal from here. Which one does Jim go to Maggie?"

"None I hope," was what she answered to herself, then to her sisters-in-law.

"Jim never has money or time to go to any drinking place, so I wouldn't know."

It was late afternoon before the men returned. Obviously Jim had tried to drown his sorrow. "Maggie won't be pleased that I smell of drink," he announced to the company. "Doesn't meet with her grand ways you see she's not like lowly country folk as we are."

Maggie felt ashamed. What was he trying to do to her before his family? "Come sit down and have something to eat Jim you must be hungry?"

"No I'm not hungry. I'm bloody fed up of working the land, trying to get ahead, coming home at night to hear you moaning about the lack of money. Could we save for going to New Zealand? A grand life it would be there. We couldn't even afford to go to Montrose to see my father when he was alive. I'm bloody fed up of everything. I wish I was away from the lot of you."

"That's enough of that Jim," said Helen. "You don't know how lucky you are with such a good wife and family."

Jim seemed to fill the crowded room; he was such a big man. "Aye that's right, she's good, thinks herself too good for the likes of us, with her grand ideas."

Maggie was near to tears. "Sit down Jim I know you are upset, have something to eat and you'll feel better."

Jim pointed his finger towards her and shouted. "Oh I will be for you are always right. This is what to do! This is what we'll get. This would be grand for the bairns. Never what Jim wants or needs."

Bella got up from her chair at the window. "What you need, Jim Chisholm, is a good hard kick up the arse. You've been spoiled all your days. Wanting this and that and never pleased, tell your wife you're sorry and for God's sake behave yourself."

Helen then took up the lecture. "Our father scarcely laid to rest and you are creating trouble, through drink." Jim sat down at the tale, never letting his eyes meet Maggie's.

No words passed between them until eight o'clock after the family had left and gone to their own homes. Jim came back upstairs from seeing them off. As he entered the room Maggie was standing by the sink washing dishes.

"I'm sorry Maggie to have shamed you in front of folk. I should never have taken the drink. I feel terrible about it now, but then I feel terrible about what happened to my father."

Maggie kept her eyes on the dishes in the sink; she did not want Jim to see the tears. No apologies could blot out the hurt he caused her. "That's true Jim, you're a different man with drink, but it loosens your tongue to say what is in your mind and heart."

"Surely you can make some allowance for me today of all days, when I've buried my father," Jim pleaded.

"I've thought of nothing else all day but what a fine man he was and he was so good and kind to me, when I needed a friend the most. I wish he was here with me now." She folded the cloth and walked over to the fireplace to hang it up to dry.

"Come and sit down and have a wee drink with me before we go to bed lass," Jim said trying to put his arm around her.

"No thank you, I'll have to see to Mary yet, she needs feeding and changing soon."

Jim frowned. "No time for me at all, always something more important."

Maggie stopped him. "You can swap places with me any day Jim and take over the washing, cooking, cleaning and shopping with very little money." Maggie knew immediately that the words left her lips she had said the wrong thing.

"Here we go again. I can't keep you up to the standard you imagine you belong. Well that's it, I'm for off." Quickly he grabbed his bonnet from the hook on the back of the door, and then marched off down the stairs, banging the outside door as a final indication of his anger.

It took several weeks after the funeral for things to settle down between them. Initially they went through their daily routine without exchanging a word. Maggie felt sorry for the bairns but the time that they were altogether was not very long and they she hoped they would never notice that anything was wrong.

Maggie felt concern that the trouble might start Jim drinking again, however he appeared only to have frequented the public houses the night of the funeral, after storming out in a rage. Maggie had been frantic when he did not come home all night. She later found out he had slept all night in the lavatory. Bridie had complained bitterly at having to waken him at six in the morning, "to get her night bucket emptied."

Jim never spoke of that night nor of his ridiculing Maggie before his family

The school summer holidays gave Jimmy and Charlie time to play about the house. The boys were quit a help to Maggie, for they played with Jessie and rocked Mary in the cradle while she tackled the daily load of washing. Bridie often remarked how clean and fresh the washing looked when hung out to dry.

As the wash bubbled in the boiler and as Maggie scrubbed the clothes on the board she sang to herself the Gaelic songs learned in her youth. She thought of the news her brother's wrote of their life, of how her daughter in Canada was growing up. It had been a hard lesson, the funeral day, so she never discussed the letters contents with Jim. Quite often her brothers would send money 'to buy something for the bairns'. Maggie had decided she would try to save it to visit Janet on Gigha.

Despite everything Jim was a good provider for his family. Never idle at a time when farmers were finding it difficult to pay for hired men.

Helen and her husband Fred had not been fortunate in getting a place at the last Muckle market. They had moved into a small rented cottage in Dall's Lane. With a large family to support, Fred was forced to apply for 'Parish relief.' The children with many others attended a kitchen set up in the old 'half-time' school for free bread and soup.

Maggie listened as the men folk talked of the 'state of the country's affairs'.

Jim was certain that nothing would bring the country back 'on to its feet' but another war. This had been his theory for years. Maggie felt less threatened at the thought of Jim being recalled to his regiment, she was sure that being forty years old would make him too old for military service.

CHAPTER SEVENTEEN

S PRING BROUGHT THEM another child. David, their third son was born in April. It was agreed he would take the name of Maggie's father. Bridie was delighted with 'her lovely golden haired boy', as she called him. "Lord knows Maggie, you should have been a Catholic with all those fine bairns you keep bringing in to the world."

Maggie was not as happy as her friend. She felt so tired trying to cope day after day with five young bairns. "How did you manage through all your problems Bridie and still stay happy?"

The old woman smiled, "Lassie as long as you are all together as a family that's the greatest gift the good Lord can give you."

Maggie considered what she said for a while. "Aye I suppose that's fine but he keeps giving me little gifts it's difficult to provide for."

"Would you have said that Maggie when you lost your twin babies?"

Maggie quickly agreed she would not. She also thought back to the nights she'd cried herself to sleep longing for her first born.

Bridie gave her a pat on the back. "Och come on cheer up, we'll have a walk along River Street with the bairns, you're bound to see others worse than you there."

Maggie did enjoy her family. The boys played well together, Jessie toddled on behind them. As they went down Bridge Street, they did no more than acknowledge the greetings of the women sitting at the entrances of the common closes. The women were all busy knitting as they joked and shared their family news.

Neither Maggie nor Bridie had ever allowed themselves to become part of this gossip exchange. Children with their bare feet ran after metal hoops balanced through the bend of a metal cleek.

"Jimmy will be needing one next," said Bridie.

"They always want to be the same as their friends," Maggie agreed.

At the foot of the Pathie, they turned along the Inch.

"Let's sit down here for a wee while Bridie, the bairns can play on the grass."

Maggie laid her shawl on the ground and sat Mary down. "There you are now enjoy the lovely evening." Bridie was rocking the infant David in her arms singing away an Irish Gaelic melody.

"I imagine this is how it would have been if my own mother was alive." The words Maggie heard came from her lips, yet she was startled by them.

Bridie stopped singing. "You've never told me of your Mammy and we've faced a lot of blood and tears together." She looked Maggie straight in the eyes. "The hurt and loneliness in your heart would be less if you shared it Maggie."

"Yes I expect you are right, but it's so long been my secret, I couldn't let people know of it."

"Surely you've spoke of your family to Jim?" Bridie was determined not to let Maggie withdraw at the first real chance of discussing her origins.

"No, not completely for if I told him then it would make him think even less of me."

"That's not what I see your marriage like Maggie, you cannot blame a man for having a drink to send his father's spirit back to his maker."

Maggie picked Mary up from the grass," I've forgotten all that," she lied. "It's just sometimes he thinks I act as if I'm trying to be a cut above the rest."

"Well are you?" got in Bridie quickly.

"Of course I'm not Bridie. I just want to get on and better myself and make a good life for the bairns. I don't mean them to want for the ordinary things that others take for granted, the way I had to."

"You should be telling your man all this, not me lassie, he's the one that shares your life.'

Maggie agreed this was what she had to do.

The curfew bells started to ring from the Cathedral tower. "Lord help us it's eight o'clock, Jim will be home and no tatties ready." "Come on bairns, hurry up the back braes." Bridie laughed. "Can't keep your Lord and master waiting, eh." Jim was still not home by the time they reached the house. Maggie had time to have the bairns washed and in bed before he appeared.

"You look as if you've had a hard day," was her greeting.

"I have lassie, we are having to do the work of two men, with no extra money to save the farmers a few pounds."

He sat down by the fire unlacing his boots as he spoke. "The harvest is almost in though, we should be done by the weekend."

"Does that mean you will be here on Saturday evening then?" asked Maggie.

"Who knows the answer to that? Why, what's so special on Saturday?"

"Oh nothing really, I just thought you would see a wee while of the bairns, that's all. They are in bed when you leave in the morning and asleep by the time you're back at night."

Jim was stripped to the waist washing himself at the sink. "Aye I'll be a complete stranger to them before long."

After Jim ate his meal, he sat smoking his pipe. "I've been wondering if I'll get another fee come the term Maggie."

"Of course you will Jim, everybody knows you give a good days work for your wages."

Jim agreed with her then added, "It's not so simple as that though. They want married men with families cottared so they can use the wives and bairns to work for little or nothing, when need be."

Maggie was a bit astounded by this news. "You wouldn't think of moving to tied house, would you? Don't worry about it yet Jim." Maggie was sewing pieces on to her patchwork quilt. "I have never done any farm work since I left Culburnie, twenty years ago."

"You'll not be doing any either Maggie. You know my views on wives working. Your job is to be with the bairns. As we've just said they see nothing of me for days on end. Above all, they need you, their mother."

Maggie realised how cut off Jim must feel from his children. "Of course they need you as well."

Jim knocked his pipe empty on the bars of the grate.

"What makes you think that Maggie?"

"I know fine Jim, for I missed my father much more than my mother when they died." There it was out.

Two hours later as they lay in bed, Jim holding Maggie in the protection of his arms.

"You've had a hard life Maggie but never forget that I truly love you."

She snuggled closer to his body. "Oh I sometimes come out with things I don't really mean when I'm angry. You've been so good for me, I want to give you the best of everything but never seem to get out of the bit."

"I just need to be with you and the bairns Jim, as long as nothing can change that we'll be fine. Things will work out for us, you'll see."

CHAPTER EIGHTEEN

MAGGIE WAS GLAD to see the first signs of spring. As she predicted Jim was still working on the farm and they had not been forced to move from their home in the High Street.

How long this was to last was questionable, as the men folk, who stood about the Southport in the evenings talked of nothing else but 'there would be war with the German Kaiser, before the year was done'"

Jim saw this as his chance to make a break from working on the land.

"I'm still on the reserve you know lass, I'll be among the first to be called up," he told her.

"Surely twelve years away from soldiering and being over forty now will keep you out," she answered.

Jim was annoyed that his wife should believe he was too old to defend his country.

"Lord Maggie, it's experienced men like me they'll need. Not young laddies in the Boy Scouts. At forty one I'm in the prime of my life."

Maggie knew he was determined to go, whether recalled or not.

There was no choice given.

The first week of August, Jim was notified to join his regiment immediately at Pirbright.

It was only the arrival of the letter that caused Maggie to grasp the seriousness of the situation.

Britain was at War. With every able bodied man over eighteen years of age, her husband Jim, was required to fight the Germans.

Like all the other wives Maggie would have to cope with bringing up the bairns alone, until the War was over and the men returned victorious. "It will all be over by Christmas lass, it's the chance we've been waiting for. Once back in the battalion I might be able to stay on. You'll get a sergeant's wife's allowance every week"

Think about it Maggie, we will be better off than ever before." She hung onto his arm. "You won't be here though Jim. What if anything happens to you? What will the bairns do without their dad?"

Jim put his hand on her shoulder.

"You'll be like the rest happy to get on with it. What is going to happen to an experienced campaigner like me? I'll show the Huns what they are up against. Jim Chisholm, who thrashed the Boers."

They both laughed nervously.

"You should thank them, for making you so happy to get away from Brechin and us."

"That's not true Maggie. I don't want to leave you. I just want to get a chance to do what I'm good at. Soldiering."

Brechin Railway Station was crowded with families seeing their loved ones off to War.

Jim was far from the first to embark.

The Volunteer Regiments had marched through the town to join the 'regulars' in training three weeks earlier in July.

It was thought that they were already across the English Channel and fighting in the front line.

Jimmy and Charlie were revelling in the excitement. "How long before you have killed all the Germans Dad?" they asked.

"Oh I will be as quick as I can lads," he answered.

"Do you have granddad's gun?" quizzed Charlie, "he would have killed them all."

"I suppose you are right son."

Jim couldseethecolourinMaggie'sfacechangeatthementionoftheword killing. Jim picked Jessie up in his arms.

"Come on now, a big kiss for dad, it's got to last for a long time until the next one."

This was Jim's favourite child, his first-born daughter. Jessie could charm the birds off the trees. "I'll send you one every night, when I go to bed Dad, you will get it where ever you are."

Mary hung on to her mother's skirt, frightened by all the hustle and bustle going on around her.

"Kiss for dad Mary. You'll remember me when I get back, I hope."

Maggie could not hold back her tears any longer.

"You'll better come back Jim Chisholm, for I am no use without you."

As they kissed goodbye, David in Maggie's arms was squeezed between their two bodies.

"It's the closest I've been to him since he was born Maggie. There between us. Where he belongs."

The town silver band struck up with the tune 'Will ye no come back again'.

The emotions and feelings running high, the music caused what had been trickles of tears to develop into a steady flow, accompanied in some cases by body wracking sobs.

The train sounded its whistle as it passed the cattle market and disappeared under the bridge.

"Come on Mam, let's get home for some tea," said Jimmy, trying to console Maggie. He took Jessie by the hand. "Come on Charlie, you help Mary, Mam cannot mange to carry her and the bairn."

The square outside Brechin Station was crowded with women and children.

"Stay together bairns and not get lost. It's bad enough losing your father. How could I explain to him that I wasn't able to watch you for five minutes until we walked home." When they reached the Southport, Bridie was standing at the entrance to the close. "Come on Birdie's been waiting for you all. You boys can play out the back for a wee while. I've made a spot of tea for your Mammy, for I thought she would be wanting some, to be sure."

"Oh I do Bridie, thank you. You are such a good friend. I'll never be able to repay you for all your kindness." Och, what a fuss to be sure about a wee strupach when you are in need of one.'

Maggie looked into the old woman's face. "You know Bridie, I haven't heard that expression for years. My mother used to say that when I was a little girl. To be honest that's about the only thing I remember about her now."

Bridie knew that this was neither the time nor the place to speak of Maggie's past, as she was so upset by the departure of her husband.

Maggie would have to be very strong to cope with five young children.

"It's the future you have to think of Maggie, my lass. How well you will have everything in order, when Jim comes home from the War."

"Do you think it will be long before it's over, Bridie? You seem to know the answers to most things."

Bridie dangled David's fat little legs over her knees, as she patted his back, when rocking to and fro, in front of the fire.

"Only the good Lord knows the answer to that. The papers say it will all be over by Christmas."

"Jim won't be able to get a fee at that time if he's sent home then."

Bridie chuckled. "Well when would you like the Lord to put an end to it all? Let me know and I will light a candle and pray that you get your wish."

Maggie felt the colour rush to her cheeks.

"Oh I want Jim home, it's just that a sergeants Pay for a month or two would be fine and there would be no work for him here in the winter. I had set my heart on a visit to Gigha and visiting my aunt. With the extra money I could take the bairns to see her."

"That's a grand idea, it will do you all good. Just do that when the schools are off on holiday.' "I don't think Jim will be home for October, do you? I'll just write to Janet and tell her we will be then.'

The thought of visiting Gigha again would keep Maggie happy over the next few weeks.

The boys were excited at the idea of a long journey by train and steamer. "How many days will we be on the boat Mam?" quizzed Jimmy.

"Only part of a day son. It might feel forever once we are started on the road though."

"Will we stay in Glasgow?"

"Only long enough to get from the rail station to where the steamer leaves from. Maggie reckoned she was to have many questions to answer before their journey was completed.

"What if we get lost in Glasgow?" chimed in Charlie.

"Don't be stupid. How could Mam get lost there? That's where we lived before we came to Brechin. Mam was born there and so were we."

"Is that right Mam? Do we come from Glasgow?"

Maggie curtly replied, "Well yes, in a way that's true"

Charlie was like a terrier with a bone and would not be put off easily. "Why did we leave and come here then?"

Maggie as usual embellished the truth and kept her secrets to herself. "I suppose because it was a far healthier place to live. There was work for your dad, and granddad was needing company."

There was no necessity for the children to know the facts behind their move from Glasgow. After all Maggie had long ago come to accept the stress and frustrations that Jim had suffered trying to maintain his family, by the income of two men's work.

Perhaps Jim would succeed in his desire to remain in the Guards.

Only time had the answer to so many different things.

CHAPTER NINETEEN

O CTOBER STARTED AS a beautiful warm sunny month. The brightness, however, was only relative to the weather and he hearts of those too young to accept the disasters and carnage enforced upon those commanded to 'defend the rights of man' upon the fields of France and Flanders.

Each day brought more news of families throughout the town, who had been bereaved of fathers and sons. Men who had been the breadwinners, now lying dead from gas or gunshot wounds, rotting in the muddy trenches, which zigzagged the sea of red covered poppy fields.

Maggie could not entertain the idea that such an end would come to her Jim. Of course, he was an experienced soldier. The Boers had pitted their wits against his regiment and failed. How should the Kaiser's troops have more success?

Duke's factory 'bummer' had sounded the dinner break, when there was a knocking at the door. This unexpected interruption from setting the table for the boys caught Maggie by surprise.

"Who can that be David?" she said to the child in the cradle.

The telegraph boy looked very official and serious.

"Mrs Chisholm. This is for you from the War Office."

Maggie looked at the boy in disbelief. This could not be for her.

"Just wait a minute son, the broth will be boiling over."

She want back upstairs to the fire and pulled the pot to the side. David was still asleep.

"Well what's the message son?" she asked knowing in her heart the only thing that it could be.

The young boy was most experienced in delivering unwelcome news.

"Are you Mrs Chisholm, 110 High Street?"

She nodded and managed to emit a very squeaky "Yes".

"Well this is for you," he said handing over the bright yellow envelope.

"Will there be an answer?"

Bravely Maggie tried to ear open the paper with hands that seemed to be detached from the command centre in her brain. Her eyes skimmed over the written words as she spoke aloud the message they conveyed.

"The War office wish to advise you that Sergeant James Chisholm has been reported missing in action and presumed killed."

The silent boy stood studying her ashen face. How he hated this job. If only he was old enough, he could enlist and join the others from Brechin fighting in the front line.

Eventually in a quiet voice, he asked, "Is there any reply, Mrs Chisholm?"

"No laddie, there's no reply, nor is there an answer to something like this."

Slowly she climbed the stairs with leaden feet.

"Oh God, what am I to do now?"

She looked at her infant son who was now awake, lying gurgling and cooing.

"Laddie stay happy as you are now. You will not need to be told yet this awful news about your father."

She picked up her son, with the crumpled message still held in her hand.

"We will better get Jessie and Mary from Bridie's. The boys will be in any minute for their dinner."

The old woman could see that her young friend was not her usual cheery self as she walked slowly towards the cottage door.

"What ails you lass?" She asked as her eyes dropped from Maggie's white face to the bright coloured envelope crumpled in her hand.

"In the name of Joseph, Mary and Jesus, it isn't Jim is it?"

Maggie could not speak. She unclenched her fingers on the bulletin of death and offered it on outstretched palm to Bridie.

Silently she read, then pulled the child from his mother's arms.

"Come away, I'll come back with you and see to the bairns."

She steered Maggie and the girls back to their home.

Jimmy and Charlie bounded up the stairs.

"Mam there's a circus coming to town," shouted Jimmy.

"Can we go Mam? It's to be beside the paperie," said Charlie, excitedly pulling at her overall.

"There's to be animals and clowns all doing funny things."

"We will see boys. Everything seems like a circus today, with people like animals doing funny things. Come on now, sit down at the table and sup your soup. It will be time to get back to get back to your lessons before you are ready."

Well into the afternoon Maggie and Bridie still sat by the fire drinking endless cups of tea.

"You know Maggie lass, the wire never said that Jim was definitely killed, to be sure. We can still hope and pray that he is alive."

Maggie set her cup down on the fender and pulled Jessie up onto her lap beside Mary.

"I've spent most of my life hoping for things that are never granted to me. Everything turns sour. All that I love and cherish is taken from me."

"Stop this now," scolded Bridie. "You'll always have the love of your bairns. Think how I feel for you. Life for me would be a weary miserable existence, but for you and yours being near."

Maggie knew this to be true.

It was more than a week later that the letter of notification that Jim was alive and a prisoner of war, arrived at the house. Despite reading it several times Maggie could not take in the news. She ran to Bridie's home.

"You were right once again, Jim is alive. He is in a prisoner of war camp in Germany. He will be there until the war is finished. That means he will not be involved in any more fighting."

The old woman hugged her friend.

"I'm so happy for you lass, but I don't think that Jim will be so pleased at being caged for the duration. Still as you say that will probably be him finished with any front line action."

"Oh Bridie, I can go on holiday now with the bairns knowing that my Jim is alive and reasonably safe. Thank God foe his mercy."

"You deserve a change in fortune Maggie. I'm glad you will be able to get away for a change. Do you all good and I will enjoy hearing all about it from you and the boys when you get back."

The train pulled slowly to a stop at Forfar station. The children were so excited at this great travel adventure.

"Is this Glasgow now Mam?" asked Jessie.

"Don't be stupid Jess, you girls are all alike. You know nothing", snapped Jimmy, as he pulled Mary from the carriage door, by the hand.

"Never mind the bickering you two and help Charlie with those bags until I get everything together."

Maggie had David sitting on her hip and was trying to carry the bags and luggage all at the same time.

"Jessie you pick up the basket with the picnic in it. I am sure that you are a big enough girl to manage it for Mam."

Charlie laughed, "Don't let Mary have it for you know how she loves to eat everything. There would be nothing left for us."

This comment brought a smile to his mother's face.

"That's not a nice thing to say about your sister," she told him.

Mary was such a good-natured child, who had been no bother since the day that she was born. Despite being of plain appearance she was in her own way equally as attractive as Jessie. Mary had the most beautiful shade of auburn hair. When people mentioned this to her she would be so shy and look down at her feet, while her face turned red with embarrassment. It was true that she enjoyed her food and her sturdy frame was proof of this fact.

"Hurry along now and stay back from the edge of the platform for the express will come in so fast that the wind might pull you over on to the rails."

This was one of the times that Maggie missed Jim's firm handling of the children. Indeed it required a regimented exercise to transfer five youngsters from Brechin to Glasgow from there to Campbeltown on McBrayne's steamer.

The final part of the journey would be by bus to Tayinloan then the ferry crossing to Ardminish.

Maggie hoped that the food she had packed would be sufficient. Despite the shortage of money she still considered it easier to picnic than cope with excited children in some café or tearoom.

As the train was steaming towards Glasgow, Maggie's mind travelled back in time to the days when she journeyed from Culburnie. She would have been about the same age as Jimmy now. He was certainly ill equipped to face life on his own and be expected to care for David as well. She comforted herself that such an event would never happen.

There had been no news from her brothers in New Zealand for several weeks and this worried her. The troops from there had been involved in fighting in Gallipoli. Perhaps Janet would know if they had been 'called up' or not.

By afternoon the rocking of the steamer made the children tired and fretful.

Maggie tried to get them to lie down on the seats in the saloon. Eventually they all fell asleep. An elderly woman sitting nearby said "You'll get a minute to yourself now lassie."

"Yes it has been a long day already." She answered.

"Where are you going with them all?" enquired the friendly stranger.

"We are going for a holiday with my aunt."

Maggie was never one for giving away too much of her families affairs, even though she knew that the lady was only making polite conversation.

"Does your aunt stay in Kintyre then?"

She decided that this woman was not to be put off easily.

"No she lives on Gigha," was Maggie's curt reply.

"I come from Islay myself," the woman went on, "I know quite a few people from there though. What is your aunts name?"

"Her name is Janet McMillan, she's the blacksmith's widow."

What is she going to say now, thought Maggie.

David turned over on the narrow bench type seat and almost fell on to the floor. Maggie jumped up and tried to move him back again.

"I watched you when you got on the boat at first and I was sure that there was something familiar in your face. Now I know what it is. If you are Janet McMillan's niece then you must be a McKinnon from Tormisdale."

"I don't know what to say to you for I am staggered that by looking at me you can work out my family relations."

The woman looked at Maggie.

"Oh I'm not as clever as all that. Most of the people on the islands know each other. I went to school with Janet's younger sister Marion. What a tragedy her dying and leaving those nine bairns."

She spoke as if Maggie would be aware of all the family happenings.

Maggie could feel herself beginning to feel tense. What if this woman knew her background?

"I wonder if you could keep an eye on the bairns until I go to the toilet?" she asked.

"They'll be alright with me, never worry. Take a wee stretch of your legs and get a cup of tea if you want."

Maggie smiled. "Thank you very much. I might just do that."

I'll take some time away from your questions, she told herself.

As she strolled on deck she remembered the woman's words that all island people knew each other. Perhaps she might know of her old friend Neil McLeod, or she might even have some news of John and Tibby McLeod. Since moving to Brechin they had completely lost touch with their good friends.

Probably Tibby would be on her own, as John would have been called up to go to France. Neil McLeod would be too old for active service.

When she got back to the saloon the children were still asleep as she had left them

"Good wee lambs they were. They must be tired with the journey from Glasgow." Said the woman.

Maggie turned Mary over for fear she might roll off the bench to the floor.

"They had an early start this morning and it will be late before we reach the island."

"Did you manage to get a cup of tea for yourself?"

"Yes I did and I'm very grateful for your help. My husband is away at the war and I miss his help."

"Aye lassie there's a lot more like you and some never to get their menfolk back again."

The woman sat quiet for a spell knitting a sock she had produced from a bag at her feet.

Maggie sat with her eyes closed for she knew the friendly soul would continue talking if she appeared awake. Perhaps she should ask about her friends. She was unsure if she really wanted to learn about Neil's life after he left Glasgow. True in times of despair she had considered if life would have been different had she accepted Neil's offer of marriage. On the occasions that she found herself entertaining those private thoughts, she felt embarrassment of disloyalty to her husband.

Such feelings swept through her as she heard her own voice ask, "Do you know Neil McLeod, who inherited his father's estate on Islay?"

The woman manoeuvred her knitting needles around, and then started another row, before answering.

"I'm sure that everybody on the island knows Neil and his background. Is he known to you?"

Maggie was still surprised at herself for asking the question.

"Well yes," she stammered, "I used to be in service as a cook."

The woman interrupted. "That would be about the time that he was a butler in Glasgow, would it not?"

The discussion continued.

"Yes," Maggie answered, "It was a good few years ago now."

"They have been good years for Neil then," the woman went on," he has put a manager into the home farm and opened the big house as a very posh hotel. Not for ordinary folks, you know. Foreigners from England, America and such likes."

Maggie could imagine Neil organising a household to make any visitor's holiday comforts well catered for.

"If I see him who will I say was asking for him? I just can't say the widow McMillan's niece from Gigha, can it?"

Maggie nodded, "That will be fine. He'll know who you are meaning alright."

She looked out the porthole into the darkening sky.

"I had better get the bairns wakened for we will soon be in Campbeltown. If I could just ask you to be so kind as watch them until I go and wet a cloth to wipe their hands and faces, please."

"Off you go lass. They'll be fine."

Maggie's mind was not on the washing of faces. Neil McLeod, now a man of means. She should have asked if he was married. At least she had the blessing of her bairns.

As she left the steamer at Campbeltown, Maggie turned back and waved to her travelling companion. Neil had never married, and he was now a very rich man. So be it, she thought.

"Come on we will soon be in Tayinloan, then the little ferry to Gigha. Auntie Janet will have a big tea waiting for us all, when we get there."

"Good," said Mary, "I am so hungry."

"Never changes, does it Mam," said Jimmy.

Maggie herded them together towards the open charabanc that would take them on the next part of the journey.

"Hurry up now, there's no time for arguing."

It was well after ten o'clock, when the children were eventually settled in their beds at Janet's home.

Maggie could see little difference in her aunt's appearance. She did not look her age.

"It's so peaceful and quiet, when they are asleep, is it not?" said Maggie.

"You might think so but there are worse things than noise," replied her aunt.

"Sitting on your own with no one to speak to, no one to come in, or to have to prepare a meals for. Lassie you will always have your family, noisy troublesome or not, they will always be there for you to car for."

Maggie lay in bed in the quiet darkness beside Jimmy, Charlie and David.

They were in the 'outside bed', in the corrugated iron shed next to the house. Jessie and Mary were in the ben house bed beside Janet.

Would this be the sort of accommodation she would have occupied had she married Neil McLeod.

Probably she would have slept in some enormous four-poster bed, with servants to pander to her every need.

Where would Jim be sleeping to night? Maggie could feel her throat muscles tighten and her eyes moisten.

There was no answer to those questions. One thing was certainly clear in Maggie's heart. Money and position were not her idols. She had no regrets of marrying Jim Chisholm. The children who came from their love were worth more than money could ever buy. She pulled David closer to her chest, stretched out and touched Jimmy and Charlie. "God bless you my bairns, and bring my Jim home safe to us soon."

Maggie could not remember when last she had prayed sincerely hoping that someone was "up there" to answer.

"You never listen to what I ask God, but please don't fail me this time."

CHAPTER TWENTY

THE TWO WEEKS flew past like time was on wings. The children were brown as berries with running free on the foreshore everyday. Maggie enjoyed the company of her aunt and her willing help with David.

Each afternoon when she was away from household chores she made the effort to take the bairns on some sort of adventure. They had collected all shapes and sizes of shells from the tide line and carried enough driftwood to keep Janet's fire blazing all winter. They brought up to the garden creels of seaweed, that according to the locals made potatoes grow better and faster than anywhere in the country.

Maggie believed that everything about Gigha was better than anywhere else in the country.

An old fisherman who sat on the jetty waiting for the lobster boats to come home, made a firm friend of Maggie and the children.

"The island needs young folk," he had told her. "All our young must leave and go to the mainland and the cities for work."

"Surely when the war is over they will come back," said Maggie.

"No fear lassie. It goes much deeper than that," explained the old seafarer. "There are very few young men who left here directly to join the forces. Och they are fighting for their country sure enough, but they had already left Gigha to work in the factories and shipyards or they joined the Merchant Services. Like you they only come back on holiday or to visit their families."

"I would love to come back and stay here for good. Maybe when my husband gets back, he's a prisoner of war, we will try to settle here beside Janet."

"That would be as good for her as it would for you. What does your husband do, when he's not soldiering?"

Maggie thought for a minute.

"Well he's good at most things, but he's mainly worked on the land as a ploughman."

"There's not much land for ploughing here lass, but the factor is one for breeding of heavy horses. Maybe he would be able to work with him."

"We will have to wait for this war to end and our men to come home before we can make any plans."

The old man looked at Jimmy and Charlie running through the whins searching for rabbits.

"Aye they'll no believe it, but that's the best time in their lives they are having now. No worries nor cares. A few more years and they will be worrying about how to support a wife and family."

Maggie laughed, "I hope not for a while yet, for they are only ten years old."

"I expect that you are like me, putting in a hard days work when you were their age?" the man went on, "people forget so easily when they are looking to improve things for their bairns."

Maggie agreed that what he was saying was correct. She could well remember those early mornings in the cold, running to the byre, at Culburnie to get the cows milked before she had her breakfast, then went to school.

"Hard work never harmed anyone, you know," said Maggie." I've had my share of it and I'm sure I'm a better person foe the efforts I've made."

"That may well be true lass, but I'm sure that someone else is a damned sight better off with money in the bank, because of the sweat on your brow."

He sat quiet for a while then said, "This island is owned by one man who benefits from every bit of work done by man woman and child who lives here. We are all dependent on him for the right to stay in the place where we were born. He wasn't born on the island. He was born to a family who had plenty of money, enough to buy the island. My family the McNeills have been here for at least six hundred years. We have worked the land, fished the waters but we have no right to remain on Gigha should the master tell us to go.

Maggie felt sorry for the old man, but she realised that he was trying to tell her perhaps the island life was not as idyllic as it appeared on the surface. "My husband Jim would never work on a farm that would mean we had to live in a tied house, to be turned out at the farmer's whim," she told him.

"Well your husband won't be looking for work here I'm afraid, for every house on the place belongs to the laird."

Maggie and Janet sat y the fire knowing that the morning would bring an early start for their journey back to Brechin.

"It will be a long winter waiting for spring and your coming back with the children Maggie. Maybe by that time the war will be over and Jim will be with you."

Janet poured out a glass of whisky for both of them. They sat slowly sipping, while talking.

"If the war is over and Jim is home, then it won't be so easy for me to come here."

"Surely Maggie, it would be better with him to help you with the bairns on the journey?"

"That's true Janet. I'm sure he would help me and be more than anxious for the benefit of such a relaxing holiday, but we just could not afford the fares if it wasn't for Jim's army pay."

Janet set down her glass, threw another peat on the fire before continuing,"

Well Maggie, call me a selfish old woman if you like, but I hope that your man is in the army for a lot of years yet."

Maggie with a raised voice answered, "How could you wish that on me, if as you say you care for me and mine?"

"The world is a hard place, you of all people should know that much. I've never known a great deal of pleasure in my lifetime, other than the satisfaction of being able to give a good days work to my master. My marriage was if it has to be truthful, not one of love, but of convenience for both Alex and myself. Charlie was the one bright and shining light of my life and for reasons known only to God, he was taken from me. Over the years Maggie I've got to know you so well. You are a hard working gentle girl who hasn't let the knocks you've been given in life, turn you sour and bitter. You'll try to help anyone in need and your children certainly will always have your undying love. Sometimes you are far too soft with them, but I can understand that you want them to have the many little loving pleasures that you were denied as a child. Selfish as I am, for I want the love of you and your children, to have them around me for the time that God has allotted to me to remain on this earth. I want someone of my own blood to be here with me."

Maggie was unsure what to say to Janet for what the old woman desired was an expression of her own innermost feelings. She leaned across and touched her aunt's hand, which rested on the arm of the chair, despite knowing that any sign of affection might be rebuffed as a sign of unnatural weakness.

"Janet I know what you mean and how you feel, for until I met Jim and married for love, I felt so alone. The long weary hours spent wishing I could just meet and speak with someone of my own. What I would have given to hear what you have just said, when I was a young girl."

Janet removed her hand from below Maggie's.

"We've wasted so much of our lives and time that could have been spent together lassie."

Maggie squeezed her aunt's fingers; "You wouldn't want to keep me here away from my man and the bairns away from their father. Would you?"

"No I don't suppose I would, but it's so lonesome sometimes when the dark winter days are here. I wonder if I'm going to see you all again. I really love you all you know, the dark winter nights are when I ask myself if I could have done more for you and your brothers, when your mother did those shameful things. We were all left to face up to her sinful actions. She betrayed us all, but most unforgivable of all, she deserted her bairns."

"Oh come on Janet. What is in the past has to be forgotten. Who knows things might have turned out just the same in any case. I most surely would still have married Jim, for we are meant for each other. The war would still have gone on, with the men folk away fighting, so I still would have been on my own here with the bairns visiting, just as I will as often as the school holidays and pennies permit."

"Och I'm a silly old woman, forgive me. Of course you'll be back soon. Little David will be toddling around and I can walk him up past the old smiddy, up to the school and then the church, where all can see me with my bairns."

She got up slowly from the chair, "Come on, get away to bed with you for it will be a long day tomorrow. Don't let the ramblings of an old woman upset you."

She patted Maggie on the shoulder, "Well not all blethers for I am proud of you, and how you have faced up to your responsibilities in life. I hope that Jim will be home soon and be with you when you come back in the spring."

Maggie put her arms around her aunt's neck before kissing her on the cheek.

"I promise, I'll be back early in the year and please remember that we are two of a kind Janet for I need you as my own, just as much as you need me."

Maggie slept little that night thinking of what had been said the previous evening.

Poor Janet, she had summed up her life those many years before, then when Charlie died, that she was working to keep alive waiting for death.

Had it been the same thoughts that her mother fostered in her mind before committing herself to the cold dark waters of the Clyde. Had it been the thought of complete devastation and uselessness following the death of her father that caused her to end her life.

Maggie could not even remember what her father and mother looked like, yet she could recall, from somewhere the memory of a drunken figure lying in the box bed.

The death of her father was not the reason for being deserted by her mother. Janet was right. What ever it was that caused Mary McKinnon's depression, drinking and irresponsible actions, was seeded long before the death of her husband.

Maggie knew that she could never leave the bairns to face an uncertain future alone. Perhaps her aunt had spoken the truth, when she alleged that 'she could be too soft with the bairns'. Since Jim went away she had often considered that at times she did not spend as much of her time with him as she might have done.

Jim Chisholm was the only man for her. Each day that they were apart she became more convinced of this fact.

In the early morning, when Maggie left the 'outside room', to go into the cottage, it was raining and there was a gale blowing.

Janet was already out of bed and had the fire burning.

"Lord knows lassie you are to have a rough journey home."

Maggie glanced out of the window as she dried her hands and face.

"Aye Janet, it would seem as if winter is to be upon us earlier than we expected. I hope it's not to be a rough crossing, for the bairns sake."

Maggie's wish was heard by no-one, for the crossing to the mainland and from Campbeltown to Glasgow, was the worst that she had experienced.

The children were sick with the constant rocking and rolling of the boat. Maggie, herself did not feel well at all well, however, with everyone feeling the same there were no offers of help with her ailing brood.

When they arrived at Brechin station, the Chisholm family were a pitiful sight.

"Hurry on now," encouraged Maggie. "Along Damacre Road, down City Road then we will be home. Come on now boys you help the girls and I will manage David and the luggage. Half an hour and you will all be in your own beds."

Jimmy was struggling to lift Mary up.

"She'll need her supper Mam, you know how she won't manage to sleep if she's hungry."

"That's quite true. We will have what's left of Auntie Janet's picnic for the journey. Come on now, hurry on Charlie and Jessie."

Less than an hour after the arrival of the train at Brechin, the children were in bed, fast asleep.

Maggie was happy to be home at her own fireside, with a cheery fire blazing in the grate.

She poured the boiling water from the kettle on the hob into the teapot, then set it on the chrome plate in front of the bars to allow the tea to infuse.

There had been three letters behind the door when she opened it.

One from New Zealand, one from the Red Cross and one in unfamiliar hand writing.

The Red Cross were advising her that the camp where Jim was interned, had been visited by an official deputation, to find that the prisoners there were in good health and appeared well cared for.

David's letter was full of how he wished that he could be fighting for his country. He had left working for the Hydro Electric Company and was now in Dunedin, where he hoped that both he and Alex would settle for good.

Maggie poured out her tea. She had kept the mystery letter until last.

It was from Bridie's daughter, and had been written only five days after Maggie left for Gigha.

On the morning following her departure, the police had been asked to break in to Bridie's cottage, as the neighbours were concerned at not seeing her out and about.

Apparently the old lady died sitting by the fire.

The note went on to explain that after a private burial service, the family removed all their mother's personal effects from the cottage and gave up the lease. They regretted that they were unable to contact Maggie, as they knew that she was the only real friend that their mother had in Brechin. However, as the cottage had been given up, they could not stay on to tell her in person of Bridie's death.

The note fell from Maggie's hand.

"Oh God, what next will you do to me?" she sobbed.

Despite the fatigue of the day's journeying, Maggie could not sleep. She lay beside David tossing and turning. Poor Bridie. She had been so lonely at times and in the end had been by herself.

Janet would most probably face the same fate. Yes she would try to get back and visit as often as possible.

If only Jim was at home, how different things would be. When would this damned war end? Well at least she had the children with her. Poor Jim did not have his freedom, nor the ones who were with him.

She decided that she would take the children and have their photograph taken, then send a print to their father and also one to Janet. Jim would be amazed at how much they had all grown in the time he had been away. It seemed as if she had just closed her eyes when it was time to get up and get the bairns porridge ready.

There were all the daily chores to be done, with no relief from them by a friendly chat with Bridie.

Maggie accepted just how cut off she seemed to be, while still living in the heart of the town. She knew that she only had herself to blame. Keeping her affairs to herself was part of her nature that she could never change now.

Passing the time of day with neighbours and shopkeepers was as near as she ever got to making conversation, apart from talking to the boys.

Jimmy and Charlie were very good at keeping her up to date with all the daily news.

Maggie did not relish the thought of telling them of the passing away of their dear friend, who had become almost like a grandmother to them all.

Thank goodness it was Sunday. At least there would be time for her to explain before the boys had to go to school on Monday.

No doubt some other children there might break the news to them if she left them unprepared.

Strange to think of Jimmy as being ten years old already.

Margaret would be a young lady by now. It had been many months now since there had been a letter from Canada, with news of the family there. It had been even longer since Maggie had given any thought to Culburnie and the McDonalds.

What events would take place in the next ten years, she asked herself. Then she decided it was just as well that the future remained a mystery.

It was after breakfast before the boys wanted to go outside to play, when Maggie explained to them Bridie's 'passing away'. She found it difficult to control her voice, when answering their questions. It was obvious that the boys, especially Jimmy had some knowledge of the meaning of death.

"There are lots of boys at the school who have no dad now, because they were killed in the war. At least Bridie didn't have to fight and get shot by the Germans."

Maggie was able to reply, "That's right son, she died in her own home." Her thoughts however were different; she fought all her life to survive though, with little to show for her struggle, then a lonely death.

"Right away and play and don't get into any mischief with those Bridge Street bairns. Charlie I don't want to hear that you have been near that weaving shed, being cheeky to that old man."

Charlie with a face of innocence, smiled, "We would never Jimmy Badger, Mam. Isn't that right Jimmy?"

There was not a direct answer from his brother. Jimmy grabbed his hand. "Come on we will see if the Gallacio boys are out on the backies."

What would she do with Charlie? Maggie had a laugh to herself. Charlie was full of fun. She knew by his face that he would have been involved in tormenting the poor old weaver, with his beard and unshaven face, he did look like a badger.

Sooner Jim was home to take them in hand the better.

Maggie busied herself trying to get the wash sorted out. She spent sometime playing with Mary and Jessie.

"My goodness girls it's almost dinnertime. What will those boys be at?" Maggie did not have long to wonder.

She could hear Jimmy as he came thumping up the stairs. He burst into the room carrying a big sack.

"We have lifted all the tatties, carrots, neaps and onions from Bridie's garden, Mam." Charlie was trailing another sack up the stairs.

"Oh laddies you should not have done that. They were not yours to take. This is as bad as stealing."

Jimmy looked sheepishly at his mother.

"I didn't think so Mam. After all we did most of the work in the garden.

We did it for Bridie and now she isn't here I think that they should belong to us. Bridie won't be needing them. There's no-one in the house to use them."

Maggie thought for a moment. "Well this time I suppose you are right, but remember I won't have you stealing and taking what isn't yours."

"We would never do that Mam, they would just have been taken by somebody else or left to rot in the ground. You are always telling us not to waste food."

Poor Bridie. They were arguing over a few potatoes that the old woman had in her garden.

What a token of remembrance.

Would that be all that she would leave behind on Earth to show for a lifetime of struggle to 'better herself'?

CHAPTER TWENTY ONE

IT WAS A long weary winter, with nothing to feel cheerful about. The war in France dragged on with each day bringing more drastic news of disasters at the battlefronts. Many local men had fallen, victims to the extreme cold weather and the conditions in the mud filled trenches. The predictions that the war would end by Christmas were far from being true.

Maggie like many other women did her best to bring some seasonal cheer to her children. With the loss of her friend and Jim imprisoned in a foreign country she felt very isolated from adult conversation. Relationships with Jim's sisters had never been very strong and she always felt they were ill at ease in her presence making social contact with them a very rare event.

Occasionally she would talk to her neighbour, who also lived through the close. Mrs Gallacio like herself bringing up a family. They were able to talk about the children. The boys of both families had become firm friends. Maggie did not feel such an incomer as her Italian counterpart.

Brechin similar to many other Scottish towns the place chosen by the Gallacio immigrants to set up their ice cream and fish and chip business. It was a hard life, with the war in Europe making things even more difficult for the family.

Being confined to the house by the cold weather gave Maggie more time to write to her family. There had been the usual gift of money for the children from their New Zealand uncles.

One of the unexpected surprises of Christmas had been a letter from Canada from her daughter Margaret. It brought feelings of joy tangled with a curious sense of embarrassed sadness.

Mary had decided now that their adopted daughter was sixteen it was the correct time to tell her of her natural mother. Curiosity, seeking conformation of Mary's explanation of why Maggie had been forced to part with her, and the question of whether or not she had any brothers or sisters had prompted Margaret to write directly to her natural mother.

Maggie had never imagined that this might happen. Certainly Jim knew of her child's existence, but how could she explain to Jimmy and the rest of the children that in Canada they had a half sister aged sixteen, who had been raised by someone else.

After much soul searching she decided it would be wise to keep her secret for telling at a later date.

Janet kept in touch by a weekly letter telling of all the island happenings. Maggie knew enough people on Gigha to feel it was news from home.

What she longed for was some information about Jim. Since the letter card from the Red Cross stating that he was well and the camp satisfactory, there had been no further communication.

A she sat by the fire, in the quiet of the evening, with the bairns tucked up in bed, Maggie sang to herself as she knitted jumpers and socks. Her hands were never idle during her waking hours, with cooking, cleaning and washing. She tried to give some time to each of the children by themselves. They loved to hear all the highland tales that Maggie heard as a child by the fireside at Culburnie. John McDonald had been a grand storyteller, with a handed down personal knowledge of Scotland's history. The bairns were growing so fast and starting to be independent.

Jimmy and Charlie were both doing well at school. Jim would be pleased to hear that when he got her letter.

How he would accept the fact that Charlie had taken on to 'run with milk', she could not be sure. She could just hear him. "My laddie up at five in the morning to run filling up flagons of milk, then away to school to sit sleeping all day. Never ever, I just won't have it. It's slave labour Maggie, I want something better for my sons." Maggie was sure that the novelty of the work would not last long, and then she need never tell Jim. She was surprised when Charlie told her that along with a boy from Bridge Street, he was picked for the job by the local dairyman.

"I'll get paid Mam and if you are lucky you get houses in the Latch Road or Park Road, you can get tips and presents from them at Christmas."

Charlie was a good boy, so very different to his older brother. Jimmy was always very serious about things. He had a good brain for his work in the classroom, although never showed much enthusiasm for anything that would take any effort on his part.

Jessie would be starting school after Easter. She would tell the teacher what was what. Maggie was amused by the thought of her girl sitting in class. In appearance Jessie was a most attractive child, who was blessed with a very happy nature. Everyone who passed the Southport would talk to her as she played or ran an errand to the shops. She could carry on a conversation with adults or children and be completely at ease.

"Mrs Petrie, from Bridge Street told me today that the War would soon be over and all the dads would be coming home soon, Mam."

"What made her say such a strange thing to you?" asked Maggie.

"Well she asked me to watch her baby, Lizzie while she was in the 'Soshie'. The bairn was crying all the time and when Mrs Petrie came out with her messages, I asked her if Lizzie was missing her dad and was that what was wrong with her. She said it was and I would soon have my dad home from the war as well."

Maggie tried to explain that it might be a long time before that would be true.

1917

The weeks and months went by with no real hope of the War ending. Maggie as she had promise spent all the school holidays with her aunt on Gigha. The boys were growing faster than she liked to think. Jimmy would soon be fourteen and leaving school. He had no ideas about what sort of work he would like to do. Charlie had got him started on 'the milk', with him but Jimmy just would not get up in the morning. He had tried a paper round, but was sacked for always being late. Perhaps he might get a start as a message boy, then move on to an apprenticeship as a grocer. Maggie would talk to the owners of the better class shops like Mitchell, or Adam and Smith the next time she went shopping. If it were necessary she would even approach the manager of the Co-operative Society, which was almost next door.

Charlie was a worker, he had been told by the head master at school if he maintained his progress, then he might be able to sit for a bursary to carry on with further education. That would certainly please Jim.

Would Jim be pleased with how his children had developed in over three years enforced separation from his family and home?

Certainly Jessie and the boys could vaguely remember their father, but Mary and David had no idea what the word father meant. To them it was just a name.

They were very close to each other, almost never apart. To Mary, David's word was her command. David was a sturdy little fellow with a beautiful head covered in golden curls. Both children were very like their father and his family, as was Charlie. Maggie had no recollection of what her family had looked like but she assumed that Jimmy and Jessie were more in their image. Janet might be able to comment on this.

Maggie considered Jimmy going to work and how this would be the end of the trips to Gigha. Certainly she could not leave him to cope by himself, when the rest of the family were away on holiday.

She worried about Jimmy starting out on his own as she had been around the same age when she was first sent from Culburnie croft to the 'big house'.

People talked of the good old days yet from her recollection Maggie found it difficult to remember what made them so celebrated.

Five o'clock in the morning to after ten at night running to serve every whim of the gentry, for a warm bed and your keep. Jimmy just would not have survived.

Maggie decided that she would have to be more firm with her oldest son and make him face the realities of life, whether he liked it or not.

It was just after nine o'clock when Jimmy came running up the stairs.

Maggie got up from the fireside chair where she had been sitting mending school clothes.

"What time is this to be coming in?" before he could answer her she added, "I have told you before about this. You cannot get up in the mornings. Things will have to change laddie."

Jimmy went to the wall press and took out the bread and jam. He slowly cut and spread the bread.

"Och Mam, you know fine I would be playing billiards with Ernesto. It's his table but he can't beat me yet."

Maggie put the loaf and jam back in the press.

"That's maybe so Jimmy, but he'll be up before you in the morning peeling tatties and helping in the shop before you are even turning over in your bed. In short Jimmy he's not afraid of work. What about you?"

Jimmy sat down on the fender.

"That's not fair Mam, you know I tried to get something to suit me."

"It's the life of the landed gentry you are looking for son, I'm afraid that is a life you must be born into to enjoy."

"Aye Mam, that would suit me fine."

Maggie put the kettle on the fire.

'Well Jimmy I've got news for you. You are starting a job on Monday. Your cousin Jim was here yesterday to tell me that they are needing an orra loon, where he's feed at the Mains of Edzell and he spoke up for you. Mr Craighead said he knew your father well and on his reputation as an honest hard worker he is prepared to start you without even seeing you."

Maggie had considered the offer long and hard. This might be the making of her son, away from home and in the bothy with other men. Certainly these days, on the farms there were only older men and young lads, for the young men were all away in France and Flanders. Jimmy was almost in tears.

"How will I get home at night Mam?" he asked.

"There's no chance of that son, you'll have to be like the rest and live in the bothy during the week and come home on Saturday afternoon. You bring your washing home with you and I'll have it washed clean for you going back on Sunday night."

Jimmy sat staring at the fire, the half eaten piece still in his hand. "What about the billiards Mam, I won't be able to practice."

"There's more important things than games in life son. You have to learn to support and make a future for yourself."

Near to tears Jimmy kissed her on the cheek. "I'll away to my bed then. I'll see you in the morning," was all he managed to say.

"Good night son and don't waken Charlie to chatter for he will be up at half four for the milk."

Maggie was glad to be left in the room alone. How she had hated telling her first-born son that it was time to leave the nest to fend for himself in the cruel cold world.

Carefully Maggie folded Jimmy's change of shirt and socks before placing them in the case that she had carried her belongings in those many years ago when she travelled between Glasgow and Culburnie. She slipped two bars of Highland toffee and a packet of biscuits into the neck of the shirt. When he finds them he will know that I am thinking of him, she reasoned.

Four o'clock on Sunday afternoon came all too soon for her. Jimmy had tied the suitcase to the carrier of his father's bicycle. Maggie had given him strict instructions; under no circumstances was the bicycle to be damaged in any way. The first priority, as far as he was concerned, was with the first wages he received, he would buy for himself a good second hand model.

As they stood at the end of the close waiting for her nephew Jim to appear, Maggie tried hard to make her conversation seem unemotional or stinted.

"This is a grand chance for you now son, when your dad comes home he will be so proud of you being in a job. Look well after Dad's bicycle for you know yourself how he cleaned and polished it. No letting the other lads borrow it for going into Edzell. Always be mannerable to Mr Craighead and his wife and remember your pleases and thank you' when eating in the kitchen. Don't forget to give yourself a good wash at the end of the day's work and when you get out of bed in the morning. Pay good heed to what I'm telling you. Now I want no news of you carrying on with the dairymaids or lasses from the farmhouse."

During all the time his mother had been talking, Jimmy stood with eyes downcast, watching his foot slowly nudging the pedal of the bicycle round and round.

Maggie prodded him in the small of his back.

"I hope you are taking in all that I am telling you Jimmy, for from the time you leave to go to your job you will be on your own to make the most that you can of your life. You go with all the bet wishes and blessings that any mother could give her son. Do well for yourself laddie."

Maggie was fighting hard to keep from showing that her tears were ready to burst and flow like a river.

Jimmy showed no emotion what-so-ever.

"Here's your cousin Jim coming now, so you'll get away." She kissed him quickly on the cheek. "I won't embarrass you on the street but you know fine that I just want to take you in my arms and give you a big good luck cuddle." From the pocket of her overall she took a small brown leather purse. "This was your granddad's purse and I have put a pound in it for you so that you won't be starting off in the world penniless. Take good care and spend it wisely. On you go now, I'll be waiting with a good tea ready for you on Saturday."

CHAPTER TWENTY TWO

EVENTUALLY THE CHILDREN were finally tucked up in bed, with everything peaceful and quiet. There had been a bit of arguing between them, which was instigated by Jessie. "I don't see why Charlie should have the big bed to himself now that Jimmy does not sleep here," she said. Charlie who never let things bother him answered, "That's all right then, you and Mary can sleep in the big room and I'll sleep in your bed."

This did not appeal to Jessie for it did not resolve what had been bothering her. "No Mary and I are fine where we are. I don't see why David should get to sleep with our Mam all the time. He can sleep with you."

Charlie agreed that this would be perfectly alright with him, but where would David sleep on Saturday nights when Jimmy came home?"

Jessie replied that they could think about that later, as in any case David wanted to sleep in 'the big lads bed'.

Maggie worked away listening without making any comment. Certainly Jessie would get what she wanted out of life. Mary had been primed by her to persuade David that this was what he wanted.

How would David accept that he could not sleep with her once Jim returned from the war?

She would agree to the bairns sleeping arrangements, until it proved to be a satisfactory solution.

Maybe if David had a small single bed in the big bedroom, then there would be no problem with Jimmy's bed space.

Maggie was not given long to consider whether the plan would work for in the early hours of the morning David crawled into bed beside her. With his sturdy little arms around her neck and his face pressed against her cheek, he whispered "I just love you Mam," then he fell asleep.

The week dragged on, with cold winds and dull rainy weather. Jimmy was forever in his mother's thoughts. Would he remember to put on dry clothes, if soaked when out in the fields? Would they be working him too hard? He was still just a young boy.

It was five o'clock on Saturday evening, when she had the chance to get answers to her questions. Jimmy came running up the stairs with his bundle of washing under his arm.

"Oh Mam, I'm glad to be back. I've missed my games of billiards."

"Is that all you've missed son?" she replied quite astounded.

Maggie lifted the kettle from the fire. "Well the tea is just ready. We have been waiting for you to come home before we started."

Jimmy crossed to the table and surveyed all the extras for the special tea, to mark his being established as a working man.

"Och, I thought I would just get a game while the tables were free, seeing that I haven't had one for a week. Could I not get my tea later?"

Maggie felt anger at the inconsideration of her son. "No you cannot eat later.

Take off your jacket and get sat down at the table."

She poured the tea into the cups.

"What will people think of this as a home if you can only rush in and be out again in five minutes. You will get away to your friends once we have heard how things went for you at Edzell. Then when you have eaten and hear what's been happening here in your absence, if it's not too late, then and only then can you go out for an hour or so."

One whole week without Jimmy had given her time to think about how she would tackle her oldest son's failings.

The realisation that she was mainly to blame for his lack of consideration for other than himself did not make things easier.

Maggie had only to recall the moments of warm and tender love in which her son was conceived, and of how much she had wanted him for her own child, to melt away thoughts of contradicting his wishes or commands.

Jimmy left the house just after six o'clock.

"See you, when I see you Mam."

Sunday morning allowed Jimmy to lie late in bed.

He had said very little of his first week's work experience. She parcelled up the clean and ironed washing for his afternoon departure.

It was after midday when he appeared in the living room.

"What's to eat Mam?"

Maggie pointed to a place at the table. "Just sit down there and I will see to you."

Maggie knew if he was seated at the table then she had more opportunity to question him and get some type of answers.

"What is the food like at the Mains?"

She turned the sausages sizzling in the frying pan.

"Just rubbish Mam, brose, porridge and tatties. Not like the things you make for me Mam. I don't really want to go back."

Maggie straightened up from bending over the fire, holding the frying pan.

"Let me make this quite clear to you Jimmy. Whether you like it or not, you are going back. That is that. If you don't go there to Mains of Edzell to your work, then certainly will not spend another night sleeping in this house. Do you understand?"

"But Mam it's horrible, I have to be up at five to light the fire and have the breakfast for the men coming back from seeing to the horses. Then I have to work all day in the fields, with some porridge, tatties and cheese in the farm kitchen at dinnertime. Then at lousin' time at night I have to hurry back to the bothy and light the fire and have the kettle boiled for the lads tea. I never get a minute to myself."

"Think on this son, that is what life is all about. The more effort you put into working at making life a success, then the more you will get out of it. I have worked non-stop all my life, with never a minute to myself, yet I don't feel that I am any worse for it. Come on now enjoy your breakfast and we'll have no more talk of not going back. What would your Dad say?"

Jimmy poked the sausage on his plate.

"Dad wouldn't like it either. He never stayed in the bothy did he? He always came home at night. I could get a job where I would be home at night."

Yes, thought Maggie and I would never get you out of bed in the morning. "I've told you Jimmy, no more of this nonsense, you are going to work. Your father had his reasons for not staying in the bothy and they are nothing to do with you. It looks as if the war might soon be over and just think how proud your dad will be that he is coming home to find a working man in the family he left as bairns."

"I don't think I will be home next weekend for the grieve said we will be starting the harvest and will be working from dawn to dusk until it's all in."

"You'll just have to make the best of it then son. Think there will be extra pennies to you when the crops are all in. What will you buy with them? A bike for yourself?"

"No I think I would like my own billiard cue. There's a billiard room in Edzell, just across from the muir. I could maybe play there in the evenings. I suppose I could have Dad's bike as long as he isn't using it."

Maggie was glad that he was accepting he had to go back to work and thought it best not to tell him that the bike was on loan on a temporary arrangement. "Yes I suppose it will be fine meantime."

The end of the harvest looked as if it would herald the end of the war. Newspapers were predicting that Germany could not withstand another winter in the mud and water filled trenches.

The end of October and Maggie, like other wives hoped everyday would bring the cessation of war. Would Jim have changed? What difference would he see in the bairns? How would they accept having their father home?

Eleventh of November it was all over, the War to end all Wars. The women of Brechin prepared to welcome their surviving men home in style. From cupboards and attics, bunting and flags were produced. The factory owners' wives played their part in supplying material. The town was gaily decorated over all, however, no amount of frivolous nonsense could hide the sorrow and unhappiness of those who were cruelly denied the pleasure of again meeting their loved ones.

The war did not discriminate against classes for sadly the loss of family to the so-called 'upper class', was equivalent to that of the poorest in town. It had been printed in the Brechin Advertiser that during one of the British campaigns, the loss of life to the local regiment 4/5th Black Watch, was from twenty three officers nineteen were killed or wounded, other ranks amounting to four hundred and thirty, only two hundred had survived wounding or death. These figures were only of one confrontation with the enemy, from many battles over four years of continuous fighting.

Would Jim consider himself fortunate to have been held captive for four years in Germany? What price had he paid for his enforced interment?

The first communication arrived the third week in November, in the form of a postcard informing Maggie that Jim was back at the Guards head quarters and was being discharged as being medically unfit for further military service.

"Will Dad be here for Christmas?" asked Jessie.

Maggie told her that she hoped he would be back home long before that.

Many of the families were already united with their men folk. By day the station and Park Road thronged with people eager to welcome home their triumphant warriors. In the evening families still congregated hopeful that their men had travelled on the London express to the main line station, in time to make the connection to the branch line.

Despite the cold damp weather, Maggie stood on the platform each night at eight o'clock, waiting for the local train from Montrose to arrive.

At first the bairns thought it a novelty being allowed to stay up late waiting for their father's return. By the fourth night they were reluctant to go to the station again.

"I don't want a father anyhow," said David. "We don't need one, do we Mary?"

Mary true to form answering," If you say so David it will be alright."

Jessie intervened for she vaguely remembered her father. "Don't be stupid you pair, of course we need him. He loves us and wanted all the time to be with us instead of being away in that other land with the enemy. Charlie you tell them about our dad.'

Charlie was pushing about one of the trolleys used by the porters.

"I suppose he's alright. He goes to work most of the days so we don't see much of him anyhow."

He turned to his mother, "Will he bring back his gun with him Mam?"

Maggie like the children was tired of the standing waiting.

"I'm sure I've no idea laddie. I don't care what he brings if only I could see him safe and sound right here in front of me".

"Here's the train now coming through the bridge; I hope Dad is on it," shouted Jessie from the far end of the platform.

Maggie could feel her legs starting to shake with involuntary movements.

Please God let him be on the train. Oh God, what will he be like after all those years. Will he be changed any? I hope he doesn't think I look older. Maggie's mind was bombarded with thoughts of questions and doubtful answers.

At first as he stepped down from the carriage, Jim did not recognise Jessie and Charlie, who rushed towards him shouting. "It's our very own Dad, come back."

He threw down the bag he was carrying and pulled them both close to him

"Jessie what a grand lass you have grown, and Charlie you're almost a man."

"Our Jimmy is a man now dad and works on the farm," Jessie informed him.

"Well there will be lots of things to tell me, but first I want to speak to your Mam, so you two run along in front," Jim said to them.

Maggie stood rooted to the platform, holding a child on either side, by the hand. The tears were running on her cheeks as she spoke. "Mary and David, this is your dad."

Jim bent down and kissed them both on the head.

"Dad will have to get to know you both. Won't he? You run on now and catch up with Jessie and Charlie and we will all get away home."

"I'm staying with my Mam and so is Mary," said David.

"Do as you are told David, don't be a baby, we will be right behind you," said Maggie, then she turned and looked straight at Jim.

"I've tried to picture this so often and what I would say first to you Jim. Now all that I can manage is thank God for sending you back to me safe, for I need you so."

Jim's arms folded around his wife and held her so close she felt that she was to suffocate.

"You know I'm not one for words Maggie lass and I'm sure there are none that would ever explain or tell how much I have missed you. I'll always love you," he whispered in her ear, while still holding her close in his arms.

"Oh Maggie, the thought of you waiting for me is all that kept me alive through these years of hell. Come on lass, let's catch up with the bairns and get home, we are going to be a family again.

Maggie felt relief when David, exhausted by the excitement, settled down to sleep with Charlie. As she had prepared the children for bed she watched Jim sitting by the fire smoking his pipe. He looked so thin and gaunt, his large body frame stripped of muscle. She would make sure that he was well fed and cared for until he got back to health.

"Come on sit down here on the hearth beside me," he asked her. Maggie sat down on the fender stool and rested her arms across Jim's knees.

"Well what do you think of them? Do you like what you see?" she asked.

"Aye, you've done a good job on your own with them and it pleases me that the boys aren't feared of work. I'll tell Jimmy that on Saturday when he comes home. Strange him starting in the bothy at mains of Edzell, for I was there myself as a youngster. It's the biggest arable farm in Angus, you know."

"So I believe, and according to Jimmy he works it all by himself. How about Jessie and Mary?"

"Jessie will go far, she is more like you than ever I imagined and form what I've seen this evening could chat her way to anything she ever wanted." His answer pleased her.

"Aye, I suppose you are right and I hope with us behind her then she will reach her goals in life."

"Mary, well she's a lovely little girl, quiet does not say much unless prompted by David. There's a lad for you. Made up his mind the minute I stepped off the train that nothing was to come between him and his mother."

Maggie immediately sprung to her youngest child's defence. "You've got to be fair with him, he still has to learn about you. I've tried to explain what his dad was like."

"Och Maggie, I'm not criticizing you, I'm just commenting on how the wee lad can stand up for himself. I can see that he could be a force to be reckoned with."

Jim did not appreciate how true these words were.

Chapter Twenty Three

THE EXCITEMENT FINALLY died down, the bairns were asleep in bed and Maggie and Jim sat by the fireside. "There were times, Maggie, when over the last four years I despaired of ever seeing you all again. It's just too much yet for me to take in that I'm here in front of my own fireside with you and the bairns beside me."

Maggie took his hand in hers, as she turned from sitting on the fender to look into his face.

"Thank god that it is all over Jim and we can get on with our lives again."

Jim stroked her hair. "That's not going to be easy, you know lass for I'm going to have to get a job soon. Who will want to employ me, who is labelled as being medically unfit?"

"Jim, you will soon be back to your usual self once I get a chance to feed you up a bit. That big boned frame of yours looks so empty. Plenty of good milk, meal, tatties and pork, then you'll be as right as rain."

"You sound so sure lassie, when we are back to where we were when we moved to Brechin from Glasgow. No job, no money and no prospects."

Maggie stared him in the face. "Listen to me Jim Chisholm, there are many wives and mothers in Brechin, who would be delighted to be sitting together tonight with their loved ones, just as we are now. I know that the future is not to be easy, however the main thing will be that we are facing it together. I have a few pounds put by from your army pay. We will manage away for a week or two until you are on your feet again."

Jim, for the first time since his 'home coming' laughed. "I might have known that you would have planned something lassie. If you had been in the army the war would have been over long since."

"There's on thing for sure those Germans that starved you until you are just a rickle of bones would have got what for."

Maggie lay with her head in the crook of the sleeping Jim's arm. He was so relaxed and peaceful. They had sat talking far into the night. Sometimes recalling shared memories of the past; other times relating incidents that had happened in their lives apart, which might interest the other.

Jim was anxious to see his first-born son Jimmy. "I just can't take it in Maggie, that he has started work. Though it's not what I would have thought a position with grand prospects, at least he is supporting himself. Charlie will have to stick in and win that bursary. Education is what makes the man. I never appreciated that more than when I was confined in that damned camp. Some of the lads there came from moneyed families. They had every chance in life, education the lot, yet they hadn't made the most of their chances. Then there were the men who came up through the ranks, spent their spare time reading and studying. Salt of the earth the educated working man. Jimmy could do worse than join my old regiment."

"Och Jim, he's far too young for that. In any case the war is over now and all the men will be coming home again."

"That's it Maggie, where will there be work for everybody?"

Later as she lay thinking over the conversation, Maggie knew that it would not be easy for Jim to find employment. It was years since she had left her position as a cook but if necessary, with the children all of school age, she might manage to find some type of work to help out until Jim was back to normal.

The door opened and closed quietly. David's curly head appeared at the bottom bedrail.

"What's he doing in my place Mam? I don't want to sleep in Charlie's bed. He can get out of there and go through the room with Charlie."

Maggie did not want to waken Jim; she tried hard to make her whispering voice sound angry and raised.

"Get back to your bed through the room and no more carrying on. I don't want you wakening your father up. Now go before I have to get up and give you a smack."

David started to cry. "I don't want him here in our house and neither does Mary."

Maggie moved as if to get out of bed. "I've told you what will happen if you don't get going."

David ran from the room, banging the door as he left.

"I heard all that. I think I'll have to have words with that young man and let him know that I don't allow just anyone to creep into the bed of my wife."

Maggie sighed with relief; at least Jim was taking the children's bewilderment at having a man about the house light-heartedly.

"I will have to be patient with David, for he is a very clinging laddie. He has been closer to me than the others. Perhaps I have made him that way with you being away." Jim pulled her closer to him "I want to be closest to you Maggie. After all I was the one who loved you first, before they were even thought about."

"You forget my handsome fellow that maybe what you are saying is not correct, for even when we were young your thoughts were never far from wanting to make babies!" she teased.

"Och lassie, you cannot condemn me for that. What man would be any different when married to a lovely lowland maiden, like you? You forget how old I am and now medically unfit for any kind of service. Mind you a little cuddle might do wonders for my recovery."

Jim 'lay on' in bed until Charlie and Jessie were away to the school. Maggie was busy by the sink in the window, washing up the breakfast dishes, when he eventually wakened.

"Lord what time is this for me to be lying in my bed. Half the day gone, when I could have been washed, shaved and dressed, ready to go around some of the farmers on my bicycle, looking for work."

Maggie had a sense of relief that she was facing out the window. "For goodness sake, this is your first morning home in four years; surely you don't have to rush away the first day to get a job. In any case, Jimmy has borrowed your bicycle to get to his work in Edzell," she hesitantly replied.

He swung his legs out from under the blankets and the patchwork quilt. "That's no good at all. He will have to get one of his own. Every

Tom, Dick and Harry will be on the look out for work. They will all be like me, glad to take anything in the district. I haven't changed in my ideas Maggie, that I won't take work with a tied house. Neither do I want to be away from you and the bairns in some bothy, after spending four years held captive by the Germans."

Maggie now setting the table for his breakfast replied. "Jimmy only borrowed the bike, he does mean to get one of his own, when he has saved up enough money. After all it was just sitting in the shed while you were away."

'There are lots of differences to be made now that I am back. Jimmy will better have saved enough by now to get a bicycle of his own for Saturday, for when he comes home with mine, he certainly won't be going back on it."

"Come on then eat your porridge, for your bacon and fried bread is ready. Things will sort themselves out in their own good way," she said trying to humour him.

"Don't speak to me like one of the bairns Maggie, for the only way that I am to get things right is if I am to be first around the places asking what work is going. I can't walk around the whole of Angus in less than a week, but with pedal power at my feet I'll make a damned good try."

"I've told you already Jim, I have a bit of money 'put by' and we will manage for a week or two. It's the Muckle Market feein time soon. You'll get a place then."

"Dinna be so sure o' that. The farmers have managed for the duration of the war, wi' the young lads and auld men. They'll no be keen to get rid o' them on lower wages and pay the full entitlement to a man who has been away from the land for four years."

"Well this being Friday, we will see what Jimmy has to say tomorrow when he comes home. At least you have the weekend without work worrying you. I'll away across to Websters' and get a paper for you to see if there is anything in it to interest you. Mary and David are playing at the door, so keep an eye on them for a minute."

Jim sat at the table finishing his cup of tea. Certainly he enjoyed his breakfast, and Maggie was right in that with her cooking she would soon get the weight he had lost back. Mary and David appeared at the table and curiously eyed their father.

"Are you having your dinner Dad?" asked Mary. "Mam never told us it was ready."

"No, Mary, I am just at my breakfast, but you can have a piece with jam if you are hungry. Do you want me to spread it for you?"

"Yes please Dad," said Mary, who could never think of refusing food of any description. "David will take a piece as well, won't you?"

David moved away from the table. "No I don't want one. Where has my Mam gone?" he asked looking his father straight in the face.

"Your Mam has just gone out for a minute to get a paper son, I'm sure you'll manage until she gets back won't you?"

"I don't like it when she goes away from me, but I'll manage to watch Mary for her."

"You won't have to worry about being looked after when Ma's away to the shops David, for I'm here now and as I'm your dad I look after you all, Mam as well. I'll keep you all safe from any harm."

Mary sat down by the fire eating her bread uninterested in what conversation was going on between her father and younger brother.

"If you are going to stay here then do you think you could make a cartie for me? Charlie said he would but I've never got one yet."

Jim was quick to catch on this was his opportunity to perhaps impress and be accepted by his youngest son.

"Oh I think that maybe if we got some wheels and wood I could manage something. You would have to help me make it. Would you manage that?" David's eyes lit up with excitement,

"Oh I'd easy manage and Mary will help to look on the 'backie braes' amongst the rubbish for wheels. Come on Mary, we'll have to get wood and wheels for our dad."

Maggie was almost knocked over by the pair of them as they rushed past her on the stairs. "Where are you two rushing off too?" she shouted after them.

"Our dad is needing wood and wheels to make a cartie and Mary and me are away to the 'backies' to look for some for him," shouted David before banging the door shut.

"Well you certainly didn't take long to find work, did you?" she said as she entered the room.

"What are you speaking about?" Jim asked.

"I've never seen David so excited in his life. He tells me that 'his' dad is needing wheels and wood to make a cartie. Surely you don't mean to go seeking work on that?" she joked.

"Come here and I'll show you the kind of jobs I like best Maggie. I feel so pleased that I've managed to get Mary and David to call me 'our dad'. Only Jimmy to see again and I'm beginning to feel that my life is to start again after a four year pause."

Saturday teatime was the first time ever that the complete Chisholm family had sat down together at the table to eat. Maggie was in high spirits, for that morning she had the added bonus of a letter from New Zealand to tell her that her brother David was to be married.

"This is just like a party," said Jessie "Everybody happy and laughing together. That's because you are home dad. We have all waited so long for you to be here with us."

"Jessie you have no idea how long I have waited and wanted to be here with you all. What's more I cannot let this occasion go without saying that your mother has done a grand job of bringing you up when I could not be here. You are a family to be proud of with my grateful thanks to your mother."

CHAPTER TWENTY FOUR

THE MUCKLE MARKET brought with it nothing but disappointment, for Jim could not find any work in the near locality, to where he could commute each day. Jimmy was not taken on again at the Mains of Edzell he could not manage to get any other farmer to offer him a fee.

Jim was full of despair. "God knows where we go from here? I might try tomorrow and see if I can get a few days at the beating on Southesk or across at the castle. The 'nobs' will be out in force for their shooting before Christmas. They'll no doubt be needing folk to scare the birds on to the muzzles of their guns. Jimmy you can come with me, for two wages are better than one."

"Oh Dad, do I have to go? I don't want to go trailing the woods all day shouting and raising the pheasants. I might get shot."

"For God's sake Jimmy don't be such a whine. You are coming and not lying in your bed all day waiting for your mother to arrange work for you. It's time for you to act as a man. I know it's not easy but if you show eager to give a good days work in return for pay, then it doesn't matter how lowly the task is. How do you think you could manage to make your way in the world without earning your keep?"

Jimmy did not enjoy his father talking to him in this manner, for his mother as a rule seldom criticised her oldest son. "Well I could always be a professional billiard player, they make a lot of money, and there's nobody in Brechin that can beat me."

Jim jumped up to his feet. "I don't want to hear more of this bloody stupid talk about you spending your time playing games in those dens for ruffians. Do you hear me Jimmy?"

Maggie feared for her son, as Jim grabbed him by the shoulders and shook him.

"You'll save your energy for paid employment of an honest means. Little wonder you lost your job at the Mains, for the grieve told me you were out until all the hours at the billiard saloon in Edzell, then you wouldn't get out of your bed for yoking time in the morning. That's no damned good in any man. I will not stand for laziness in a son of mine. Do you understand?"

Jimmy's face was ashen; his lip trembled as he tried to reply.

"Don't stand there blubbering like a lassie. Do you hear what I'm saying? If you do answer me." Jim shook his son again.

Maggie rushed forward to grab her son from any further bodily harm his father could inflict on him.

"Don't interfere Maggie, this is business between me and my son. That is if he wants to stay part of this family, he will have to accept that he earns his keep and the privilege to remain part of the family."

"Oh come on Jim, you are not in the army now speaking to one of the young recruits, this is our son Jimmy."

Maggie could see Jim was rapidly losing his temper with her. "I'm well aware of who he is, unless he changes his ways and acts like a Chisholm, who were never afraid of work, then he will have to face the consequences. Do you understand laddie?"

Jimmy who was still held by the shoulder at arms length by his father, managed to whisper, "Yes Dad I do."

Jim released his son from his grip. "That's all right then, as long as we understand each other. Just remember that I am head of this house and you answer to me. Not to your mother, who has been far too damned soft with you."

Maggie knew better than to voice any opinion while Jim's temper was raised. She busied herself putting coals on the fire then washing her hands in silence.

Jim took down his jacket and bonnet from the hook on the back of the door. "I'm away," he said.

Maggie ran to the top of the stairs. "Where are you going Jim? When will you be back? Will I keep your tea for you?"

"You'll see me when you see me and not before it," he shouted back up the stairs before closing the outside door.

Jimmy came through from the room. He was crying. "I'm sorry Mam. I didn't do anything to upset Dad. It was him that picked on me."

"Stop your snivelling. Your father spoke a great deal of sense. I just hope you take notice of what he told you. Take a leaf out of Charlie's book and work harder."

"What book of Charlie's do you mean Mam? You are always telling us not to destroy or tear pages from books. Nobody in this house can make up their mind about anything. I'm away out."

Maggie pulled him back from the top of the stairs. "You are not going to play billiards, for I am not to face your father when he comes back and knows you have defied him. Get a rag and clean up that bicycle. At least make some attempt to please your dad."

"I'm sorry that he ever came back," he snarled as he turned to go back in to the room. "I hope he gets a job at the beating and someone finishes the job the Germans couldn't do by shooting him."

Not only was Jimmy surprised by the force of the open handed blow to his face, but Maggie was shaken by her own reaction. "Don't ever let me hear you say anything ever again wishing harm to another person, least of all your own father. Do you understand?"

Jimmy nodded and went back into the room totally dejected. Now his father had turned his mother against him. What would he do? If only he could have gone back to the bothy in Edzell. He decided that he could go out and see if one of his friends in Bridge Street could get work for him at the woodcutting. They were away all the week living in a bothy. That would mean he would only have to suffer his father on Saturday evenings.

The ten o'clock bells rang long before Maggie heard Jim's step on the stair. He took off his bonnet and jacket hanging them up before he spoke "I'm sorry lassie if I upset you earlier, but I will not take back what I said to Jimmy."

Maggie poured water from the boiling kettle into the teapot before replying. "I know what you said was right Jim, but I don't want you to make an enemy of your own son. Where have you been all evening?"

"Well I just had to get out to cool down, before in my anger I did something that I would regret. I walked out to my sister Bella's. In a way it was maybe meant for I managed to get a fee at the same place as her man.'

"Oh Jim that is really grand, you will mange to bike back and forwards and we will all be fine together."

"Maybe so Maggie. I am not having Jimmy hanging about here idle living off us. He has to learn what life is all about."

She was quick to agree with him. "No one knows that better than him, for he was out tonight asking one of his friends to get a start for him at the wood cutting with Black's at one of their sawmills.'

Jim sat down and unlaced his boots. "I hope it works out for him. I'm pleased to hear that he did something on his own for once. You cannot keep him tied to your apron strings forever you know."

"I'm aware of that Jim, it's just that I can remember so well having no young life through having to work every hour that God gave us. I want better for our children."

"That's no different to what I as their father want for them. They'll never stand on their own two feet if you keep doing things for them. Let them suffer a little to let them appreciate the good things in life. Let them make their own decisions."

"Well Jimmy got out the dusters and cleaned your bicycle for you without any prompting. It will be fine for you on Monday morning."

Maggie knew in her heart that this was not strictly true. She wanted Jimmy to win back favour with his father. "When will he know about this work he is after?" Maggie handed him his covered plate from the fireside oven. "I hope that it is not too dried up, I wasn't sure when you would be back," she fussed over the cutting of bread, spreading it with butter, before answering the question.

"Well tomorrow afternoon if he can borrow your bicycle for a couple of hours, he will go out to the sawmill and find out what the situation is. His friend is going with him. If Jimmy is to get a start then he will come back for his things and he will get a hurl on the bar of the other laddie's bicycle back to the bothy."

"That is no use at all. If he gets work then his first wages will have to go towards getting transport for himself."

Maggie sat quietly knitting, while Jim ate the dried up meal. Eventually she broke the silence. "With you getting work Jim, I still have the extra money laid past for an emergency. Maybe I could use some of it to get a good second-hand bicycle for Jimmy."

Jim rose from the table and crossed over to his high backed wooden fireside chair. "You will do nothing of the kind. What money he has earned already was squandered away in that billiard saloon. I've tried to tell you let him work it out for himself. By the time he's sat on the bar of a bicycle for two hours his arse will give him a message that it's not a suitable way to travel."

That was how it was; when Jimmy left on Sunday evening it was across the bar of his pals bicycle. By Christmas it seemed as if Jim had never been away, in fact on the evenings he arrived home wet, tired and bad tempered after a day's toil in the fields, Maggie found herself wondering why she had so desperately longed to have him home.

Jim noticed that she was not her usual bright cheerful self. One evening after she had scolded David for annoying the girls he could see she was near to tears. "Are you feeling well enough Maggie? For you look awful tired and harassed these past few nights, when I've got home."

"I suppose I do feel a bit off colour, then at my time of life it's just to be expected."

Jim nodded, "Aye lassie age is beginning to tell on all of us. You'll be forty-two 'n I've just had my forty-sixth birthday. Never mind you are just as old as you feel. I think we have a cart load of trouble to cause in our time yet."

"I hope we get long enough to know our grandchildren anyhow, do you not?"

"I suppose I do. I've never really thought much about it to tell the truth. I haven't even wondered what a grandfather is supposed to mean."

"I have thought about it a great amount lately, after all even although we never speak about it my daughter Margaret is old enough now to be married and have a family of her own." Jim grabbed her around the waist and sat her down on his knee.

"So that's what's been at the back of the dismal face. You are frightened of being a granny."

"Nothing of the kind, I'm just a bit off colour. In any case how could I be worried about being a granny, when I've never even really known one? Your father is the only grandfather I've ever had any dealings with, he was a grand old man."

"You are right there Maggie, I never appreciated what a great old man he was until it was too late to talk to him about it. Och this conversation is getting too morbid, come on away to bed with me my bonnie lass, and I'll let you see how young you are, and what a good account an 'old man' can still give of himself at loving and pleasing you."

Maggie put her arms around him and kissed him on the cheek. "You, Jim Chisholm, always have one thing on your mind and it never varies."

Jim returned her kiss. "Maggie be glad of that for I'm not the one for sweet fancy talking, nor do I suppose I have told you this in many years, but I love you more now than when we first met all those years ago."

Later, as Maggie lay in bed beside her husband Jim, she knew that there was a magnetic attraction to this man, the father of her children. She knew over these long four years why she had longed for him to be back beside her.

In the darkness of the room she could feel her cheeks redden at the thoughts of why and how he could bring pleasure and satisfaction to her life. She slipped her arm from beneath his head. The movement caused him to stir and moan softly. Maggie kissed him on the ear then whispered softly, I'll always love and need you Jim Chisholm, until the end of time."

CHAPTER TWENTY FIVE

THE SPRING SUNSHINE brought a quick thaw, which heralded a disaster for Brechin's factory workers, living in the lower areas of the town. The weather had been severe, with snow lying on the ground for many weeks. The sudden freshening winds on the glen hills melted the deep drifts and swelled the burns feeding the river, causing serious flooding all along the banks of the Southesk.

Before it entered its winding way past the ancient castle of Brechin, the Southesk as it had done for centuries, spread its waters over the lands bordering its passage to the sea at Montrose.

Farmers faced the loss of livestock and crops washed away in the floodwater.

Within the city of Brechin, manufacturers mourned the loss of machinery and materials soaked by the river in spate.

Householders from River Street and the low lying parts of the town were stunned at the destruction of their homes, that they had strived so hard to fashion into warm refuges from the noise of the weaving sheds, being turned into waist high filled water tanks.

Perhaps it was fortunate that the Chisholm household sat high above the reaches of the swollen river, for spring brought another swelling and indication that changes in their life style was predictable.

Maggie had accepted that her fertile years were ended and that her listlessness was due to the changes taking place within her body.

With no close friend to advise or discuss her problem with, Maggie tried to carry on with her daily routine as normal. She felt so tired and lacking in energy, with most days never seeming to be able to finish her routine household tasks. The dragging feeling in her back become greater each day that passed. Her clothes became tighter at the waist each morning when she dressed.

Maggie was certain that a tumour in her 'belly' would take her from her family before the year had ended. How long she could keep this secret from her family was on her mind every wakened hour. How will Jim cope with the bairns? This was one of the foremost questions she asked herself. Perhaps he will get another wife? Would she accept another woman's bairns and be good to them?

It was mid afternoon, the sun shone outside on the busy streets. Maggie could hear the chatter through the open window as people went about the town on their business, She lay on Charlie's bed resting, for the heat and this thing in her belly had sapped all the strength from her swollen legs. Things were just going good too, before this struck her down. Jim was almost back to his former physical fitness. Jimmy was managing to hold down his job at the woodcutting. Charlie was promised a step up in life, if he managed to pass the school bursary exam.

Jessie, Mary and David were all settled at school and seemed to accept that their father was the one who made the rules.

"Oh God," she said aloud, "How could you do this to me, when things are going in my favour. I've never been a bad person to deserve this punishment. I haven't attended church, nor have I had my bairns baptised but surely this punishment is too drastic for things I've done in my lifetime. You left me without parents or family as a child. I ask you God please do not leave my bairns without their mother."

Maggie was still asleep on Charlie's bed when Jessie found her. "What's wrong with you Mam? Are you feeling unwell? We were looking for you when we came in from school." Maggie was startled and ashamed that she had been found out sleeping in the afternoon.

"Oh dear, I must have nodded off. I had a bit of a sore head with the heat and just lay down in the quiet for half an hour. I'll get up and get your tea ready in a minute."

Jessie tucked the covers up around her mother. "Just stay there where you are, I'll bring you a cup of tea. You don't look well Mam, your face is all 'puffy' looking, Charlie will be here in a minute or two and he'll know what to do."

"What a fuss you are making," she told Charlie. "I'm perfectly able to get up and make Dad's supper myself. My head is better now."

Charlie handed her the third cup of tea he had brewed for her since getting home from school. "Look Mam, don't argue, stay where you are and rest until Dad gets in. He's the boss you know and will see that you are not able to get up yet. By tomorrow, if you stay where you are, then you will likely be better.

Maggie was not fit to get up the next morning and was somehow relieved to know that Jim was now aware of her problems.

"I'm not going to work today until I've heard what the doctor has to say," he told her.

"You can't just stay off. I'll be fine and you'll hear what news there is at night when you get home."

"Maggie, I'm not leaving you until the doctor's been. What on earth possessed you to keep this to yourself for weeks? I'm your man. I care about you and have the right to know. There's little work anyhow with the fields flooded, so stop worrying."

It was late afternoon and the doctor had not visited. Jim had given the bairns their dinner and sent them back to school. Maggie lay in bed watching him at the sink washing up the soup plates. He looked so awkward, with his big hands rinsing the plates in the basin.

"This will be fine practice for you when you have to manage on your own," she told him.

"Will you stop that nonsense at once Maggie. I don't want to hear another word like that out of you. Whatever this is we will face it together. You've been a fighter all your days and I don't want that defeatist talk now."

Jessie, Mary and David were met at the door by their father. "You'll better stay outside here a while, for the doctor is with your mam. I'll tell you when he has gone. Behave yourselves," he said as he disappeared back up the stairs again.

When he entered the room Maggie was sitting up on the bed. The doctor was sat on the edge of the bed beside her, holding her hand. Jim could not understand what was going on for the doctor was laughing. "Come away in Jim and let me congratulate you."

Jim thought the man has gone stark raving mad. I'll throw him out before he does Maggie any harm. "What in Hell's name are you on about man? Congratulate me and my wife ill. You'd better explain yourself."

"Jim, its easy to explain. Your wife is pregnant. You are to have another baby. Like many other women with men who have returned from the war. This is to be the year of the new baby boom."

"But she can't be expecting, she's past 'the change'."

"I'm pleased to tell you she is and you'll have proof yourself about October, when it puts in an appearance. Maybe you are at the change Maggie, but nature plays this trick on women and catches them out when they least expect it."

Jim sat down on the fireside chair; tears were streaming down his weatherbeaten cheeks. "Thank you so much for your news doctor. I'm sorry if I was a bit sharp with you. Maggie and I were convinced it was something sinister she had growing inside her."

The doctor got up from the bed and shook Jim's hand. "I know that man, for Maggie had told me. Congratulations, but in saying that I still want you to understand she'll still need good care."

He turned to Maggie. "You're not exactly to be a young mother are you Maggie? With care though everything will be fine. Stay in bed for a day or two resting. I think the worry of your imagination running riot being removed, you'll feel better and more able to cope. Bye Jim, I'll let myself out."

Jim crossed from the fireside to the bed and took Maggie into his arms. "Maggie I was so feared that I was going to lose you."

They held each other close for a few moments, without speaking. Jim pulled himself away from her and laughed. "Remember you silly bitch how we spoke about you wanting to be a granny. Never for a minute did we think you would be a mother again."

"Aye Jim, it'll take a bit of getting used too. What will the bairns say?"

"Well I can remember when Charlie wanted a dog instead of a bairn. Do you think he'll have changed his mind this time?"

"Probably not. The one whose nose will be 'out of joint' will be David, for he's been the bairn of the house for so long."

'Well lassie, he'll just have to accept that changes happen. Just the same as he had to learn that he could not sleep with you for the rest of his life with you."

Maggie took his work-roughened hand and squeezed it. "Maybe if he and you had slept with Charlie this would not have happened."

"Do you wish or believe that Maggie?"

"Of course not Jim. I was only trying to pull your leg a bit. We've had enough serious talk in this house over the past twenty-four hours to last for years. Go on get the bairns in until we tell them the good news that they are getting a bairn to join them."

The noise of clattering feet and jostling to be first up the stairs made Maggie realise how worried her bairns had been.

"Are you feeling better Mam?" said Mary, who had managed to keep the others behind her until she reached the door first.

"Yes, the doctor says I'm going to be fine soon. You are to get a little brother or a sister about the end of the year."

"I thought as much," said Charlie. "Every time you have the doctor Mam, then that's what happens."

"Well I'm glad you will be prepared for it, for I'll need a lot of help. I'm not going to be able to run about behind you lot, as much as I have been in the habit of doing."

Jessie run forward and turned the sheet evenly over the edge of the blanket. "Och mam, I'll be able to look after it every single day for you. I'll even stay off the school on washing days, to let you out to the washhouse. That's what some of the girls in Bridge Street do to help their mams.'"

"We will have to think about that one," said Jim who was trying to get the fire stirred up enough to heat the kettle. "What do you think about the baby in the house David? You are very quiet, saying nothing."

David looked at his father, and then walked across to the bedside. Slowly he climbed up beside Maggie. "You'll not want me for your bairn any more then Mam, will you? If you are getting a new bairn."

Maggie pulled her youngest child into her arms, close up to her chest. "Well David, you aren't a bairn any longer, you're a big laddie now and I'm so pleased with you and how you have turned out I thought we might be lucky enough to get another bairn, almost as good."

Jessie was setting the tea things on the table. "We want a girl, don't we Mary, and after all there are enough boys here now."

Jim intervened before a row broke out. "That's something we will have to wait and see. Come on now and behave yourselves."

"David, you get off that bed and act as the big lad your mother says you are."

"Who will tell Jimmy about the baby?" said Charlie.

"Oh he will find out soon enough. After all it won't be here for a good few months anyway. We will have to get clothes and everything ready."

'Where will the bairn sleep Mam, will it get in bedside you like I did before I was big?" asked David.

Jim started to pour out tea into an odd assortment of cups set out on the table.

"Come on and get your tea just now, and forget about questions for a while. Get some jam from the press Jessie and we will put it on scones that are left from Mams baking yesterday. Cheese bannocks, scones and home made jam, you lot don't know how lucky you are with your mam being so good a baker."

He looked across at Maggie sitting up in their brass-ended bed, winked to her then laughed, "She's so damned clever that she didn't even know that there was a bun in the oven."

CHAPTER TWENTY SIX

MAGGIE FOUND THAT the warm summer weather trauchled her more each day that passed. Her swollen ankles and feet kept her in the house, depriving her of a walk in the fresh air. "I hope that this bairn appreciates what I'm going through to bring it into the world," she told Jim as they sat at the table, after their evening meal.

"Well I know one thing for sure the lassies are certainly looking forward to its coming. I've never known Jessie to be so excited about anything for a long time," said Jim.

"Charlie and Jimmy don't really like to talk about it. Do you think that they are maybe a wee bit ashamed that a couple of our age should still be adding to our family?"

"Lord Maggie, you do speak rubbish at times, why on earth should they feel that?"

"You of all people should have the answer to that Jim. When men are working together is that not the sort of thing they talk about? Jimmy is working all day with men, who are living away from home, some from their wives, which makes me imagine what the conversation will be. You know what it was like in the army, for you've told me before how the gossiping was all about 'bedding women'."

"Aye if Jimmy lives up to the Chisholm standards then I've no doubt he'll have tried it himself."

"Jim Chisholm, don't even think of such a thing. What's more I believe that you would be pleased to hear that he had."

"Maggie it's a natural thing in life. What would you say if our boys were different from all other men and never fancied a woman?

That would worry you just as much as the thought of them lying down wi' some farm lassie or a kitchen maid."

"Was that what you did when you were their age?"

"Does it matter to you now, where I got my experience? There's one thing for certain I've never had an eye for any other since I met you Maggie Chalmers at John McLeod's wedding."

"It's years since anyone called me Maggie Chalmers. Sounds so strange. I've been Maggie Chisholm for so long now, it's difficult to remember anything else. What are we to call this new bairn if it's a girl?"

Jim scratched his head, "Well maybe if we asked Jimmy and Charlie, or the whole lot of them it might make them feel more as if it was really their bairn."

"That's a fine idea, but I'm asking what you would want to call the bairn."

"It does not really bother me much lassie, whatever you think would be right, then I won't mind. Had you anything that you fancied?"

"It's all so long ago now, but I thought maybe we could name it after John or Annie McDonald, who brought me up. They were fine folk and it might be lucky to use their names."

"I suppose that's as good an idea as any. Remember how we named one of the twins after Donald McDonald, and to please Bridie McMahon we called the other George after the doctor"

"Poor wee mites, they never had much luck, did they?" Maggie struggled to her feet to fetch the teapot from the fireside. She filled her cup. 'Do you want a drop more tea?" she asked before continuing the conversation.

"I suppose if it wasn't so Irish Bridget is a fine name for a girl."

Jim held out his cup for filling, "My father would never have been happy with a papish name like that. You know yourself how he was such a kirkman, and when I was young he was very involved with the freemasons at Tarfside. No I dinna think Bridget is a good choice, although I liked Bridie, she was a grand person."

"Och well then we will settle for John or Annie, and that's it."

John Chisholm was born on the fifteenth of October, on a bright autumn morning. Jim left Maggie and his new son in the care of the children, supervised by a kindly neighbour Lizzie Wishart. There was work to be done lifting the tatties, and Jim could ill afford to lose his wages.

"You'll be fine with Charlie and Jessie to fetch anything you need. Mary will play with David. Mrs Wishart will see that they get the broth I've left for them. I'll be home at night just as quick as I can lass. Now you just rest as much as you can, while the bairn is sleeping."

There was not much rest for Maggie. Jessie and Charlie bickered constantly about who would stay in the house. Eventually Maggie told Jessie to go out and play with her friends. At least Charlie could not argue with himself. No sooner had Maggie closed her eyes and put her head back on the pillows, when Jessie appeared back in the room. "Can my pals see our new bairn Mam?"

Maggie opened her eyes to find the bed surrounded by girls of varying ages and height. They did however, all appear to have one common factor, noses which were glazed with green trailing snotters on to their upper lips.

"Just stand well back from the cradle and have a quick look at him. Bairns as wee as John need lots of sleep to make them grow, so don't waken him. Once you've seen him then off you go again out to play in the sunshine for a wee while. It will do you all good."

When Jim returned at night Maggie was laughing as she related the day's events to him. "There they were, hanging over the cradle. I was frightened that John would catch something off them."

"They have to be hardy bairns these days, with all those fatherless ones now, in the town. Nothing much for the mothers to feed and clothe them. Some of the Bridge Street women were out lifting the tatties today. I suppose they had to leave the bairns on their own, until night."

"Some neighbours or old granny would be keeping an eye on them I'm sure. It's the same at the berry picking time. Mind you the bigger bairns go with the mothers to the rasp fields."

"We will maybe get some of ours at the berries next summer. It would always help to buy something for them to wear at school," Maggie tutted.

"Well if they fight and argue on the field as much as they have done today, they won't have time to make much money. We'll see what next summer brings, it's a long way off yet."

David did not adjust well to being the second youngest in the family. He was still not recovered from the separation from his mother, to attend school, when his brother John made his appearance. "Why can't I just stay at home with you Mam? I don't want to walk all that way up to Bank Street just to listen to that teacher wifie. I'd rather be here with you."

Maggie lifted him up onto her knee. She knew that the holiday break from lessons had unsettled him. "You know fine that all big laddie's have to go to learn and read."

"But Mary could tell me what the teacher says, when she comes home in the afternoon."

"That might work I suppose, but you wouldn't like your friends to think that you were a mammie's boy and had to stay here with me. Now would you?"

David sat quiet considering what had been said. "I wouldn't care what anybody said to me about being here with you Mam, for I love you most of all in the whole world. If you want me to go to school though I'll go just to please you."

"It's for you own good, and Dad and I will be so proud of you when you are top of the class."

"Will you be as pleased with me, as you are with John?"

At last Maggie had got to the seat of the trouble. "Of course we are pleased with you. We never stopped loving you, in fact that's why we got John, we were so pleased with you, we hoped that he would turn out the same. You do like him don't you?"

"Well I suppose so, but I never get on your knee now, and I have to sleep with Charlie. Mary likes him and I'm frightened she might let him take my place in her games, just as you let Dad sleep with you instead of me."

Poor David, he was so mixed up with his feelings, and felt as though his family were pushing him out. Maggie put her arms around him and squeezed him close to her chest. She could feel his heart pounding as she gripped him tightly. "Oh son, there's no one could take your place in my heart. You each have a little part of me that is special for each of you alone. Mam loves you all because you are part of her and anything that hurts or harms you she feels the pain with you. There's that same little bit of me in each of you linking you together, along with a special part of Dad that makes him protect and love you. Now do you understand? With all our little bits of us the same we belong together as a complete family."

"I suppose so, I'd better away and see what Mary is doing with my cartie. She thinks she is a horse and wants to go round to Wordie's yard at the station to see if we could get a load of coals."

After his first day back at school, Charlie came running up the stairs ahead of the others. He was out of breath by the time he reached his mother's side as she stood by the fire stirring the contents of a pot. "Mam the headmaster has given me a note for you and Dad. He wants to see you both," he gasped.

"What trouble have you got into at school son?" said Maggie putting the lid back on the pot and out stretching her hand for the envelope that Charlie had retrieved from his trouser pocket.

"Honest Mam, I've done nothing wrong. He sent for me to come to his room and told me that as I was unable to 'stay on' at school he wanted to see Dad and you about a job he thought might be arranged for me, that would give me a good start in life."

Maggie read the note in silence. "He wants Dad and myself to see him at his home one evening, when we can manage to discuss your future work prospects. Oh Charlie it all sounds so grand. What will Dad say about it all? He was so disappointed when despite the bursary we knew we could not afford to let you stay on at school."

Charlie put his arms around his mother's neck, and then kissed her on the cheek. "Look mam, I don't mind a bit, for I have never been friends with all those 'toffee noses' that are staying on, anyhow."

"That's not the point son, your father wants you to have the education that he never had. You work hard, and we have no doubt that you'll succeed in what ever you try. We just didn't have the money for all the extras to give you the same as the others in your class. It would have meant that your brothers and sisters would have gone without for your education. I hope you understand."

"Mam it doesn't bother me about the bursary and staying on at school, but if you and dad going to see the headmaster means I'm to get offered a good job, then please talk dad into going. Will you?"

"Of course we will son. We want the best for you. I wonder what sort of job it will be. Did he say anything at all about it?"

"No Mam, just what I've told you and that he gave me the letter."

It was arranged that Maggie and Jim would visit the headmaster's home on the following Friday at seven o'clock. This would give Maggie time to have the younger children in bed and Jim time to wash and shave after his supper.

As they walked up the High Street, with Maggie linked on to Jim's arm he commented, "We are as if we were away to the theatre or something. In fact it's the first time in years we have gone out together of an evening all spruced up in our best."

"That's very true Jim. Remember when we were first married in Glasgow and you would take me out to the theatre and the music hall shows?"

"Aye we enjoyed life then. Nothing like that now. We canna' even manage to give our bairns the learning they deserve."

"Come on now Jim that's not true. We do the best we can for them. No father could work harder to provide for them."

"Well there's something wrong somewhere in a country where every child cannot have an equal opportunity in life because of status."

"I hope you are not to be in this frame of mind when we reach the dominies house in Gallowhill, for he is obviously thinking about our Charlie's status and ability in life, before he wants to discuss the prospects of a job for him."

"Aye I suppose I'd better wait and see what he has to say before I get on my 'high horse'. Like you I just want what is best for the laddie."

The eight o'clock bells were sounding as the pair hurried down the High Street again. "Can you imagine Charlie a bank manager Jim? I've never been in a bank in my life. They seem out of our world and if he wants it there's a job for our son to work there everyday."

"Yes I must admit that teacher mannie seems to have a great interest in our lad.

There would be very little wages for the first few years, but unlike the school there would be no expenses either. Charlie could work his way through the banking world like serving an apprenticeship. Sounds Good."

"So did what he had to say about our Charlie. Hard working, honest, trustworthy, always ready to help others and most of al a good sense of humour. Yes Jim Chisholm, missing the theatre and Glasgow has done us no harm"

"It has certainly done our family good for we have something to be proud of about the way they are facing up to life."

Chapter Twenty Seven

"I HOPE THAT I'M lucky today at the Muckle Market Maggie, for there are so many farmers who are 'scraping hell for a ha'penny.'"

"Why should that be Jim? We were the ones that won the war, but we're no better off. In Davy's letter he was saying how all the men who went back to New Zealand after the fighting ended, were greeted like heroes and given gratuities and land grants."

"Aye that's maybe so, but things are getting so bad that the farmers are asking the men to take a cut in their wages so that they can keep their jobs."

"That's awful. Will you have to work for less money?"

"No not if I can help it. Of course if I don't get an offer of a place at what I'm earning now, then I might be forced to think again. We're over a barrel, and they know that damned fine."

"I never knew that things were so desperate Jim, although I can see by prices in the shops the cost of everything is going up. I'm glad of the tatties, neeps, meal and milk we get. Keeps the pot filled."

"Och things should work out. Jimmy seems to have settled down and made up his mind that he has to work. I'm not so happy though about Charlie keeping on that milk job in the morning before he goes to the bank. I know to my cost the consequences of having two jobs and the employers finding out."

"We will just have to let him be until after Christmas. The laddie does not want to lose all the tips and little gifts he gets. The milk money will help him to buy a new shirt and tie, for he can't go on wearing his school clothes to the bank."

Maggie was so proud of Charlie's success in being a 'white collar' worker, she blocked from her mind that it was a problem to meet the 'job requirements'.

The English kirk jumble sale had been the means of acquiring a dark coloured suit, and a pair of smart black leather shoes. Most of the so called 'better class' in Brechin worshipped at St Andrews Kirk and gave freely of their surplus goods for purchase by the poor. The suit, Maggie had washed and pressed so as to rid it of 'anything' of the previous owner. She was not so happy about the shoes, for she could remember how Annie McDonald said that "the bad and ills in folk came out through the sweat of their feet."

Who had owned the shoes prior to the sale had her puzzled. Had it been someone who had died of an infectious disease, or been killed in the war? The shoes had been scoured on the inside with carbolic soap, then stuffed with paper and dried before the fire. She could not be over cautious with the health of her banker son.

John was a good baby sleeping almost day and night. Jessie could not give him enough attention during the short intervals he was awake.

"Do you think he knows me yet, Mam?," she asked while sitting by the fire cradling the infant in her arms.

"I'm sure he must, for the little one has spent more time in your arms in his short life than anywhere else."

"I just want him to know how much I love him Mam."

"Oh Jessie I'm sure you'll both have a long lifetime for you to convince John of that."

"What are you keeping running looking out the window for mam? You've been at it about a hundred times."

"I'm anxious to see if Dad is coming back yet for his tea. He has been away to the feein since nine o'clock this morning. I thought he would have been back long before now."

"He'll have met some of his cronies that he's worked with and be having a fine news about old times. You won't see him coming in the dark anyhow."

What Jessie did not know was that Maggie feared that her husband had not managed to find 'a place' or that he was 'newsing' with friends in one of the many bars.

"What you say lassie is probably right. I'd be better occupied rattling down the pullover I bought at the jumble and get on with knitting school jumpers for Mary and you."

The eight o'clock curfew had rung and the children were all in bed when she heard Jim's feet on the stairs. It seemed an eternity before he reached the door of the living room. "Well Maggie my lass. That's me fixed up for another six months. I feel quite pleased with myself, for there's no many today that have been able to drive a bargain with wages the same."

"I'm so relieved things have worked out well Jim. Will you still be able to stay at home at night?"

Maggie could see that Jim had celebrated his success. "Was it a good feein bargain then?" she asked, frightened to mention that he had been drinking.

"Oh just the usual arrals, meal and tatties," he hesitated as if to say something more, then sat down on the chair to untie his boots. "You'll be needing your tea, with nothing to eat all day. Come on sit across at the table and I'll get you something from the oven."

Jim grabbed her hand as she moved past to the fire. "Maggie I've been hanging about since three o'clock. I was wanting to come home but was so ashamed, that I couldn't face you."

"Why ever not Jim? You knew that I would be anxious waiting to hear your news."

"Well I spent the fee money in the pub. I was so delighted at getting 'fixed up' when Unthank asked me for a dram, I could see no harm in it. Well time went on and I had a pie and a few more drams with the lads. We were just talking about Flanders and the war. Before long it was half past two and one half crown gone. I spent the other one trying to pluck up courage and get over my guilt before facing you and the bairns."

Maggie put her arms around his neck. "I'm not to say that we could not have done with the money Jim, but what's gone can't be helped. It would have been worse if you never got a job. There would have been no five shillings nor six months wages. I don't grudge you your freedom and time with other men for you work hard every other day of the year. Come on now sit over for your supper."

As the days went past Maggie thought often of how she would have spent those five shillings. In her heart what she had said to

Jim was true that she did not begrudge him a little time to himself. However, it wrangled in her mind that she should be wrangling at jumble sales and remaking other peoples cast off clothing to send their family out clean, neat and tidy, when Jim could selfishly spend five shillings on his own pleasure.

The Christmas envelope from New Zealand had the usual 'penny for the bairns', along with a long letter. It certainly sounded as if her brothers were meaning to settle down and marry. What would nineteen twenty hold for their future? It all sounded so good on the other side of the world.

Maggie knew better than begin any arguments about emigration, but did say to Jim that it was good to know that her brothers were getting on fine in New Zealand. Jim made no comment, but Maggie feared that the first time that he lost his temper over something she was liable to pay the price for suggesting that they should move there.

The house was all scrubbed and given an extra polish for Hogmanay. Although there were never any callers or unexpected guests at their home, Maggie believed that the New Year should start with everything fresh and clean.

It was after ten o'clock when she eventually sat down with Jim by the fire. "What a carry on, all this scrubbing and cleaning. You look fit to drop. The house isn't needing anything done. For God's sake sit still and enjoy the rest of what's left of the year. I'd be away to my bed but there's no saying what Jimmy and Charlie will be up too. Then there's all that noise from outside the Eagle Inn and the Southport Bar at throwing out time. Then there'll be all the people coming to and from the Cross after hearing the New Year 'rung in'. Come on sit beside me at the fire."

"Well I suppose you are right, there's nobody but yourself and the bairns to see the house anyhow." Maggie sat down on the wooden nursing chair opposite Jim. She reached across to the fender stool, opened it and pulled out her knitting.

"For God's sake woman, can you not be idle for one minute in the yea? Am I to be demented by the clicking of pins until the end of the year?'

Maggie smiled, then set the wool and pins down on her lap. "The past five years I've never had any complaints of how I ended my year."

"Can you remember how we brought it to a close last time?" chuckled Jim.

"I can that and you've no chance of a repeat performance. I'm getting to old for carrying bairns Jim Chisholm."

"Come on sit across here on my knee for a wee while. When I was a guest of the Germans for all those four years. I used to wonder just what you would be doing. You know in all that time I could never picture you sitting with your arms folded. There are so many things that you can do, and so many times you can come up with the answers to what seem impossible situations. Could you just sit still with me, so that I can hold you in my arms and feel you are all mine. No speaking, just stay with me, close together, how we should be, not until the end of the year, but until the end of time."

Maggie felt the colour rush into her cheeks. "I've never known you to be the one for the fancy talking before, what have I done to bring all this on?" "Maggie as you say I'm not one for the talk, but I just think you should take it a bit easier. We could never do without you and some days you look so tired I wonder if you'll live to see many more. You are more important to me than a scrubbed doorstep or a shining blackleaded grate. I know how proud you are of our home, for you've worked so hard to make it comfortable. Pleas try to think of yourself for a change, please try to take things easier. I love you very much. There I've said it."

Maggie kissed him full on the mouth. "There are times when you are so much the gentleman that I fell for, all those years ago. The home would not be here if it were not for you being such a hard working provider Jim. The credit has to be shared with you. Don't fuss about me always doing, for I've never ever had time to sit idle. Maybe I am a bit too proud but that is something that has developed throughout my lifetime from a start with nothing at all. I've never forgot what it feels like to be referred too as a pauper, and I want our bairns to appreciate a good clean loving home."

It was about one o'clock when she could hear Charlie and Jimmy's voices on the stairs. Maggie knew from the giggling and stumbling that they had been drinking more than 'cuddle m' dearie' ginger wine. The living room door opened and in they came, their noisy entrance wakened their father.

"Happy New Year to you Mam," said Jimmy as he lay across his father to reach her at the back of the bed against the wall. He kissed her cheek, then slid back on to the floor.

Charlie whispered from beside the sink, "Happy New Year Mam. I'm sorry that we wakened you. Hope we didn't disturb the 'old man'."

Jimmy now leaning on the table for support, tried to straighten himself up. "What the hell would that matter anyhow? He's disturbed us enough in the past, without an apology."

"Is that so lad?" said Jim as he sprang from the bed. "Then I'm going to live up to your expectations."

He grabbed his son by the shoulders lifting him clean off the floor. "Now my cockie fellow, first you'll tell your mother that you are sorry for coming home in such a state, then you and I will go outside to the wash house and I'll give you a lesson in manners. You'll also tell me where a lad of your age was served drink and I'll put a stop to that."

Charlie stood rooted to the spot, still beside the sink, his mouth hanging open.

"What business is it of yours to get on to me for it's not beyond you coming home after a good bucket and upsetting everybody?"

Maggie could feel her whole body shaking. "For God's sake Jim keep your hands off him for he's drunk and doesn't know what he is saying."

"I agree that he's drunk lass, but damned fine does he know what he is implying. I just hope that he is man enough to realise I take lip like that from no man, least of all my son." Charlie ran forward and pulled his father's arm. "Put him down Dad and don't upset our mam. Jimmy is all mouth, he's been with the men from the sawmill and they were all giving him and his pals drink."

"Well if he's going to play men's games Charlie then he's got to realise that a sharp mouth can be given a few big smacks to close it. Outside with you boy, for a good lesson you are badly needing."

Maggie crawled to the edge of the bed trying to grab Jim's back as he made for the door, with Jimmy hanging from the end of his arms like a rag doll. "Please stop this now Jim. It's our laddie for God's sake. Speak to him tomorrow when he's sober."

"Just stay where you are Maggie. Charlie you get to your bed after you've made sure that the others aren't wakened. I'll be back when this young bugger knows to respect his mother, father and home. Out you to the wash house."

After what seemed hours, but by the clock was only five minutes, Jim re appeared and got into bed. "Stop worrying lass, he's through the room in his bed, with a couple of belt marks across his arse. Only his pride is hurt. He'll have a damned sore head in the morning. It was far better that he got his lesson from me than one of those wood cutters, who might have broke his nose or marked him for life. He's my son, as well you know. I do care."

Maggie could not speak, she only managed to move her head slightly, without indicating whether she approved or otherwise. Long after Jim had fallen asleep, she lay awake. Could this be an omen to what the year would bring? She had been so happy in the last few hours of the old year.

As his father predicted later in the in the morning Jimmy looked as if he was about to die.

"Well was it all worth it big man?" taunted Jim. "Do you still think that you are fit to back chat your elders?"

Jimmy sat at the table trying to swallow the contents of a cup filled with sweet tea.

"Well come on son, tell me, do you?"

"No Dad. Anything you say Dad. Just leave me alone for I'm so ill I won't be able to go back to my work."

Jim smartly replied, "That's what you think, you'll be fit enough all right once I get you in a tub of cold water a few times, that will start the blood flowing through your body instead of blocking up your head."

"You'll kill him if you do that. It's freezing outside and that wash house boiler will take hours to heat."

"I've no intention of filling the boiler, nothing like a dip in ice-cold water to clear a hang over. Right son, come on you've already agreed that Dad knows best."

"Not again, Dad, please. I'm sorry for what I've done and said," pleaded Jimmy.

"Aye I believe you, now trust me. As you told me I'm not a stranger to drink and believe me there is nothing like a cold plunge to bring you back from feeling as death was near."

When he reappeared in the living room poor Maggie was the on who looked as if the 'great reaper' was about to scythe her down.

"Ready for your breakfast now eh! Come on sit down at the table and I'm sure Mam will rustle up something for us. Won't you Maggie?"

As she bent over the frying pan at the fireside Maggie was sure that it was beyond her understanding to figure out the workings of the mind of a man.

CHAPTER TWENTY EIGHT

C HARLIE LAY IN bed with the patchwork quilt pulled right up to his chin. He had been out in the early morning to the milk delivery, but after returning home he announced to his mother that he 'did not feel well enough to go into the bank today'.

This came as no surprise to Maggie for she had noticed over the few weeks, since the start of the year, a change in her boy, who was by nature happy and care free, to a solemn quiet and withdrawn individual. She had given him a hot drink and despatched him back to bed until the younger ones got off to school. It was after nine o'clock when Maggie called Charlie through from the room. A bright fire burned in the grate, and she had made a fresh pot of tea.

"Come on now and sit down and tell me what is wrong with you laddie, for we have plenty of time to speak of it before I go up to the Bank to let them know you are not fit enough to go in this morning."

Maggie's imagination had run riot at all types of disasters that caused Charlie's enthusiasm for banking to disappear. Had he found the cash too much of a temptation? Was the book keeping beyond his ability? Had he forgotten his manners to the older members of staff?

"I don't want to go back to work at the bank Mam." he told her. She could see that he was fighting hard to keep back the tears.

"Why ever not? It's not many that have such a good chance to get a start in life, as you've won for yourself. What has brought on this sudden change of heart? You haven't done anything bad. Have you Charlie? Tell me and what ever it is I'm sure that we will be able to sort out something."

Charlie's face reddened at the idea of his mother thinking he would bring disgrace upon his family. "I've not done anything to be ashamed of Mam. It's just that I don't want to go back there to work."

Maggie knew that she could believe him if he said that he committed nothing that would offend her. Charlie was a good hard working boy. Perhaps he had been working too hard. "If you are finding it difficult to keep up with things, then you should give up running after Wallace's milk cart, in the early hours. That would give you more time to yourself."

"It's nothing to do with the milk Mam. Giving it up would make things even worse," he answered.

"Well for God's sake what is the problem? This is just not you at all. Your father is concerned as to why you are different. Lord knows he sees little enough of you, so it must be sticking out a mile that there is something upsetting you, before he sees it."

"I just want to leave the place and get some work on a farm or in the sawmills or anything at all away from Brechin."

"You haven't been fooling around with the lassies have you and got one into trouble? Tell me now for that is one thing that will show itself before many weeks have passed."

Charlie's face changed colour from red to an angry white. "You don't have much faith and trust in me. Do you Mam?"

Maggie could immediately understand the hurt and damage she had inflicted on her son. Quickly she jumped forward and put her arms around him.

"Oh Charlie, never think that. I'm so proud of you and what you have achieved. Why, not ever in your life until today have I had reason to worry about you. That's what makes it all such a puzzle. I want to help you sort out what ever it is that's brought you to this decision."

Two hours later as she walked up the High Street to go to the Bank, Maggie knew that her dreams for Charlie would have to be altered. All those weeks that she had imagined her son to be so happy with his newfound position in life, had been weeks of human misery. The work had presented no problems in itself, for according to Charlie, the chief clerk had complimented him on his neat, tidy and accurate penmanship. His fellow workers were always very friendly towards him, but as he had put it, when talking down to him.

Maggie had asked for an explanation of what he meant by this, for she certainly was not to have anyone ridiculing her son and making him feel inferior. However, Charlie appeared to find it outwith his lifestyle when the others started talking about their evenings at the drama club, or singing practice for the Musical Society. Such refined activities were not what had been encouraged in her children. The billiard room or playing on the 'back braes' were the only hobbies known to her family. Then of course Charlie had felt out of place with his jumble sale suit, despite Maggie's alterations to make it fit, and the clean well pressed appearance, he told her it was obvious to others that it was a 'hand me down'."

These problems Maggie felt could be overcome in some fashion. The one that she felt was not within her scope to solve was the usual one of finance. Charlie's friends from school, who had been lucky enough to find jobs, were working in the mill, or on the land or like his brother woodcutting. Although their wages were small, after paying 'board' to their mothers, they all had a shilling or two left to spend on themselves, at the weekend. The meagre wage paid by the bank did not stretch to allow this bonus for Charlie. Even with the 'milk money', Maggie and Jim reckoned that they were out of pocket subsidising their son's chance on the ladder to success. To provide spending money was an extra beyond their means.

As she approached the Bank, it seemed as if Clerk Street was shrinking, for when she reached the entrance, Maggie was still unprepared, considering what excuse she would make to speak to the manager.

If only Jim could have been with her. She knew that this would not be possible for it was the 'sowing time' and he was in the fields from dawn to dusk.

The smell of polish and the shining wood and brass, took her back in memory to a long forgotten time of crisis, when she was sent for Granny Fraser.

A young man at the counter with a wave of his hand beckoned her to come forward. "Good morning madam. How can I be of assistance to you this morning?"

He certainly was immaculately groomed, with tailored jacket, over a white shirt, with hard starched collar and a blue silk tie. He smiled as he waited for her to reply. "Could I see the manager please, if it is convenient?"

The young man nodded. "May I ask if you have an appointment madam and if not who may I say wishes to see him?"

"I'm sorry I have no appointment, my name is Mrs Chisholm and I wish to see him regarding my son Charles, who is employed at this branch."

The young man immediately extended his arm across the counter. "I'm so pleased to make your acquaintance Mrs Chisholm. I hope there is nothing wrong with Charlie, we were a bit concerned and surprised when he never showed up this morning."

He certainly was a friendly lad she thought. "That is why I wish to speak with the manager, to explain Charles's absence. I'm sure he will be quite all right."

The young man left the counter and disappeared behind a screen at the back. Suddenly he reappeared from a heavy wooden door in the corner. "If you could just take a seat," he suggested as he guided Maggie into the corner, where there was a velvet covered chair sat beside a large table, with blotting pad, ink well, pen and tray.

As she sat down he handed her a magazine from the top of a pile, on a chair at the far end of the table. 'The Tattler', she hadn't seen since days in service." The manager will see you soon just as soon as he is free Mrs Chisholm. He apologises for keeping you waiting."

Maggie turned over the pages of the magazine only glancing at the pictures as she flicked them over. Without lifting her head, she tried to survey her surroundings. Certainly the clerk behind the counter had been most polite and helpful. Would the manager be as easy to approach, and understand the problems that Charlie had to face?

Her eye caught something familiar on the last page of the 'glossy society paper'. Amidst photographs of so called social events right in the middle, the smiling face of Neil McLeod and his bride. Ghosts from the past sent a peculiar shiver through her body. It was many moons since she had even given Neil a thought, probably not since the start of the war when she met the Islay woman on the steamer. She looked more closely at the face of her once dear friend. He certainly appeared happy and although not in the first flush of youth, his wife was a bonnie woman.

Maggie felt happy that at last he had found someone to share his life. Perhaps it meant that she should see the announcement, though not the ideal morning to ponder over old times with the worry of her son's future hanging in the balance.

The young man behind the counter came from the heavy oak door. "The manager will see you now Mrs Chisholm, if you will just to follow me please, I will conduct you to his office."

What am I to say, she thought. Her breathing felt as if something was restricting the intake of air. She had never been so nervous as this before. Surely age was beginning to take its toll.

The manager was a small dapper man, who met her at his office door with outstretched hand. "I am so pleased to make your acquaintance Mrs Chisholm, do come in and take a seat. William will you perhaps arrange for two cups, as I'm certain a cup of tea would be appreciated, and this is the time I have mine to revive and refresh. Is that so?"

He smiled at Maggie, who in her highly nervous state managed to nod her approval.

Three quarters of an hour later as she slowly walked towards her home, her mind was in turmoil. The Bank manager had nothing but praise for Charlie's work and ability. He spoke quite freely of how for the first time in years he had 'in his charge', someone with prospects of a very bright banking future.

He showed marked disappointment when Maggie explained the circumstances, that Charlie felt so inferior, that he had taken to his bed, and only wanted to get away from Brechin. "Wages are standard throughout all branches, my dear," he explained. "My hands are tied, much as I would like to help Charles, out of this predicament, I cannot at the present moment come up with an answer. Perhaps a day or two to think over will do Charles some good. Come back and see me on Thursday morning at ten. If Charles feels up to his usual hard working standards, then we will be pleased to see him back at any time before then. I would still appreciate a chat with you on Thursday even although Charles resumes his duties. The welfare of my staff is of prime importance to me, and it grieves me to learn that he has been so unhappy and I have allowed the situation to go unnoticed."

Maggie tried hard to relay the conversation word for word to Jim, as they sat together in the late evening.

"How pleased I was to know that at least one of our family was to get a break away from the hard graft of manual labour. You say that Charlie is determined not to even consider going to give it a try?"

"I've given myself a sore head, with worrying and trying to get him to see reason, but no, he has made up his mind. He told me that nothing would persuade him to go back."

"There's no point in me getting him up out of his bed then, to go over what has already been said. God lassie, what a chance, I wish I had been as fortunate as to have the learning and brains, to try a job like it."

"We can't live other peoples lives for them Jim. We have tried to do our best for him, but Charlie has a mind of his own. I would rather that he was happy. No doubt someday he'll maybe see that it would have benefited him to persevered with what to him was a big problem."

Charlie wrote out his resignation the following night and put it through the letterbox in the Bank door. He did not wish to speak to the manager and had little time to do so. That morning he had told Wallace, the dairyman he was unemployed and was immediately offered work at Haughmuir.

Maggie had prepared his shift of clothes for him and by Thursday morning he was settled in the bothy and at work on his 'new place'.

With no-one to care for John it was impossible for Maggie to keep her appointment with the manager at the Bank. She knew that her disappointment not only stemmed from Charlie's decision but she also could not get out of her mind what opportunities would there have been with a marriage to Neil McLeod?

CHAPTER TWENTY NINE

1924

"THERE WAS NO way I could get a fee at a farm near Brechin Maggie. I was offered a cottar house with the job at Arnhall but I didn't want us to give up our home and our independence. The bairns would have had to change schools and everything. So that's it, I'll just need to live in the bothy for six months, and hope that the tail end of the year brings us a bit of luck."

Jim was sat by the table, looking so dejected the picture of abject misery. He had been away at the feein market since the early hours of the morning. Before him on the table was his uneaten meal.

Maggie put her hands to rest on his shoulders. "We've faced worse situations than this Jim. At least you'll have a wage coming, and that is more than many will be saying tonight. We will have Saturdays and Sundays together and that's no less than we have just now. That's more than we managed for the four years you were away kept prisoner in Germany. Get on with your supper, there's no point in making yourself ill thinking about it."

"That's part of the problem lass, I spent four years separated from my family, supposedly for the rights of freedom for man. Here I am still a slave to the system, in order to provide a meagre existence for my wife and bairns. Surely something is wrong somewhere?"

"I agree with you Jim, but how can one man like yourself change the pattern that has been set for years." She poured tea into his cup. "Get on and not waste that food," she added before he could reply.

"I don't know lassie, but somehow that government in London will have to accept that a man is entitled to work and earn the means of supporting his family. There were lads there today that I've known for years as hard working honest men, almost demented by the thoughts of not having a place to go to on Monday morning."

"It's a sad state of affairs right enough, but we have been fortunate that there's work for you and both the laddies."

"Jessie will be leaving school at the tattie holidays. Maybe by that time things will have improved."

Maggie sat down at the table opposite Jim and poured herself a cup of tea. "That's right I was hearing the young lassies from around Bridge Street who left school at the last holidays, are having to go to Kirriemuir to work at the weaving."

Jim looked surprised. "What with three linen factories in the town? I'm not keen on Jessie going to live away from home all the week. It's different from the boys."

"They don't live in Kirriemuir all the week Jim, they get Meffan's bus every morning at five o'clock to get them there for the six o'clock start. Then the bus picks them up again and has them home in Brechin for seven o'clock at night."

"God knows what kind of existence that is for young women. I tell you life for working people is getting worse instead of better."

Monday morning at five o'clock Jim was preparing to set off on his bicycle for the farm at Arnhall, beyond Edzell. His farm 'kist' would be picked up by the horseman with the cart the following day, after the cattle market. Maggie had been up and out of the bed and made him a cooked breakfast.

"This will be the last, I suppose for a week. Back to the porridge and brose," he told her as they sat together at the table.

"You know Maggie I feel the same as I did at twelve years of age, when I left my father's house to start at the bothy. I haven't made much headway since then, have I?'

"For goodness sake Jim, don't be so fed up. It's only for a few weeks until the spring, when the work picks up a bit. I'll have something nice cooked for you on Saturday, when you get home. There's a musical evening on at the City hall. Maybe we could go to it together. Jessie will look after John and David. What do you think?"

"Well I suppose it would be something to look forward to all week. We deserve some time to ourselves and a break from perpetual struggle to survive."

"That's it settled then I'll have your good boots cleaned and things set out ready for you coming home Saturday afternoon."

As promised the farm cart picked up Jim's bothy kist, which held his change of clothes, razor and a few personal items. This was also where he would store his ration of meal, milk and cheese. Every bothy resident was responsible for looking after his own victuals and supplying his own crockery and utensils. It was the rule by custom that everything was served and eaten from a bowl, with a spoon. Some farmtowns took a pride in that their 'bothy lads' never washed their bowls from one term day to the next, six months in all. This was not for Jim, for Maggie had packed for him a cup, plate, fork, knife and spoon.

The week went past more quickly than she expected. Jessie had persuaded her to rearrange the sleeping arrangements, to allow the girls to have the 'big room'. David and John were moved into the 'wee bed room'. The garret where some of Jim's father's belongings had been stored was tidied up and an old bed mad up for Jimmy and Charlie's weekends at home.

"It's quite comfortable Mam, I'm sure after sleeping in bothies it's a big improvement," said Jessie trying to convince her mother that her brothers would find sleeping in the loft, with old junk, acceptable.

"I expect that there's some truth in what you're saying, but I'm not happy about them away up there sleeping below the slates." Maggie could well remember how cold it was sleeping in the loft at Culburnie.

The roof there had been lined and packed with straw for insulation and was still freezing in the winter.

"We will see how it works out Jessie, but you might have to move back to the wee room again if it doesn't."

Saturday morning Maggie had the house scrubbed from corner to corner. Mary was such a grand worker and made Maggie's life so much easier. In the afternoon Jim's Sunday best clothes were on the bed beside his polished boots. Maggie had the tea all prepared before she washed and changed into her only dress. "You are looking real bonnie Mam," said David. "What are you all dressed up for?"

"Dad will be home tonight son and he is taking me out to a function in the City Hall," she answered.

"But you never go out Mam. Who will be here with me?"

"You're right David, it's so long a time since I was away from the house you can't remember it. However, Dad and I are allowed an evening to ourselves and you will be fine here with Jessie, Mary and John. Maybe Charlie will be in the house as well. We will know when he gets home. Jimmy will be playing billiards at Gallacio's so there will be nothing coming over you until we get home."

Jim had still not appeared.

"Maybe he's had a puncture in the tyre of his bike," said Jessie trying to make excuses for her father.

"Maybe he's fallen off the bike," said David.

"Or maybe he's fallen by the wayside and got drunk," added Jimmy.

"Stop this at once," said Maggie. Jimmy had voiced her worst fears. Jim was so depressed when he left home at the start of the week, she had thought that he might return home worse of drink. As the days passed though she had become more confident that he would not let her down.

I t was almost ten o'clock when Jim staggered up the stairs. "Well lassie," he shouted, "I'm home and no doubt you will be ready for me."

The table was still set for his evening meal and his clothes lying on the bed.

"Yes Jim, I've been waiting for you to come home. The bairns are in bed for they couldn't keep their eyes open any longer."

"You would have liked that Maggie if they had their eyes opened to see their father drunk. Wouldn't you?"

Maggie did not answer for fear of saying something that Jim could take objection too.

"Cat got your tongue, or do you not think me good enough to speak to now?"

"I'm just getting you something to eat; you must be hungry," she answered.

"Och I'm not hungry. I've lived high this week on brose, porridge, bannocks and cheese. I've worked six in the morning to six at night, then slept in a room ten feet square with four other men. Do you know the cattle are better cared for than farm hands?"

"Why did you not come home then when you had the chance, to a good meal and a cosy fireside, where your family were waiting for you?"

"Because I went for a drink before I could face you, I'm so ashamed that I'm reduced to the same work I did as a laddie. There no you have it."

"There's no need for shame Jim Chisholm, you are a good father and provider for your family. It is your concern for their well being that has forced you into the job you've taken. Far from feelings of shame I'm proud that you are my man and father of our bairns." "I don't deserve you lassie, yet I'm so miserable when we are separated. I just felt so downhearted that I felt a drink would make me feel better. As usual I couldn't stop at one then it was too late."

He looked across at his clothes lying on the bed. "You were ready for the soiree in the City Hall. I spoil everything for you. Lassie to say I'm sorry won't make up to you, but I truly am and somehow I will try to make up for your disappointment."

"Och well Jim there will be other times for us to get out together now that the bairns are growing up.'

"Are they all bedded?" asked Jim.

"Well the girls, David and John have been sleeping for ages. Charlie did not come home because it's his weekend 'on' working in the dairy. Jimmy has gone again so I suppose that will mean he will be working extra as well."

"Maybe," was all that Jim replied.

"What do you mean by that Jim?" she asked.

"Well I suppose if I was truthful I would admit that he is very much his father's son, and enjoys the comfort of strong drink at the cost of meeting his responsibilities."

"Don't you think he's working then? Surely he wouldn't stay away in the bothy, when he could be at home here with his family." Not wishing to have Maggie more distress, Jim agreed that she was probably 'right as usual. Jimmy would be working'.

After eating the meal prepared for him Jim sat by the fire. "Tell me Maggie when last did Jimmy pay you any money for doing his washing and feeding him when he comes home?"

Taken aback by this direct question Maggie stammered, "Oh, it was not so long ago Jim, that he paid me."

"With all this extra week end work, then I would think that he will be well able to afford you a little extra then. Don't you think?"

Maggie could not answer for she knew that Jimmy had given her no money for months, in fact she had on more than one occasion had to give him a 'loan' of two shillings before he left for work on Monday mornings.

"You never change Maggie lass; stand by your men folk through thick and thin. God knows why? Your loyalty is so misplaced. Here's me couldn't even come home to take you out for an hour. Selfish to the backbone standing drinking, spending money we can ill afford to waste. Your son Jimmy will be standing in some bar or billiard room exactly the same spending money that you could put to far better use. God knows how you put up with us and can always find excuses for our behaviour. Surely there are times when you feel like running away from all this. There's nothing you cannot turn your hand too. You could have a good life for yourself Maggie."

"Stop this talk at once Jim. You know full well that the most important things in my life are you and our family. Without you I would have nothing to live for. You don't know what it's like to have 'no one of your own' to care for."

"Maggie I would be quite happy just to have to care about myself."

Little did Jim know that what he had said, while still influenced by drink, had hurt Maggie deeply. Did Jim no longer care for her and the bairns? Certainly he did not appear to be bothered by how little he seen them. His first concern had been to get to a bar and by drink to raise his feelings of depression.

Long after Jim was asleep in bed, Maggie sat by the fire thinking over just how things were in her household. She worked from morning to night keeping the place and bairns clean and tidy. Clothes were patched and remade while the cloth still had some 'body' left in it. Any woollens were refashioned and knitted into other garments. Occasionally she would take in washing from the big houses in latch Road or the Manse. Anything to make an extra shilling that would help to keep up appearances. Yes Jim was right in what he said; both he and Jimmy were selfish benefiting from her forgiving generous nature.

After hours of sitting at the cold burnt out fire Maggie could foresee no answer to her problems. Never could she leave her bairns. How could her mother have deserted her and her brothers?

CHAPTER THIRTY

THE YEAR BROUGHT no change to Jim's work conditions. He was still living away from home during the working week in a farm bothy. Saturday and Sunday nights were spent in Brechin, but his frequent visits to the bars made his homecomings anything other than welcome stays. Maggie found herself longing for relief of Monday mornings, when Jim and his two older sons would be away back to work, leaving her at peace with David, John and her daughters Jessie and Mary.

Jessie like most young Brechin girls had started work at the weaving. As her mother had predicted earlier, she was one of the many transported each day to the factory twenty miles away at Kirriemuir.

Maggie listened to Jessie's chatter as she was eating her evening meal.

"The girls go dancing on Saturday nights at the Masonic Temple Mam, they want me to go with them."

Maggie frowned. "Do you not think you are a bit young lassie to be going out dancing at night?"

Maggie could well remember how much she enjoyed the music, dancing and company, when she was a young girl.

"Och Mam, all the girls on the bus will be going and I'm old enough to work, surely I'm old enough to go out dancing with them, we will all be together."

"You don't know what your Dad will say about it though. He would not want you out late on a Saturday."

"Why would that be, in case I met him staggering home drunk from the pub? At least I would be coming home first before going out on the spree."

"Stop that at once Jessie Chisholm. I will not have you saying things that are disrespectful to your father, and in his own house."

Jessie got up from the table. "For goodness sake Mam, what do you think we are, blind? We see what happens every weekend. Dad has lost all interest in us, or this place we call home. It is only a sleeping place after his Saturday drinking. Sunday sees him recovered enough to face work on Monday again.

Maggie's face was red with anger. "Jessie I will not have you saying such things about your father. He works hard and it's not his fault that he cannot find work in Brechin where he would be home each night. That's what he would want. He just gets depressed being away all week, then needs a drink to cheer him up."

"Please yourself what you want to think mam, but you cannot change my mind. We see what goes on. We aren't bairns any more, you know. I'm going to the dance. I don't care what he thinks about it either."

Maggie cleared up the tea dishes from the table. As she washed them up in the sink she could feel a lump arise in her throat and tears well up behind her smarting eyes. It was true that her family were no longer an age when they were oblivious to the rift developing between their mother and father. Maggie had tried so hard to keep from them her feelings of being ill at ease when Jim was in the house. She hoped that they had not overheard them argue when he arrived home late after drinking and become abusive to her. There had been more than one occasion when he had lifted his hand to strike her. Fortunately Maggie had fended off the blows, but for days had bruising on her forearms.

How could she betray him to his children? Jim was not a bad man. Circumstances had brought them to this desperate situation. The next feein' market might bring him work near Brechin, where he would be able to get home each night and enjoy the comfort of his own fireside. Jim never took drink before he was forced into living away from home. Maggie could not even think about what life would be like should Jim be able to live at home and not give up drinking. She would never be able to cope with him. If only there was someone to discuss the problem with or even if she could speak of it in coincidence with a friend. Since Bridie died she had never allowed herself to form any kind of relationship between herself and neighbours. It was no use trying to get Jim's sisters to understand for they had more domestic problems than they could cope with themselves.

In some respects she understood the bitterness Jim felt at how life had treated him. He was hard working and could not be accused of being lazy or shirking when it came to a days toil. He was a big man who was looked up too by his fellow workers. However, Jim always felt that rewards he received for his efforts did not reach his expectations. Jim had always wanted to make something of his life. Probably if he had still been in the Police force things would have suited him better. The fact he was called up for army service when his country needed him, then after four years as prisoner of war, without pension discharged as being no longer medically fit to serve, was a great irritation to him. Little wonder the frustrations of life's circumstances drove him to the bottle. At least he forgot the struggles for a short time. Why did he take it out on her though? Jim could be so nasty, for no reason at all. Her brothers in New Zealand were a favourite topic for his drunken ranting and ravings. Jim could not miss a chance to ask why she did not 'pack up and go to them, instead of being saddled with a drunk like him.'

"Over the months Maggie had given up trying to convince him that she only wanted to be with him and their family. No way did she consider him to be a 'no good drunk'."

Was this true?

Jessie seemed to think very little of her father. She would never discuss it with Jimmy for there was little love lost between them already. Jimmy hardly acknowledged that his father was there when they were all in the house.

Charlie was very loyal to them both for he never made any reference to his father's behaviour. Maggie was certain that Charlie volunteered to work weekends to avoid being involved in arguments that were established part of the daily routine when Jim was at home. He appeared anxious and on edge when in his father's company.

Maggie sat many hours trying to work out some of solution to the problem. She considered writing to her brothers and asking what the prospects would be for them moving to New Zealand and finding work and a new life together. It would be good for them all to have a fresh start. There might be a better chance for Jessie and Mary, other than facing twelve hours each day in the noisy, dusty atmosphere of the weaving shed. The possibility of an accident with the machinery was forever foremost in her mind. Those poor girls tired after a days work, then travelling to and from Kirriemuir, it was little wonder that someone did not fall asleep and get caught in the wheels or driving belts of the looms.

David and Alex would surely help with finding a place for Jim and the boys. The letters they sent always mentioned full employment. Certainly they had their own families to care for now, for David had only recently got married and was so pleased to be coming a father himself. Alex had a good job with New Zealand Post office, which gave him security for his wife and two sons and daughter. Alex would be a wonderful father, thought Maggie, for he had kept in touch with her daughter Margaret in Canada all of her life. At least she was away from the arguing and drunken squabbles that faced the rest of her family. Would she ever see any of her own kin again? The question was always in her mind the same. There would be so many things for them to talk over. What did they all look like now, with age and the ravages of life, leaving altered features?

The face that returned her look each morning from the mirror, as she combed her hair, was not the fair skinned fresh complexioned bright-eyed one she longed to see. In its place was a dull wrinkled skin, with eyes hidden between 'puffy' eyelids and pockets of fluid settled on her cheekbones. Perhaps the climate in a new country would be good for her.

She would go to the library in the afternoon and borrow some books about New Zealand. Once she read for herself what there was on offer, then she would write and find out what was on offer, then she would write asking her brothers for advice. Jim need not be told until there was something definite to discuss.

As she busied herself about the house. Maggie's mind kept forming pictures of them all in a small farm, with the boys and Jim working the land and managing the sheep. The girls would be busy spinning and weaving the wool out in the warm sunshine. Oh how wonderful it would all be if only they could get a start.

The more she read about the country, the more her mind was set on going. There seemed to be a new purpose to her life. Jim would feel as though he had regained some self-respect. She had read for herself that New Zealand government gave land grants to immigrants, who had a knowledge of agriculture. Jim Chisholm certainly had that.

When all the family were together for their Sunday meal, Maggie decided to casually mention the plan that had burned in her head for over four weeks. "This is grand us all together as a family should be. Don't you think so?" she remarked filling the soup plates.

"We could do with a bigger table for a start," replied Jim, who had John sitting on his knee, and Charlie crushed against his shoulder.

"Hurry up with mine Mam, for I'm needing away to meet somebody," said Jimmy.

"He'll be meeting a girl," teased Jessie.

Charlie punched Jimmy on the shoulder, before saying, "You must be joking, he's too damned mean to spend money on anyone but himself."

Jim spooned soup into John. "Yes I agree with you Charlie and I think it's about time that he put some pennies on the table for the food he's so desperate to gulp down. Your mother has not seen the colour of his money for months. Is that so Maggie?"

Maggie did a quick turn about from the table to put the pot back on the hob of the fire. She uttered no sound.

"Speak up woman, it's the truth that Jimmy here has not given you a penny piece for his upkeep for months?" challenged Jim.

"Well maybe he's forgotten once or twice to leave something," she finally managed to answer.

"Right James my boy, we will have the money on the table now, that what is owed to the family. You have always known that you 'pay your way' or else. Take back that soup now Maggie, he can have it when it's paid for.

Maggie stood rooted to the fireside rug. "The laddie is hungry Jim. Let him have his dinner then we will sort out the money together."

"This will be sorted out here and now." He added in a voice although not shouting was already showing signs of irritation.

The family sat spoons in hand motionless waiting for the next move between their father and brother.

"It's very simple lad, just put your hand in your pocket, take out your money, lay it on the table and we can all get on with eating."

Jimmy sat, eyes lowered at the oilcloth cover on the table. "I don't have any money Dad."

Jim set down his spoon, handed John over to Maggie, who welcomed some reason to move and occupy her hands.

"I thought as much, you wouldn't have had it yesterday when you were betting on cards, would you?" sneered Jim. "I suppose I did, but that's where I'm going after dinner to win it all back. I'll give you something, honest Mam."

"Live horse and you'll get corn, eh. Tell you what Jimmy; you'll get food and a bed when you pay what you owe your mother. Until then I would be obliged if you did not bother us here with your scrounging ways."

Oh please God don't let this happen thought Maggie as she stood looking out the window, across the back braes to the trees twisting and turning in the wind and rain. The boy cannot be turned out of his home on such a night.

"We'll manage to sort things out later Jim. Just all eat up your dinner."

Maggie's stomach was turning over with knotted nerves. So much for mentioning a start in New Zealand now. "Maggie you are not to interfere in this matter. Jimmy knows full well that he does not work all week to throw money away gambling on cards and billiards, while you struggle to make ends meet and the rest of his family provide for him. The choice is his own. He puts forward his money or he does not eat and live in this house. That is my final say on the matter."

Jimmy rose from the table with such a jump that the chair fell backwards banging on the fender of the fireplace, causing the pot of soup to fall into the fire. Steam and hot ashes were everywhere. John began to scream and the girls were sobbing.

"For God's sake stop all this now," said Charlie. "What a carry on, makes me wonder what I come home for anyhow."

Jim was standing by the table; he looked a giant of man. "That's your decision to make laddie, you can please your self about coming here or not. Certainly I know that you never let your mother be out of pocket by your presence."

"Well Dad, it's not worth the price, listening to you laying down laws to others that you cannot keep yourself. You won't be seeing me here again if you are near the place. So long mam, I'll be in touch with you," he pecked her on the cheek as he passed her to get to the door. Jimmy lifted his jacket from the hook on the back of the door and left the room without saying a word.

Mary went to her mother and put her arms around her shaking shoulders.

"Come on and sit down Mam, Jessie will see to John while make you a cup of tea and clean up this mess. Things will sort them selves out. The boys will be back next week end, you'll see."

"Only if they play the game with your mother, Mary," said Jim, who had once again seated himself at the head of the table and was continuing to sup his soup.

Jessie, who had been fussing over John to stop him crying, sprang across the room to face her father.

"Just when do you intend to start playing the game then, dad, and being a bit more considerate of our mother? Stop treating her like an unpaid slave."

Jim was taken aback by this attack, from his elder daughter; he had always expected some harassment from Mary, who was always very loving and protective towards her mother.

"You have heard what I had to say to the boys Jessie and if you feel that things are not to your liking in this house then you are well able to support yourself somewhere more suited to your plans."

Jessie leaned forward directly facing her father, 'That would suit you fine, getting us all out of the way, then you would have nobody to stand up for Mam. You certainly would be no help to her rolling in drunk on a Saturday night, causing trouble on Sunday before you creep out sober on a Monday morning again. No I'll stay though it's just to keep a check on how you treat our Mam, so mind how you go."

Maggie was rendered speechless. Certainly Jessie had slapped Jim into place. He made no move to get up from the table.

When they were eventually left alone in the room Jim finally spoke.

"Maggie I never intended that this fiasco should ever have happened. I know how much it means to you to have the family all together. I only wanted to put Jimmy right about the gambling. Of course Jessie is quite right in what she had to say about me. God knows how we are to get out of this mess I've brought us into."

"I don't know Jim. Certainly things cannot go on the way they are." Maggie decided it was not the time at present to mention New Zealand or her plans for a rosy future.

CHAPTER THIRTY ONE

THE LETTER FROM Gigha arrived in the morning post, informing Maggie that Janet was in poor health. Duncan McNeil a nephew, from the McMillan side of her family had thought it best to advise her of her aunt's condition. Feelings of guilt and remorse at how little time she had spared to even think of her old relative filled her with shame.

Life at home in Brechin had not been easy for Maggie over the past few years. Jim was still managing to find work but no longer worried about living in the farm bothies. The rift and break up of the family had never healed. Maggie believed that it was long past a time when she could manoeuvre her family back together. The problem did not come from one source, but several. Jim continued to drink too much on Saturday afternoons and evenings. As Jessie had said years before, the so called home in the High Street provided a convenient 'stopping off' place for recovering after his binges. Despite his drinking, however, Jim always gave Maggie the money for the rent and housekeeping. John, now at school was with Maggie the only two left for Jim to support.

Jessie and Mary were still employed at the weaving and were now spared the early morning journeys to Kirriemuir. Smart's factory in River Street had increased their labour force in the spring of 1929, offering jobs for women and girls. This allowed the girls to come home for their breakfast, dinner and then teatime. Maggie enjoyed being busy preparing meals for them and listening to all their chatter and news.

David was working at Black's sawmill in the town. Jimmy had been instrumental in getting him a start at fourteen. David also had his meals at home. Only on the occasional weekends did Maggie's two elder sons visit their home. Neither appeared to be ready to settle down with wives and set up homes of their own. This was a disappointment to her as she formed the impression that her marriage and home making efforts were the cause of the boys' reluctance to end their bachelor days.

"You'll just have to go and visit Janet, that's all there is about it Mam," said Jessie. "We'll manage away fine here, won't we Mary?"

Mary could see that her mother was upset by the news of her aunt. "You'll get away on Friday, when the school breaks off for the summer holidays. Keep John off the last morning. You have six weeks to stay on Gigha, if you want then. A holiday will do you both good."

"Oh Mary, I couldn't do that and stay away all that time. What would your father say?"

"Let him say what he damned well wants, we'll be able to handle him," said David. 'It's about time you left him to see what this place is like without you running after him at weekends."

"Don't say things like that David, in your father's house. I have to consider him, after all he is my husband."

"For God's sake mother, you never get any better, letting him take the loan of you. You are far too soft with him the 'part time dad and Jim the lad"

"Stop miscalling your father. I don't have the money to pay the fares in any case. Just forget all about it. I'll write to the McNeills and find out exactly what is going on. They are on the spot and look well after Janet's needs."

Mary got up and put her arm around Maggie, "Now Mam you know that's no answer for you would be wondering if what they told you was correct. Janet is your only living relative, apart from us. They must want you to go or they would not have written to you in the first place. Janet is in her eighties now and you won't have much more time with her. You'll just go with John."

"Mary is quite right Mam. We'll put the fare together for you and post on money to you every week until you feel ready to come home," said Jessie.

Maggie started to cry, "Oh lassies I can't have you doing that for I'd never be able to pay you back. I appreciate the thought though. You are good to your mother."

"Stop the greeting now, before John comes in. He'll think this a great adventure getting away on holiday and on a boat across the sea at that. You are going on Friday. Mary, David and myself will see to everything. Now get John's stovies out to cool for he won't have time for anything other than back to school to tell his chums he's going on holiday on a boat."

David laughed. "Aye and it won't be Haggart's rowing boats at the 'paperie' either."

Maggie and John waved goodbye to Jessie and Mary as the train pulled out of the railway station early Friday morning.

It still bothered her that she had been unable to discuss her enforced holiday with Jim, before departing for Gigha.

David and the girls assured her that there was no point in delaying the departure until the following Monday, with a possible outburst of drunken verbal abuse from Jim to send her on her way'

"Oh Mam, this is such an adventure, going on a different land across the ocean. Are you excited too?"

Maggie looked at John's flushed and glowing face, with so many looks of his father.

"Yes I suppose I'm excited son. I just wish I'd spoken to your dad before we set off though."

"Och Mam, our dad won't worry about not getting. He wasn't with you when you took the rest of them to Janet's when they were my age. They told me about it all and the good fun they had there. I just can't wait to get on the boat. Dad will be fine. He manages in the bothy all the week so he'll mange the Saturdays and Sundays without us."

"I suppose you are right son," answered Maggie in an abstract fashion. John never remembered a time when his father was in the house other than Saturday and Sunday. If the drinking had been bad then probably their meeting spoiled by Jim's abusive behaviour. Maybe he was looking forward to a break from such disruptions in his young life.

The journey was long and tedious, but John found every stage more exciting. Glasgow rail station and the city streets with trams and buses a fascination. At the quayside he looked at the steamer in amazement.

"Could that ship go right across the sea to America?"

"No I don't think so John, but it goes on to Islay, after Campbeltown and Gigha. That's where your grandmother and Janet came from."

"Why don't I have a Granny? Other people at school all have them and Granddads."

"Well yours died a lot of years ago."

"Why did they die Mam?"

"Oh John, I don't know I expect God wanted to take them back to be with him."

"He won't want to take you and my Dad back to be with him, will he? Because I need you both."

Maggie swallowed hard, thinking to herself thank you John, for I was beginning to despair that not one of our children felt the need of their father.

"Don't worry John, nobody will take your Mam and Dad away from you. I know how much a bairn needs both. Now away and see if you can get a wee peep at the ship's engines. I'll just sit here until you get back."

Janet was sitting by the fireside when Maggie and John entered her home. She slowly rose to her feet trying to straighten her bent frame. "Oh Maggie lass I'm so pleased to see you and the bairn. Come away John until I see you in the light." She pulled John close to her side. "My you certainly have the looks of Jim Chisholm about you. If you grow up a fine upstanding man like him then you'll be alright, eh Maggie?"

"He's growing up far too fast for my liking. Cannot keep him in boots and trousers," she replied, feeling no need to disclose to her aunt any flaws in the picture she had formed of her husband.

"That's true lassie and growing bairns are forever hungry, come away and get something to eat. I'm not so able to bake bread and bannocks myself now but I have good friends and neighbours who wouldn't see me wanting."

"You had done the same for them when you were younger no doubt. It will be their way of repaying your kindness to them."

"I suppose that's one way of looking at things lassie, but I've always lived by what the good book says 'to love thy neighbour as thy self', and to 'do unto others as you would wish done to you'. It haunts me sometimes to think that is not always what happened to you in your life, but I do pray for you and yours Maggie, every night that God spares me on this earth."

Maggie held her old aunt in her arms, "Oh Janet I'm so pleased to be here with you for a while."

As promised the family regularly sent on money to Maggie. However, she had little need of any with no shops to spend it. Janet would not hear of accepting anything for the food that she prepared for Maggie and John.

'Lord knows lassie it's a pleasure for me to be doing something instead of sitting seeing pictures in the fire. I feel so much better of both your company."

Maggie had noticed an improvement in her aunt's condition. She herself could feel much better. More at ease with the daily happenings. Time to be away from problems could show them up in a very different way. There were ways of solving problems if they were thought through and the causes removed. Maggie made up her mind that she was to try and spend more time with Jim. Perhaps he felt shut out from his family and sought company in the bars as a substitute. The question that Maggie could not answer. Did Jim still care for her enough to try again and save her marriage?

On the fourth week of her stay the postman delivered to her an envelope addressed in Jim's bold handwriting. Maggie could not open it for fear of the message within. It was afternoon when Janet was having a lie down that she eventually plucked up enough courage to discover what Jim had written.

Sat in the sunshine on the rocky beach, slowly she tore open the envelope. Two five-pound notes fell from the folded page. Jim hoped that Janet was feeling much better, that John was enjoying his holiday and also that she was finding the change a benefit. No mention was made of family at home nor any query as too how long she intended staying on Gigha. The short message was signed 'your husband Jim'.

By the end of the fifth week Maggie was ready to go home. "John will have to get back to school you know," she explained when telling Janet of her leaving. "I'll be relieved to know what the rest of the family have been up to in my absence."

"It's none of my business Maggie, but I'm to ask anyhow. Are things alright between Jim and you?"

Maggie blushed, this was the moment she had dreaded and had hoped to be able to avoid.

"Why, what makes you think that something is wrong?"

"The fact you seldom mention his name, and if it does crop up then you change the subject to find something to urgently need doing. I've lived a long time and lived through many situations not to notice certain signs."

"Well I suppose things have been going through a rough patch, with Jim having to work away from home, and the family beginning to try and show they are grown up and know what's best. I don't think it's anything that Jim and I cannot work out between us."

"Tell me Maggie, I can remember a time when your whole day's conversation was about the wonderful Jim Chisholm. I know that doesn't last forever but can you imagine life without him at all. I only ask this through being a widow for longer than I care to remember."

"Oh Janet, these weeks here with you have given me time to try and work out my feelings for Jim. I believe that I haven't made things easy for him by devoting so much time to our family. With only two days each week to be together, a house and family to keep. I feel somewhere I've managed to make him feel shut out. He prefers the men's company in the bar to mine and his children.'

"You'll have to make up your mind Maggie what you want, after all your family are an age to be setting up their own homes. Jim and you could have many years of each others company, free from stress that children put on a marriage."

"I've thought all these things out for myself Janet, but I'm glad you have said them, for it makes me more determined than ever to try and sort things out when I get home to Brechin."

"Don't you be laying all the blame at your own door for it takes two to make a marriage work. Sad to say it only takes one to break it. I think you both have a chance to sort out your problems though. I'll say an extra prayer for you both."

The thought of Janet's prayers always brought a smile to Maggie's face. Like so many of her age and those with an island up bringing, her aunt had firm religious beliefs. These beliefs were also akin to other inherit island customs. Each night following a spell on bended knee with bowed head, at her bedside, Janet would bless her communion with God by downing a large glass of the best Islay malt Whisky. These 'blessings' were delivered from the Islay ferry by horse and trap in two stone jars, once a month. The place of manufacture and origin known only to the buyer and seller, and of course the Lord, who knowest all.

CHAPTER THIRTY TWO

IT WAS SO good to see the girls standing on the station platform as the train pulled in. "There they are John, wave to Jessie and Mary," she said excitedly, as they were both trying to lean out the carriage door at the same time.

"They see us, Mam for they are running to meet us."

Maggie was so happy to be back home again, for she had worried what had been happening. The girls hugged them both and kissed them on the cheeks.

"My but you have grown John," Jessie told him. "And you are both looking so well after all that fresh air."

Mary linked into her mother's arm. "We missed you Mam, but it's a bonus to see you looking so well and not tired. How was Janet?"

"Och well as one could expect for a woman of her years, I suppose. I'm glad that you both talked me into going for she's a lonely old body with no children to look after her. I'm well blessed with you ones. How are the boys surviving and your father?"

Jessie was walking ahead carrying the bags and listening to John's stories of his island adventures.

"They are fine. Dad was a bit surprised when he discovered that you were away and him not knowing. Once he got over the shock of realising you could decide things for yourself he was all right. Said he would write to you. Did he?" she replied.

"Yes Mary, Dad did write and he sent on money for John and myself to spend on enjoying our holiday. He does care you see."

"I can tell you this much Mam, he got a bit of a fright when you weren't in the house when he came home. Jessie reckons he believed that you had left him for good and David kept him wondering for a whole week end before telling him that you were away to auntie Janet."

Maggie's voice was raised in anger; "There was no need for keeping Dad in a state of worry. That was a wicked thing to do. Dad doesn't have much to bring him pleasure these days. I knew I should have waited and explained myself."

Mary squeezed her mother's arm, "Don't you be silly Mam, he has told Jessie how much he needs you and how badly he has treated us all with his drinking. Maybe things will be better for his worrying. Come on forget about it now. You've had a good break away from Brechin and things will soon be back to normal. You'll have that wash house boiler fire lit before six tomorrow morning and your arms up to the elbows in soap suds if I'm not far wrong."

"You have the measure of me Mary, that's where all my thinking and planning is done, leaning over the scrubbing board. I get so carried away in my own thoughts I've almost rubbed a hole in the leg of the minister's long johns."

Mary laughed "We knew he was a holier than thou kind of creature without any help from you."

The house was shining like a new pin. The tea was set and ready on the table. Jessie filled the kettle and put it on the fire. "We promised David that we would wait until he gets in before we start our tea. He's really missed you Mam."

"I suppose he has and he's had you girls running after him. I've never been away from him before, but I won't always be here. I had no Mam to care for me from the time I was ten. Nae mammie's kisses for me."

As Maggie said the words she could see Jessie's lips tremble.

"Oh Mam, we'll need you for years and years yet. You'll enjoy when you have grandchildren to sit on your knee."

Mary joined in the conversation, "That maybe won't be so far away with her having a steady lad now. Will it Jessie?"

"Be quiet and don't talk rubbish. Mam will be thinking I've got myself into trouble when she was away."

"Well Jessie. Have you?" Maggie was quick to ask."

"Of course not. Just because I've been out dancing once or twice and to the pictures with a lad doesn't mean anything"

Mary couldn't wait to get the story told, "She had him here for his tea with David and myself the other night. She was frightened that Jimmy or Charlie would come in. They would have let Dad know."

"Is this true Jessie, what Mary is telling me?"

"Yes Mam, it is true but there was no harm in it Jim is a fine lad. He gets fed up sometimes as he has to spend time in lodgings."

"Well we had best put this to rights and ask him for his dinner on a Sunday when Dad is here. That way there will be no more need for telling tales. He will be your guest with my approval. Does that please you?"

Jessie was blushing, "Maybe he won't come. He'll be frightened of meeting you and Dad."

"We were young once you know. We understand what it's like. There's no shame in bringing your friends home for a cup of tea. Better that than hanging about dark closes."

"I won't be seeing him until Sunday night for he goes home on Saturday to Aboyne to visit his family."

"Well that's fine it will give me time to see Dad and make him aware of what is what. Aboyne is away north of Aberdeen is it not? What is he doing down here in Brechin?"

Jessie had still not got over her mother's acceptance of her friendship with a young man and broke into her prepared promotion speech of all the virtues of 'her' Jim Mill.

"He works with the thrashing mills and can drive lorries. His father has a farm, but his older brothers work with his father. He comes from a big family, but is very well dressed and very well spoken. He goes where the mills have to be taken to different farms. Of course he always comes back to the yard at Brechin when the work is over. He is very honest Mam." Maggie stopped her, "For goodness sake Jessie draw breath, I think we've had enough background meantime."

Mary interrupted, "She'll not stop Mam. We are getting fed up with Jim Mill morning, noon and night. I swear she even speaks about him in her sleep."

Maggie laughed, "It must be serious then and all in five weeks."

Again Mary volunteered information, "She's known him longer than that, just never dared to say."

"Well we will see for ourselves when he comes for dinner. David will be up the stairs any minute. Fill up the teapot. I see you've got his favourite, an apple tart from Belford's bakery."

"Mary ran up for it; you spoil him Mam getting one for him every day. We thought it would be a good sign that you are back again."

When David came hurrying through the door Maggie for the first time appreciated how handsome a man he was. His golden curly hair and fair complexion. Although not as tall as his father, David was well built. The work at the sawmill had developed his shoulder muscles. He ran forward and lifted her from the floor in a bear type hug. "You're home at last. How I have missed you ma. Where's our John?"

"Put me down you ruffian, before I give you a clip round the ear. John is putting his clothes away in the drawers. More than you do without nagging."

David kissed her cheek. "You have no idea how much I missed that nagging. Mind you Jessie and Mary together almost made up for you."

"Come on then, let's all sit down and have our tea. Tomorrow Saturday night, Dad, Jimmy and Charlie will be here with us. We will all be together again."

David was washing his hands and face at the sink, while Maggie filled the teacups.

"Dad thought you had ran out on him, you know. Couldn't believe you could do something on your own without his approval."

"So I believe, you didn't do much to stop him worrying either. That was a wicked thing to let your father suffer, David. You could just have told him right away that I was called to see Janet as she was ill.

"Did the old bugger good to worry for once about his actions."

"Stop that swearing at once, especially when referring to your father. Do you understand David?"

"Yes Mam I understand and so does he now, that there is to be no more bowing and scraping to him. He is just the same as the rest of us here and will treat us with some respect. No more drunken abuse or he'll be out on his ear in the street. What is more I told him that to his face." "Oh David what are you saying? What have you done? Your father does not need to be cut off any more from his family. He needs to be here with us. That is the problem He feels he's not good enough for us. I believe you did mean well but don't interfere between your father and myself. We managed before we had you."

David set down the towel, took Maggie's hands in his, "Look mam, Jessie, Mary and myself cannot stand it any longer watching you run yourself into an early grave, while he stands about public houses, then comes home drunk and shouting all kinds of lies about you. We love you mam and just will not see it happen. Dad agrees that he has not been playing the game. Neither he nor our Jimmy. He is the cause of trouble between you Dad, and Charlie stays away because he cannot stand the rows. We just want the best for you, what you deserve. We think think that's what dad might want as well, but has a funny way of showing it. The fear of losing you, we think, has made him see sense. Let's hope so for I mean what I said he'll go out through that door." The chatter went on at the table without Maggie really hearing it there must have been some sort of confrontation between Jessie, David and Jim. Certainly Mary had hinted as much on the road from the station. Jim would not have enjoyed being warned by David about his behaviour. Yes he was more of a man than she ever imagined.

Saturday afternoon Jim appeared as Maggie was starting to prepare the evening meal. "You're home again then Maggie, I'm so glad. How was Janet?"

"She's not bad Jim, just a done lonely old woman. You are early I haven't got the tatties ready for the pot yet."

"Yes lassie I just couldn't get down the street quick enough to see if you were here. Maggie I'm sorry for all the upsets I've caused you. Never mind the damned tatties. Come and sit down with me a minute or two, while we have a bit of peace and quiet on our own to speak to each other." He took the knife from her hand and led her across to the fireside chair. "You know Maggie in the thirty years we've been together we've had many ups and downs but I was never so frightened in my life as when I came home and you were not here. I thought you had left me. Oh I wouldn't blame you if it had been true. I've said many times to you that you would be far better off without me. I couldn't live without you. God alone knows why I go and take dink, for it brings me more misery than I can handle. It's even turned my own family against me." Maggie sat with her head bowed, "Jim I just don't know what to say to you. I do know that we have been growing further apart, with little or nothing to say to each other. I had made up my mind after getting your letter that perhaps I was at fault and did not give you enough of my time. Now our family is grown up and we should be able to spend time enjoying each other's company."

Jim smiled, "They are grown up alright, David has already told me to mend my ways or he'd throw me out on the street. He could do it as well. Working away all week doesn't give us any family life. I will try and keep away from the public houses Maggie. Not because of what David said but to save our life together. What do you think of trying again to put up with me?" "Oh Jim, the faults are at both our feet. We will just have to be patient with each other and not take things for granted. I could never leave you. I'm sure you know that fine. The bairns in their own way were just trying to head us in the right direction, back to each other."

"Well I hope they have succeeded Maggie lass." He kissed her on the cheek.

"I'd better get on with the tatties. Oh we are getting Jessie's young man for dinner next Sunday. Did you know that she was courting?"

Jim stirred up the fire, lit his pipe with a stick before answering, "No I didn't but if he's serious about our Jessie then he'll need a will of iron to handle that one. She's a grand lass and feared of nothing or anyone, if she's made up her mind about something. A good tonguing or two I've had from her. Who is this lad anyhow?"

"Oh some farmer's son from Aboyne, who drives a motor and works with thrashing mills."

"He's a bit far from home down here if his father has a farm?"

"Oh Jessie has nosied into all that, he has older brothers who work the farm with his father. She's seeing him tomorrow about coming to meet us.

Jim chuckled "Just as well I'm to be on my best behaviour then." Maggie turned from the sink and looked him in the face.

"I'm only joking lassie, I've never been more serious in my life about trying to change. What would I have without you and yours? Nothing I would have nothing and be nothing. I promise you that things will be different."

CHAPTER THIRTY THREE

J ESSIE'S ENGAGEMENT BROUGHT a flurry of activity to
their High Street home. Maggie enjoyed entertaining her
daughter's young friends who suddenly started calling and
spent hours through 'the room' giggling and chatting.

Jim's sisters had also paid her the honour of dropping in for a
chat.

"I believe your Jessie has landed herself a farmer's son for a lad,"
announced Bella as she sat at the table waiting for tea to be poured
for her.

"Well she's become engaged to be married to a fine hard working
young man, whose father works a farm in Aberdeenshire."

"My, our Jim will be real pleased with that," said Helen.

Maggie filled her cup for her and handed it over. "Jim is happy
that his lassie seems to have found a decent man to share her life with.
There are so many without work or prospects these days it makes life
difficult for the young ones starting a home together."

Bella reached across the table and helped herself to a buttered
scone. "You have a short memory Maggie. Things are no more
difficult than they were when we were young. I think in fact that they
have things easier. What do you think Helen?"

"Well my family that are already married are having as big
a struggle for survival as we did. Things cost much more now and
there are farm workers that have no free meal, milk and tatties, and
the bairns are going hungry. Factory work is fine but the wages don't
pay enough for the food they need. If the Soshie stopped their 'black
books' for tick and had no dividend for checks for the money spent in
their shops, how would ordinary folks like us live?'"

Bella was quick to answer her sister, "Maggie never buys from the Soshie, she gets no dividend, yet she has managed to bring up her family. Seems as she's to get a farmer's lad for her son-in-law into the bargain."

"You have to give Maggie credit for what she has done Bella. We have always admired how her bairns have been 'turned out' in good clothes. Well fed and good mannered."

Maggie could feel herself blush, where was all this praise leading. She had long known how her sisters in-law considered her to be a snob and a cut above the rest.

"They are no different to any other family," she managed to say before Bella pose the answering question.

"We will be getting an invite to the wedding party to meet this young man and his family, no doubt?"

So that was what the visit and the flattery were all about.

"Oh I'm leaving all the planning and such things to them to sort out. Our Jessie is not the one for having people interfere in her business. It's not the first time that Jim has mentioned that she is very like you in that respect Bella." Maggie could see that Helen was amused by her quick thinking.

"Have they managed to find a place to stay yet?" asked Helen.

"Not so far, they are still looking. Eight weeks yet before the date they have set in October. Hopefully something will turn up for them," answered Maggie.

"After such a long engagement let's hope it is a place to stay and not something else that crops up," said Bella still squirming from being put in her place.

"You are such a bitch Bella. If you can't say something good then you should keep quiet. I think it's time we left you in peace Maggie. No doubt we will be hearing or seeing you before the happy day. If I hear of a house for them I'll let you know as soon as I can. Come on Bella you've to bike back to Dumbarrow before it's dark. Maybe it will give you time to think."

"There's no need to rush off," said Maggie trying to be polite, but wishing they would just go.

Helen lightly kissed Maggie's cheek, "No we must be getting on, Bella would sit all night if I let her, then have to stay overnight with me, because she couldn't see the road to bike in the dark."

"Aye it's no joke living away out in the country. You 'townies' have it easy. At least I'm saved from having to walk the eight miles, by borrowing one of the laddie's bicycles."

"Come on then, for he's maybe needing it to go courting a farmer's lassie, then Maggie will be able to quiz you."

As she ushered them down the stairs Maggie said, "I'm sure if they are to have any sort of party then Jessie will be in touch with you both. Thank you for calling in. Be careful going home Bella, and if you hear of a house Helen, we'd be grateful to you for letting us know."

Helen was as good as her word. A few days after the visit, Maggie got back from her daily pilgrimage to Belford's bakery, for David's apple tart, to find a note saying that a house opposite the Railway station was being vacated. Helen had even gone to the bother of finding out that the lease of the property was being handled by Kinghorn the solicitor.

Jessie was so excited by the news she could not eat her dinner. "I think I'll just take the afternoon off and go and find out about it. What do you think Mam?"

"Well you need all your pennies, to be taking time off your work. You will have to see what Jim thinks; after all it will be his home. I'll go up to the office this afternoon and find out for you all about the rent, lease and if you want to make an appointment for you both to see the place. How will that do?"

Jessie looked unhappy at the thought of having to wait until evening for any news.

"Oh mam, Jim is so busy just now harvesting, he'll never be able to get time to see it. All right I'll see hear what you have to say at teatime. You're right about the money for we will have furniture and everything to buy."

The house was just ideal for them starting off married life. Maggie kept to her word and had gone that afternoon to the solicitor, who had given her the key to view the property. There were two large ground floor rooms that face the entrance to the rail station. The late afternoon sun filled the rooms making them warm and welcoming. The living room had a white porcelain sink in the window. Maggie thought she would have enjoyed standing working at the sink, while watching all the comings and goings from the station entrance. The shared toilet was inside the close next to the door that led to the wash house and drying green.

"I tell you Jessie if it wasn't for you needing a place to set up house I would be asking your father to look at it for us. No stairs and such a nice place to stay."

"How would you all manage to fit in there?" asked Jessie frightened that her mother might go after the house for herself.

"Well you won't be living here much longer, Mary is walking out with that young fellow Stirling from Forfar. I don't suppose we will have her company if they have marriage in mind. David and John would just have to move where your father and I made our home."

"You never change, do you mother? Really you could go wherever you want to live, for Dad doesn't care where he sleeps off his Saturday night boozing. You would be soft enough to move house and let him take the loan of you."

"Jessie you are not to say such vindictive things about your father. Do you understand? Maybe with you all off my hands we will be able to spend more time together."

"I just hope that he manages to stay away from the pubs and drink the night of the wedding. I don't want any arguments in front of Jim's family. Mary will have Stirling with her as well and she will not want a red face."

'Your father will not let you down. Believe me." Said Maggie most emphatically.

However, in her heart of hearts she knew that her guarantee was only lip service, for Jim's promises of abstinence were worthless.

The wedding day being Friday, Jessie did not go back to work after dinnertime. She had been paraded from the factory, up Bridge Street, with an old curtain draped over her head. Bright coloured paper chains were hung over her shoulders. She was made to carry the customary gift of a chamber pot filled with salt and a celluloid dolly. This was the token which would bring good luck and healthy bairns to the newly weds. Her friends from the weaving shed had also collectively given money to buy the couple a fireside rug and a set of pots for their new home.

Maggie had not been idle. The big bedroom had been cleared of furniture. A large trestle table, borrowed from the Temperance Hall across the street, was in position against the fireplace wall. A cold buffet such as she had prepared in the days when she cooked for the gentry was set out and covered over.

"I've left your clothes and Mary's in the wee room," she told Jessie. "The boys and your father will just have to get ready in the wash house. Their clothes are hanging up in the attic. I've lit the boiler fire for plenty of hot water, so that you can have a bath in there before they all come home. I'm just concerned that I've made enough trifle, cakes and things. Your father is to bring a half bottle of whisky, port and sherry, when he comes back about four o'clock."

"That's early for him, he never usually gets in until about nine o'clock on a Saturday. Even then by the state of him it's a wonder he made it."

"Jessie your father will be here he promised. It was himself that made the arrangements to be finished early. It's not every day that his daughter gets married. What ever you think of him lassie, your father has always loved and cared about you. It would not be fair of you to leave the home he has provided you with until today without letting him know how you appreciated what he has done for you."

Jessie put her arms around her mother's neck.

"Oh Mam, hold me close just for a minute. I know who made our home what it is and who it is who needs to be thanked for our upbringing. You made us what we are Mam. You are the one who never thinks of yourself. You would work your fingers to the bone to provide for us. It's not the first time you've come up from the washhouse with your knuckles bleeding from scrubbing other folks washing to make an extra penny. Don't make Dad out to be something that he's not. The credit is yours mam. Thank you. I can only hope that if I'm blessed with bairns I can manage to give them as much love and comfort as you have given to us."

Maggie lifted the corner of her overall and wiped the tears from her face.

"Away you go and get washed Jessie Chisholm, making me look worse than I really am, with bleary eyes. Of course you'll have bairns and a good life ahead of you for you have chosen a good man. Hurry up now and you'll see Dad will be in by the time you are washed. He might just get a minute or two with you himself to tell you what he has to say. Don't be too hard on him for he hasn't had things easy either. Now off you go."

It was just after four o'clock when Jim came up the stairs.

"I'm here lass, got finished at mid yoking. Left before the lads even had their pieces started. I've brought the drink for the toasts. Sherry and port, for we've no idea what Jim's mother will take. We can't make a fool of our Jessie before she leaves the house. Where is she anyhow?"

"She's in the washhouse having a bath, she'll be up in a minute. I think the nerves are beginning to get the better of her, so be patient with her."

"Lord lass, these last few days I've thought so much about how I've missed her growing up. So many times I have repeated in my head what she told me before I went away to the war. "I'll kiss you every night Dad and no matter where you are Dad you'll get that kiss. Do you remember Maggie?"

"I do that Jim and I think you should tell Jessie that for she is feeling so unsure of herself and how you feel about her."

All the activity of getting ready was over. Jessie and Mary had left the house accompanied by their mother and father to arrive at the vestry of the Cathedral for six o'clock.

The four Chisholm boys sat in the living room patiently waiting for their return and the start of the celebrations.

"Jimmy, you and Charlie should be wearing green garters, for Jessie is younger than you both and married first."

"Would suit Jimmy fine, with those fancy patent leather dancing shoes he's got on, with that suit he got on the never, never, from the flying draper," said Charlie.

"If the old man finds out he's not paid for them there will be hell to pay. You had better keep up the payments boy, or the tailor will be after the money from our Mam. No way is she going to pay it for you. Isn't that right Charlie," said David.

"Alright David, he has got the message just make sure that there is nothing goes wrong to spoil tonight for Mam. You are not to cause any bother with dad, Jimmy. No taking too much to drink. If our dad should have a few drams and on an occasion like this he is entitled to enjoy himself, none of your cheeking up to him. Alright."

Jimmy got up from the edge of the bed where he had been sitting next to John. "I'm sorry that I said I would be here. I could have been playing billiards instead of being accused of being the family troublemaker," he said.

John leaned forward and pulled him down by the back of his jacket. "Just sit down and let them finish what they have to say Jimmy,"

"Seems as though you are all ganging up on me. You've all been speaking behind my back.

Charlie moved forward towards his older brother.

"Yes maybe we have, but we intend that nothing goes wrong to spoil what is the most important day in our sister Jessie's life. Our Mam has worked so hard for this day and up to now any fights or arguments in this house have been caused in some way because of your selfishness. Remember this and for once go out of your way to please our Mam, by being the man she thinks you are and everything will be great. David is right in what he says about the clothes. You fall behind once with the money and we promise you if mam finds out and has to pay a penny piece we will punch the price out of your hide."

With all the promises made and agreed about future lives together it was time for the party to begin. By seven thirty everyone was thoroughly enjoying themselves. Jessie and Jim were waltzing around the floor to the music from a borrowed gramophone. Maggie and Jim were seated by the window with the groom's parents.

"I hope they are always as happy as they are tonight," said Maggie.

"We are so pleased to see him settling down with a wife and a home of his own. Jessie is just what he needs, she is such a hard working lass. Nothing scatter brained about her like a lot of the young women these days," volunteered Jim's father.

"Aye you are right there," replied Jim. "She's very like her mother, not only in looks but nature as well. My Maggie usually has the answers to most things and can turn her hand to anything. If Jessie lives up to her mother's teachings then your laddie will have a grand life."

Maggie could feel her face turn scarlet.

"What on earth are you blethering about Jim Chisholm? What will these good folks think of us?"

"Oh don't think we haven't noticed ourselves that Jessie is prepared to tackle anything. That was what we liked about her the first time

Jim brought her home. She was out in the fields helping with the rest of the family, as though she had been born to farm work, instead of her being born a 'townie'. She's also such an attractive looking lass. Our laddie has made a good choice. We think they will be very happy together."

The party went on well after midnight. Everyone joined in the singing and dancing. David spent most of the evening in the company of one of Jessie's weaver friends from the factory. When Mary and Maggie were washing up some cups for the ever-flowing tea, they both spoke of the attention he was paying to the girl.

"Who is she anyhow, Mary?"

"Oh she's one of the girls from Bridge Street. She works beside Jessie on her pass'. She's not to be there long though for she wants to be a cook and is leaving to go to the Asylum at Hillside for training. There you won't need to worry about your precious laddie being taken from you for she's going away from Brechin."

At five o'clock Maggie managed to crawl over to her space at the back of the bed. Jim had been asleep for two hours. It had only been about one o'clock after his daughter and her 'new' husband left to go to her own home that he began to show the signs of having drank too much. She was surprised at how well her boys had behaved and managed to keep the party going. Yes it had been a grand affair. No arguments or bickering.

They were a family to be proud of.

CHAPTER THIRTY FOUR

MONDAY MORNING FOLLOWING the wedding brought a letter from Canada. Its arrival made Maggie aware that she had not heard any news of her daughter for over a year. Certainly, she was not prepared to be informed that by the time she received the mail, Margaret was most likely a mother herself.

There were expressions of much regret by Margaret at not advising Maggie earlier she had been married for over a year. Finding a home and all that it entailed had kept them busy. Margaret had met her husband at the House of Commons in Ottawa, where she was working as a stenographer. Frank her husband was in charge of the library. Their marriage had taken place only six weeks after their first meeting, they were so happy and eagerly awaiting the arrival of their baby.

Maggie sat by the fireside, with the folded notepaper in her hand. Sounded as if things had turned out well for her lassie. Married to someone who had an important government position. She was a stenographer. John might be able to explain what kind of work that entailed. John Fraser must have passed on his quick brain and learning ability to his daughter.

How many hours of worry had been wasted on trying to project what life might have to offer her children.

They all seemed to be well equipped to manage by themselves.

The wedding party made it clear that Mary and David were not to be long in choosing partners for their future lives. There would be a new generation of bairns to care for.

The little Canadian she might never see in the flesh, but she would most certainly write and ask for photographs to be sent on to her as soon as possible. With a husband with a 'moneyed' position there was even an outside chance that someday her daughter might bring the baby to Scotland, where she herself had been born.

She would have easy access to any family produced by Jessie, Mary And David.

Strange that Jimmy and Charlie were not thinking of settling into homes with wives of their own. They had never shown any signs of interest in the local girls.

A knock on the door disturbed her reverie. "Are you in Mrs Chisholm?" echoed up the stairs.

One of the neighbours in passing, handing in a little gift for the 'newly weds'.

"Just a little thing for luck to them. Young couples these days need as much of that as they can get, eh?"

Maggie accepted the small parcel from the woman she recognised as one who lived in Bridge Street.

"That's quite true with so many unable to find work. I'm thankful that mine are all working," Maggie told her.

"Aye I expect I should feel the same for mine that are an age for working have something to go too. Lizzie is getting on fine at Sunnyside learning the cooking. Not that I see much of her for when she does come home, for your laddie, the red headed one, takes up most of her time."

Maggie immediately recognised who this friendly woman was, "You must be Mrs Petrie, I'm so sorry for not realising who you were. Do come in and have a cup of tea."

"No, no that's not needed I just wanted to hand in the wee thing, you see your Jessie worked beside my oldest lassie Annie, before she married and went away to live in Dundee. They were good pals and went to the dancing together. I'll have to get back for the bairns dinners. They'll soon be out of the school."

"Well you'll have to come back when you have a bit more time and let me make you a cup of tea. Tell me how is Annie, for I've no doubt Jessie will want to know?"

"Oh she's keeping not so bad this time, not as she was when carrying Nan. Sick all the time. I think they are hoping for a laddie this time."

"My goodness, so you are a granny already, and still family at the school. You don't look old enough to be a granny."

"Well I don't suppose I feel like it either for Annie's lassie Nan is older than my youngest one. You'll maybe find yourself in the same boat if Jessie 'falls' soon."

This was not a thought that Maggie would even entertain.

"I don't think that is very likely Mrs Petrie. You'll have to excuse me now for I can smell the soup; it's maybe sticking to the pot. Do come in someday when you have more time. I'll have a word with David taking up Lizzies time. If you want?"

"Mercy no dinna' do that. You canna interfere with the young ones love life. They'll sort things out for themselves. Just as we did. I'll take up your invite for a 'fly cup' and drop in sometime. Bye for now."

As she busied herself setting the table Maggie thought of the woman's words about her becoming a mother again. Mercifully there was no chance of that happening again. She did regret not being able to talk about her grandchild. She could not even tell her own family of the existence of their 'half sister', as it had never been explained to them. Jim was the only one aware of Margaret and her whereabouts.

"There's a present for you and Jim from Mrs Petrie in Bridge Street,"

she told Jessie when she appeared for her dinner.

"That was nice of her Mam. Her daughter Annie was my pal before she got married and went to live in Dundee."

"So I believe," said Maggie, "But there's someone else who is very friendly with one of her lassies, eh David."

"So what?" answered her son with a face the colour of a beetroot. "Has to be to have anything to do with him," giggled John.

"That's enough of that John. Leave David alone. Who his friends are is his own business. Get on with your dinner or you'll be late back at school."

"Annie has a little girl and is expecting another soon, Jessie. Her mother was telling me."

"She's a nice lassie Annie, so is her sister Lizzie, David's girl. There's a big family of them. Seven all living in two rooms with no running water or anything."

"That can't be easy for Mrs Petrie and her 'late' bairn younger than Annie's."

"They're very clean Mam," said David, "and they don't all live in two rooms. Jimmy the oldest son works at the sawmills and lives away from home. That's one of the reasons Lizzie went into cooking so that she could get free board and a room to herself," David volunteered. "She won't be having a bed to herself for long if you get your way David," said John as he jumped out of the way of his brother's clenched fist. "John I will not have any suggestive talk here in front of the girls. Get away to the school. What does Mr Petrie work at then?"

Before Jessie or Mary could answer David replied, "He works with the 'black squad' in the factory. Since the War it's the only work he could get. He's got the Military Medal for saving Archie Duke's life when they were fighting in the trenches. Of course Dukie was the commanding officer as well as the owner of the factory, so he gave Mr Petrie a job when the fighting was over."

"You seem to have ferreted out all about them," said Mary.

"Just the same as you have found out about your lad's folks in Forfar, Mary."

The peace and quiet of the afternoon was most welcome.

David certainly appeared to be very interested in his girl's family. They were so similar to her own. The father, who was honoured for acts of bravery during the War, forced through lack of opportunity to accept the favour of a lowly labouring job in the blacksmith's squad. Their two roomed home, without basic facilities, offering shelter to the parents and seven of a family. Little wonder people left to set up homes abroad, where rewards for work were more in balance.

Since the afternoon when Maggie 'viewed' the house for Jessie and Jim she had considered many times her conversation with her daughter. "You could live anywhere, Mam."

Could she take John and start a new life for them both in Canada or New Zealand?

If Jim cared enough about them, as when sobering up on Sunday's he professed to do, then he would just have to follow them.

John would soon be leaving school and looking for work.

What was there for him in Brechin? Lack of money put an end to any career Charlie could have had in banking. Jimmy seemed to get by with what he earned doing various labouring jobs, so long as his time for billiards was not curtailed. The girls would be happy enough coping with homes and families of their own. If David were serious about his girl friend then maybe they would marry and emigrate as well.

Did she have the courage to make her move and put to test the theory that her family would follow her to another country and a better life?

By Christmas Jessie knew that she was expecting a baby.

"I'll have to try and keep on at the factory until after Easter," she told her mother. "There's no need for thrashing mills at this time of year. Jim is talking of us moving back to Aberdeen, where he could maybe get a job driving one of Charlie Alexander's fish lorries down to England."

"You are giving me good and bad news all at one time. How could I look after your bairn to let you work if you move away from Brechin?'

Jessie could see that her mother was upset by her news.

"If Jim had a steady well paid job then I wouldn't need to work. I would be free to take care of the bairn myself. That's what I want Mam. You never worked. You were always here when your bairns needed you for anything."

"I don't know so much about that Jessie, but knowing you I'm positive you'll do what you think is right. I'm very happy for you both that the baby is on the way."

"What do you think of being a granny, eh? Something for you to tell Dad. Maybe he'll act his age and be a bit more responsible when he's got a grandchild."

Maggie took Jessie's hands in hers.

"I have something to tell you lass. I think it is one of the most difficult things I have ever had to explain in my life. I suppose I'm frightened of what you will think of me after you hear what I have to say. It's a secret that your father has kept for me all our married life."

"For God's sake mother, you make it sound as though you have committed a crime of some kind. Whatever are you on about?"

"Well in a way I suppose you are right. You see when I was a young girl and in service, I had a baby and had to give it to someone else to care for. She's married and now a mother herself."

Jessie's face turned white. "Oh Mam," was all she could gasp for a minute, then "Where is she now? Do I know her? Is she our father's bairn? Is so why did he not bring her up?"

"Jessie, Jessie give me time. This is not easy for me after all those years of trying to think of the right way to tell you about Margaret. She is in Canada. No you don't know her and no your father is not hers."

Maggie felt so tired and wearied but relieved that at long last her secret was out.

"This is just too much for me to take in Mam, I can't believe that you of all people would have an illegitimate bairn."

"Well it's true I can assure you. I was just a young country lassie who was 'taken in' by a good-looking man's 'sweet talk' and charm before he cleared off to avoid facing his responsibilities. My foster sister Mary McDonald brought up the bairn as her own. When they emigrated to Canada, Margaret was just an infant and I never saw her again. She has written to me though."

"What does our father think about all this?'

"Well before we married I told him the whole story. He was quite prepared to have Margaret brought back and raised as his daughter. Her home was with who she thought was her mother and father in Canada."

"You said she writes to you. Where are the letters?"

Maggie took the letters from their hiding place in an old handbag. "Read them through while I make a cup of tea for us. News of having a new bairn, new sister and a niece all in an hour is just enough for any mortal to cope with."

After reading the letters and finishing off her tea Jessie handed the envelopes back to her mother. "So you are a granny already, Maggie, mine will not be the first."

The use of her Christian name conveyed as a term of endearment indicated that Jessie was struggling to come to terms with the revelation.

This caused them both to shed tears. "Why have you kept this to yourself for all those years, you silly old woman? Do you not understand how much we all love you Mam? Torturing yourself."

"I was afraid how you would judge me, giving up my own flesh and blood. Believe me Jessie I had no choice at all. Many a night I've cried myself asleep for my bairn."

Jessie wiped her mother's cheeks. "Come on now that's all behind you now. Once Mary and the boys are told then we can speak quite freely about your grandchild. Is it a boy or a girl?"

"I don't know for I've never had the courage to write and find out."

"Well you have plenty of time in the evenings to get writing. Leave it to me to tell the others. Everything will be fine. Is Dad the only person you have ever told?"

"No I told your auntie Janet before I even met your father.'

"Did she make things difficult for you, with her knowing?"

"No not really but she used to go on about children being gifts from God to be cared for and looked after. My conscience found it hard to cope with such lectures knowing that I had betrayed my child by giving her away."

"That was the only thing you could have done. How could you have managed to support a bairn with no man behind you and having to work all God's hours? Margaret has had a good life and upbringing and from her letters has done a pretty well for herself into the bargain. The rest will see it the same. Dad is a fly old devil keeping something like this to himself all those years."

CHAPTER THIRTY FIVE

MAGGIE HAD NEVER felt so excited about the arrival of a baby since carrying her own. Jessie was round to the High Street home everyday to report her daily state of health. "You have knitted and made enough clothes for a regiment of bairns, Mam. It's just one that I'm having you know."

"Och, Jessie you wouldn't grudge me the pleasure of making for the wee one. Mind you by the look of the size of you it's not so wee, might even be a regiment.

"Could be twins. I had one set of twins you know."

Maggie looked across at Jessie as she sat looking out the window.

"Oh I'm sorry for mentioning it to you lass at such a time. Your babies will be fine and healthy. It's going to be a big lad like your Jim or your father."

"Well we will know for sure in the next week or so. I hope it's at the weekend when Jim is home. I hate when he is away driving lorries."

"Do you think he wants to be away? You should be careful in what you say to him Jessie. You are very lucky with a man who has a well-paid job and is prepared to work night and day to give you a good wage.

"I know what you say is right Mam, when the baby arrives it will be company for me."

"Company," Maggie laughed, "You won't have enough hours in the day to finish everything that babies need done for them."

"You managed fine with all of us and I can remember when you had granddad to look after as well."

"Surely you cannot remember as far back as that Jessie, for you were just a bairn when he died?"

"Well maybe you are right Ma, it's probably hearing the boys talking about it, how he went off the head and set his house on fire."

"Och Jessie, he wasn't off his head, just a poor lonely old man who couldn't cope with life on his own. I'm surprised at you thinking of such things that are so long gone in the past."

"How far back into your life can you remember Mam, How did you feel when you were waiting for your first bairn to be born?"

Maggie moved across the room to stand beside her daughter, placing her hand on Jessie's shoulders.

"What kind of daft notions are you sitting there dreaming up to yourself? Your baby is going to be fine and healthy. When I had my first bairn there was no good and loving mam to help me. Circumstances were very different but I still

had love and attention from my so called Mam, Annie McDonald."

"You have never told us of your real Mam, Auntie Janet's sister. Why was that? Do you remember her or how your mother and father both died, leaving you orphans?"

Maggie could feel her whole body trembling the moment she had dreaded most of her life was now upon her. How could she tell her children of how both her parents had taken their own lives and left their children destitute?

"You must think I have a wonderful memory lassie to think back over fifty years. The only mother I had was at Culburnie. It was some kind of accident in Glasgow that caused us to be left on our own."

"Did you never ask Janet what happened to them? I am sure I would have."

"Yes Jessie I'm certain you would. However, you know the sort of person Janet is and unless it is something she wants you to know then you are wasting your breath asking. All this questioning you must be thirsty. I'll make us both a 'fly cup'. Jessie sat quiet in the window space watching the activity in the street, while Maggie made the tea and spread butter on two slices of home made ginger bread.

"That is one of the things I remember from being a bairn, the smell of your baking Mam,"

"Lord lassie are we still on this journey into the past?"

"Well if I don't ask we would never know for you never tell us much about when you were young. Maybe a bit about your brothers being in New Zealand but how long did it take for us to know we had a sister in Canada or who her father was. You must have been just a bairn yourself when you had her."

"What difference does it make to you now wanting to know all about my past?"

Jessie leaned across the table and grasped her mother's hand in hers. "Maggie, I know you better than you know yourself and the man that was the father of your bairn must have loved you at one time. What happened to him that you were left on your own to face the wrath of your family and the kirk?"

"There was no wrath from my family as far as I was concerned. They stood by me just as I would you. I suppose if Donald had managed to get his hands on him things might have been different. You know how my adopted sister brought up Margaret as her own, in Canada."

"Aye, and what about the father?"

"Well he was the tutor to the young lairds at the 'big house' where I worked near Inverness. After I moved to a better job in Glasgow he would come to meet me sometimes and we would travel back on the train together when I had a few days off to spend at Culburnie. Och there was trouble about another lass he had been seeing before me and he cleared out of the district."

"Then what happened did he not get in touch with you if he loved you so much?"

"No things were not so simple as that. He went away to fight in the Boer War."

"Was he killed fighting there side by side with Dad?"

"For mercy sake Jessie, it had nothing to do with your father, I didn't even know him then."

"Well I do know for in 1921 there was a flu epidemic with hundreds of people in Glasgow dying. In the paper it said 'High Ranking Police Officer Dies of Flu'. Thinking maybe it was someone your father might have worked with, when he was in Glasgow police, drew my attention to it. There it was in black and white. No doubt about it. It was Margaret's father."

"Does she know about it then Mam?"

"No Jessie I suppose that now I have told you we are the only two on earth who know. Now can we end this conversation?"

"I suppose so but first let me tell you that I can understand how desperate you must have been to hand over your bairn to someone else. I know how much you love us all Mam and it must have torn you apart. Nothing or nobody will ever take my bairn from me. That's for sure."

"Will you never leave 'it' with its granny for a while?"

Jessie laughed, "Away you silly old wife, whenever 'it' needs spoiling, then round to you it will be. Pampered to the last. I can understand things you have had to face all by yourself. How you never wanted anything to do with the kirk, like getting us baptised, not mixing in with other people for fear they found out your secret, trying to get us to better ourselves. You are a wonderful Mam. You are going to have a big job on bettering that as a granny."

Maggie and Jessie hugged each other close for a minute without uttering a word. "You had better get away to your own house and get some tea ready for Mary, she'll be in a hurry to meet her young man, it's good that she is sleeping with you until Jim gets back with the lorry."

"You'll have company with John tonight after tea, no doubt David will be away biking to see Lizzie at the Asylum."

"Don't say it that way Jessie sounds as though she was a patient."

"She must be a bit daft to have fallen for our David, who is Mam's favourite."

"That's not true, you all mean the same to me. David is a fine lad though. He is good to his mam."

"Oh I'll have to agree with you on that but he can wrap you around his little finger. Wait until you are knitting for his bairn."

"Jessie you are awful. John will be home soon I'll need to get his tea sorted. There are no auctions today so the mart will close early."

"Aye Maggie, you never got Banker Charlie but you will soon have Auctioneer Johnnie."

"Your dad and me are so proud of him. He never tells you but dad is proud of you all."

"I suppose you are right as usual. Well I'm off. If I don't have to send Mary running round for you during the night then I'll see you tomorrow forenoon."

Maggie watched and waved to Jessie as she walked up City Road. Yes she was looking forward so much to handling the bairn. Jessie was a strange one wanting to know about her past. It was true Jim was looking forward to the new arrival. She remembered how he walked about their humble home in Glasgow, with his son Jim balanced on a cushion. Of course he was proud of them and loved them. It was such pity that he could not show his children how much they meant to him.

The evening meal was on the table when David and John rushed in together. "Great Ma, I'll wash first for I'm seeing Lizzie tonight. John nip down to the drying green and get that white shirt for me. Mam you can iron it while I'm eating."

"David I'm not your servant. There are other shirts."

"Yes I know Mam I just wanted him out of the room to show you this." From his dungaree pocket he produced a blue ring box. A diamond and sapphire engagement ring sparkled up at her. "I'm hoping when I come home tonight that Lizzie will have agreed to marry me."

"Oh David son, what can I say to you?' Maggie wiped the corners of her eyes with the dishtowel.

"Mam just say you are pleased for me. I love Lizzie as much as I love you."

He looked so happy standing there at the kitchen sink stripped to the waist washing himself. He was the one most like his father in looks and nature.

"Well I do wish you well son, but I wish Lizzie all the luck in the World when she takes on someone like you with your orders for shirts and Belford's apple tarts. Always be good to her David. Don't take someone you love for granted."

Maggie kissed him on the cheek. "Now get your tea and remember you'll have to ask her father's permission first. They are kirkie folk and will want things done the proper way. As it should be. When will we see Lizzie next? Hopefully when dad is here at the weekend."

David winced. "Well I suppose we had better face the 'old man' on Saturday or Sunday not that it will make any difference to him I expect."

John came into the kitchen with the shirt. "All right if I eat now Master David?" he said.

When Maggie had cleared away after the meal and sat by the fire with her knitting she felt tired. Well it had been an eventful day and she could not sleep soundly at nights waiting for news that Jessie had started.

There would something of interest to discuss with Jim on Saturday night. How would he react to David's plans for marriage and setting up his own home? Relations between Maggie and Jim had improved since David's ultimatum. There lay the problem they were so similar in every way yet could only see the flaws in the other. There would soon be only two of them left in the High Street home during the week. Unless of course Jim managed to find work nearer Brechin. Mary and her Jim Stirling were already looking for a house in Forfar, where they would live after marrying. So typical of Mary she wanted no fuss just a quiet ceremony in the vestry then on to their new home together, Of course nothing could be finalised so long as she had to 'look after' Jessie overnight until the bairn was born. The speed her family were marrying this would inevitably be the first of many grandchildren.

Maggie smiled to herself. What a wonderful thought.

Chapter Thirty Six

MAGGIE AND JIM were walking together along Damacre Road. They were both dressed in their Sunday best. "Tell me again Maggie, who the little fellow looks like? Is he like his mother and your side of the family or has he a bit of me about him?"

"Lord knows Jim you are so excited you would think that you were going to see the King himself instead of a six pounds bairn."

"I'll have you know this Maggie no Royalty means anything at all to me but the six pounds infant that you are talking about is my grandson Jimmy. I never had the chance to really enjoy our own bairns, but it will take wild horses to keep me away from this wee lad."

Maggie did not spoil Jim's moment of pleasure by telling him that in the near future Jessie, her husband and the new baby would be moving to Aberdeen, to make it easier for them to spend more time together as a family. He would find out soon enough.

The infant looked so small cradled in his grandfather's arms. Jessie put her arm on her father's shoulder. "You look so good nursing bairns Dad.'

"Oh you wouldn't remember about it lassie but I've had a fair bit of experience. Not the first time I've cleaned your backside and changed your 'hippens'. That's right is it not Maggie?"

Maggie was sat in the armchair by the fire, turning the baby clothes hanging on a drying screen. "That's true Jessie, your father was a dab hand with bairns. When you were all little I suppose I could have never coped without his help."

Jessie was far too happy to spoil the occasion by arguing and saying she found it hard to believe. The evening soon passed, with the proud grandparents watching Jessie bath Jimmy and settle him for the night.

As they walked home again Jim said "I can remember when we walked along here when I came home from the Great War. I was so pleased and happy to be getting home to my wife and bairns. Here's me now walking home the same road after seeing my grandson put to his bed. It's a grand feeling lass. The bairn is as bonnie as I've seen, but he has the looks of his father's family. Not that it matters a bit to me."

Maggie could detect from his tone that he was a bit disappointed. "Well maybe the next one will have your handsome figure and good looks. I'm sure with Mary marrying next month that Jimmy will not be our only grandchild very long. We will have to make the most of him while we can."

"Tell me what you mean by that Maggie? There's nothing wrong with the bairn is there?"

"No, no Jim nothing wrong with him he's a fine healthy wee laddie. No, it's just that Jessie was saying with Jim away all week with the lorries to Aberdeen they were thinking of getting a house there. That would mean Jim would see more of Jessie and the bairn than he does now."

They turned into the close at the Southport and up the stairs to their home.

Maggie busied herself poking the fire into a cheerful blaze, and then boiled the kettle for a cup of tea. Jim reappeared from through the room where he had put away his good clothes. He was wearing his moleskin work trousers and a vest and on his bare feet.

"You look pretty fit to be an old grandfather," teased Maggie as he leaned past her to light a taper for his pipe.

"Oh well I have to be in tip top condition, to live with an old granny."

They both sat quietly watching the flames dancing around the burning coals.

"You know Jim, this bairn is the best thing that has happened to us for a long time."

"As usual you are right Maggie. I was thinking about it when I was changing my clothes. I'd be a liar if I said I will not be disappointed if they move away to Aberdeen, but if it means they are all to be together, then I'm all for it. That was our trouble you know. It started with us not having time for each other, then drifting apart."

Maggie gave his bare foot a kick off the fender. "What do you mean apart? I'm still within kicking distance to keep you in line."

"Och Maggie lass, you know fine what I'm saying. This has been one of the very few enjoyable evenings we have spent together in years."

"That's true Jim but it could be the first of many in the rest of our lives together. Our bairns are finally grown up and we only have each other to please. It was just the times we lived in and lack of proper work that kept you away from home."

"Aye Jim Mill has the right idea he is taking what is precious to him to where the work is."

The year was good to the family. Mary was married and living in Forfar. David and Lizzie were still intent on marrying and setting up home as soon as they had saved enough money to buy furniture. John was doing well at his job at the auction mart. Charlie and Jimmy spent very little time in Brechin but both seemed happy to have work.

Maggie and Jim spent Saturday evenings and Sundays together. Jim was fascinated by the antics of his grandson. He just could not get enough time to be with him. Fortunately the move to Aberdeen had never taken place.

"See how he is toddling around Maggie. He really is a clever little chap." Maggie smiled at the sight of Jim crawling about the floor.

"You're like a bairn yourself. Jessie and Jim would have had a better laugh at you than the picture they've gone to see at the Regal."

"Hear that? He said Gaa Gaa. He knows me."

"Aye you are gaa, gaa, but it does my heart good to see you happier than you've been for years.

Jim picked the toddler up in his arms. "Come on then a kiss for your Gaa, Gaa bonnie lad."

Jimmy pulled at his grandfather's cheek with his podgy fat fingers, and then pushed his lips against the 'stubbly' chin.

"Oh you're my precious little man right enough. The weekend cannot come quick enough for me to get home and see how much you have grown while I'm at work." "That's true Jim you've never had a drink for weeks. Home for Friday night teatime. Saturday night playing with Jimmy."

'Yes Maggie and I get more pleasure from being a granddad than ever I got from any bottle. I was thinking that maybe tomorrow we could take the bus to Montrose and take Jimmy to the beach. I'm sure he would like to see the water."

Maggie gave him an affectionate clap on the back.

"When did you ever take any of our own bairns to the beach? Yes even the apple of your eye his mother Jessie."

"I suppose things were different then and I've got time to make up for my mistakes in the past. Just let's enjoy the bairn together lass."

With Jim away working week days Maggie had more time for her own pursuits.

After the household washing and ironing on Monday she decided that she would go to Forfar on the Tuesday morning and visit Mary when she was home from the factory for her dinner break.

Maggie opened the door with the key that Maggie had given her and proceeded to fill the kettle. She was quite startled when Mary appeared behind her still wearing her nightdress.

"For God's sake Mary you just about frightened the life out of me. Why are you not at your work? I brought pies and apple tarts for us to have our dinner together."

"Oh Mam I couldn't eat anything for I've been so sick. Every time I lift my head off the pillow. Even a drink of water won't stay down."

"Oh aye," said Maggie "how long has this been going on?"

"Just for the past two days."

"Have you seen the doctor yet? Don't you think it would be a good idea?"

"Och Mam, it will pass in a day or so then I'll be back at work as fit as a fiddle."

"Well you may be right Mary my lass, but I wouldn't be surprised if it's a bit longer than a day or two before you are better of this lot. Into bed with you and I'll bring a cup of hot sweet tea. You should get Jim Stirling to fetch you one in bed before he leaves in the morning."

"He doesn't have time for all that nonsense before getting to the factory to start at six. He'd think I was taking the loan of him."

"Well lassie it's been him taking the loan of you that's got you in this state today."

"Dinna be daft Mam, what has he to do with me being sick."

"Mary lassie, I've been there myself can you not work it out for yourself. You are expecting."

Maggie hugged Mary close to her. "Aye your father is going to have twice the pleasure before long. Young Jimmy will have a rival to compete with."

"You must think me awful stupid Mam for it never dawned on me that's what was wrong."

"Lord lassie there's nothing wrong with you, it's the most natural thing for a healthy young married woman to 'fall' with a bairn."

"We wanted me to be able to work for a while yet to get all the things we need for the house. Bairns need so much. Look at all the things Jessie need for Jimmy."

"Och away and lie down, things will turn out fine. The sickness never lasts long. You'll get back to the factory to work for a few months yet. It's amazing but bairns always bring a way of their own with them. Yours will be no different I'm sure, it will be well provided for. I'm so happy for you lass."

As she travelled back to Brechin on the bus, Maggie could imagine Jim's face when she gave him the good news on Friday night. She had promised Mary to keep her secret until the weekend to allow her to tell her father and Jessie herself.

As they sat at the tea table together David gave John a nudge on the arm

"Maggie was at Forfar today John, she's not saying very much about it.

Looks awful pleased with herself though. Have you noticed?"

John looked up, "Did you see Mary at her dinnertime mam? How was she?"

"Fine. How would you want me to find her then?"

"Alright of course," said David, "But you'd think you had spent the afternoon sitting in an empty room the amount of news or conversation you have given us. Did Mary and you fall out or something?"

"What nonsense next? Have you ever known me to fall out with Mary? She's fine. We just didn't have much time to gossip."

"Well then Mam I have a bit of news for you. Lizzie and I have had the chance to rent a room off River Street, at School lane. If it's all right then we will take it and plan to get married in September. Just Maggie and you then Johnnie lad."

"What is that supposed to mean David?"

"Well Dad is never here through the week. Weekend man only, Monday to Friday you'll only have John to spoil and cater for."

On Friday night after the family had left for their own houses, Maggie and Jim sat by the fireside. "We're getting like Darby and Joan, with the house to ourselves. Best enjoy the peace now for with more bairns there's not to be much of it in the future."

Jim chuckled, "Well if the next generation are all the same as young Jimmy then we are to be very lucky. It would be fine if Mary got a lassie."

Maggie looked across at him. "I can remember all those years ago, your father was so pleased that Jessie turned out to be a girl."

"Lord that was a long time ago. He couldn't understand why we didn't call her Margaret. Do you remember?"

"Aye I do that Jim, as if it was yesterday. Strange how I tried to keep the secret of Margaret from our bairns all those years. They quite accept that they have a sister in Canada. I heard John telling a friend just the other day after we got the letter with photographs of young John and Isobell."

"Aye you are a granny more than I am a grandfather. Jimmy makes up for any number of bairns."

"The years are slipping by so fast. Think of all the changes in our family since last year at this time.

"Well there's been a great deal of good to be pleased about."

"Yes the bairns have mad me feel so proud. Most of all though they've made me feel so happy and proud of the way you have turned away from drink and become a wonderful grandfather. Just the way I always imagined it would be. Your father was a wonderful man, with the bairns you know that, and there are times that you can be so like him."

"Well perhaps that's true Maggie I may be like him but I hope I don't end up in the Asylum as he did. Maybe if I'd gone on drinking that's what would have happened.

"Oh Jim, that will never happen. You have me and all your family around to care for you."

"Maybe so but I'll not forget David's threat to throw me out on my ear if I didn't pay you a bit more respect. He's quite a lad. I hope he takes his own advice and looks well after that wee lassie he's going to marry.' He paused for a minute; "I suppose that'll be more bairns for me from that partnership, as well. Och come on to bed Maggie we're not too old to shock them with one of our own."

CHAPTER THIRTY SEVEN

MAGGIE FELT SO glad to sit by the fire after clearing the table following the evening meal. David had been in such a rush and his excitement when getting ready to see the minister had done nothing towards easing the tiredness, which seemed to have overcome her. It would be the same from now until Friday when David and Lizzie married. Happy as she felt for them, the wedding just seemed to be at a time when everything was 'on top of her'. Mary was managing grand with her baby. He was such a good boy John. So different from Jimmy. John certainly had the build and looks of his grandfather. Now he was six weeks old Maggie stopped going to Forfar every other day, just to lend them a hand. Poor Mary worried so much about her infant who in spite of his mother fed, slept and was thriving like a mushroom. From the fender stool she picked up the People's Friend that David had thrown to her as he rushed in from work.

"There you are Maggie you'll get your feet up on the stool and read some of the 'sob stories' that appeal to you when you've the place to yourself tonight. By the time I get back you'll have tried all the knitting patterns and made jerseys for the bairns."

He was a good lad and she would miss him from the home. However, he was like his father in so many ways. David was of the same belief that 'the World owed him something'. One thing that was certain and Maggie never doubted, he loved her so very much.

Could he devote the same kind of love to the girl he was going to marry.

A noisy clanging bell in the street disturbed her. Maggie crossed to the window and watched the 'white van' from the Forfar Fever hospital manoeuvre its way down Bridge Street. Some poor family with illness in its home. Maggie recalled hearing, in the shops, of how some children in River Street had taken Scarlet Fever. It was so damp down there at this time of year. It was a relief to know that where David and Lizzie were to set up home was away from the worst flooding area. In any case their one room home was upstairs.

It was after eight o'clock when Maggie was aware of hearing footsteps on the stair. She must have nodded off, for the fire was low. John rushed across to warm his hands.

"What a horrible night out there. I would have been better staying here warm and cosy rather than going to the pictures."

"Was it worth watching. Tell me about it then, while I make us some tea."

"It was 'Tarzan the Apeman', all about a boy who was in an air crash. He was left in the jungle when his mother and father died in the crash. The apes and monkeys raised him and he could talk to all the animals."

"Sounds quite an exciting story."

"It was even more exciting when they stopped the show and the manager stood in front of the screen and asked for a family from River Street to go home at once. Wonder what they were being thrown out for?"

"Maybe they weren't as you say 'thrown out'. It could have been that they were needed urgently at home. I heard the 'Fever Van' from Forfar going down Bridge Street earlier tonight."

"Do you think that's what it was mam?"

"Lord laddie, I don't know but there was certainly worry and trouble for some poor family in River Street, tonight."

When Maggie was waiting to be served by the butcher the following morning, she could not help overhearing a conversation about two families in the Vennel, taken ill with diphtheria and rushed away to the Hospital at Forfar.

Other women started to join in the conversation regarding how foolish it had been to close the Brechin Fever Hospital as it made visiting so difficult.

The butcher added his words of wisdom "Of course you cannot get in to see people in isolation anyhow. You have to look at them from outside through the window."

"That's true," said a woman at the counter. "When my laddie had Scarlet Fever last year. I went up and down the path outside looking in every one of the ward windows, searching for my bairn. I couldn't see him anywhere in any of the beds or cots. I broke down and started to cry for I thought he had died and nobody had told me. Well I managed to get attention of a nurse and asked where Peter was. I just did not recognise my own bairn for they shaved off all his hair. Said it was to break the fever. Just about the end of me I can tell you."

"Never mind mistress," said the butcher, "He's still there today so they must have got something right to cure him."

"I suppose so," answered the woman, "But my heart goes out to those poor families struck down with diphtheria, for its very few come home from Forfar having survived such a killer. We can only hope that it does not spread through the town."

In the afternoon as she stood by the fire turning scones on the girdle Maggie could hear the bell of the 'Fever Van' ringing as it passed in the street. The noise stopped suddenly just below the kitchen window. Maggie wiped her 'floury' hands on a cloth as she ran across the room to look out at what was going on. A uniformed nurse and the driver of the van disappeared into the close.

Maggie could feel herself shaking at the thought of some of the neighbours' families having fallen victim to the killer illness. Passers by and shoppers stood on the far side of the street watching, oblivious to the risk of infection.

Eventually the nurse reappeared carrying 'the bairn' from next door. Maggie recognise the fair curly hair of the four years old little girl. Bessie was the youngest of eight and was the only daughter born late, after seven grown up sons. How could something such as this happen? Bessie was a well nourished, much loved bright little girl who was adored by her family. The van doors slammed closed leaving Bessie's parents standing forlornly on the pavement. They would not be able to hold their bairn again until she was free from infection and cured.

Maggie sat down on the fireside chair, the tears started to run down her cheeks as she recalled the misery and devastation brought on by the death of a child.

"Now David I want you to run round to Jessie and tell her not to bring Jimmy here to the High Street with the diphtheria being her," said Maggie as she sat at her evening meal with her two sons.

"What difference do you think that will make Mam?" said John. "None of us have got it in this house."

David looked at his mother and nodded approval of her plan.

"It's all right Mam, I will go round for you. It's not worth the slightest risk. They have closed the picture houses and everything to try and stop it spreading."

"Does it just affect bairns Mam?" asked John.

"No laddie it can be anyone of any age so you be careful when you are sorting out things for auction. The Fever Hospital takes the bedding and everything for fumigation. I'm not sure but the Sanitary folk might even fumigate the houses."

"Have you seen that bothy dad sleeps in.? The Sanitary would have a field day in there," said David.

"Oh your dad will be alright. He's a hardy tough one. Don't worry about him."

"Mam I wasn't worrying more surprised that he still chooses to live in such a midden all week with a comfortable home here."

"Well David, he never had much choice in the matter. Your father's not one who could survive without work and the 'bothy life' was the sacrifice he had to make to be able to earn a living."

Friday was the day preparing for Jim to come home. He would be disappointed that Jimmy would not be there to play after tea. Jessie had taken notice of her mother's advice and kept Jimmy away from what was considered a risk of infection. Maggie had been round to see them in Park Road on Wednesday night. Jimmy was such a little character he was playing wit a woolly sheep pretending he was a sheep dog crawling about the floor and barking.

"Your father will get a laugh when he sees you on Friday" Maggie told her daughter.

"I suppose he will Mam, Jimmy has made such a difference to our dad. He will just have to come round here after tea and play with him instead of at home. I think Jim will probably be home early Friday and we might get out by ourselves for a wee while with Dad and you looking after Jimmy."

The feet on the stairs were not Jim's. Maggie was surprised to see Mary come through the kitchen door.

"Lord lassie, this is a surprise, I wasn't expecting to see you at this time but you know I'm always glad to see you. Come on and sit down" Maggie knew as Mary moved further into the light of the room that something was far from right. Mary's face showed that she had been crying recently. Maggie held out her arms beckoning her daughter to come to her.

"Come away to Mam lass and tell me what's the matter" she noticed that young John was missing. "Is something the matter with John?"

Mary moved forward and grasped both of her mother's outstretched hands. "John is fine Mam and safe at Forfar with his other granny. Mam it's Jessie and her Jim that needs you now." Mary was trying to say something more but the words were not coming out from her lips, because of the body racking sobs.

"What do you mean Mary? Jessie and Jim need me now. Dad and myself are going round after teatime to mind Jimmy and let them have a wee while to their selves."

"Oh Mam this is so hard I'm trying to tell you. Little Jimmy is dead. He died this morning in Forfar with diphtheria."

Maggie wondered if Mary had gone funny.

"Mary what in God's name are you talking about? Jimmy is fine I was playing with him the other night. He's at Park Road, never anywhere near Forfar."

"Look Mam sit down. The shock of this has not really got through to me yet. Jessie had the doctor to see Jimmy this morning because he was fevered during the night and coughing. He was taken to Forfar in the forenoon. Jessie got the first bus to Forfar after he was lifted. She was in such a state she never thought to send you a message. At dinnertime I went round to Whitehills Hospital with her to find out what was what" Mary started to sob loudly. "Oh Mam when we got there the sister told us Jimmy was dead"

After what seemed a lifetime of silence, in the distance Maggie could hear sounds echoing through her head. "Mam are you alright? You're not going to faint are you?"

Eventually Maggie managed to reply. "No I'm not all right Mary, my lassie, but I'll have to pull myself together to help my bairn Jessie and her man. Oh God knows if there is one how such a thing could happen."

Maggie looked towards the kitchen door "Oh lassie here's your father now, this news will be the death of him"

Jessie and Jim had packed the last of their furniture on the lorry. Maggie stood beside them on the pavement outside the door of what had been their home.

"Now remember what I've told you both. You are away to a new home in a new place and a new start. I'll finish what has to be done cleaning up here and take the key back to the landlord. Off you go now. You look after Jim and he'll look after you."

"Mam you'll se that there are always flowers at the cemetery for Jimmy. We wouldn't want to think that he was forgotten."

"Listen the pair of you. Jimmy will live in our hearts, with us forever. We must be thankful for all the pleasure he packed into us during his short life. Now off you go."

Maggie turned on her heel and went back into the house, where the living room was bare except for the low nursing chair that still sat beside the fire. She sank to her knees and rested her head on her folded arms covering the seat, where her daughter had so happily fed her baby from her breast.

"Oh please, if there is such a thing as a God, hear my prayer now, stop this dreadful disease that is destroying so many loving families. Please let the children have their young, happy and free lives.'

How long she remained on her knees Maggie did not know. She was disturbed by knocking on the window. It was David with his young wife Lizzie.

"Come on Mam, open up the door", shouted David from outside.

"Lizzie and I want to talk with you. Let us in."

Maggie wiped her face and unlatched the door.

David folded his arms around his mother and held her close to him.

"We thought we would find you here, when you weren't at one hundred and ten. Did Jessie and Jim get away alright?"

"Yes they were away in good time. It wasn't until after they were gone that I couldn't hold back my grief. My heart is so full for them, with hope and wishes for their future happiness."

"Come on let's get you home," said Lizzie. "A cup of tea will do you good. David and I will come back and finish up the tidying, once you are settled at your own fireside."

"You're a good lassie, Lizzie. I just feel so tired and weary these days."

"Well you certainly have not shown it and there's no denying that without your example to follow not one of the family would have managed through the past few weeks."

"Och David I'm a silly old woman for you have all suffered as much as me. You never even had a celebration party after your marriage with us all being grief stricken."

"Well Mam we have something to celebrate now for Lizzie has just been to the doctor and she is expecting. That's what we were at the house to tell you."

Maggie held her hands out to them both.

"Oh my bairns I'm so happy for the pair of you. Seems as though I am to be allowed an event to look forward to happily."

EPILOGUE

IN 1950, ALEXANDER Chalmers retired from his position with the Post Office, in Dunedin, New Zealand. In the spring of that year he set off on a 'Round the World' trip with the intention of visiting his sister's family, in Scotland and in Canada her daughter Margaret and family. He flew to London and travelled by train to Aberdeen, where all Maggie's children from her marriage, excepting David, had settled.

Unfortunately, Alex never achieved his dream, for he died of a heart attack on the taxi journey, between Aberdeen rail station and his niece Mary's home.

Alexander Chalmers was buried in Brechin Cemetery, in the same lair, with and next to his sister Maggie.

They were together at last.

Jim Chisholm, after Maggie's death, continued to work on the farms of Angus. During the Second World War, being too old for active service, he managed to get employment, with the armed services, working at Edzell Aerodrome. In 1946, no longer required by the Government War Department, Jim again returned to working on the land and living in farm bothies. The rift in the relationship between Jim and his older children was never mended. His youngest son John maintained a distant contact with his father. Eventually, after he was unable to work on the land, Jim became a resident in a home for 'old soldiers'. Even then, his need for work prompted him to undertake the duties of relief boilerman at the home.

In the late summer of 1950, Jim suffered a stroke and died quite suddenly. His family buried him with his wife Maggie, in Brechin Cemetery

Lightning Source UK Ltd.
Milton Keynes UK
UKOW03f1417220614

233847UK00001B/34/P